EXCHANGE

By the Author

Stick McLaughlin: The Prohibition Years

Exchange

Visit us at www.boldstrokesbooks.com

EXCHANGE

by
CF Frizzell

2016

EXCHANGE

ISBN 13: 978-1-62639-679-1

THIS TRADE PAPERBACK ORIGINAL IS PUBLISHED BY
BOLD STROKES BOOKS, INC.
P.O. BOX 249
VALLEY FALLS, NY 12185

FIRST EDITION: JULY 2016

CREDITS
EDITOR: CINDY CRESAP
PRODUCTION DESIGN: STACIA SEAMAN
COVER DESIGN BY MELODY POND

Acknowledgments

There's a substantial tale behind every novel, and *Exchange* has a healthy one, but none of it would have led to an ISBN number without the encouragement (and yes, the insistence) of Bold Strokes Books. Thank you to publisher Radclyffe and her ace admin, Sandy Lowe, for their dedication to our romance genre and their faith in my attempt to do it justice.

I'm indebted to editor Cindy Cresap for her patience and meticulous eye in helping craft this story, which, no doubt, landed on her busy desk like a twenty-pound hunk of clay.

Exchange is what happens when two people discover their hearts so aligned, there is no turning back, and only braving the consequences will enable their life together. It's also a story that hits close to home, not only for my new wife and me, but for many who seek their own "happily ever after." If you're one of them, reading this now, I thank you for giving *Exchange* a deeper look, and I sincerely hope it lightens your heart.

In keeping with the story, let it be written in headlines that my better half, Kathy, deserves credit for this novel. Unquestionably, without her devotion and courage, *Exchange* simply never would have happened. XOX

For Kathy.
We never dreamed "bus buddies" would someday exchange vows.
Together, everything is possible.
Love you, always.

CHAPTER ONE

Shay Maguire emerged from the dance floor throng, spent and overheated, and returned to her seat at the bar. She shook her head at her old friend Coby's smirk. "What? I didn't cruise sixteen hundred miles to get laid, for Christ's sake." She wiped her face with a cocktail napkin.

"Uh-huh." Coby held out her bare wrist and checked the time on an invisible watch. "Could've fooled me."

"Shit. Montana women are tireless."

"I think you must've set a record. She followed you into the ladies' room and you were out in a flash—and back dancing with someone else. You dog."

Shay frowned and drank what was left of her beer. "I wasn't interested in 'dancing' in the restroom."

"God. Remember the old days? Age must be catching up to us."

"I've developed a healthy respect for that 'four-oh' on the horizon."

"Eh. There's no reason you can't enjoy being single again."

Shay glanced back at the lively dance floor. "I've got nothing against light and flirty, but no hookups. Now it's all about bigger, adult decisions."

"Well, I'm glad that common sense brought you out here and might make you stay." Coby sighed dreamily toward the bartender, her partner, Misty. "God, she took me by storm, so you never know what might happen. I'm just saying."

Shay shrugged and raised her empty bottle. "Another round, please, Ms. Misty. Colder the better." She watched her step to the ice chest and reach in, the form-fitting black leggings outlining an alluring figure. "Misty's just a doll, you know. It amazes me that a low-life musician like you ever landed a lady so fine."

Coby slung an arm around her shoulders. "Goes back to our natural Boston-bred charm, old pal. Misty and I clicked and something said 'stay,' so I did. Same can happen to you."

"Right. I really *am* serious about starting over, you know, getting down to business."

Misty wiped ice chips off their bottles. "Coldest ice in the territory." She winked at Shay. "You're a popular commodity on the dance floor tonight."

"Hell, it's been ages since I spent *any* time on a dance floor. I'll pay for it tomorrow, I'm sure."

"We'll whip her into shape," Coby assured Misty.

"Well, your secret's safe with us." Misty leaned forward slightly. "From where I stand, the ladies love your leather."

Shay tilted her head in doubt at the compliment, at herself. Black leather hugged her from hips to boots with that flushed satin texture of flesh, a second-skin-tight that forced nerve endings to the surface and detailed her ass, thigh, and calf muscles. She'd been uncertain, selecting leather for her first night at the Exchange, the bar Misty owned and operated, but everything about coming to the quaint little town of Tomson had screamed "change," so she went for it.

"Where *do* all these lesbians come from? It's just miles of nothing around here. I didn't expect this."

"They come from all over," Coby said. "Now and then, some locals will stop by for a drink, to dance…probably just to check us out. But in general, folks don't interact with the nighttime *clientele*. The sidewalks roll up at six o'clock and we're surrounded by businesses, so it all works out. No neighbors complaining about the parking or the music."

Misty beamed proudly. "We're a very popular wireless café by day and very gay-friendly dance lounge by night. Personally, though, I love that we've cornered the lesbian market. There isn't a women's club for at least a hundred miles."

"And you bought the place." Shay was still overwhelmed by the concept, admittedly envious.

"Oh, back then, it was no gold mine, believe me, but being the bartender here, I wanted my own shot at it. Plus," Misty ran a finger along the back of Coby's hand, "by the time it became available, I had someone in my life who gave me the strength. Dreams *do* come true sometimes."

Shay sat back. Making those dreams *last* was a different battle because just finding the courage was tough.

"It can be done," Coby said quietly, as if reading Shay's mind. "You were a huge success in Chicago, so you've done it already. You can again if you want."

"Tomson may be stuck in its ways, not quick to change," Misty added, "but people generally are very supportive of that entrepreneurial spirit. I think it comes with the territory. You'll see."

Shay wondered how "supportive" townspeople would be of her, *the dyke from Chicago.* "At this very moment, I'm not sure what I want, but looking around could be fun."

Shay figured her "looking around" could start right here. This scene wasn't really all that unfamiliar, but the vision of her own business, establishing roots in a town like this was.

The Exchange bustled around her, the antique jukebox in the corner supplying an endless string of familiar tunes, and Shay let herself be swept away by the simplicity of it all. It was refreshing and edged that troublesome self-doubt farther from her mind.

"How did we ever make it past twenty-one?" she mused aloud.

"Your college connections," Coby said before drinking.

"Ah yes. And you were the rowdy rocker attracting all the girls."

"Jesus, those were wild times."

"And, boy, have we changed. These women here...I'll admit they aren't what I thought I'd find. Not many beer-swigging farm-boy butches in this crowd."

"They're in the minority here tonight," Coby said. "You danced with that blonde in the rhinestones twice, and that little brunette who's about to wiggle out of her jeans, and the cowgirl in heels—"

"You keeping score? Did you notice that I couldn't get off the damn dance floor?"

"Sure. Like you're going to ignore that hot redhead who keeps looking this way, aren't you?" Coby snickered into her beer.

"I may have had my fill of dancing tonight."

"Oh, right, Miss Light 'n Flirty."

Several women cajoled each other at the far end of the bar and drew Shay's attention from Coby's teasing. Next to them, an athletic-looking woman in a Dodgers ball cap and faded rose USC T-shirt sat nursing a beer. She filled out the shirt nicely, Shay thought, lost in her prolonged evaluation of the woman's trim build. *Probably a tennis player.* The face was angelic, and when she tipped her bottle to drink, sapphire eyes glittered beneath the tiny recessed lights overhead. Mesmerized, Shay watched her absently flick a short, honey-blond ponytail back off her shoulder and survey the many dancers.

Something urged Shay to stand, to take that walk, but the press of a small palm between her shoulders turned her on her stool.

The redhead lowered her lips to Shay's ear. "I think it's our turn, don't you?" She claimed Shay's hand and led her away.

❖

From her seat at the far end of the bar, Melissa Baker watched the latest pairing leave the club hand in hand. This time, however, she didn't add it to her running list of Exchange success stories. She felt a pang of disappointment at their departure. She'd enjoyed the view for the past two hours, from the moment she'd spotted the good-looking stranger and attached that rugged body in tight leathers to the customized Harley parked out front. The door closed behind them and she turned back to her beer, unable to shake the image from her mind, an image in which *she* had left with a handsome mystery woman of her own.

"She's hot, huh?" Misty quipped.

"Mixology school teaches bartenders how to read minds? You do it too well, Misty. And Keary does the same damn thing when you're not here."

Misty wiped the bar top around Mel's beer bottle. "Honey, when she walked out, half the women in the place took on your same look."

Mel readjusted her ball cap and shook her head at the effect one sexy, mature butch could have on a room full of lesbians. What an interesting psychological article it would make for her newspaper. It would have been amusing if she herself wasn't helpless to improve her own plight.

"Good dancer," she conceded.

"Not that you were watching or anything."

Mel finished her beer, put cash on the bar, and slid off her stool. "Another player."

"Well, she's got the look, I'll give you that."

"She didn't waste any time leaving with the redhead."

Misty pressed her hand atop Mel's, holding her from leaving. "Why didn't you ask her to dance or at least talk? Who knows? Might've been you leaving with her."

"Sure."

"What? You don't think she noticed you sitting here alone?" Misty struck a dumb face.

"Really, Misty. Stop. I doubt she'd think I was her type. I'm not one of her dancing babes." She pulled car keys from her pocket and tapped Misty's hand. "Besides, whatever would I do here in Tomson with that much butch, huh? But thanks for the thought—and the beers. Hope you get out of here at a decent hour tonight."

Once outside, Mel inhaled hard and let the cool air of the spring night flush the tension from her chest. Misty was a dear friend and had only the best intentions, but damn if her words didn't churn her orderly mind into a twist. The time spent crowd watching certainly had been relaxing, and she'd only had to decline two dance offers, but these nights always closed with a return to her solitary reality.

She headed up the sidewalk toward her Subaru, the vacancy between two parked cars telling her that the heavily chromed Harley had left. No doubt cruising lazily through the dark, nothing but the two of them pressed warmly together, carefree. Reality was a bummer, even if the woman was a player. *Someday*, she told herself, *you'll be able to let loose.*

At her car door, she paused to scan Main Street, quiet and deserted, shopkeepers she knew like extended family now home asleep at addresses she knew by heart. Quaint and homey Tomson, in many ways still stuck in the nineteen seventies, and that wasn't necessarily *all* bad, but at moments like this she wished certain attitudes had advanced with the times.

She settled in behind the wheel, wondering if someday she'd see success from her efforts as editor of the *Chronicle*, Tomson's newspaper, if her passion for this little town was well spent. The newspaper gave her purpose, but above all, it lent her the means to actually *do* something with her life that mattered. She couldn't afford to let it or the town or herself down.

Mel sighed hard in the silent car, sitting in the driveway now and staring blankly at the homestead she shared with her grandmother. The idea of a late-night rendezvous with that tall, dark-haired stranger from the Exchange sent an odd rush through her system, one she hurriedly dismissed. It irritated her, thoughts of that woman refusing to fade. *Oh, the talk that would start. "You see our newspaper editor making time with that butch dyke?" It'd be all over town the next day and half my advertisers would bail. And my life would be destroyed.*

She couldn't afford to be associated with a woman, least of all a woman as androgynous as that stranger. Ill will would spread like the plague and she'd have to woo outraged advertisers and readers with discounts, freebies, and puff pieces to win back their financial and public support, while her pride and joy bled soy ink down the drain.

It had happened with her arrival as editor six years ago. The simple change in status quo forced her to spend most of that first year scrounging, groveling, and skirting delinquency with bill collectors before things leveled off. It had taken everything she'd had—every ounce of pride and energy and every damn cent in her savings—to publish a professional, community-minded product consistently, week after week, and gain their trust and their business. She remembered too well how her father watched and waited, oversaw her every move, and measured her success from his retirement condo in Miami.

His last remaining tie to Tomson, aside from the family homestead, the *Chronicle* was her grandfather's creation, and owning it had been Mel's driving objective since high school. To her absentee-owner father, who resisted change with every ounce of Tomson's territorial ancestry, the newspaper was Mel's litmus test. He dangled it before her optimistic spirit, as if challenging her to snatch it free of his grasp. She knew she would, that *she* was meant to move it forward, but she agonized over traveling the "straight and narrow" road he demanded. And she had less than one year of "travel" left before her contract with him placed ownership in her hands. Until then, she knew he'd sell the paper out from under her unless she maintained the historic homestead with her grandmother and preserved the conservative, well-respected Baker family reputation—and under no circumstances "shame the family by experimenting with deviant behavior." He'd backed her into a closet as a grad student and locked it with the *Chronicle*.

The newspaper was her future, today just as solid and reliable as any townsperson, but, she wondered, what did that say about her heart and soul? Had she effectively sold her soul to the *Chronicle*? And as for her heart, well, being herself couldn't even figure into this equation. Not for the foreseeable future, at least.

She hated these internal debates. They tore her conscience to shreds.

Mel locked the heavy farmhouse door behind her and went silently up to her bedroom, careful not to wake Nana. Lying in the dark, she added Nana's eighty-five-year-old opinions to the pile of worries in the back of her mind.

Chapter Two

Shay followed the moonlit wooded trail from Coby and Misty's backyard and felt her spirit lift when she finally found the modest campfire in a secluded niche along the lakeshore. A few hours at the Exchange, and the drinks and propositions that came with them, had her tired and more alone than she'd expected. Finding Coby relaxing by the fire, Shay eagerly settled into the sanctuary of her best friend's company.

Coby poked at the burning logs with a stick. "Hey."

"Hey yourself. I followed the light of your fire." Shay sat down heavily beside her on a tree trunk. "Brought you a beer."

"Bless you." Coby raised the bottle and saluted the lake. "Another tranquil night."

"I like this…your burning place. I like this town of yours, too, Cob." Shay tossed a stray branch into the flames and shook her head at her thoughts. "I've only been here a week and already I'm getting good vibes about Tomson. I can't explain it."

"Hanging at the Exchange wouldn't have anything to do with it, would it?"

"Hell," Shay shook her head, "going out for a few dances now and then is pretty harmless, but I think I've gotten that out of my system. And just so you know, that one night I took Paige out for a ride was it."

"Paige?"

"Paige Hackett. That redhead."

"Uh-huh."

"It was just a ride, although she wanted a whole lot more. That's probably why she hasn't been around—and believe me, I'm glad. Just being here feels too good to mess up, and I'm not looking to complicate things." Shay watched Coby prod the coals. "You two have such an amazing life here. Storybook stuff, Cob."

"I think you're staying. At least for a good while."

"You're pretty confident that this city girl can hack it?"

"Yup. It's happening," Coby said softly. "The land plays a big part. I'm convinced. The air, so much sun, so many stars. It changes people. And now you're hooked."

"Hmm. I'd need a job, though. I won't be a freeloader on you two."

"You can't be a freeloader, stupid. You're family."

"No, seriously. For me to stay on with you guys a while, I'm paying. End of discussion."

Coby prodded the fire again. "Thanks, but you don't even know what you want yet, let alone if there's anything local to be had. Why don't you just hang on to your savings while you look around."

"No pay, no stay, my friend." Shay leaned forward on her knees and stared into the flames. "I tucked away almost all of that huge insurance settlement I got for when the time is right, for when opportunity knocks again, so there may not be lots of cash in hand, but there *is* a significant stash. Starting a business from scratch is an uphill grind, I know, but I did it once and I intend to do it again."

"So sorry about all that, Shay. I know it set you back in a lot of ways. Do you ever hear from Lee?"

Shay sipped her beer. "Opportunities in the New York art world are a lot more appealing to her than my burned-out motorcycle business. Those punks torched a lot more than they ever knew."

"Well, at least it all led you here."

"There was nothing left, no reason to stay, and I certainly didn't want to go home. Plus, hell, I missed you, Cob."

"I've missed you, too." Coby set a hand on her shoulder. "I hope you give Tomson a chance because I'd like you to stay."

"Well, Tomson can't be some right-wing hotbed if you're this happy here. Am I reading it wrong? They're pretty accepting of us?"

"Y'mean being gay out here?" Coby shrugged. "Eh. I'm sure Chicago and Boston are a helluva lot more progressive than Tomson. We have a serious percentage of ignorant assholes, but we all try to stay out of each other's business." She sent Shay a mischievous glance. "The Exchange *does* push our luck a bit, though."

"No doubt. Just like a female mechanic looking for a job."

"You never know, Shay. Sonny's garage just outside of town might be interested in more help. God knows that big ol' boy could use it. But check the papers. The *Chronicle* has some help-wanted stuff, and the *Tribune* out of Billings has a bigger section. It's bike season, so that's a plus, but who knows what might pique your interest. You can swing a hammer and drive all kinds of rigs. There may not be much locally, but you never know."

Shay nodded toward the shrinking flames. "I'll take a look tomorrow."

❖

Melissa fought *not* to snort like a bull.

The envy of at least half the women in Tomson, Mel's luminous hair snapped like lightning off her shoulders as she spun away from the counter and raged out of the town hall. The confirmation she'd just received splashed gasoline on her fire. The impact-laden shopping complex, entitled The Tomson Heights Trade Center, the latest ground-gobbling brainchild of Slattery Enterprises, had just spent all of two hundred dollars on the last of the permits needed to proceed. Mel steamed.

Two hundred dollars, my ass. Developers blow their noses on two hundred dollars. Here in sweet little Tomson there's no such thing as a twenty- or fifty-thousand-dollar fee, nothing that would even make the almighty Della Slattery blink, let alone think twice. Once again, for just a pittance, Cruella-Della will do as she pleases here in her hometown. You, too, can desecrate some of the most pristine, picturesque land in the entire USA for a song. Just two hundred dollars and go right ahead, plant a bunch of cheap look-alike houses or a shopping center out of concrete and asphalt, don't worry about how much our shopkeepers and landowners can handle. She cursed town leaders and even the voters for ignoring her often controversial editorial opinions in the past, for not adopting protective bylaws and fees that would have guarded against such corporate rough-riding.

Composing next week's editorial torrent in her head as she stomped down the granite steps, Mel nearly collided with Tomson's selectmen chairman on his way up.

"Morning, Miss Baker." He stopped and tipped his golf cap. "Our lovely newspaper editor's on a mission today, I see."

Mel collected herself quickly. "Mr. Nelson. So good to see you. How's business these days?" The man had her so conflicted, her stomach protested at the mere mention of his name. He held the controlling vote on most town affairs while walking the fine conflict-of-interest line as manager of the two-year-old Home Depot. As such, in the ultimate catch-22, he was the leading advertiser in her newspaper. Revenue from his sales inserts alone covered the rent for her small storefront office.

"Oh, things are moving well," he said. "Business is growing. We're catching on. Spring's a busy time of year, you know, so I can't complain."

"That's great for you." *Should I tell you how the local hardware store is struggling now?*

"Say, I trust that *this* is the year you'll join us duffers for the Indigo Club's annual Harvest Ball. The wife and I were just talking about it this morning. She's on the decorations committee, you see, already getting things in gear, so I hope you've marked your calendar."

"Well, I'll be—"

"Your grandparents always attended. It's when we raise most of the Winter Fuel Fund, as I'm sure you know."

"I plan to cov—"

"I know each year you promote our fundraising free of charge—and we're so grateful, believe me—but we'd love to have you join us. Bring a date and dance the night away." He winked and Mel's stomach rolled. "I'm sure Elsie has told you plenty of good stories about our annual shindig."

"My grandmother brings out the stories every season," she said. "I'll see what I can do this year."

"Excellent." He stepped closer and Mel knew he had more than dancing on his mind. "On a different topic, if I may, Mel, I just want to say your editorials these past few weeks have been, well, let's say concerning."

"I hope the topic of developing Tomson is always concerning, Mr. Nelson. It's a very weighty, far-reaching issue."

"No argument there. But I just hope you realize how upsetting it is, having our newspaper advocate against jobs and increased income for our families. A sizeable percentage of townspeople are counting on those construction jobs and looking forward to opportunities you're quite adamantly against. From what I'm hearing, it's not sitting well."

"I understand and can certainly sympathize, but the broader picture is critical. I realize times are tougher than ever, and projects the size of Slattery's offer tempting relief, but Tomson can't afford to blindly green-light every project that comes to the table."

"Our town boards give no one a free pass."

"Not deliberately, but too many projects—mostly by a developer I don't need to name—have wound up, let's say, less than advertised, and proved burdensome to residents and the town as a whole. There's a serious need for oversight every step of the way, not to mention what's required for the future." She hoped he recalled his own woes, the roof reinforcement required after Home Depot's first winter, the layoffs executed after that so-so initial spring. Construction materials and business projections Slattery used to bring the Home Depot to town had been costly and seriously lacking.

"Just putting you on notice that some folks are seriously upset with the *Chronicle*."

"I appreciate the heads up, Mr. Nelson. Thank you. I truly hope people see there's no need to be divided about this. And now, if you'll pardon me for rushing off, I have—"

"Oh, by all means. I certainly can appreciate a busy work schedule." He tipped his cap again as Mel backed away. "Give Tomson some positive press now, young lady."

The Chronicle *will say what needs to be said.*

Honestly, the man gave her the creeps, but she walked a fine line herself. She offered a polite wave. "Give my best to the family, Mr. Nelson."

Mel drove back to her office in a daze. The hypocrisy of her position overwhelmed her whenever she let it. And now was not the time. She reminded herself that the *Chronicle* was Tomson's local weekly, and on the day she signed the contract with her father, she'd shouldered the responsibility of making it the informative, thought-provoking member of the community that it was meant to be. She simply had to live the life he dictated a bit longer to inherit the paper free and clear, but that had nothing to do with taking her role seriously.

"Young lady," my goddamn ass. I've got a grandmother here,

Nelson, in a homestead dating back to before you were born. I'm as invested in Tomson as you are with your damn Home Depot, and I'll fight to protect it any way I can. Jesus Christ, why do these stuffed shirts always come on like Dad? It's a wonder he's not blustering around here, too.

She fumed over the notes in her hand: the battle with the territory's largest employer was ramping up. Prior to Home Depot, Slattery Enterprises had built several residential developments, complete with their share of design issues, and now, with the Heights complex, was about to introduce the first Walmart to this part of the state. She shuddered to think of the impact it would have on Tomson's already straining infrastructure, and wished those ramifications had received deeper investigation during the initial permit process. Hell, she thought, the site prep alone posed a serious environmental risk, so close to the Rohan River, but it, too, had been fast-tracked forward. Like every Slattery project.

"Are you getting out of the car today?"

Mel woke from her daydream to see her photographer, Mike, standing at her driver's window, hands on his hips, frowning.

"I said, are you get—"

"Yes. Yes. I heard you. Sorry." She flung open the door and grabbed her purse and notebook off the adjacent seat. "Think I spaced out there for a minute."

"Try ten minutes. I was going to just wait you out, but I got a tip to head over to the cop shop. They're moving that guy they busted down to Billings in about..." He checked his watch. "Well, now in about ten minutes."

"For Gronlund's horse rustling case?"

"This guy's the only one they caught. Supposedly, there are five of them, but this one decided to talk."

Mel shooed him away with her free hand. "Go. Go. Get something other than a mug shot."

Alone at her desk, Mel stared down at the current issue on her blotter. She'd left it open to the Slattery Enterprises full-page color advertisement about the July Fourth festival. The three thousand dollars it added to the *Chronicle*'s bank account eased the grind of paying bills, signing paychecks for Mike, her correspondent, and herself, but it brought to mind the measly two hundred Slattery had just paid for the final go-ahead to build the Heights. The corporation paid more to win the town's favor via the festival than it did to affect its future.

She turned to her keyboard and her fingers flew. It was never healthy for a community to live by a single source of news, this she knew, but right now she was thankful the *Chronicle* was the only paper in town. Popular or not, what she *had* to write might rile more than a few readers and advertisers but needed to be written. She was gambling with the *Chronicle*'s lifeblood, her own income, but, ethically, she didn't have a choice.

CHAPTER THREE

S hay sat back down in the porch rocker with her second slice of pizza and tipped her beer bottle toward Coby in the opposite chair. "His name is Tom Rogers. He's Slattery's maintenance foreman. I couldn't believe it when he asked if I was interested. It was too good to be true, less than an hour after I landed Saturdays at Sonny's."

Misty shook her head. "I can't believe it either. I didn't think that Five Star bunch would, well, take to you." Her cheeks pinked. "I mean, no offense, Shay, but you're not the all-American girl."

Coby pointed at her. "Course not. She's the all-American dyke."

Shay shook her head at them both. "It seems Rogers is beyond that. He was pretty forthcoming, took me outside to show me around and talk privately. I guess the mechanics work under a different boss, Angelo Sorvini, but we weren't introduced." She caught Coby and Misty sharing a knowing glance. "Rogers told me the owner, Della Slattery, liked my resume and said hiring me was a good idea, considering I obviously had Sonny's endorsement. Lucky I stopped by his garage first. He carries some weight around here, doesn't he? No pun intended."

"Yeah, he's a big boy, for sure," Coby said, "but there's a reason that place has been the lifeblood of his family for generations. The town loves him, and everybody depends on his work, although if he doesn't take better care of himself, he won't be working much longer."

"He was nuts about my bike and we hit it off right away. I even helped him pull a motor before I left. He seemed to regret not being able to offer me full-time. He really could use the help."

"Must've felt like Christmas when the Five Star said yes."

"I couldn't believe it. I answered all Rogers's questions and showed him a few things, but this Sorvini didn't join us. I got the impression he's not the sociable type."

Coby grumbled as she chewed. "Probably not thrilled about having a dyke around. He's the town asshole."

"Really? Well, sounds like Della shut him up. Rogers turned all red telling me. It was kind of cute."

"It sure sounds promising, Shay." Misty pushed off in the glider and sipped her wine. "But Sorvini can't be fun to work for. Just so you know. This will be full-time?"

Shay nodded. "He said Sorvini's mechanics always have equipment needing something, and when they don't, there's a ton of prep work for the Fourth that needs doing. Apparently, the ranch crews are expected to do all that, plus gear up for Slattery's project called the Heights, and they're swamped. So I'd be helping out his carpentry guys, too, and doing miscellaneous things, I guess, like painting, hanging signs, even playing the gofer."

Coby took another slice of pizza and leaned toward Shay. "Wait till you meet Della."

"A home-grown success story," Misty said. "I think her great-great-grandfather helped establish the town. Lord knows, the Slatterys owned most of it at one point. Just the Five Star Ranch alone is about thirty thousand acres. More money and land than she knows what to do with."

Coby chortled. "And very attractive. She's late forties, a high-fashion corporate buzz-saw."

Misty hoisted her wine glass. "You must've made a good impression, Shay. Rogers showed you around?"

"Yeah, you could say. He had me run the mill saw and then tell him how I'd re-roof the main barn. *Then* he had me back up a flatbed and load and unload a D-8 bulldozer, just to prove I knew how to handle them."

"Way to go, Shay." Coby sat back. "Any guys give you trouble?"

"Nah." Shay shrugged. "A couple times I found guys whispering to each other, but overall, they seemed friendly enough." She set her empty bottle on the table. "One kid, Freddy something, he was ballsy enough to tease me about my haircut. I like him, too, like Rogers. There are other crews working there, but I didn't meet any of them."

"And you didn't go face-to-face with Sorvini?"

"Just saw him from a distance. He's got a mouth on him, lots of swagger, real beefy. What's his story?"

Coby snorted. "He's part of the old-school breed still hanging on to the days when 'men were men,' you know? He's bought up some land in the area, and I think he's out to make a name for himself."

"Even if he bought every piece of Tomson that's left, he still wouldn't overtake Della," Misty said. "Maybe he does see himself as king of the hill someday, but there isn't enough property available. Bet he'd love a piece of the Heights project, if he doesn't have a vested interest already."

Coby nodded. "I wouldn't be surprised either. Getting in on the actual development might be his thing."

"Regardless, Shay," Misty added, "I hope this leads to bigger things for you."

"I guess I should have reservations."

"Well, remember. Sorvini aside, Della's top dog. Even though Slattery Enterprises employs a lot of folks, I doubt any of them actually likes what she represents, the high life, big money, projects that always seem to have problems. People don't have lots of job choices around here, so they're sort of stuck working for—"

"The Dragon Lady," Coby finished.

Shay debated how much of herself she really should risk, how big a step she should take. "She's that bad, huh?"

"She's determined to develop the town, Shay," Misty continued, "bring in commercial business, and townspeople are between a rock and a hard place, living with that, the jobs it could bring versus changes to everyone's life and the town itself. Check out the *Chronicle* sometime." She nodded toward the newspaper on the table. "You'll see."

❖

Nana lowered the *Chronicle* and eyed Mel at the stove. "Helen talked my ear off at the salon once you went back to your office this morning."

"Why do you let that old bag get to you, Nana?"

"Melissa, hush! Helen Carrington is my age."

"But she's an old bag, Nana. You're a sweet grandma."

"Well, I had no choice. I was getting shampooed when she popped in. Lissa, she just *knows* you and that grandson of hers, Sheridan, would make a lovely couple at the Harvest Ball, come September."

Mel swung open the oven door and slid in the stuffed chicken. "Nana, you know better than to insist. I am not now and have never been interested in anything to do with Helen Carrington or her grandson or attending that damn ball."

"Be reasonable. All of Tomson would love to see you there. You're a celebrity in town, dear, the prettiest girl—"

"Nana, please." Mel sipped her iced tea as she imagined attending on the arm of another woman. And why, of all women, that butch at the Exchange came to mind puzzled her. She shook her head at the reaction that would get. "You know, I always support their effort and they seem to overlook that. They get more free publicity from the *Chronicle* than I can afford as it is."

"There you go again with the newspaper."

"Need I remind you again this year of what that publicity is worth?"

"You need to socialize, Melissa. Get out more, have fun, like all the girls do."

"Nana, come on. I'm twenty-nine and a businesswoman in town. Let all the 'girls' do as they please and leave me out of it."

"Well, since you are so hopelessly, stubbornly committed to putting your lifelong happiness at the mercy of this newspaper, you might think on this: your father would be overjoyed to see a picture of you hobnobbing with the well-do-to for one evening. Especially with a handsome date at your side."

There it was again, Mel thought, that infernal internal debate. Nana had a point, Dad had their agreement, and Mel had her pride. She could go alone, even though her father would probably call and chastise her for creating gossip that would linger till the next Harvest Ball. But his attitude and potential gossip aside, she'd spend the entire evening engaged in petty conversations with shallow women, and dancing with and then fending off drunken flirtatious men of assorted ages. She'd be bored to death, degraded, insulted, and probably mauled for the price of her one-hundred-dollar ticket. She doubted that her father's satisfaction or a handful of advertising promises would make it money well spent.

"Why don't you have your sweet photographer, Michael, take you?"

"Nana, you've been to enough of these over the years. You know how pompous, how superficial everyone is. It's a fashion show for the women and an evening of eye candy for the men."

Nana straightened. "Well, what's wrong with that? It's for a good—"

"We go through this every year, you and I."

"Listen to me, Melissa Baker. You know your father will call as soon as that edition arrives in his mailbox. You should make the most of the Harvest Ball." Nana tapped the *Chronicle*. "Besides, you publish many more editorials like this week's, casting aspersions about development and big chain stores, and you could be begging for advertisers."

Mel spun to face her. "I'm surprised at you, Nana. If Grampa still ran the paper, he would be keeping just as watchful an eye as I am about Tomson development."

"Now you're being melodramatic. You're letting the *Chronicle* go to your head."

"Hardly—and you know it. Letting builders, officials, and residents jump up and down with their eyes closed is incredibly dangerous. It's the epitome of bad municipal planning."

"It's not your job to fix the world, Lissa."

"It's the *Chronicle*'s job to provide the right information, to at least try. You saw how fast Slattery put up those two subdivisions some years back, and then those apartments, and you know the structural troubles they've had, the drainage and water issues. You know how high our tax rate has gone, how stretched our resources are, the schools, police...God forbid our fire department ever has two fires at the same time."

"Calm down, young lady. I agree Della moves too fast sometimes, but we can only do so much without jobs and being able to afford things. We have to face facts."

"The *Chronicle* is obligated to present them, even if they're ugly, and I refuse to wear blinders, especially when a project this size could become another Tomson problem child. Advertisers are free to take their money elsewhere, but I have faith that differences in opinion won't lead advertisers to alienate potential customers."

Nana opened the paper to the full-page Fourth of July advertisement. "How much longer do you think Della will be advertising like this?"

The Home Depot's sales insert slid onto the table, and Nana pounced on it triumphantly. "Will this faith you laud so highly pay your salary, your printing bill, when these ads stop?"

"So, I shouldn't pay attention to what's going on? What happens if the Rohan gets 'tweaked' during site work? Or polluted by the same substandard drainage system Slattery managed to sneak in at the apartment complex? Or if the fishing hole by the train depot disappears under tons of excavated dirt? Della's talked about building right there. Did you know that? By the tracks. So it's all part of her master plan. What about Tomson's master plan? Who watches out for that?"

"Lord, you get too worked up." Nana turned away and picked up her knitting. "This watchdog crusade of yours will cost you, Lissa. We have to make sacrifices, compromises. That's all there is to it."

"Well, the *Chronicle*'s not going to compromise. It will continue to keep its eyes open and do what's right for Tomson."

Mel set her palms on the edge of the sink and took a breath. *Families, ranchers, all count on the* Chronicle. *Advertisers need it, and aren't likely to suddenly go silent. And yes, that Fourth of July ad money is short-term, but Slattery's mammoth complex promises a mother lode of revenue by next summer. I'd be a sham of an editor to turn a blind eye to development.* She gulped the rest of her iced tea. Staring hard out the window, she realized how emotional she'd become, how drained she now felt. *Boy, do I need an alternative focus in my life.*

CHAPTER FOUR

The roadside boundary of Jed Maclin's ten-thousand-acre horse ranch with its idyllic pastoral vista always caught the attention of passing motorists, and Shay's was no exception. Postcard pretty, she recalled Coby saying. Occasional flower boxes bursting with reds and yellows sparkled in the sunshine along snow-white rail fencing that framed acres of plush, rolling green. Coby had also said Maclin's lower eighty, this portion she now saw as she rode along the straightaway, became Slattery land last month. Nicknamed "The Heights," the setting was destined to be completely erased within a week or two.

Ahead, the assortment of SUVs and pickup trucks along the road drew Shay's curiosity, and she slowed the Harley as she passed. Dozens of people crowded around a Land Rover, and their angry voices rose over the Softail's low rumble. Then the wild gesturing, the swinging of picketers' placards began in earnest.

A woman darted between two parked trucks, and Shay jerked to a stop.

"Everyone needs to let them know!" the woman shouted at her. A girl ran out next, the sign she wielded decrying devastation of the land. "It's her future at stake!" the woman railed, pointing to the girl.

A man charged toward them and yanked away the girl's placard.

"I'll take that! We're just doing our goddamn job!" he screamed in her face. She threw herself at him, fists flying. The woman joined in. He heaved the girl to the ground, and Shay dismounted in a hurry. He then swung around to the woman. "We're just the surveyors, y'stupid bitch!"

The girl jumped on his back and he slung her off. He cocked his fist at the woman, but Shay shoved him away from behind.

"What the hell are you doing?"

He spun around and teed off with the placard. The wood post caught Shay in her left temple, and she hit the pavement in a heap. She vaguely heard the stern tone of a police officer as her mind blurred, colors of clothing, vehicles, trees all dissolving to gray.

"Hey, man," the deep voice barked, "you okay? Hey, you hear me?"

Shay forced herself up on one elbow and squinted up into the Ray-Bans. The side of her face felt wet. "Are you talking to me?"

The officer straightened and removed the sunglasses, his expression a bit chagrined.

"Oh—you hang on there, miss. Ambulance is on the way and they'll take a look at that gash on your head."

Shay sat up, and the palm she pressed to her temple came away bloody. "I'll be all right." She rose to one knee but wobbled. The officer set a heavy hand on her shoulder.

"You stay put. Hear me? We got a couple others to look at, but you'll get checked out. Stay down." He went to meet the ambulance and directed the technicians to a man with a suspected broken nose and a woman holding her wrist.

Shay squinted to focus and was relieved to see the Softail was as she'd left it. Nearby, a firefighter swept up windshield glass from the Land Rover.

"What the hell is this all about?" she asked.

He stopped in mid-sweep. "Shay Maguire?"

"Freddy?"

The Five Star carpenter crouched at her side, his volunteer firefighter's coat pooling on the ground. She was glad to see him.

"Shit," he said, studying the blood trailing down her neck. "You gotta have that checked. How the hell did you get mixed up in this?"

"Believe it or not," Shay said, wincing, "I was just passing by. So much for being a Good Samaritan."

"Well, damn." He pulled a neatly pressed white handkerchief from his pants pocket and blotted at the blood that was reaching Shay's collar. "Tomson's temper is all riled up these days, and you sure picked the hot spot to cruise by. These are the surveyors Della hired, and, well, some folks are intent on stopping the job, no matter if they can't, legally."

"Just my luck."

"You're lookin' pretty woozy." He gave her the handkerchief. "Don't think you ought to be driving your bike anywhere soon."

"Yeah. Swell." She reached to dab at her wound, and an approaching EMT told her to stop.

"I'll let them see to you," Freddy said, rising. "All right if I move the Harley off the road? I'll take care that she's stable on the stand."

Shay assessed him cautiously, leery of anyone touching her prized machine.

"Honest," he tried again. "I'll be careful."

"Okay," she said finally, the EMT now in her face. "Thanks, Freddy."

"Can you stand, miss? Walk with me to the ambulance?"

Accepting the guide to her feet, she winced at the pain slicing through her brain and let him lead her to the others gathered at the back of the vehicle.

A tall, slim man in jeans, a large satchel hanging from his shoulder, backed away to the edge of the gathering and raised his hands to his face. A photographer, Shay realized, and watched him flit to another spot and take more pictures.

The EMT gently tilted Shay's head away, and firm fingers manipulated her scalp. *Having so little hair to worry about must be a relief for him.* She managed to keep her eyes open through the lancing pain even though, with her view limited to a nearby truck tire, there wasn't much to see.

"Excuse me. I'm sorry to bother you folks."

"Hey, Mel."

"Thought you'd show up, Mel."

"Hi, guys."

Shay wanted to see the source of this smooth, confident voice, the woman everyone sounded pleased to see. The voice grew in volume, and Shay assumed the woman had turned toward the injured.

"I'm Melissa Baker from the *Chronicle*. Anyone want to share their story here? Exactly what happened? How did the demonstration end up this way?"

Great. We've made the news, Shay thought, frustrated she couldn't move her head to face this woman.

"Not right now, Mel," a man told her. "We're almost done here and transporting one."

"Jesus, John. It looks like a battle scene. What are the extent of the injuries?"

Shay almost shook her head. *Everybody friggin' knows everyone.*

"Sprained wrist, lots of cuts and contusions, a head gash. The broken nose we're taking."

The woman, Mel, didn't respond, and Shay figured she was writing. Meanwhile, the EMT working on her moved her head again, but her vantage point didn't change much. Damn, she wanted to see what was going on.

"Thanks," the reporter said. "I'll catch you back at the firehouse for names."

"Miss?" It took an extra second, but Shay realized the EMT was speaking to her. She hadn't noticed the work on her scalp had stopped, it was too numb. She looked up at last. The reporter was gone.

❖

Mel paced herself in the summer-like heat and strolled across the supermarket parking lot. High above her, a workman secured a large poster for the Fourth of July celebration on a light pole and she noted that advance work for the festivities had begun in earnest. *Della's sparing no expense.*

Hot work in a bucket truck for that poor guy, she thought. He wiped his brow, then scruffed the bandana over his bristly haircut, shiny with perspiration, and stuffed the cloth into a back pocket. In jeans that hung off nonexistent hips and a red sweat-darkened sleeveless T-shirt, he was lean and rugged with toned, glistening arms, and Mel wondered how many women—and men—noticed. A glimpse of his tanned face stopped Mel short as she neared the store's entrance.

She dipped her sunglasses to the tip of her nose for a discerning look. *The Exchange. So the player in leather works for Slattery? Unbelievable. Too bad.*

The quick beep of a car horn made Mel jump.

"Hiya, Ms. Baker!" Three girls waved as their Corolla squeezed by her and headed out of the lot.

Mel hardly had time to return the wave when a frail hand cupped her elbow and urged her toward the store's door.

"Sure picked the wrong spot to stand, Miss Baker."

"You're so right, Olin. Thank you."

"Morning, Mel."

The superintendent of schools and his wife approached, shopping cart filled with bags. The cordial expression on his long, haggard face seemed forced, and she had a good idea why.

"Hello, Hardin, Susan. Good to see you."

He stopped his cart at Mel's side and was about to raise a finger to make a point when his wife pushed it back down.

"Mel," he began on a sigh. "Quite the editorial about Slattery this week. Can't say we see eye to eye, however."

"That so? I'd love to run a rebuttal, if you'd care to send one, Hardin. You know how people love to read letters to the editor."

"Hmm." He straightened and stared across the parking lot, his own internal debate quite obvious.

"That's a wonderful idea," Susan injected, tugging on his shirt for emphasis. "Hardin, if you really want to go through with supporting the Heights and Slattery, you should put all you've been saying in writing. Let other people see."

"Absolutely," Mel said.

"You know that project will help build our tax base, the school budget," he reminded Mel. "I know you're familiar with the high school's expansion needs. Can't for the life of me understand why you'd fight a cause that can do so much good."

"All my points are in the editorial, Hardin. Tomson needs to keep a closer watch on things, not jump on the bandwagon for the here and now." She glanced at his overflowing shopping cart and was thankful for an excuse to end what Hardin could extend for hours. "You need to head home, so I won't keep you any longer, but please consider writing. Won't you?"

Susan edged the shopping cart out of her husband's hands. "I'll talk him into it."

Mel entered the supermarket and sighed heavily at both the relief from ending his debate and the air-conditioning. Pulling out a cart for herself, she spotted the postcard advertisement stuck to the far end of the wagon. More July Fourth promo. And her mind drifted back to the handsome woman in the bucket truck, a surprising addition to the Slattery payroll.

As much as she wanted to dwell on that topic, she concentrated on completing her shopping mission promptly, and managed to be back behind her desk within the hour. The editorial half-written in her mind wouldn't wait.

Two hours at the keyboard proved useless, however. She ran both hands through her hair, frustrated by words that wouldn't come.

"You've been swearing at that tube all afternoon," Mike said, passing her desk. "None of it's printable."

"Be quiet. I can't help it. I refuse to suggest a truce of any kind."

"Well, you can't promote business as usual either," he said, stopping at the doorway to his workroom, "not when it's blood-and-guts warfare."

"I know. Go take pictures for me."

"Did you pick what you want yet? I put some for this week in the system hours ago."

She waved him away and opened the photography folder on the screen.

An array of thumbnail shots popped up, and she sat back to check out the slide show. Angry faces, placards in motion, arms raised in protest, some defensively, several dozen shots. She chose six, showing the pros and the cons, some with Maclin's acreage as backdrop, and one of the aftermath at the ambulance.

She stopped the slideshow and blew that one up. She knew all the emergency personnel shown, but only two of the four injured individuals. One woman stood in profile, having her wrist taped. The other sat with head turned away and slightly dipped as dressing was applied to his scalp. She swiped through her tablet and found the list of those treated by the EMTs. According to her notes, Meredith Walker of Tremlett Road suffered a severely sprained wrist. The head wound victim was a Shay Maguire of Sunrise Trail.

Mel looked back at the screen and enlarged Maguire's image. She knew everyone in the four homes on Sunrise, including Misty Kincaid and Coby Palmer from the Exchange, but didn't know this man. Then the long torso, the very short black hair, the slight curve of breasts struck her. Along with images of the bucket truck, the leather...

"So it's you." She sat back and examined the photograph, the body, the pose. "Shay Maguire. Damn. Did Della send you to keep the peace, tough guy?"

Mike stuck his head around the corner. "You say something?"

Mel straightened quickly and minimized the shot on the screen. "What? No, just mumbling to myself."

"Still?" He ambled closer and leaned on his palms on her desk, looking at the thumbnails she'd selected on her computer. "Want me to print those out? Or do you have a layout in mind already?"

"We'll go with this one as the lead," she said, thinking fast. "It shows everybody's anger, you can read the placards, see the surveyors' equipment, and Jed's property, too. These other five…Let's do something with them for page five, op-ed, say half page. I'll write the cutline."

Mike nodded. "Got it. I'll put them together now." He left her alone with the photos and her thoughts.

Mel went through all the thumbnails again, this time with a different objective. Near the end of the slideshow, she found a shot taken over the shoulder of a crouching firefighter. Shrouded by dark brows, narrowed hazel eyes seemed to search the responder's face, glazed and lost, so compelling Mel found it difficult to look away. The stern nose and pained, tightly pressed lips barely held Mel's concentration once she focused on the angular jaw smeared with blood.

Welcome to Tomson, Shay Maguire. Mel's professional instinct flared. She wondered what led to the injury, exactly how Shay came to be involved. The image spoke volumes and demanded to be published, but an oddly personal whisper drowned it out. *Are you all right? God, there's a lot of blood. Where are you right now, Shay Maguire? Where did you come from? Bet you were excited to be working for the Almighty Slattery Enterprises.*

Suddenly, Mel was helpless against a wave of empathy. Imagining herself a stranger to town and landing a job with the biggest name, she knew she'd have felt more than a bit disillusioned, disheartened to end up bloodied on the side of the road, even if she did have a harem of dancing girls to soothe her wounds.

But honestly, this isn't how Della works, not this rough stuff, unless this is your style…No, you wouldn't have been on the short end of that stick if it were, would you? You're too mature, too strong, too rugged. You're too gorgeous, is what you are.

Mel sighed toward the ceiling. "And you, Mel Baker, are pathetic."

She shut off the computer, knowing the editorial wouldn't be written today, not with Shay Maguire imprinted on her brain, and grabbed a copy of the paper and headed across the street for coffee.

With her back to the adjacent booth in Marie's diner, Mel fine-tuned her eavesdropping skills. She never knew where local gossip would lead, and these two silver-haired ladies behind her, much like Nana, thrived on collecting every whisper, every rumor. Ann Turner's husband Dick owned the venerable Tomson Hay & Grain, a mainstay in town with deep roots, while Ann's lifelong cohort, Francine Morgan, owned the sewing shop at the old mercantile building. Faithful *Chronicle* advertisers, the popular businesses provided bottomless sources of "information."

"I drove Dickie out to Sonny's this morning to pick up the Chevy," Ann said in a hush, "and you'll never guess who—or maybe I should say what—we found. Sonny has a woman there, a *woman mechanic.*"

"No!" Franny was aghast.

"Mmm-hmm. But get this—we had no idea—she looks just like a man. *And* she rides a motorcycle. My Dickie didn't know what to do."

"You don't say! Oh, poor Dickie."

"I know. Just like a man, I tell you. Shortest hair I ever saw on a woman, hand to God. And, well, she had a pretty smile, but, Lord help me, there she was, all filthy in her coveralls and talking to Dickie about the engine just like a man. No doubt in my mind, she's a *lesbian.*"

Mel grinned into her coffee cup at Ann's whisper.

"Bet you two couldn't get out of there fast enough."

"That's the truth. I thought it a bit, well, creepy, if you ask me. I can't imagine Sonny hiring someone like that, perverted and all. Lord Almighty."

"Thank heavens his father isn't still with us," Franny whispered back. "Dear old Leo is probably rolling in his grave, having the likes of that in his place."

"Dickie said Sonny hinted he's thinking about selling, did you know?"

"After all these years?"

"Well, he's awfully big now and I heard his heart's giving him trouble. I just hope whoever buys the place brings in better help. Charlie Bailey has worked for Sonny for ages and he's a lovely man but he could never afford to buy it. And now, this...this *woman*, well, she seemed to know her job all right, but...Imagine? We don't need that kind settling in. Dickie said her name was Shay Maguire."

Mel choked and coffee dribbled down her chin. She quickly wiped it off.

"I see," Franny said on a sigh. "Please tell me Dickie gave his hand a good washin' after that."

Jesus Christ.

"Oh, he wants to keep plenty far away from that kind, you know."

"They'll convert you, Ann. Did you know that? Just last Sunday, Pastor spoke of places for curing sick ones like her. He said they haven't been very successful, though, so we all have to be on our guard."

"I think the...the Exchange, that wireless place they claim is a café, I think that's the culprit. That's where they're sneaking into town. You know it's a barroom at night, don't you? Have you ever passed by in the evening?"

"Heavens, no."

"We go by every time we drive home from Lily's house and, let me tell you, Franny, there are cars everywhere and the music blares out through those old walls. Can't imagine what goes on inside."

"Well, I hope Dickie learned a lesson and he'll go elsewhere, next time the truck acts up."

"You bet your boots, we won't be going back. I do feel sorry for Sonny, though, losing our business, but he needs to see the light soon, or all his customers will do the same. Last thing God-fearing folks of Tomson need is that element taking over. We have enough to worry about already."

Mel looked down at the half-page Tomson Hay & Grain ad in the *Chronicle*, a high-revenue fixture for years on page three. Would it be there if Dick Turner knew *she* was a lesbian? And the quarter-page ad for Franny's Knit-n-Needles shop, also a regular on page seven, would that disappear?

She kicked herself for not butting in, admitting to having overheard their conversation, and correcting their ridiculously misguided statements. *Despite what's at stake, people need to know the facts. Bet Shay Maguire would ignite if she heard their crap. An intriguing vision...* The women were leaving, and Mel's internal debate heightened to a deafening roar.

"Oh, Franny, look. It's Melissa!" Ann set her fingertips on Mel's shoulder. "We didn't know you were here, dear. How are you? How's Elsie?"

Mel didn't know where to begin after such a saccharine greeting. Aware she'd hesitated, Mel fumbled.

"M-morning, ladies. You're looking summery today." Both women preened at her words. "And Nana is well, thank you." Mel felt herself slip too easily into her business persona, heard meaningless words escape. "Did you hear that she won at bingo last Sunday? Four hundred dollars. There's just no living with her now."

Ann patted Mel's cheek. "You are such a darling granddaughter. She must be so proud."

Franny leaned closer. "We're all proud of you, Melissa. And thankful we have the *Chronicle* on our side."

Ann nodded vigorously. "Well, enjoy your day, dear. We must run along."

The gingham curtains fluttered as the door closed on the continuing chatter.

"Such a sweet young lady."

"Truly. I hope she brings a date to the ball this year."

Mel blew out a breath. She reached for her coffee, but the cup was empty.

CHAPTER FIVE

"Maguire!" The bone-jarring yell seemed to rattle every tool in the mechanics' barn. Sorvini stomped toward the ten-wheel dump truck. "Where the hell you been? I've been looking all over the fucking ranch for you."

Knee-deep in the engine well, Shay set a hand on a fender and hopped to the floor to meet him. She straightened, bracing for war, and gestured at the truck. "I was giving the guys a hand. I think it's all—"

"You weren't assigned that job this morning. Were you."

"Are you asking me or telling me?"

He stepped closer. Shay didn't like it. Or him. And she didn't appreciate his looming presence or his barrel chest getting any closer.

He stabbed a finger in her direction. "You give me shit and I'll throw your ass outa here so fast you won't know what hit you."

Shay raised both palms. "Not giving you anything, Angelo. Just asking. And no, I wasn't assigned the ten-wheeler today. But I fixed the auger for the guys at Arena B and figured I'd help with the truck. They were pressed for time, and we couldn't reach you on your cell, so—"

"So you took it upon yourself when I could've made better use of your time elsewhere." He rocked back on his heels.

"Look, I said we tried—"

"I don't give a shit what you *tried* to do. I don't have time to waste, hunting you down. Now clean your shit up and get your ass to the office. Della wants to see you."

"Della?"

"What, are you fucking deaf now?"

Shay grabbed a rag and did a fairly good job of removing the grease from her hands. Her mind raced. She stepped outside, hearing

Sorvini mumble "fucking dyke," as the door closed behind her, and wondered how anyone worked for the man. Then she wondered how much longer she would. Or should. *As if what Slattery Enterprises wants to do to Tomson isn't hard enough to swallow.*

Fourteen acres away, she cut the Softail's engine and rolled silently up to the sprawling, finely landscaped ranch house that served as company headquarters. She'd never been inside and oddly found herself curious about the décor, the personnel she'd never met. Della. The Dragon Lady. She dismounted and brushed off her smudged shirt and jeans.

A young receptionist stopped typing when Shay entered, and ran a presumptive look from the top of Shay's frazzled hair to the tip of her dirty boots.

"Good afternoon. May I help you?"

"I'm Shay Maguire. Angelo Sorvini said Ms. Slattery wanted to see me."

"Ah." The receptionist waved toward a chair, an array of bangles clattering on her wrist. "I'll let her know you're here." She disappeared around a corner.

Shay conscientiously brushed off her ass before sitting on the antique love seat's brocade cushion. She'd just settled down when the young woman plopped back into her chair.

"She'll only be a minute. You work here, don't you?"

"A couple weeks now. I guess I'm here as a Jack-of-all-trades."

"A *Jill*-of-all-trades. I'm Lisa and I have kinda the same title—for the office, though. Where're you from? You have a cute accent."

"Yes, where are you from, Shay Maguire?"

The seductive alto from the doorway surprised Shay so much she jumped to her feet and blurted out, "Chicago."

"Oh," Lisa inserted on a breath. "Ms. Slattery, this is Shay Maguire. Shay, Ms. Slattery."

Shay enjoyed the view. Della Slattery was Madison Avenue stunning in silk blouse, designer jeans, and tall, high-heeled boots. With a gold pendant at her throat, matching hoop earrings, and flawless makeup, Della could have knocked Shay over with a flick of her French nails.

"Chicago. Follow me."

Once in the posh, wood-paneled inner sanctum, Della pointed to one of the two leather wingback chairs in front of her ornate mahogany desk.

"Have a seat. Excuse me one moment." She snatched up a folder and left, only to return in seconds, sweeping into the room with a cell phone to her ear. "That's not what we agreed, Angie. No, we can't. Fine. We'll go over it later this afternoon." She hung up and clipped the phone to her waistband as she sat.

"Are you a lesbian?"

"Seriously? Are you allowed to ask that?"

"How old are you?"

"Or that?"

"Are you single?"

"We've only just met, Ms. Slattery. Are you asking me out?"

Della stood and her stoic expression dissolved, replaced by one fit for Hollywood lights. Shay thought the transformation remarkable.

Della offered a handshake. "How do you do, Chicago?"

Shay stood and clasped the refined fingers firmly. "Well, thank you. Quite the unique introduction, Ms. Slattery."

"Forgive me. It's not even one o'clock and it's been a bitch of a day. I was just trying to lighten the mood. I apologize."

They both sat and Shay chuckled. "No apology necessary, but I have to admit, I've never met a woman so direct."

"Well, I'm afraid I'm too direct sometimes, and my intentions are often misconstrued." Again, she rose, but this time crossed to the well-equipped bar at the back of the room. "I really shouldn't offer because you're on the job, but what the hell. May I offer you a drink?"

"I'll pass, thank you."

"Pardon me while I indulge." She poured two fingers of Scotch into a leaded crystal glass and returned to her seat. "So. We finally meet. You've been performing magic for Angelo, I hear. They tell me you moonlight at Sonny's as well."

"I don't perform any magic. Just my job, Ms. Slattery. And all the work keeps me busy—and scrubbing my hands."

"Well, we're lucky to have you, Chicago. Did you know that both Sonny's father and grandfather helped out at the Five Star in their days? I find it reassuring that you come to us on his recommendation."

"Well, thank you. And no, I don't know much about Sonny's past. He's an unusual guy, but I have all the respect in the world for someone running his own business."

"What did you do in Chicago? And what brings you here, to Tomson of all places?"

"I had a motorcycle shop, quite successful after just eight years, actually. Built it from scratch, but it was torched one night and the dream ended. I'm here visiting friends, looking for a new start."

"You don't say?" She sipped her drink and shook her head. "I'm impressed. No wonder you're such a supporter of Sonny's operation."

"I've worked my way up. Running a small business takes all your effort. You invest your heart and soul, and I appreciate that a great deal."

Della set her glass down and folded her hands in her lap.

"Big business is much the same, Chicago." Della opened the latest edition of the *Chronicle* to a five-picture arrangement of the altercation at Maclin's ranch.

"I believe that's you," she said, setting a glossy fingernail on the ambulance picture.

Shay leaned forward. "Yes, it is. I hadn't seen the paper yet. I'm surprised that was worth printing."

"Can you tell me why one of my employees had to be fended off by my surveyor?"

Shay felt the small hairs at the back of her neck stand up. The slow-healing gash on her head throbbed as heat and irritation crawled up her spine. She leveled a stern look at Della.

"I'd like to get a few things straight, right up front."

"Let's."

"First and foremost, my opinions about the Heights, or anything else for that matter, are just that: mine. No one else's for the taking. Secondly, what I do on my own time is my business. And third, I was assaulted by *your surveyor* when I happened to be driving by and stopped him from punching a woman."

Della sipped again, never looking away from Shay. "I see."

"Forgive me if I doubt that."

"Your story contradicts the information I received."

"I'm surprised your information source isn't top-notch."

Della raised a sharply groomed eyebrow. "Apparently, that's worth looking into. You're quite sure of yourself, aren't you?"

"Truth is, Ms. Slattery, if your surveyor had punched that woman, I would've knocked him into next week. But then he split my head open. Now, if you want to get your information source in here, I'd be glad to set him straight, too."

"You just *happened* to be at the Heights at that time?"

Shay stared back, reminding herself that this haughty queen of Tomson controlled her paycheck. She cleared her throat, exhaled hard, and stood up, unwilling to break their eye contact.

"I'm not sure what you intended to accomplish with this little meeting, but I think I've said all that's necessary. I'd like to get back to work."

"Sit down or there'll be no work."

Shay hesitated. She scanned the lavish room, wondering if this would be her only chance. She sat.

"Listen, Chicago, I won't be undermined by my own employees. I want to make that clear. Slattery Enterprises is a multimillion-dollar operation for a reason. Now, I respect your principles, your work and work ethic, and, yes, even your style, but I require respect in return."

"Absolutely. That's fair. But at the risk of being blunt, a Slattery Enterprises paycheck doesn't buy my opinion or my personal time. And that has absolutely nothing to do with the immense respect I have for what you've built here."

Della held Shay's straightforward gaze for an extra beat before heading to the bar for a refill.

"Care for that drink now?"

Shay chuckled under her breath, the tension in the room eased noticeably. "Sure. If the boss offers, why not. Jack, please."

Della stopped at Shay's chair. "Frankly, I hope you'll choose to stay long-term. You're experienced, strong-willed, sharp, and talented. You could go far here, Chicago."

❖

The Chandler Construction facility reminded Mel of a military compound as she drove through the tall chain-link entry. The sprawling complex had grown to mammoth proportions and earned bragging rights to nearly all new development Mel had witnessed in the twenty-plus years she'd been in love with the territory. At a brawny six foot three, Ed Chandler was the General George Patton whose army reconfigured heaven and earth at the jingle of a lucrative contract.

"He's on a conference call, Ms. Baker," the receptionist told her, smiling as if their pre-arranged meeting could be set aside. "If you'll have a seat, I'll remind him of your appointment." She was back on the phone before Mel could speak.

With a resigned sigh, Mel sat and checked her notes for the interview. Several men in Chandler coveralls noticed her on their way out and their muffled comments had Mel shaking her head at the routine she'd come to expect. She'd been here several times over the years, and each visit meant fending off alpha males. Each time she hoped it would be different. *Someday, when you can speak your mind.*

The youngest of the group removed his ball cap as he approached. She recognized the wispy frame and hopeful look. He'd stopped into the *Chronicle* office a few times, hinting about the Harvest Ball.

"Morning, Mel."

"Good morning, Andy." She fought the reflex to tug her skirt down over her knee.

"Waiting on the boss, I bet."

"I am."

He glanced toward his friends watching from the revolving door. "Well, um, I bet Ed won't keep the likes of you waiting long, not if he knows what's good for him."

"I appreciate that, Andy." She checked her watch and cursed Chandler for throwing her morning off schedule. "I hope not." She knew what was coming.

"Hey, listen, um, us guys, we're putting together a letter to your newspaper."

Mel straightened in her seat, taken aback by the unexpected topic. "That's great. We look forward to receiving it. Can you give me a hint what to expect?"

"Well, yeah. It's about you being against us, wanting to stop the Heights and all."

"I think you've misunderstood the *Chronicle*'s position, Andy. It's not about actually stopping the work, or against the working person at all."

He scratched his head. "Well, sure it is. We're counting on that work. Hell, Johnson over there already got a new F250 picked out, needs it bad. And Ronny's figuring they'll be able to pay for day care after all, once the project gets rolling. The *Chronicle*'s putting the work in a bad light and that's just tryin' to take money out of our pockets."

"And it ain't appreciated." One of Andy's friends loomed over his shoulder. "We think it's time our newspaper stuck up for the workin' stiff, instead of spoutin' off about things that won't matter till years from now." The other two men arrived, and Mel felt drastically outnumbered.

The one with "Ronny" embroidered on his coveralls put his hands on his hips. "Sure hope the Heights goes as planned. With another little one at home, my wife has to find a job, and she's got her eye on one of the new ones, but we gotta afford day care, too. You have to stop riling everyone up."

Mel stood and looked at each of them. "Development needs to be done right, guys. You wouldn't dream of doing a mediocre job, cutting corners, and the like. I know none of you would. Well, Tomson has to be more careful that that doesn't happen. Problems have already risen and more will, unless the town keeps its eyes open and speaks up."

The stockiest of the men stepped forward, his expression hard. "So I should call *you* the next time my truck dies out on I87 in the middle of friggin' nowhere?" He snorted. "You got some rethinking to do, Miss *Chronicle*. Maybe if you had something to lose, you'd smarten up." He turned away and called the others to follow.

Mel just watched them go, wished there was a happy medium to be found. Her palms were moist, and she brushed them against her skirt, relieved to see the receptionist rise at her desk.

"You can go up now, Ms. Baker."

Mel exhaled hard as she crossed the lobby, grateful the elevator doors sat waiting. They closed promptly, and she leaned against the wall. Change never came easily, especially in Tomson, she thought, and people wasted no time aligning themselves and formulating defenses. She reminded herself that she'd chosen the right side.

She headed for Chandler's office doors and exchanged greetings with Mae, his secretary, who'd been a fixture behind the desk since before there was a desk.

"Hi, Mel. Sorry to keep you waiting." She lowered her voice. "He gets on those calls with Angelo, and they never quit. Go on in, honey."

Great. Chandler and Sorvini. What a pair. Who knows what either one has up his sleeve?

"Thanks, Mae." She rapped twice on the door, summoned her composure, and stepped inside.

"Melissa." Chandler's voice boomed even when he whispered, filled the room just as much as he did. "My Lord, if you aren't just a ray of Montana sunshine. Come, walk those gorgeous legs over here, and sit." He ran a massive palm across his white whiffle-cut hair. As he reclaimed his seat, he scanned her from head to toe, and Mel forced down her distaste for him.

"Morning, Ed. Thank you. How've you been?"

"I'm good. Thanks. It's all good. And how's your little *Chronicle* doing? Last week you made it up to thirty-six pages, didn't you?"

Mel's jaw clenched. "It's nice to know you noticed."

Chandler tossed a hand toward her. "Eh, you'll be a regular at forty-eight once Della's project opens." He leaned toward her. "Which is why I'm surprised you keep beating a dead horse, all fired up against the Heights. It'll be good for your business too, missy."

"As Slattery has been good for yours," she quipped. "As for the *Chronicle*'s growth, it's wise to remain guarded. We both know what that complex will do to the small businesses in town."

"Tomson can't live in nineteen fifty, Melissa. You've got to convince that lovely head of yours that things cost more today, and what Tomson collects just doesn't cut it anymore. Hell, just paving a damn road costs twice as much as it used to. I know these things. What those little shops are paying for taxes now? Hell. Folks have to start paying more."

"And if they can't? What happens then, Ed? They suffer. They're forced to move out."

"Hey, that's the way things are today. But you just look down the road: the town beefs up its commercial district, adds a hotel or two, maybe? Say…a theme park, more housing? Industry will blossom. You have to think ahead. Della's real sharp that way. She knows what she's doing and, right here," he patted his desk, "she has the means to make it happen."

Mel's mind reeled at the vision of theme parks and factories. *Is that why Sorvini's sniveling around? Is it all currently simmering on Della's back burner?*

"I didn't come here to debate the issue, Ed."

"Well, then, Melissa. Tell me what you need from me today?" He sat back. *Impossibly cocky.*

"Can you give me an idea of your timetable, the latest specifics about the plan? And your expectations about hiring?"

He unrolled a large tube of drawings on his desk and spun them around to face Mel. "We're heading out there real soon, in fact. Site prep begins in a few days." His thick index finger grazed over Jed Maclin's acreage. "It'll just take us a few days to take all this high ground down to road grade."

"So gravel trucks, the plan still is to—"

"Yup. To dump by the tracks, filling in that useless swamp."

"Quite a haul," she said, remembering the casual nature of the Conservation Commission hearing on that very issue. "The swamp… That's about fifteen miles from Jed's place—using residential back roads."

He shrugged. "It'll probably be a loud, messy parade route, you're right, but not for long. And some of what we take up we're keeping on site for the berm along the back boundary."

She pictured Maclin's pristine white plank rails bordering the road as Chandler peeled back the next page and let it drape off the end of his desk. *It's just the beginning.*

"Our septic, leaching, and drainage systems will set up like this," he went on, pointing. "The parking lots will be taken to these varying grades to channel runoff this way."

"Toward the Rohan."

"In that direction, yeah, but you've seen all this before."

She clearly remembered seeing the preliminary plans many months ago, when Della's engineer presented them at public hearings, but to provide readers with accurate, up-to-date information, she needed more time to gather pertinent specifics like gradient percentages, percolation speeds, set-back distances, building dimensions, parking capacities.

The list was lengthy. *Get to the town hall for your own updated copy, pronto.*

"Foundations are going in here, and here, and the big one for Walmart over here," Chandler said. "I want them poured by the Fourth. Once they're ready, we can get the steel crews going on the skeletons."

"These two sites," she said, tapping on the drawing, "they'll each accommodate retail stores?"

"That's right. Four in one, two bigger ones in the other."

It struck her that the structures would be occupied the instant the building inspector gave the okay. "So, you're tackling all three at once?"

"You bet we are. It'll be all hands on deck. Going to bring in a couple dozen more framers and welders. Each building will be roofed, closed in before Labor Day." He chuckled at Mel's surprised reaction. "Oh, we'll make it."

"That's one hell of a schedule, Ed. Della's aiming for a Christmas opening, isn't she?"

"You got it. And it can be done. As long as Chandler Construction's running the show, it will be."

Back in her Subaru, Mel snickered as she drove. Ironic, that townspeople were hardly concerned about such a high-rolling corporate machine, yet feared Armageddon and the destruction of their upright society should the issue turn to equal rights. *How could an out lesbian survive in this place?* She sighed, clinging to the hope that time would bring acceptance and the most important changes in her life.

She pulled over at Jed Maclin's picturesque roadside pasture and took in the look of it, knowing this opportunity was fleeting.

Heavy-duty pickup trucks sat scattered across the field, workers' hammering having displaced the normally tranquil sounds of birds and the occasional snorting horse. The postcard-like white fencing was disappearing. The easy roll of the land coated in lush green velvet pulled her from the car, and she meandered to the far end of the fence and onto the property, up to the higher ground that Chandler said would soon be hauled away.

CHAPTER SIX

Each whack of the eight-pound hammer Shay applied to the fence rail felt like it was being applied to her head. Her wound, though more than half-healed now, still throbbed, her skull still complained, and today's job of tearing down Jed Maclin's pretty white fencing hurt almost as much.

Tom Rogers stopped along the line to assess his workers' progress. "Kills me, too. I hate what she's doing to this land."

The twelve-foot plank finally surrendered and dropped into the grass at Shay's feet. She hefted it onto her shoulder and paused at Rogers's side before heading to the waiting truck.

"She make him an offer he couldn't refuse?"

"Angie negotiated the deal."

Shay grumbled about Sorvini being Della's personal hit man as she went to the truck. She flipped the oak plank onto the pile and came back, shaking her head.

"Sad to lose this acreage, though. Good thing he has thousands more."

Rogers waved his hand across the site. "The Walmart suits wanted this spot real bad, just a skip out of town, not far from the crossroads and the highway."

"But don't you think it's odd? A shopping center out here in horse country? It's not that far out of town, but still..."

Rogers shrugged. "All I know is the town okayed it. No grounds not to. Damn town has no protection, hasn't passed a damn bylaw about development in thirty years, and now we got no choice. The newspaper's been crying about it for over a year."

"So, Della got what she wanted."

"Everything's approved, so I don't imagine there are any illegal shenanigans going on." He elbowed her arm. "I suppose business is business when all the cards are stacked in your favor."

Shay doubted Della would skirt the law, not with something as precious as her shopping complex. Now, Sorvini, she wouldn't put anything past him. If anyone would just *take* what he wanted, *make* it happen, regardless of rules or even common decency, it would be him. Such a damn shame.

"What's in it for Sorvini?"

Rogers cocked his head. "Lots of folks wonder."

"So, Della sees Tomson as her domain, huh? She's born and raised here?"

"Just like her daddy and his daddy. But family legacy, generation farmers, all that doesn't seem to account for much in Della's book, not like it did to those before her. The fight in the newspaper's taken a nasty turn lately, what with Mel Baker pointing that out in spades." He snickered. "For the prettiest gal in town, she's got balls. Slams Della with anything she can get her hands on. It's a dirty fight nowadays, Mel getting down to ethics 'n all."

Shay vowed to read the *Chronicle* more thoroughly next time she got her hands on a copy.

Rogers counted silently, pointing to each section of fence. "Seventeen more, Shay. You guys need to shake a leg. Chandler's rigs will start showing up at the crack of dawn tomorrow, and they'll probably start grading this down right away."

Shay pulled out her hammer and started in on the next section.

"And by the way," Rogers added, "new rules because of that mess with the surveyors. Nobody but us steps foot on the property. Della wants trespassers arrested on the spot, absolutely no exceptions."

"How to win friends," Shay said between blows of her hammer. She popped one end of the plank free and was headed for the other post when Sorvini's voice blasted across the field. All heads looked up.

"You!" He pointed up the rise and yanked his cell phone from inside his suit jacket. "What the hell you doing up there? Get down here!"

Shay simply stared, taken by the sight of the lithe woman rising in the sun, hair a brilliant white gold against the cerulean sky. *Holy shit.*

Rogers jogged to Sorvini's side. "What's your problem? That's just Melissa Baker. Leave her be."

Shay connected the vision to the soothing voice she'd heard but hadn't been able to see at the ambulance.

Sorvini stormed forward as Melissa descended toward him. She pressed a palm to her thigh, preventing her skirt from catching the breeze, and shielded her eyes with her other.

"Sorry, Angelo," she said, reaching level ground and appearing far more amused than guilty. "I couldn't resist."

Sorvini shook his phone and yelled. "I'm getting Sheriff Davis out here right now."

"Why? Hi, Tommy."

Rogers smirked over Sorvini's shoulder. "Hi, Mel."

"Why?" Sorvini railed. "Because Della wants you arrested. That's why. You of all people. She'll love this."

Shay folded her arms and shook her head at the man's style. *Sorvini, you're such a prick.*

"Arrested?" Melissa laughed lightly. "Really, Angelo. I'm not causing any trouble and you know it."

"Yeah," Rogers said and slapped Sorvini's shoulder. "What's she done?"

"Doesn't matter."

"Call him, then," Melissa said. "I'll wait."

Sorvini glared for an extra second. "Damn right I'll call him." He punched in a number and pressed the phone to his ear, then walked several steps away, lowering his voice to a mumble.

Workers gathered behind Rogers, several of them greeting Melissa. Shay joined them, but kept to the rear of the group just to watch. Melissa's assessment of everyone was quick and sharp—and familiar. Shay dug through memories of faces she'd seen around town, of those foggy nights at the Exchange. That solitary woman in the ball cap came to mind, but she dismissed the tennis player she recalled for this dazzling lady who now observed everyone, including Shay.

The playfulness in Mel's expression softened to curiosity when their eyes met, and when she nodded a hello, Shay felt her breath catch. She nodded back, pleasantly surprised when Melissa didn't immediately look away.

"Gee, Mel," Rogers said. "Della really did tell us to ask no questions and have trespassers arrested, but I'm sorry Angie is doing this. It's stupid."

The workers concurred in unison. Obviously, none of them would vote to remove such a strikingly beautiful woman from the property. Shay chortled toward her feet.

"Let him do what he has to do, Tommy," Melissa said. "Thank you, though. Don't you worry about the police."

Rogers nervously rubbed at the stubble on his chin. "Yeah, but…"

Shay was enthralled. Like hungry schoolboys, the men hung on Melissa's every word, every shift of her legs, every motion of her hands. She had them hopelessly wrapped. *Yes, me too.*

"I'll talk to Della," Melissa assured them. "I'd no intention of causing anyone any trouble."

"Cruiser will be here any second," Sorvini bellowed as he rejoined them, staring at Melissa the whole way back. "I don't know what you thought you'd accomplish, sitting up there. What were you up to, anyway? Think you'd eavesdrop and get details of the job here? Were you spying or someth—"

"Oh, for God's sake, Angelo. You're going to have a stroke if you don't calm down."

The comment drew muffled guffaws from the crew.

Eyeing him suspiciously, Melissa sank back on a hip and crossed her arms. Shay thought it was the sexiest pose she'd seen in ages. "Is there something I *should* be spying for? You doing work you shouldn't be?"

Sorvini's look narrowed. Before he could respond, however, Rogers tapped his shoulder and Sorvini jumped and let loose.

"You stay out of this, Rogers. Damn lucky I came out here to check on things. Now get your bunch of flunkies back to work. We're waiting for the cops." He spread his glare over the gathering. "You heard me. Get the hell back to work!"

Reluctant to move, Shay found herself a bit spellbound and thoroughly enjoyed Melissa's discreet palms-up "oh well" to Rogers. And then that crystalline look fell upon her again. All thought of returning to the fence vanished. *Hello, Melissa.*

Sorvini yanked Shay's arm. "Think you're special? I know what you're gawkin' at, friggin' dyke." He reached for her again. "I told you to get—"

Shay stepped to within inches of his face. "Touch me again, you son of a bitch, and the cops will be arresting *you*."

"Hey! Break it up!" A hand locked onto Sorvini's shoulder and pulled him back. Officer Jennifer Hennessey held him firmly at the end of a stiff arm. "What's going on here?"

Caught speechless, Sorvini looked back at Shay and growled. Hennessey shook him by the shoulder.

"I asked you a question, Mr. Sorvini."

He took a moment and a deep breath. Then turned to Melissa. "She's trespassing. I want her arrested."

Melissa shrugged. "Hi, Jen."

Hennessey turned to Sorvini. "It's Ms. Baker you want arrested? You mean I drove —"

"Goddamn right, I do. So does Della."

Hennessey put her hands on her hips and seemed to ponder the situation. She removed her hat, wiped her brow with the back of her hand, and squinted up at the sky. Finally, she looked back at Sorvini. "Seriously?"

Rogers snickered from somewhere behind them.

Sorvini snapped at him over his shoulder. "Get the fuck out of here, Rogers." He stiffened and barked at Hennessey. "Yes. *Seriously.* What is it around here? The law's the law. Why am I telling *you* that?"

Hennessey took pains to settle her hat back on her head properly, letting Sorvini boil at her side.

"Well, okay. If you think Della wants to press charges here, I'll do it, but..."

"But what, for Christ's sake?"

"Well, I was just thinking about all that's involved, you know? Transporting the prisoner to jail down to Billings tonight, the court filings, the attorneys, not to mention—especially in Ms. Baker's case—the extra stuff Ms. Slattery will have to deal with." She leaned against his shoulder and whispered. "Hear what I'm saying, Mr. Sorvini? You know, for Ms. Slattery's sake? It might not be the type of publicity she wants right now, what with all this important stuff she's got going on." She straightened and surveyed the pasture casually. "But if you insist, then—"

"All right. Stop." Sorvini's expression twisted from fury to frustration. "Goddamn it." He shook a finger at Melissa. "You get off Slattery property and stay off. Hear me? Newspaper or no damn newspaper, next time I won't be so charitable." He nodded at Hennessey and turned to leave, but spotting Shay still standing nearby brought him up short. "And you I don't trust. Get over there and do what you're paid to do. And you better keep your friggin' distance from me."

Shay glared back at him. "Officer? Did you hear that?"

Hennessey sighed loudly. "Mr. Sorvini. Let's quit while we're ahead, shall we?" She watched as he went to his car. "Such a dangerous temper on that man."

"Thanks, Jen," Rogers said. "You're good." He winked and headed for his truck.

Hennessey looked pointedly at Melissa. "You stick to reporting the news, lady, not making it."

"Yes, ma'am." She saluted. "Thank you, Jen. I'm glad it was you who responded."

"Me, too, otherwise, you'd be riding in a cruiser right now." She turned to Shay. "We haven't met. I'm Jen Hennessey." She offered a handshake and Shay accepted.

"Shay Maguire."

"New in town?"

Shay struggled to concentrate. She could feel it as tangibly as fingertips, Melissa's gaze sizzling along her spine, down her legs, while this Officer Hennessey, imposing at probably six feet tall and some two hundred pounds, demanded her attention. "Eh, yes. I didn't realize working for Slattery Enterprises would be such an exciting job."

"Well, nobody needs this kind of excitement. Watch out for Sorvini, Maguire. His temper is his best asset."

"I'll remember that. And thank you for being so cool under fire. Great job."

Hennessey nodded and glanced back at Melissa. "Could I have a word, please?"

"Of course, Jen." Melissa hurried to her side and they conferred quietly as they walked away.

The air around Shay abruptly stilled, emptied its electrical charge, and she inhaled and exhaled to settle herself. Oddly, she missed that tingle, not to mention the very sight of Melissa Baker in her white blouse and baby blue skirt. The legs were sensational, the body to die for, and the smile, outright killer. But that attitude, the self-assurance and sassy confidence, well, they made all the difference in the world.

Bet she brightens everyone's day. She quashed a rising, pleasurable fantasy, a curiosity that threatened to hurl her off track. *Damn if she doesn't look as fine going as she does coming.*

❖

Shay turned the key, and the hefty Ford motor fired right up. She stared hard at the dashboard, as if daring the beast's vital organs to complain about the overhaul she completed.

"Singing a sweet song," she said, pleased that Sonny would have another satisfied customer in a few hours, and drove off the lot to put the big truck through a test run.

She took the road out of town, past the last few farmhouses and rolling pastures until just open prairie was all there was left to see. Hot June air blew into the cab from both sides, tossing the owner's discarded receipts, coffee cups, and empty cigarette packs around like a tornado. Shay wondered what such a storm would be like out here, so far from the skyscrapers and claustrophobic neighborhoods of Chicago. She didn't really want to find out. The mere thought of a Montana winter was enough to make her shiver in this eighty-four-degree sunshine.

How do they do it, live with the land as they do? Has to be in their blood, born and raised to it, like Yankees are to the bone-chilling wet of February slush. Coby's taken to it, though, which means I should be able to, too. Sonny is just a natural, like the Five Star guys. And probably even that knockout at the newspaper, Melissa Baker.

Warmth crept through her chest at the image of the attractive blonde nestled into a fur-lined parka, standing in knee-high boots in glittering snow. She curled the truck onto the crossroad that would take her back to town. *Probably has a cowboy stud for a husband and a golden-haired little angel for a daughter. And Jen Hennessey in her macho uniform probably has her doing a slow burn, unable to ditch the cop who stalks her behind those shades.* She chuckled at herself. *On the other hand, what if the fabulous Ms. Baker plays for "our team"? Was there more behind that look she sent Hennessey?* Shay had to admit she didn't know nearly enough about Melissa Baker to be thinking such things. *Do not even consider finding out.*

With little else to catch her eye, Shay took a long look at a small abandoned farmhouse and its sagging barn as she passed, and wondered how the forlorn little place had come to be swallowed up by acres of wild range grass. Towering evergreens guarding each corner of the neglected porch could tell quite a tale, she mused.

Not much farther along the road, the formal entrance to the Maclin ranch drew Shay to a stop. The well-groomed entry was landscaped with semicircles of verdant lawn, shrubs, and flowering plants that hung from stacked fieldstone columns. She studied the gravel drive that disappeared over a rolling hill many acres away and envisioned a sprawling log home with a million-dollar view.

She looked back toward the little farmhouse and thought of Slattery Enterprises's quest for Tomson land. A part of her hoped Maclin—not Della—owned the abandoned tract abutting his acreage. Surprised to feel a twinge of desperation, she hoped he appreciated its potential as ranch expansion or as a homestead, instead of commercial development. *It's not beyond saving, yet. Bet it was a cute little spot, in its day.*

She shifted the Ford back into gear and headed for the garage, but her mind remained on the solitary farmhouse in need of care. She wondered if Della had propositioned Maclin for the place…or if Sorvini had.

Or if I should.

"Isn't *that* a thought," she said into the rushing breeze, and shook her head at images of re-framing that roof, painting the porch, setting up housekeeping. "Who're you kidding? One step at a time, idiot."

But the fanciful notion wouldn't retreat. Such a sweet little piece of Tomson sure sounded appealing, far from apartment life in Boston and the condo in Chicago. Even if, down the road, she decided Tomson wasn't for her after all, she could sell the place for a profit.

She pumped Sonny for details of the abandoned farm later that afternoon and discovered she was rather excited about owning a tiny piece of "big sky country."

"Sonny said everyone pitched in to help keep up the place when the husband died, but when Mrs. Von Miller passed, too, Jed bought it."

Shay finished setting the table for supper and waited for Misty or Coby to comment. "I didn't get out of the truck, but I took a good look and it has terrific potential."

"It's been vacant for almost four years," Misty said, "and Jed has yet to do anything with it."

"At least he didn't let Della get her hands on it." Coby filled Misty's wine glass and joined them at the table.

"That's what Sonny said."

"Are you serious about looking into it?" Misty asked, and she and Coby stopped loading their plates.

Their abrupt silence drew Shay's attention from her pork chop. "Huh? Oh, well, I don't know, really. Hell, what do I know about living in Montana, let alone on a farm?"

"It's only ten acres now," Coby said, noticeably excited. "You could handle it."

"You don't think it's a little soon for you?" Misty asked. "I mean, you've only been here since spring."

Shay shrugged. "Eh, probably, but it's tempting. A great investment, at least." She toyed with her mashed potatoes. "Finding a shop is still my top priority, though, and I suppose I could live in that until I found a permanent place. Sonny suggested I look into the apartments Slattery built and I just might do that. He was really encouraging about me running my own shop."

"He doesn't see you as competition?" Coby asked.

"No. In fact, it sounded as if he's thinking of slowing down, working less."

Misty glanced at Coby. "With his health problems, he should just retire."

"Well, maybe you could take over for him," Coby said.

"And you're not renting some apartment," Misty added. "You live here. If and when the time comes, and you want something long-term, *then* sink your roots into a real place."

Shay squeezed Misty's hand. "I love you both for that, but this is your home—"

"Shut up and eat," Coby said. "Maybe Sonny will ease up on himself, give you and Bailey more hours. Would you quit the Five Star if he did?" She sat up straight. "What if Sonny offered to sell you the garage?"

"Damn, woman. Slow down." Shay shook her head. "If he made me an all-in deal, I'd consider it, yeah."

"Listen," Coby said firmly. "Don't be feeling obligated to Slattery for giving you a shot."

"Don't worry about that. I do like the ranch job, the physical work and being outside so much, but the pay is minimal when I'm looking to bank as much as I can. And Slattery money comes at a price, so I'm open to change, as long as it's the right one." She pushed her plate away and leaned back in the chair. "Hearing Sonny rant about Slattery...And then that rancher, Gronlund, came to pick up his truck, and he went on and on...All that talk about Slattery can have you feeling like a hypocrite pretty fast."

"It's not easy, our job market being what it is," Misty said. "That's why the town is so torn, wanting other opportunities desperately and knowing Della's promised to provide them, too."

Shay sighed. "I'm trying not to feel desperate myself." She ran a hand back through her hair and thought it best to lighten the mood. "I like it here, a lot, and want to stay. Where else will I find such a great lesbian bar?"

"Cascade," Coby answered flatly, and Misty threw a napkin at her. "I'm just kidding! But really, there is one in Cascade but only on Friday nights."

Shay smirked at Misty. "Why do you put up with her?"

"You're right. I should trade her in for a new model."

"Hey!" Coby feigned a pout across the table. She tapped Shay's plate with her fork. "Speaking of model, you must've run into Mel Baker by now. She owns the *Chronicle*."

"Coby," Misty said sternly.

"What? She's hot and single."

Shay's head snapped up. "No way. She's the owner? And she's family?"

"Coby," Misty cautioned again.

"Well..." Coby shrugged. "*We* know she's family."

"Mel isn't out and you know it."

"Well, she should be. It's just her damn grandmother—"

"No. It's far more than that. It's her readership, her advertisers. You know she has to court them."

Coby waved her off. "It's not nineteen eighty anymore, Mist."

"It is here in Tomson."

"Mel's a sweetheart. She can bring folks around. She doesn't have to live like she does."

"She has a lot at stake, so she feels she does."

"Well, she's wrong."

Shay threw up a hand. "Stop, please." She looked from one to the other. "Melissa Baker from the *Tomson Chronicle* is a closet case?"

Misty's fork hit her plate hard. "I hate that phrase. It's just so unfair."

Shay sat back, duly reprimanded. "I didn't mean for it...Damn."

"I think she'll come around soon, Shay, but it should be on her terms. No one else's."

"I agree," Coby said.

Shay looked on haplessly. "I agree, too, of course."

"But," Coby continued, "Nothing says you couldn't, you know, make her acquaintance."

Shay wasn't so sure. *Why am I even thinking about it?*

CHAPTER SEVEN

Shay downshifted and the Softail crept onto the dirt-covered site that used to be Maclin's pasture. The lush swells were gone now, the landscape as flat as the adjacent prairie, rising only at the unfinished earthen berm many acres away on the back boundary. It depressed her to see what had become of the tranquil setting.

She rolled to a stop at the "job shack," the project's future headquarters. She'd spent most of the day working on it with a Five Star crew before being called back to the mechanics' barn for an emergency, and even though she longed for a hot shower and clean clothes, she just had to see the finished product. She jiggled the doorknob but found the one-room oak structure locked up tight for the night.

Disappointed, she strolled around the building, inhaling the scent of fresh lumber and newly packed dirt underfoot. She peeked in the windows, glad that the early evening sun lit up the inside enough to see what had been done.

"It's actually cute, isn't it?"

She whirled around at the voice. Melissa Baker approached, tablet in one hand and camera in the other. A satchel hanging from her shoulder bounced against her hip as she checked her footsteps and crossed the rough terrain. She walked to within several feet of the building before she looked up. Shay's heart skipped. *God, just seeing you feels good, and it's so dangerous.*

"Yeah, kind of." Shay slipped her fidgeting hands into her pockets. "Come out for the latest update?"

Melissa nodded through wisps of hair blown astray. "As long as I'm not arrested for trespassing."

Shay chuckled. "No chance of that."

Melissa slowly pivoted, taking in the landscape. "Amazing what can be done in just a few days."

"Beautiful," Shay murmured, and Mel turned to her. Shay cleared her throat. "This place—it used to be so beautiful." *Get a grip, for Christ's sake.* "Angie Sorvini waved extra cash at some of our heavy equipment guys, and they're helping Chandler's crew pick up the pace. Scary what can be done with enough money."

"That says it all, I'm afraid." Melissa took several pictures of the shack, then wandered around the end and backed away, obviously seeking a picture in which the building was directly lit by the sun. Silhouetted against the pastel western sky, she stole the breath from Shay's lungs. "I'm sorry to disturb you," she said from behind the camera. She snapped the picture and went to the window.

"Oh, you're fine, eh, not disturbing anything," Shay said, completely distracted. "I just came back to see if the guys finished. I had to leave around three o'clock and we'd only just started shingling the roof."

"Any chance of getting inside?"

"Sorry, but I don't have the keys."

"That's okay. I don't really need to show that much detail anyway." She waved the camera in a grand sweep from left to right. "This is what counts, showing the site work to date."

Shay scrambled to be conversational, but her mind was swamped by Melissa's image, neat in a tailored yellow blouse, snug jeans, and ankle-high Timberland boots. She swallowed. *How deep is that closet of yours, pretty lady?*

Melissa looked down as she tucked her tablet into the satchel, her hair flowing freely and shielding her face, and spoke from behind that fine veil. "You don't mind if I walk the site, do you?" Not waiting or even looking up for Shay's response, she started away and moved gingerly over the rough turf. Shay followed several steps behind.

"There really isn't much else to see."

"Call it professional curiosity," Melissa said over her shoulder. "As you pointed out, it used to be so beautiful."

"It's a long way to the far side, you know. Eighteen acres across."

"I don't mind the walk. I need the exercise."

Jesus, you're very well exercised in my book. She glanced to the Subaru parked at the roadside. "It'll be almost dark by the time—"

Melissa stopped and turned.

Shay jerked to a halt.

"You'd rather I didn't look around?"

"Hell, I don't care." *You can do anything you want, anything at all.* "It's just—"

"If it can be seen from the public way, it's fair game."

Shay shrugged. Where the gorgeous Melissa Baker was concerned, Shay didn't give a damn about the rules, not even her own. The feisty attitude was fun, challenging, and shoved all her discretion under a pile of hormones.

"That so?"

"It is," Melissa answered and walked on.

"Um, this really isn't the 'public way,' though. I mean, if you have to walk eighteen acres across private property to see it, how is that within—"

"Okay, so I'm not on the road." Melissa stopped again, but this time she offered a smirk. "Thought you didn't care."

"Well, I—"

"And daylight's fading."

Melissa turned away, and Shay gave up trying to *not* watch that sweet little ass. *Horses, dirt, think of something, anything but what's in front of you.*

"Want a ride?" she blurted and heard Melissa chuckle.

"On that beast of yours? I appreciate the offer, but no thank you."

"You're not afraid, are you?"

"Exercise, remember?"

Shay let it go. It was hard to think, hard to maintain focus. And risky.

There was no further jibing from either of them.

Mel figured Shay had finally relented and dropped the subject. She wondered if Shay would follow her around the whole site like a puppy. She grinned, really not opposed to the idea, as she continued picking her way across the dirt. It stretched out for acres in all directions, back toward the road, where the rail fence used to run, beyond the property line ahead toward the Rohan River, where pine and spruce stood tall, and off to the east, where she had sat not long ago, on high ground now lost to the efforts of bulldozers.

Surrounded by surveyors' orange-tipped stakes, Mel stood on

the boundary, taken by the proximity, the fragility of the river. The tranquility struck her as well, the solitary feel of the place, and she longed to just sit and enjoy it. *For as long as it lasts.*

But the rumble of a motorcycle edged into her musing and, knowing her oneness with the setting was about to end, she sighed. The only consolation was that the sight of Slattery's Shay Maguire was extremely enjoyable in its own right. Even in grubby T-shirt and jeans.

The Softail coasted silently to a stop at her side.

"It'll be dark very soon," Shay explained and swung a long leg over the seat.

Mel noticed everything about Shay as she bent and snatched a large flat rock from the dirt. The kelly green shirt stretched smoothly across her back, and the denim around her rear drew taut. The corded muscle in her arm strained as she tilted the heavy motorcycle and set the rock beneath its kickstand. When Shay stood, Mel hurriedly lifted her gaze. Shay's eyes weren't the rich emerald she remembered during that damn altercation with Angelo Sorvini. In this dimming light, they were deep and so dark they could swallow her whole.

Shay tossed a hand to the sky. "I've learned that Montana nights are pitch-black, and I'm not leaving you out here."

"I beg your pardon, but I've been out in Montana nights since I was a little girl. Besides, I have all-wheel-drive and could've driven out here myself, if I'd wanted to."

Shay stepped to within reach. "But somebody didn't think about walking over acres of this junk in the pitch black." She poked Mel's shoulder lightly, then gestured toward the road. "And now look. You can hardly even *see* your car."

Mel was taken aback by the touch, but the tingle at the precise spot of contact lingered pleasantly. She liked Shay's assertiveness, her physicality. Before her nerves jangled so much they'd be noticed, Mel boldly poked back at Shay's shoulder.

"Listen, wise guy. You haven't been around here long enough to know what a Montana night is all about."

Shay's coy expression softened, and Mel's insides softened right along with it. She returned a grin, despite the lump in her throat and the sudden wobble in her knees. *She's even more devastating up close.*

"Not long, you're right," Shay conceded quietly, "but..." She looked up at the darkening sky and then down at her scuffed boots. Mel regarded her closely, the serious set of her mouth, the shadowy hollows along her jaw. The once short-cropped hair now was long enough to bend in the breeze. Shay shook her head slightly before looking up again, and Mel took a breath at the sensation of a large warm hand enclosing her heart.

"But?"

"But…you're right. Montana nights are among the many things I'd love to know more about."

As much as she knew she should, Mel couldn't look away. She couldn't afford to hear words like those, be swayed by flirtatious innuendo, even if they were from a chivalrous, remarkably handsome dyke. *Do not go there.* Mel mentally cursed her father and their "straight and narrow" contract that kept her ultimate dream out of reach.

"Well, you're familiar with Slattery's plan for changes in town?"

A shift of Shay's jaw said she recognized the turn in the conversation.

"I gather this project is just one of Della's?"

"She's done quite a few things around Tomson, and no doubt she has more, but this is the biggest to date."

"The most far-reaching."

"You've got that right."

"She is a whirlwind, I'll give her that."

Mel snickered. "I guess I wouldn't mind so much if I knew they'd play by the rules—and if it didn't promise to change the way of life here."

"You have reason to worry?"

Saddened by the thought, Mel walked slowly toward the trees and river ahead. She still needed to get a handle on just how far they were from the boundary, from the river, but those notes in her head were a windswept mess now.

"Let's just say it's easy to pull the wool over the eyes of a town like Tomson. I haven't lived here all my life, not like most of Tomson's ranchers and farmers, but I have history here just like they do. Even if I didn't have an obligation to cover town events, I'd still watch these guys like a hawk."

"I think I'd try everything in my power to protect this land, too."

Mel gave Shay a sympathetic glance. "Says she who collects the Slattery paycheck."

"It's just that. A paycheck. It bugs the shit out of me, and sometimes I feel like a hypocrite." She sighed heavily as they stopped beside a broad pine and looked down at the water. Its forty-foot swath flowed steadily along, shimmering over river rock in the twilight. "It's pretty, isn't it?" Shay asked.

Mel nodded, pleased by Shay's immediate reaction. She watched as Shay unexpectedly took sideways steps down the embankment and splashed both hands in the frigid water. She cupped her hands in the rolling waves and drank. Second and third handfuls she rubbed into her face. The fourth, she dumped on her head and Mel laughed.

But she stopped abruptly when Shay pulled her T out of her jeans, bent forward slightly, and lifted the hem enough to dry her face. Mel seized the fleeting opportunity to appreciate a very well-defined midsection. Shay dropped her shirt and looked almost longingly at the river before scrabbling back up the banking. Running a hand through her hair, an act Mel found luxurious and quite seductive, Shay appeared to be searching for words.

"I don't want to be a hypocrite," she said, the earlier thought apparently still bothering her. "If I'm lucky, it won't be for much longer."

"You're not a hypocrite. Don't think like that. I'm sorry for teasing." Shay's discomfort ate at Mel, struck a familiar chord. "You're job hunting?" She found herself dismayed at the prospect of Shay leaving town.

"More like business hunting. Between Slattery's and Sonny's garage, I've got plenty of work to hold me over until I can start something of my own."

"What's your background?"

"I've been into mechanics and construction all my life, so I'd love to fit in here, but I'm not sure Tomson offers much. I honestly don't see how this town can afford to stay so small, old-fashioned forever. And that's a shame."

Mel weighed the words, Shay's sincerity. Looking up at her, the sturdy profile against the rising moon, Mel she wished Shay had answers, a solution, would say something to make the world stop its dizzying spin. But things just weren't that simple. There was no grand solution, no guarantees, and Shay was just a fanciful sidestep in this charge toward "progress."

"Nobody wants the town to change, but nobody has moved a muscle to ensure progress comes in correctly, either."

"We can only try our best for what matters. I think what you're doing in the newspaper, you know, keeping everyone on their toes, is absolutely necessary." Shay chortled at her own statement. "Some people disagree, I know, but I don't. I think what you're doing, hell, it takes guts, courage. You have a responsibility to see things are done right."

Mel warmed at the encouragement. Some days she didn't know if she had the guts, the courage to do her job correctly. Sometimes it felt like playing a fool's game. And then other times, like now, she had faith in what she was doing. In herself. She wanted to throw her arms around Shay and hug her. *Better give some thought as to why.*

"That means a lot to me. Thank you," she whispered, stunned to be holding back tears. She lowered her head before one slipped out and broadcast her frustration down her cheek.

She almost shivered at the feel of Shay's fingers beneath her chin, tipping her face up.

Shay's sultry voice rumbled into Mel's bones. "I may not know much about Montana, but I know a good thing when I see it."

Against her better judgment, Mel took the message and its tone to heart. Her spirit—damn, her body—welcomed the comfort of Shay so near. Her breath went short, and she retreated from Shay's touch, her tenderness.

"I, ah, I should get to the office. Lots of work to catch up on."

Shay put her hands in her pockets and turned with her. They walked in silence until they reached the Softail.

"Will you let me take you back to your car? On my beast?"

They eyed each other closely and Mel finally nodded. *How wise is this?*

Shay settled onto the seat and inched forward, offering an assist. Mel took firm hold of Shay's expansive, calloused hand, ignored the warmth of their connection, and slipped into position against her back. Promptly, she set her satchel between them and dropped her hands onto her thighs. *Plenty obvious I'm trying not to touch her. Might as well. At least, in this situation, it's necessary.*

When Shay started the bike, Mel set her palms on Shay's waist and gently pressed as they rolled away. It was a rough ride and Shay kept her speed to a minimum, but it wasn't slow enough. Mel wanted the ride to last. Much to the confusion of heart and mind, she relished the feeling of Shay's hard body in her hands, between her thighs, and concentrated to avoid squeezing deeper. Having discovered an unexpected sensitivity and compassion in Shay Maguire, Mel acknowledged the comfort she gleaned from her company. Shay reached her like no one else. Ever. And a yearning for more rose, threatening her self-control and her common sense. *I know there's no way...*

Shay pulled up behind the Subaru and walked her to her door. Mel tossed her satchel onto the passenger seat. *This is awkward.*

"Thanks for the lift."

Shay gave a little gallant nod. "Any time."

"And thank you for...tonight. For the company. I enjoyed this."

"So did I, very much."

Mel abruptly chuckled at herself and shook her head. "Why does this feel like—"

"I was thinking the same thing." Shay leaned against the open door. "If it was a...a *date*, I'd try to kiss you good night." Mel's eyes widened and her blood heated. "But," Shay quickly went on with a shrug, "it wasn't, so I won't."

"Thank you, I think."

Shay straightened off the door and stepped closer. "You know, we've never been officially introduced. Have we?" She took Mel's hand gently. "Honored to make your acquaintance, miss. I'm Shay Maguire."

Ridiculously enchanted, Mel squeezed Shay's hand and hated to let go. "How do you do, Shay Maguire? I'm Melissa Baker. And truly, the pleasure is mine."

Chapter Eight

Mel leaned against the end of the bar, adjusted her ball cap, and waved Misty to her.

"You told your houseguest I was gay, huh?"

"It sort of came out. No pun intended."

"What am I supposed to do now? I know she knows. That was plenty obvious."

"Just because you and Shay spent a lovely, quiet evening together, all alone, in the pasture, through a sunset, under a beautiful moon, holding hands…what makes you think that?"

"That's what she told you?"

"Pretty much. Well, I did pry a little. Did she try something outrageous? Like try to kiss you?"

Mel felt her face warm. "No."

"You're lying! Oh, my God. She did."

"No. She didn't."

Misty leaned on her hands. "But you wanted her to."

Mel straightened her cap again. "What do you think?"

"I think yes."

"*Of course*, yes. Well, at least if she'd tried, I could've told her I'm not on the market, not one of her dancing babes."

"Uh-huh."

"What the hell am I going to do now? She thinks we're friends. Well, we are, kind of. I mean, she was sweet and sincere…understanding…"

"Not to mention smoking—"

"Yes, yes. Smoking hot. Abs of stone, great shoulders, all muscle… Jesus."

Misty laughed. "Honey, you are in trouble."

"Yeah, no shit."

"Hold it. How do you know she has abs of stone?"

"I rode on her bike—just back to my car." Misty nodded knowingly. "What? I was supposed to stomp off into the dark? And you *have* to hold on, okay?"

"Uh-huh. Stone, y'say?"

"Don't look at me like that. Yes, she's a mind-numbing turn-on, but—"

Misty raised a finger. "No 'buts' this time. Go for it. Shay is Coby's best friend. They're like two peas in a pod. What's that tell you?"

Mel was shaking her head. "You know I can't, Mist. You have no idea how much I'd lose. And the *Chronicle*'s reputation is so important, really critical now." *Straight and narrow.*

"Mel. Let the *Chronicle* stand by itself. You're allowed a personal life."

No, I'm not.

"Everyone knows the *Chronicle* is me."

"You know, Melissa Baker, for someone with such a sharp mind, sometimes you frustrate the hell out of me."

"*You*? *I* frustrate the hell out of me."

"Exactly my point. The *Chronicle* wants the best for Tomson, argues for the right kind of change. Well, hello. The same can be said for your heart."

Knowing Misty was right, Mel looked away.

"The *Chronicle* won't survive *this* kind of change."

"The *Chronicle*." Misty emphasized the word. "Eventually, it—you—won't have much choice."

"People will turn against it."

"Some, yes, but by no means all. I'm sure."

"Well, no, not all, but it won't be the same, that's for sure."

As if she hadn't paced enough that night after leaving Shay, hadn't walked five laps along the early morning sidewalks, and thrown herself onto her bed at sunrise. Even Nana's call for breakfast had generated nothing more than an inconsiderate grunt. What her evening with Shay had started now would take an army to stop.

Misty draped the towel over her shoulder. "Just once more and I'll stop bugging you, all right?" Mel nodded and Misty tapped the bar. "Please listen. *You*, as the *Chronicle*, advocate tackling change head-on, regardless of how unpopular or costly that might be, because it's in the town's best interest." She set her hand atop Mel's. "As your friend, I'm asking you to think hard about this, Mel. Just whose best interest are we *really* talking about here?"

Mel fought back the tension in her shoulders, tried to accept Misty's point, difficult as it was, hearing her own worries voiced aloud by someone else. Lost in thought, she slowly withdrew from the bar and rejoined Mike at their table.

"Thanks for the beer, Mel," he said, brightening with her return. "Hope you're finally relaxing. You need to get out and meet people."

"Who could possibly meet more people in this damn town than I do?"

"You know what I mean. How long's it been?"

"I beg your pardon."

Mike rolled his eyes. "My Tammy's been out of state for months, Mel. It's no secret how long it's been for me. For you? Want me to guess?"

"No, I certainly don't. Is it written on my dammed forehead, for God's sake? Shit." She shifted uneasily in her seat and wiped moist palms on her jeans. Self-consciously, she removed her cap and tucked some rebellious hair behind an ear.

"Come on, Mel. I really think you just need a quickie."

"Oh, thanks a lot. Look, just because you made best buddies with the out-and-proud Shay Maguire at the ranch the other day, you're still not qualified to interfere with my personal life."

"She made that photo shoot happen, you know. She's cool, Mel. Very easygoing, nice to talk to, like you said she was that night at the Heights. I think you two would click big-time. Plus—and be honest—you *know* she's a stud."

"Drop it. Don't even think about playing matchmaker."

"Hey, she may not even show up tonight."

"What?" Mel squared off with him and lowered her voice. "So. You know she'll be here tonight, don't you?" She sighed. "Stop this scheming, because nothing's going to happen. It can't. And, for your information, I don't do quickies."

"Well, you don't do anything else, either."

"Excuse me? Tell me again why I shouldn't fire you." He was

being impossible. And he was right. She *was* cautious about letting anyone get close and justifiably so. It was going to drive her mad, give her a raging headache at least. *Damn. Why am I here in the first place?*

"Mel. Just get on your feet and dance. Simple. Everybody does it. There's even a few straight couples on the floor now. No big deal. Doesn't mean you have to get all tangled up, like that over there. Shay looks a bit disinterested at the moment."

"I *knew* you were trying to set me up." Mel's eye for detail collected every one to do with Shay at the bar.

Mike pressed his shoulder to Mel's. "Was that a 'hmm' or a 'mmm'?"

She nudged him away. "Shut up."

A petite blonde leaned more against Shay's sleeveless white T than the bar. Shay finished her beer, and Mel watched the tendons in her throat flex as she swallowed. Mel swallowed without thinking.

"I'd say Shay's not interested," Mike muttered.

"Huh? Oh. Yeah, seems that way. Damn, she's striking."

Mike sent an amused look her way. "So, your ultimate butch stud?"

"Mmm." She turned abruptly and eyed him hard. "Wait. What? Are you sure you're not gay? When did you become such an expert at these things?"

"Oh, chill, Mel. It's the same as any bar. Now, watch. The sweet little thing just won't take the hint. Now *this one,* the bass player from the band coming over? *They* made eye contact."

Fascinated, Mel noted the changes in Shay's body language. Muscles in her upper arms clenched as she straightened and set her bottle on the bar. In fact, the entire T seemed to tighten across her shoulders, draw snugly over her small breasts, and cling to the flat plane of her stomach. That long, well-defined torso. Mel caught her mind wandering, recollecting the feel of Shay's abs through the cotton, until the musician's hand gripped one of those shoulders.

Shay glanced from the blonde at her left to the guitarist at her right, and introduced them to each other before slipping away.

Mel downed most of her beer watching, and when Shay disappeared into the stock room behind the stage, a raw emptiness swept through Mel's system. Reality was a downer.

"Fun to watch, huh?" Mike offered. "I think the blonde's cute, don't you?"

Mel just responded with a noncommittal shrug and tilt of her head, and that act made her mind blur a bit. "I think it's time for me to go. Three beers is my limit."

"Let's order a couple burgers and slow things down. It's Friday night, Mel. What do ya say?"

"What I say is, there's something innately messed up about an engaged straight guy following the action in a predominantly lesbian bar. You're lucky I know you're a good guy, otherwise I'd have to hurt you."

She scanned the crowd, assessing her mental state. She'd always found it entertaining, seeing various exchanges play out in the crowd. No wonder Misty so named the club. But who was she kidding? Not even herself. Regardless of her reputation, her livelihood, this living vicariously through others wasn't really living at all and she knew it. And now, here was Shay Maguire, whose very name Mel seemed unable to avoid, whose physical presence, she discovered, held her attention, wound her nerves, and energized her blood as surely as some surreal, magnetic force. She needed to push all that temptation down into the hole in her heart and stomp on it.

"So, Mel. Burgers?"

Snap out of it, sister. Beer or no beer, you're losing it.

Shay reappeared from the back room, and Mel's forehead broke out in a sweat. She upended her empty bottle, desperate for one last sip.

"Okay. Beer, yes. I *do* need another."

Mike beamed and headed to the bar with a bounce in his step. She was moved by his good intentions, but it brought to mind—for the umpteenth time—just how strictly-business her life had become, how much of herself she had relinquished to her very public role. The conflict was exhausting.

Shay passed the stage again, but the bass player stepped down with one foot and blocked her path. Mel watched them both glance back to the blonde at the bar, right before the musician set a brief, flirtatious kiss on Shay's mouth.

Mike returned to the table, but Mel's gaze was riveted to the couple across the room.

"What'd I miss? She just kiss Shay?"

Mel inhaled and exhaled, glad to find a full beer within reach. "I bet they know each other *really* well."

"Yeah, but, see? What's stopping you, Mel?"

"Will you cut it out? That's not my style. I…That's just not me."

Mel watched the couple part. The musician seemed to spot Shay wherever she was in the room, while Shay's attention seemed to be everywhere and on no one in particular. Again, Mel's mind wandered as her gaze followed Shay to the far corner of the bar. Shay didn't appear swayed by any woman; maybe that was her style, no strings, no pressure. Not *necessarily* a bad thing.

She tuned out Mike's rambling observations because every shift of Shay's pronounced biceps, every body movement as she spoke with Misty caused muscles to shift across that broad back. Mel's insides growled with a hunger she hadn't experienced in ages. She attributed her arousal to too many beers, then had to clench her thighs together to squelch the surprising hum stirring between them. *Oh, this is trouble.*

❖

Misty hustled to the far corner of the bar, where Shay stood leaning on her elbows, waiting. "May I help you, *Chicago*?"

"Oh, very cute. C'mere."

"You look like you're going to burst. What's up?"

"Melissa Baker's at that far table. Is she here on a date with Mike, her photographer?"

"Why, Shay Maguire." Misty stood back and crossed her arms. "I thought you had taken a liking to a certain bass player on our stage."

Leaning heavily on both arms, Shay looked down at the wood grain in the bar top. "I think it's the other way around."

"Melissa, huh? Guys aren't her thing, remember?"

"Um, well, see, I think she's watching me," Shay whispered, then looked slightly away. "I mean, well, 'cause I'm watching her, and, I *do* know better, like, I know what you said, but—"

"God. You're blushing."

"The hell I am."

"So?"

"A dance couldn't hurt, could it?"

"It hasn't been an issue for you since you came to town, Shay. Why would it be now?"

Shay only looked down, pausing too long. "I think she's dangerous."

"I see."

Despite the flashing "No Hookups" sign in her mind, Shay couldn't deny this pull. The decision to risk contact with Melissa Baker felt like someone had made it for her. "Look, a dance isn't a big deal, right?"

"Only if you want it to be."

"Oh, you're a big help." Shay frowned. "Hmm. I don't know if I dare. She's…she's something else."

"She's had her eye on nothing but you all night."

"Seriously? No, really?"

Misty flicked the bar towel at Shay's arms. "Get away from me. God, you butches are such puppies."

Shay strolled to the end of the bar, overtly casual, and glanced up to find Mike watching. Melissa was noticeably absent. Shay raised her beer to him and accepted his offer of the available chair at their table.

"How ya doin', Shay? Have a seat."

"Thanks. I'm good. Did I see Melissa with you?"

"Oh yeah. Ladies' room. She'll be right back."

Shay tried to relax. "Good time at the ranch the other day, huh? Your pictures come out okay?"

"They're great, in fact. First black bull calf born in these parts in fifteen years, so it's something the ranchers all go nuts over. Glad it was you showing me around, though. Some of the ranch hands have a short fuse when it comes to human interest stuff."

Melissa returned to the table and Shay's pulse accelerated.

She stood and her brain faltered. Only a table and thousands of miles between them. Those mesmerizing eyes seized her, posed a million questions, offered a million answers. They *were* the eyes beneath that ball cap weeks ago. How they had intrigued her then, and dazzled during the Sorvini altercation, and beckoned all through sunset at the Heights. Now they came with a hint of welcome.

Dear God, please don't let me fall down.

"Eh," Mike tried, looking up from one to the other, "I believe you've met. Melissa Baker, Shay Maguire."

Peripherally, Shay saw her hand extend over the table as if of its own accord. Melissa's met hers halfway, smaller and warm, oh so warm, as Shay gently wrapped her fingers around it for a second time. Shay wondered if she'd pass out from the contact. She took a slow breath as heat shimmered up her arm and down, deep inside. She felt it threaten her knees.

Speak before you collapse, stupid.

"It's great seeing you again."

"Same here."

"I'm glad we've bumped into each other like this. Do you—" Shay caught herself before asking the clichéd question.

"I'm not here too often, so it's nice to run into you."

"You can say that again," Mike mumbled under his breath. "Guys. Sit down. You're hurting my neck."

"Let me get us another round?" Shay asked.

"I'll go," Mike said, up and gone before anyone had a chance to speak.

Shay chuckled at his hustle. "He's either having a great time or can't get away from this table fast enough."

"Probably both."

"Something I said?"

"He's feeling pretty good about himself, I think. Getting me here is something of a victory. Social rather than business conversation for a change. And…" She shook her head.

"And?"

"And he's going to gloat for days about getting you and me to the table."

"Ah." She bent forward. "I'm glad about it, too." Melissa dipped her head and Shay fought the urge to reach across the table and touch her hand. Uncertain and surprisingly nervous, she wrapped her fingers around her bottle instead. "I think about our evening at the Heights a lot," she said, as gently as the music would allow. Melissa looked up and Shay relished yet another surge of arousal. "I mean, I enjoyed talking with you, just being out there with someone…someone who *gets* it, too."

"It's nice that you've taken to Tomson the way you have, so quickly. Your sensitivity is…" She let the statement hang, apparently choosing not to reveal that opinion. "I've thought about that night, too."

Mike cleared his throat as he approached.

Shay winked. "Our chaperone is back," she whispered.

"Okay," Mike announced, setting bottles in front of them. "Miss me?"

"No," they answered in unison, then thanked him for the drinks.

"So, Shay," Mike began, tucking himself up to the table, "What's your impression of Della? You've met her, right?"

"I have. Quite the experience."

Melissa sipped her beer. "I can just imagine."

"She wanted to ream out the person who gave her surveyor a hard time at the Heights. She even brought out your *Chronicle* and pointed to the picture of me. She said that, as an employee, I shouldn't have given her surveyor a problem."

"You're kidding," Mike said.

Melissa dropped her hands into her lap. "Incredible."

"She implied that I should be supporting *the company*." She posted air quotes around the words.

Mel leaned forward. "So, you told her how you felt about being slugged, I hope."

"Yes, Ms. Baker," Shay said, enjoying the feel of the name as it crossed her lips, "I certainly did. Told her if that asshole had hit that woman, I would've taken him down. Instead, he knocked me senseless."

"The surveyor was going to hit a woman?"

"Hell, yeah. I'd only been out joyriding, had no idea what the hell was going on. But when I saw him raise a fist to that woman, I pushed him away. Then he swung at me."

"You're lucky you didn't end up in the hospital."

"Eh." Shay touched her wound gingerly and saw Mel's gaze follow her hand. "It's better now. I only remember it's there when I get excited." She prayed she wouldn't blush. "That's about the only time blood goes to my brain."

They laughed, and Shay placed both palms on the table, hoping it would lend her strength for what she was about to do. She took a breath and rose out of her chair.

"Enough shop talk. Would you like to dance, Ms. Baker?"

Melissa's inquisitive look had Shay uncertain of her next move.

"You're saying there's room on your dance card this evening? I couldn't help but notice how popular you are here."

How much of a player have I been?

Shay offered her hand, praying it would be accepted. "I'd love to dance with *you*."

Melissa glanced at Mike and shook her head when he waggled his eyebrows. She sent a seemingly nervous glance over her shoulder at the full room, and finally agreed.

"Thank you." She slid her palm into Shay's and stood.

Absurdly nervous at their connection, Shay clutched Melissa's hand carefully and rounded the table, then edged them into a small space within the slowly undulating dance crowd.

Don't screw this up.

She placed a palm low on Melissa's waist, hoping her jitters were hers alone to feel, and brought their united hands to rest against her upper chest. When Melissa's other hand settled comfortably around the curve of Shay's bare bicep, the sensation of skin against skin made Shay's head throb. The warm, gentle grasp held an undercurrent that roared dangerously through Shay's insides.

Melissa Baker was tender and willing in her hands, radiant in the colorful lights that flashed around the room, and Shay felt the beat of her heart increase, her breathing grow short. In an instant she could succumb to her over all others. She tamped down the yearning to draw her closer, to feel the length of her against her body. *Whoa, slow down. Remember: one dance.*

"Could I call you Mel? Would you mind?"

The slight upward curl of Mel's lips was answer enough, but Shay was glad to hear her voice it.

"I'd like that. All my friends do."

They stepped to the music slowly, carefully, Shay's nerves sharply attuned to their connection.

Unexpectedly, Melissa spoke, mere inches from Shay's cheek. "This is where I usually ruin things."

Shay looked down when Mel raised her head and their noses nearly touched. *Jesus, you are beautiful.* "That's simply not possible."

"It's where I say something stupid."

Shay danced them directly beneath the lights. "Try me."

"I'm not a regular here. I mean..."

"Well, I have a 'dance card,' so, evidently, I am."

Mel's gaze briefly fell to the flimsy space between them. "I didn't mean to be insulting. You just don't strike me as the one-woman type."

"Ah. Well, maybe I'm just letting what happens happen."

"So you're single and playing the field?"

"Are you?"

"No."

"Then, should I expect someone to come yank us apart at any second?"

"I'm married to my work, Shay. Playing the field is not an option."

"I was, too, once. But sometimes the 'real' world hits you in the face and you've got to deal with it."

"I suppose. Ultimately."

"It can be smothering, not your scene, I know, but only if you let that overwhelm you. I hope to marry a business of my own again someday. It's my number one goal, in fact, but..." *Cripes, where is this coming from? Why?* "We can't shut ourselves off from the real world, miss something fate could offer. Magic happens, you know."

"Very profound, Ms. Maguire. Magic, you say?"

Shay shrugged, a bit embarrassed to have pontificated as they danced. She supposed it was safer than drooling or letting her hands wander.

"Magic, yes. You never know where the real world will lead you."

"No, you don't," Mel whispered. "So *are* you playing the field? Testing the waters of the real world?"

"Not deliberately, no. I'm all too aware of what has to come first." *Why does it matter if you believe me?*

"You know, at the risk of saying something stupid again, I really am glad we've met."

"That's not stupid at all," Shay said, her voice dropping. "Now my turn. I've wanted to ask for this dance all night."

"My turn. Every woman here expects to dance with the handsome Shay Maguire, but...I may not let them."

Her heart pounding, Shay glanced away to take a subtle, very necessary breath. *You are such a total wimp.* She set her forehead on Mel's and sighed, swaying them to the music. Mel followed smoothly.

"Truly, Mel, there are a lot of women here but only one lady."

Cautiously, she drew her closer still, lowered her cheek to Mel's, and slid her arm farther around her back. When she squeezed, Mel moaned softly in her ear and Shay nearly forgot to breathe.

Mel's lips were so close, they brushed Shay's ear as she spoke. "Should I interpret that as a slick line or simply swoon?"

"I'm not some Casanova full of one-liners." She set her face into Mel's hair, drifted into the feathery sensation, the spring-rain scent. "Besides, I believe a lady deserves better."

Mel's nose trailed along her jaw. Shay fought back a shiver when hushed words stroked her neck.

"Then I must be swooning in your arms."

Shay released their hands and wrapped both arms around her, bringing Mel to rest against the front of her. Shay feared her voice would tremble, but she dipped her head and whispered against Mel's ear. "Is that what this light-headed feeling is?"

"Honestly," Mel set her cheek to Shay's, "I-I haven't danced like this in a *very* long time."

Neither had Shay. Not like this, anyway, not where her blood raced, her thought process shut down, and her senses screamed for more. She struggled to find the words, couldn't voice the emotion adequately.

"That makes two of us. I'd like to do it more often. With you." Thoughts of "one dance" rattled around in her brain, jostled the escalating rush created by Mel's whispers, the very feel of her, and Shay overstepped her own boundary and ignored them. She leaned back, and her stomach muscles twitched as she hurried to allay Mel's skepticism. "I'm being honest, too."

"Shay, I…I don't get out much. My time is—"

"Would you let me change that?" She searched Mel's expression for the answer, but wasn't sure what she saw. She knew it wasn't the resolute confidence she'd seen at their table earlier. There was an anxiety there that didn't belong. "Ms. Baker, might I entice you out some evening? To dance?"

Mel spent more time than Shay thought she could stand, just searching her eyes for something, possibly honesty. Shay shuffled them to the music and waited, helpless as her nerve endings wove into knots.

"Perhaps," Mel said at last.

Shay tugged Mel closer, thrilled when Mel pressed herself into her and slid both arms around her neck. *Can this night get any better?*

Hardly moving to the music anymore, Shay found it difficult to speak. This was how she wanted to spend the rest of their night. She wanted to stay lost in Mel's embrace, hold her close for hours, kiss her, slowly, softly… *Jesus, talk about ruining things.*

"You, Shay Maguire, are a dashing charmer."

"I wouldn't be surprised to hear you have a secret list of them."

Mel straightened slightly and shook her head. She tapped Shay's chin with a fingertip. "I believe you're quite special."

"No, Mel. I'm nothing special. But you—I never thought I'd meet anyone like you in Tomson."

The song faded, left them motionless on the floor, and Shay's body reeled when Mel palmed her cheek.

"Shay. It's been a long night and I really should go. Thank you for another evening I won't soon forget."

Shay set her cheek into the warm hand, and Mel's fingertips grazed her ear, sent a rousing tingle to the base of Shay's spine.

"Will we dance again, Mel?" She kissed her palm, yearning for an answer through Mel's silence. She took Mel's hands and leaned to her ear. "We could confess more stupid things to each other."

Reacting with a sweet, light laugh, Mel tugged Shay down by her shoulders and kissed her cheek.

"Good night, Ms. Maguire."

Chapter Nine

C hicago, I've decided to make you my go-between for the Fourth project, my coordinator."

Shay stiffened in the wingback chair. She hadn't known what to expect when summoned to Della's office, but it certainly wasn't this.

"Sorry, Ms. Slattery, but what's that mean, exactly?"

"Della, please." She slid a folder toward Shay. "It means I need someone with a grip on every aspect of the festivities to keep me in the loop. You've developed a good working relationship with both my main crews *and* you have management experience. I honestly don't know why it took me so long to set you up in this position, but now's the time."

Shay eyed the folder suspiciously.

"You mean, just let you know how things are going?"

"Basically, yes." She pointed to the folder. "This is status for the Fourth. It's still several weeks away, but I intend to provide Tomson the biggest celebration it's ever seen. Slattery Enterprises will be on everyone's lips, will provide a super celebration that townspeople won't soon forget. So my foremen keep daily notes of what's been done and what's ahead."

Shay simply tipped her head toward the folder, surprised to see such details weren't computerized. "I'm sure they must love the paperwork as much as you do."

"That's a given. And to my point." She flipped through the papers rapidly and looked up with a hint of frustration. "How are you at paperwork, Chicago?"

Shay raised an eyebrow. "Okay, I guess. I can read."

"Jesus Christ." Della sat back but quickly leaned forward again. "All this stuff needs to be input, granted, but, beyond that, I need someone who can run the middle ground for me. This July Fourth thing is critical PR for me in this town, and I sorely need it to go well. I run a tight ship, Chicago, and it's a fast one. I have projects reaching full stride now that require all my attention. Actually, I could use a hand with them, too, but that's secondary at the moment."

"So you want me to do what, exactly? Coordinate your massive do-or-die PR splurge?" Shay crossed an ankle over a knee and shook her head. "I've only been in town since the middle of April, Della. I get along with the guys—and I think most of them like me—but damn. You don't really know me from Adam."

Della twirled the Montblanc on her blotter. "You'd be surprised what I know about you. The fact that your motorcycle business was wildly successful played a major role in my decision. As did your master's in business from Boston University, and the fact that one of Boston's largest developers once offered you a partnership to keep you. Yes, I've made inquiries."

Shay sat dumbstruck. She'd always downplayed her background because her love was for motorcycles, not general construction or business. That Della had checked her out impressed her, and she kicked herself for being surprised. *Jesus, what next?*

"So," Della continued, "I'd like you to consider my offer. It will pay well, but requires you to be available by cell twenty-four hours a day until we're through. There's a PC you can use in the conference room next door." Her phone rang and she pushed the folder closer to Shay. "Please take a look at this and you'll get an idea of what's involved, where we stand." She answered the phone and turned slightly away to speak, leaving Shay with the folder of workmen's scribbles.

Shay read as quickly as she could, one sheet after another, trying to absorb their importance through a frazzled haze. Did she want this responsibility? For Della, of all people? She didn't doubt her own ability, but her principles seized top billing. *They call her the Dragon Lady for a reason. Being right here at her side means pimping Slattery Enterprises, and you're wrestling with being an employee as it is.* Nevertheless, the idea, the challenge was exciting, she had to admit. She'd never run an operation so big. And it would only be short-term.

Could put that cash down on a place and stop freeloading. Someplace manageable...like the von Miller farm...How big a job is this?

She forced herself to concentrate on the pages in the folder, knowing the Fourth promised major entertainment and took full advantage of the Monday holiday. Three full days of carnival and county fair were planned, to be kicked off Friday night by the carnival opening. The big events on the schedule included a bonfire on Saturday night, a concert by Prairie Fire, the country music industry's newcomer of the year, on Sunday night, and a fireworks extravaganza Monday night. A lot of prep went into *one* night, let alone three, plus a full-blown county fair ran through the whole thing.

And the papers in her hand told that story. The carnival field was awaiting an electrical contractor. The main barn needed structural repairs on the second floor and front steps. The stage and vendors' booths were short plywood and studs, and delivery was now four days behind schedule. The fields designated for parking needed fill and leveling, but the backhoe needed for that chore had just been brought in for repairs. The town health inspector was coming in two weeks to make sure accommodations for portable toilets would be up to code. And the Grange and the 4-H Club were amidst an escalating holy war for premium display space.

"So." Della cocked an eyebrow. "Are things a mess or what?"

Shay blew out a breath and shook her head.

"Well, there're some problems, yes." She closed the folder and set it back on the desk. "There's a lot to get a grip on." Della simply nodded. "If I'm going to consider this, I suppose I should ask about salary."

"How does a thousand a week sound?"

Shay swallowed hard and hid her pleasure. "Could I have a day or two to mull it over?"

"Absolutely." Della stood and Shay followed suit. "This is Wednesday. How about no later than Monday morning?"

Shay offered a handshake. "That's fine. I appreciate being considered, Della. Thank you."

She left the meeting and rode back to the maintenance barn in a daze. *Weren't you just looking for jobs in the* Tribune *this morning? So much for seeing yourself as a hypocrite. Accept this offer and there'll be no doubt.* Opinions of Slattery Enterprises that she'd heard from so many people began playing in a constant loop in her head. With a jolt, Mel's perceptive expression came to mind—and lingered.

❖

Shay slid the little five-horse motor off a shelf in the garage bay and put it in a cardboard box for her first and only customer of the day. He beamed up at his father as payment exchanged hands.

"Grease and oil," Shay reminded the boy, and returned their waves as they drove off.

She leaned against the building in the late-morning sun and downed half a bottle of water, enjoying the solitude and independence before tackling the next repair Sonny had left on her to-do list. *Della's offer is for a temporary thing compared to what I could do here. I could get used to running this place, Sonny. Maybe take it off your hands, even. Would you consider selling? Or are you going to hang on to your history here until it kills you? Maybe, by the time the Fourth is over, you'll be ready for serious business talk.*

She took a hard look around the lot, the cracked and patched asphalt, the long, rusted sign hanging above both bays, the building's chipped paint, and marveled at how Sonny managed a living on basic, quality work. Of the vehicles waiting for repair, one was a classic, beat-up farm truck, while the others were new cars, which said plenty about the workmanship here and customers' faith in it. She knew exactly what it would take to restore some vitality to the place and make it more than solvent for years to come.

Would feel a whole lot better than running round with a Slattery sign on my back.

Coby's friend Doran had made that clear last evening, when they visited the little ranch Doran and Keary owned next to Maclin's. Shay already knew Keary as the Exchange's assistant manager, but meeting Doran had been…enlightening. A quiet, brooding horse trainer, Doran opposed everything Slattery represented, and hadn't greeted Shay with open arms…

So, you going to accept her management offer? Nothing stops her when she wants something, and Della's already got you where she wants you. You see that, right? Look, they're all about greed and cutting

*corners and they've got a track record to prove it. Have you noticed
how much of hurry they're in? With Chandler over there, anything can
happen if you don't keep an eye out. Let me give you some down-home
Tomson advice. Watch where you step.*

Shay rubbed her eyes, hoping it would settle her thoughts. Even
pouring water on her head didn't help. When the office phone rang, she
voiced her thanks for the distraction. The call proved to be just what
she needed.

Once the towing company dispatcher said Mel's Subaru was on
its way, Shay cleared the rest of her schedule with renewed purpose.
How to spend a Saturday afternoon, she thought. *She has this effect on
me?* Shay didn't trust her willpower, however. When it dealt with Mel,
it had a habit of evaporating. In a way, she hoped Mel wouldn't arrive
with the car. In a *small* way.

Minutes later, Shay greeted the tow truck driver and signed his
paperwork, trying to convince herself that it *wasn't* Mel hurrying
around the front of the truck. *Nice try.*

"Morning, Ms. Baker."

"Morning to you, too." Mel tipped her cap upward and her ponytail
bobbed at the back of her neck.

Shay steadied her breathing. Mel had an uncanny way of seizing
Shay's every anatomical part, but in denim cutoffs and black tank top,
she was deadly.

Shay gestured toward the Subaru, just released from its tow. "Big
problem, huh?"

"Yeah. Damn it. As if I needed this on top of everything else, and
when I can least afford it."

"The tow driver thinks it's a broken timing belt. Unfortunately,
if that's true, it could be expensive. They're usually pretty labor-
intensive." She leaned close to whisper. "I'll fix it in record time."

Mel returned the whisper. "Why are mechanics such flirts?"

Shay reared back. "I'm deeply offended."

"The hell you are."

"Okay, lady. I'll take my time and put you in the poorhouse."

"That's extortion."

"You love it."

Mel laughed and the sound warmed Shay's insides.

"Would you like a ride home? This actually will take me a few hours, unless you'd rather sit on some grubby stool and marvel at my prowess with a wrench."

Mel frowned, as if considering her options. "Well, there *is* the prospect of watching you bent over a fender." Shay felt her face redden. "Oh, God," Mel said. "I had no idea you were that easy."

"Knock it off. I'm taking you home." Shay went into the open garage bay and returned with keys. "Just for that, I'm taking you on *the beast*." She stalked past her and mounted the Softail. She fumbled to find the ignition without looking, and scooted forward on the seat. Mel gripped her shoulder.

Shay sat perfectly still, the slight hand deliciously warm through her shirt, and Mel seated herself behind her. Small but firm fingers squeezed Shay's ribs on both sides as they pulled out of the lot, and Shay savored the sensation, imagining those hands rubbing right across her abdomen until arms hugged her tightly.

"First house on Hitchcock, please. The farmhouse on the right," Mel shouted at her ear.

Shay simply nodded. No more than ten minutes for this heavenly moment. Five minutes into town, several down Tremlett Road, and a couple down Hitchcock. Then their connection would end, Mel's touch would be gone. She concentrated on driving, on enjoying the feel of Mel seated behind her, holding her, for as long as she could.

"Ah, Shay? I think…you should detour here, before town. We passed an accident getting here, and I think they were blocking off Main for a bit."

Shay downshifted quickly and turned onto the less-traveled side street. She was more than pleased to do so. The route added five more minutes to their connection.

"You're a good rider," she called back over her shoulder.

"Thank you."

"You've spent time on a bike, haven't you?"

"Many years ago. Another lifetime. I love it."

"As a passenger?"

"Yes. Girlfriend's Triumph. No pun intended."

"Ah." Shay scrambled for something neutral to add. "Nice bikes."

"It was a rough ride."

Shay twisted around to see her, as far as she dared, their eyes meeting for only a second, but it was enough to know there was more to that story. She wanted to press but took the considerate approach.

"My first was a Honda. Then I got my hands on a Norton and nearly killed myself."

"Were you hurt?"

"Broke my arm, my jaw, a few ribs."

"Ouch!"

She appreciated Mel's genuine concern, rather amused that an eighteen-year-old's agony could feel so good today. She curled onto Hitchcock Road and kept their pace slow.

"I like the way you drive," Mel said at her ear. "I've been on too many scary rides. That's my place up ahead."

Shay wished Mel would say more, stay pressed against her back to be heard. She let the Softail crawl onto the Baker property and up to the front porch steps. She leaned forward as Mel dismounted.

"This is a beautiful place, Mel. Your grandmother lives here with you?"

"Yes. For ages. My grandfather built it himself, and I wouldn't part with it for the world. We have four hundred acres that we lease out today, but originally, a few thousand, if you go back to eighteen eighty-one."

There was pride in Mel's soulful look and Shay observed intently, intrigued. She could tell it came from having a history with the land, ancestral ground, a sturdy home built with your own hands. These were things people stood for, fought for. The few things in the world, like love, that meant more than money and power. Shay fleetingly wondered if Slattery now owned the old Baker acreage, but decided not to light that powder keg. No, she thought, a genuine historic homestead was worth everything you could give to preserve it. And she could feel the strength and determination Mel took from that, just being in the front yard. Whether it would see Mel through her own self-determination was something else, however.

She knew Mel understood what wasn't being said. And there was so much to say, not the least of which was if they would dance again. Would they share another walk in the sunset? Dare take a moonlight ride? *Back off.*

"Well, ah, I hear a Subaru calling my name," Shay said at last, restarting the Softail. "I'll call when it's ready and come get you to pick it up, if you'd like."

"Thank you, Shay. I'd appreciate that."

"My pleasure."

Her mind on Mel's precarious situation, she took the usual route back to Sonny's, glad to find no accident scene, no remnants of one anywhere, in fact. *Impressive, how quickly it was cleared.* It wasn't until she was elbow-deep in the Subaru that the possibility struck her that there never had been an accident at all, and Mel had just preferred a longer route home. *She wanted more time.* But there was also the possibility that Mel had preferred the less visible route to avoid being seen with the *dyke from Chicago.* Shay figured it wise to bring that to mind, next time fantasy beckoned.

Chapter Ten

Nana settled into her recliner in the living room and shook her head as she brought her knitting onto her lap.

"It was perfectly safe, Nana," Mel insisted, off to the kitchen to make their lunch. "I know how to be a good passenger."

"Aside from the fact that that was long ago, Lissa, when you were young and foolish, it simply doesn't look proper."

"Oh, Lord, Nana. There are millions of bikes on the road today. That stigma you place on motorcycles is long gone. Unacceptable today. You've got to get with the times." *Understatement of the year.*

"As the respected editor of our newspaper, you need to consider public opinion. You won't continue to receive that respect if you're seen gallivanting around with some rogue on a motorcycle."

That concept stopped Mel's mixing of the tuna salad. She actually *had* considered public opinion. She'd diverted their route away from traffic and observant pedestrians, but not because she was riding on a motorcycle. Suddenly quite ashamed, Mel conceded that she had hidden her association with Shay. Nana's issue with the public's perception of motorcycles didn't compare to Mel's issue. Mel knew hers was far worse.

How could she show such disrespect to someone she liked? And she really liked Shay. More than that, she was attracted to her for all sorts of reasons, including a few she couldn't explain. *If only circumstances were different. If everyone would only be respectful, open-minded. If the* Chronicle *could survive the revenue crash. If I didn't have everything at stake.* She'd love to see more of that "rogue," Shay Maguire.

She stared into the bowl, trying to remember where her conversation with Nana had left off. Vacantly, she began mixing again.

"First of all, I wasn't gallivanting. I was given a courtesy ride home from the repair shop. And secondly, riding a motorcycle is not demeaning. It's fun, exhilarating. I have advertisers who ride. I wish you'd stop thinking it's something evil. Priests ride, for God's sake."

"They do no such thing for God's sake," Nana stated, outraged.

"Well, not *literally* for the sake of God, Nana," Mel answered, trying not to laugh, "but priests do ride motorcycles. So do doctors, school teachers, everybody—"

"Melissa Baker doesn't have to be one of them."

Mel set out their lunch on the kitchen table and guided Nana in from the living room. Once situated in her favorite chair, Nana rolled right along.

"What would I ever tell Helen if she'd seen you, hmm?"

"No one but Helen cares what Helen says."

"Just disgraceful."

Mel poured two glasses of iced tea and sat down. "Enough, Nana."

"Are we having those brownies you made this morning?"

"Only if you drop the motorcycle nonsense. If the opportunity presents itself again, I'm going to enjoy a motorcycle ride. End of subject."

"I don't think—"

"Or no brownies."

"You're being cruel to an old woman."

"Yes, you're next week's lead story: 'Abused Grandmother Denied Brownies.'"

"That's fresh."

Mel tickled Nana's chin. "Who taught me the tricks, huh?"

Nana actually giggled, and Mel had to shake her head at how things had changed between them in such a short time. Only a few years ago, they were roommates, teasing and teaching each other at every turn. Bingo, church, and social circles highlighted her days now, and Mel worked hard to keep her happy.

"Your father called while you were out," Nana said, and Mel cringed. Somehow the man managed to "appear" in her life and remind her of their arrangement too often, even from miles away. She wondered if he had called today or sometime earlier in the week. Nana often confused the days.

"Did he? Did you jot down any notes?" That always sounded

better than harping at Nana to "write it down" when someone called.

"I certainly did."

Mel went to the table next to the recliner and came back with Nana's "official" notepad. That's what the pad of paper was entitled. Mel had had some printed and, being an editor's grandmother, Nana seemed quite proud to use them.

"What's this about flowers?" Mel asked, studying the handwriting. "Is he sending you some?"

"No, he wanted to make sure you planted around the house. I told him we have plenty of petunias and geraniums and that the roses should be lovely this season—but he still won't come."

Thank God for small favors.

"We'll take some pictures, Nana, and you can pick the ones to send him."

"Do you see there, how he commented on the Harvest Ball?"

Mel sighed and bit into her sandwich. *Here we go again.*

"He was quite upset when I told him you don't intend to go."

"Nana, he never went when he lived here, either." She knew he was checking up on her. Again.

"Lissa, he was in the army and then college. But you, you have no excuse. You're the newspaper editor."

"Please do not start."

"Your father asked if you were dating yet, and I had to say no to that, too." She clutched Mel's hand desperately. "Surely, someone will take you to the ball."

Mel ground her teeth at her father. "Please don't Cinderella me." She picked up Nana's hand and kissed the back of it. "You know, I'd be proud to take *you*, seeing as you think so much of this—"

"Oh, poo! The Harvest Ball is Tomson's biggest event of the year. You should—"

Before she could think twice, Mel's mounting irritation took control. "Hey, I wonder if that rogue on the motorcycle would take me."

Nana's face went blank. Then she slapped the table. "You'll do no such thing!"

"Just teasing. I'm not going, Nana. Relax." She sipped her iced tea and let her mind wander.

And it wandered back to the circuitous route she'd had Shay take for a very shameful reason. She pushed away what was left of her sandwich, her appetite gone—along with, she feared, a sizeable portion of her mind.

Could anyone live happily in her situation, she wondered. If she had her car, she'd drive directly to the Exchange and drag Misty into one of their heavy world-summit conversations and vent all her frustrations. She certainly needed to talk with someone and hoped that Misty would be available this evening.

She cleaned up after lunch and went out to weed the flower beds. The mindless work always helped her think and she needed to resolve this conflict.

Like it or not, it hurt to see she was fully capable of doing something very wrong to someone she liked very much. Sometimes she found it hard to imagine that, after a fairly affluent childhood and emerging from USC with a master's degree in communication and sociology, her life had come to this: running a newspaper in Tomson, living with Nana, and stuck in her father's closet. It seemed to be creeping in on her more each day.

The sound of a car door closing in her driveway made her check her watch. *Shay's back already?*

"God, where did the time go?" Scrambling to her feet at the side of the house, she cursed her appearance, and that she'd completely lost track of time. *Thanks to a heavy conscience.* She hated that Shay would see her like this, hands and knees caked with dirt, her clothes, arms, and legs smudged, her ponytail a disarrayed bush.

But knowing Nana was seconds away from meeting that "rogue" she saw on the motorcycle, Mel hurried around to the front yard, brushing herself off wildly.

"Shay."

"Hey, there you are." Shay detoured from the porch steps and met her in the yard. "Damn, you're such a dirty girl."

Oh, if you only knew.

"And you're too fresh for your own good."

Shay tilted forward in a mock bow. "I present your trusty chariot, raring to go."

"Boy, you do work fast."

"I promised record time," Shay said. "I called a half hour ago, but there was no answer, so I just thought I'd take a chance. Didn't mean to interrupt."

"Nana probably turned the ringer off again. I'm sorry."

"No problem, I hope. If it's not too inconvenient, could I ask for a ride back to the garage?"

"Absolutely. Just one second while I tell her."

Shay returned to the Subaru and Mel headed for the porch, wondering what Nana had seen and heard. She swung open the door and poked her head inside. "Be back in a few, Nana. Going to the garage to pay the bill."

She didn't wait for a response and promptly joined Shay in the car. "I'm sure she'll be full of questions when I get back."

"Like who the hell was that?"

"I'm afraid so," Mel said as she drove away. "She already went into a tirade about the 'rogue' on the motorcycle."

"That's me, the 'rogue.' Will she give you a hard time?"

"No more than usual. Her crusade-of-the-moment is getting me to attend the Harvest Ball this September."

"The Harvest Ball? I haven't heard of it. A formal thing?"

"God, yes. Tomson's own social gala, fancy dress-up, and chauvinistic bullshit."

"No question where you stand."

"Oh, it's awful, Shay. My position in town puts me in a quandary, though. Nana's right, saying the newspaper editor needs to attend, but I just can't do it. Just the thought of it makes me nauseous."

"Yeah, tough decision."

"The last time I went was three years ago, and I spent the entire night fending off the owner of Bissett Ford." Shay snickered. "Honestly. He's a widower in his mid-sixties and a pig." Mel curled through the Main Street intersection and waved to a woman on the corner. Suddenly, she became all too aware of her surroundings, and wondered if the woman noticed her passenger. She winced internally and kicked herself. *You're doing it again.*

"A pig, huh?" Shay asked. "All hands?"

"Oh yeah. A one-track mind."

"I gather you, well, you didn't have a date?"

"You're kidding, right? I didn't want one anyway."

"It must be very hard for you."

In a way, she was glad Shay spoke toward the windshield. If those eyes had been on her, she might have driven off the road.

Mel puffed a quick exhale upward, blowing a strand of hair off her face. The need to explain, the desire to talk, the honesty she felt she owed Shay pressed against her conscience, and dots of perspiration broke out across her forehead. Would Shay understand her predicament? Respect her decision to adhere to her father's demand? *He'll take away everything I've worked for...* A wave of shame washed through her, seeing Shay so out and honest, so relaxed beside her. They were almost to Sonny's and such a conversation required far more time than they had, even if she could summon the courage to share her secret.

"Sometimes I think struggle comes with the territory," she said carefully.

Now Shay did turn toward her, and Mel's body hummed.

"In more ways than one," Shay observed, and looked around the lot as Mel parked beside the Softail. "So...this is my stop."

"Oh! I need to pay you." Mel rummaged for a credit card in her console. "Forgive me. I completely forgot." She handed Shay the card.

"I'll be right back. It was five-twenty, total."

"Okay." Mel didn't think twice about the numbers. She didn't care. The softness in Shay's expression was all that registered, right before she spun out of the car and that long, capable body trotted to the garage.

Sweep me away, why don't you, Shay Maguire. God help me.

Mel tried to read her own look in the rearview mirror, but it was difficult. She wasn't proud of who she saw. Shay's honesty was written all over her face, and Mel couldn't say the same. It roused a degree of shame, of anger with herself that she had never experienced.

"What a mess you're making," she told her reflection. "How in God's name are you going keep this up till Dad's off your back? Eight freaking months?"

Shay bent down to her window. "Sorry, I missed what you said."

"Oh. Nothing. Just talking to myself," Mel said, thankful Shay hadn't heard. "I get into the worst arguments this way." Mel signed and returned Shay's clipboard. "Thank you again for such fast work and such a great price. You are good."

"Not if you know what you're doing and things go smoothly. Or if you're inspired."

Mel fought back a slight blush. "Well, I appreciate it very, very much."

Shay crouched at the door and gripped the window frame for balance. Mel admired her broad, heavily veined hand, the dominant look of the long fingers.

"Mel." Her voice unbearably soft, Shay paused and Mel had to make eye contact. "Come out with me, Mel. For a ride, a walk, it doesn't matter. Let's just talk."

Mel's entire body flushed with heat. Her hands shook and she folded them in her lap, as dozens of excuses raced through her mind.

"Just us, Mel. No pressure. I think we both could use it." Shay's hesitation weighed heavily. "Maybe you're free tomorrow some time? Any time?"

Mel prayed for faith in her own instinct. She did need to talk. "I take Nana to church in the morning, but…after lunch, maybe?"

"Could we meet at the stone bridge, beyond Maclin's? Does two o'clock work for you?"

Mel couldn't look away. *Somehow, I have to get past this, before it blows up in my face, before it hurts more than it already does, before I hurt her.* "I'll see you there."

"Yeah?" Shay's face brightened with surprise. "That's great." She tapped the window frame twice and stood up. "I'm glad." She stepped back and Mel started the car. "Two o'clock."

"Two o'clock it is."

CHAPTER ELEVEN

In no frame of mind to deal with another of Nana's inquisitions, Mel decided to grocery shop before heading home. That way, she could lose herself in cooking supper while Nana ranted. Thank God it was a routine errand because she had no room in her head to think of anything except Shay and just what and how much to say on their upcoming date. She was still shaking her head when she passed through the supermarket's automatic doors.

Mel waved back at the toddler in the passing shopping cart, then turned at the sound of her name.

"Hi, Helen. You're looking awfully spiffy for a trip to the market."

Nana's gossiping pal straightened off her cane. "Sheridan is home, you know, so we're just picking up a few necessities. Then he's taking me to dinner at the River House. He's here, somewhere." She looked up and down the aisle. "Probably fussing over his wine. How are you, dear?"

"I'm well, thank you. Nana's home fussing over her flower catalogs."

Helen giggled.

Gossip and shopping. Inseparable in Tomson. Mel was starting to dread these trips.

"I'm sure he'll be right along, dear. He'd love to see you again. Have you decided to attend the ball?" *That took all of one minute.* "You know he'd—"

"I'll be working, I'm afraid."

"Nonsense." She scanned the aisle again. Mel did, too, and spotted her salvation at the opposite end.

"Oh! Helen, I'm so sorry to run. Please excuse me, won't you?

I've been trying to reach Chuck Ryan about the Heights work and I've finally found him." She wheeled her cart around and patted Helen's shoulder. "Now, you take care. Have something yummy for dinner." She promptly headed in the direction of the Chandler worker she'd known for years.

"Mel," he said. "How have you been?"

"Save me, you two, please."

Chuck and his wife grinned at Mel's plight. "How long did Helen hold you prisoner?"

"Not long, thank God. She was just getting warmed up. How are you?"

"We're doing well," he said. "Plenty of work these days."

"Chuck's working like a dog out there," she said. "They all are."

"I bet. Those pictures we ran of the grading were dramatic."

"You should see the site now, Mel," Chuck said, sending his wife a glance. "I mean, I know it's just dirt but, really...different."

"I just might take you up on that—as long as Angelo isn't around."

"We heard about that episode," his wife said. "I believe that man gets out on the wrong side of the bed every blessed day."

"True," Chuck added, "and he's there with Ed a lot, so unless you want their official tour, make sure you stop by off-hours."

"Duly noted. I picked up my own set of plans, so at least I'll know what I'm looking at."

"Oh? Well, that's good," he said, nodding. "*Real* good." His attention then shifted to items in his shopping cart.

"Sorry, Mel," his wife added, "but we've got go drag our son out of the candy aisle."

Mel chuckled. "Okay, I won't hold you up. Good to see you both."

Chuck pushed the cart along behind his wife, but looked back before turning the corner. "Mel. Our quitting time is four o'clock."

She nodded. "Gotcha."

She stared after him, puzzled by his mood change and his emphasis on the site, but there really was no need to go traipsing across acres of dirt again. For what, she asked herself, more wasteland pictures? Admittedly, details of what she'd seen that evening on site with Shay weren't as sharp as she needed, and she shook her head at how distracted she had been.

Within the hour, she found herself back at the office, determined not to get snared by unwritten articles awaiting her attention, or the advertising proofs that needed printing. She just wanted to drop off the coffee and cases of bottled water she'd bought, survive supper and another round with Nana, and relax. And think.

Out of habit, she scooped up the snail mail from her desk and headed for the door.

The sleigh bells jingled loudly as she swung it open—just as the *Chronicle*'s plate-glass window exploded inward.

Shards of glass sliced into the room, and she spun away, slamming into the door. Her left cheek and shoulder met the door's edge hard, and her initial screech of surprise turned to one of pain.

She staggered back, stunned, and heard her sandals crunch glass against the old hardwood floor. Heated wind blew in through the gaping window, carrying music from a car radio, and several passersby stopped and stared. She looked around at her feet in disbelief, and outside at the growing crowd on the sidewalk.

"Whoa! Are you all right in there?"

"I'm dialing nine-one-one, Mel!"

"Miss Baker! You okay?"

"Don't touch anything till the cops come, Mel!"

"Dear God," Mel sighed, and brought a palm to the pain in her face. A headache was arriving like a locomotive. Her right calf itched, and she found a sizeable gash bleeding down her leg. "Shit." The sight melded all her shock, frustration, and pain into anger. "Any of you see who did this?"

"A black pickup just flew by," a young woman offered, and looked to the little girl clinging to her hand, "but I wasn't watching, really. We were talking."

"Yeah. I saw it," a man added. "A Silverado with chrome wheels, but I didn't see who was in it."

"You're looking awfully pale, Mel. You better sit down."

Mel nodded vacantly but didn't move. She hadn't moved an inch since bouncing off the door. A cell phone camera clicked twice and Mel searched the small gathering for the owner.

"Send me copies, would you please?"

"Sure, Ms. Baker." The teenager blushed.

Still standing in place, Mel finally remembered her own phone.

"Mike. I need you at the office right now. Faster. No fire, just one hell of a mess." She leaned back against the counter, wondering if the *Chronicle* had gone too far and how many other townspeople were this mad. "I guess we've lost the popularity contest."

❖

Shay tried to put on an agreeable face for the Five Star workers who milled around outside the mechanics' barn, but ending a *very* pleasant Saturday this way made her mad. Contrary to what Sorvini had claimed when he phoned Sonny's an hour ago, there was no emergency here. Another one of his games, she knew, because oil changes on three pickups didn't have to be done at four thirty on a Saturday afternoon. She'd had to close the garage early and go to the barn.

She heaved open all the bays, ordered the trucks onto lifts, and systematically worked each one while the guys waited, talking to each other and to her.

"Too bad you didn't get in on the big bucks, Maguire."

"A few hundred extra in your pocket," another driver added. "You know how to run the rigs, so how come Angie didn't loan you to Chandler like he did us?"

Shay snorted as she rolled the recycling barrel beneath a truck and released a stream of oil. "He's too much in love with me."

The guys chuckled.

"We were only supposed to be out there for a week, but the change in the plans might keep us working the site till Wednesday or so now."

Shay grunted as she fought to unscrew an oil filter. "Must kill him to dish out more money."

"Hell, in the end he'll make it back. Where they're setting that leaching field now will save them a ton of time."

"Yeah," another man added, "I was hoping they'd break out the dynamite, but evidently, they didn't want to make such a huge mess."

Shay stepped out from under a truck. "Dynamite?"

"Yeah. You should see the granite we hit. No fucking way we can dig that shit out."

"So, Chandler's going around it?"

"He wanted to haul it out. There's good money in stone like that, but Sorvini told him it would take too much time."

A driver shook his head as he threw his empty soda bottle into a trash barrel. "We started on the new location today. Della's hot to trot about speeding things up. I heard him tell Chandler."

One driver chortled. "Shit, it's a wonder we're not working tomorrow, too."

"Guess she draws the line at Sunday money," Shay said, wondering how far from the approved plan they were straying and if Della really knew. "Has she gone out to see the situation?"

"Ha." The driver spit out tobacco juice. "That's a good one. And get her slutty high heels stuck in the dirt? She likes how Angie has money on the brain, so she lets him do his thing."

Shay finished the oil changes and sent the men on their way, but their words stuck in her head. *Crazy to think even somebody as full of himself as Sorvini would alter approved plans.* She sighed at the prospect as she headed home, cruising along the back roads to air out all her scrambled thoughts.

She rolled past the von Miller place, a lonely sight in this honeyed sunset, she thought, and rumbled past Maclin's scenic driveway and all the way around to the Heights. Quiet backhoes and dump trucks sat scattered across the acreage, and she wished she knew more about what she was seeing.

On the chance she might find Della at work, she cruised back to the Five Star to get some things off her chest. *What can I say? You're expecting me to run your July Fourth propaganda show while you're doing what, exactly?*

She parked behind the building, beside the trademark BMW, and found Della's office door open.

"Chicago. What brings you here?"

"Got a minute?"

Della waved her toward a chair. "I didn't expect to see you until Monday morning. I hope you're here to give me good news."

Shay crossed an ankle over a knee. "It's a great offer, Della, a professional opportunity I don't think I can turn down."

"Excellent." She gleamed with excitement. "The folder here—"

"Wait, please. I need to say a few things, and…you may not be so thrilled."

Della sat back, hands folded on her blotter. "I'm listening."

"I have to tell you that I am not a fan of developing Tomson, this entire territory."

"And why is that? Should it remain ragtag for posterity?"

"Should it be desecrated for profit?"

"Oh, is that what I'm about?"

"I don't know enough to answer that, Della, but the people of Tomson apparently feel it's a foregone conclusion where you're concerned, that they're caught between a rock and a hard place."

"The people of Tomson may begrudge it, but this *is* the twenty-first century. Time does not stand still, and if they don't keep up, their lives here will pass them by. Even an old-timer like Jed Maclin agreed. Would townspeople rather see their land picked apart by a parade of outsiders? Or instead, go to someone from within, whose master plan has the best interest of the town at heart?"

"But is that what's really happening here? Can you honestly say that turning an ass like Sorvini loose out there is for the town's best interest?"

"Now, listen. Angie can be a son of a bitch, but he knows this town, how I operate, and he gets what I want accomplished. I've never had to ride herd over him."

"Are he and Chandler playing games out there? Do you know about changes being made?"

"We're meeting all the necessary requirements that, I dare say, any other developer wouldn't give a damn about."

"Ah. Your ever-reliable 'information source' has told you so?"

"*I'm* telling you that Ed Chandler didn't get where he is by mistake. He's a professional and knows the rules. And Angie is on-site to provide anything Ed needs to expedite the project. I don't have to babysit either of them."

"So, you really don't worry about them doing their own thing out there? Sorvini in particular?"

"Angie's seeing to it that this project succeeds, and no, I don't worry about what he's doing. And neither should you. The project itself doesn't even concern you."

"It does if I'm running a monumental PR job to make you look good."

Della cocked her head. "You realize you are seconds away from pissing me off."

"That was never my intention." Shay sighed inside. She hadn't reached Della at all. "But maybe somebody getting mad is what it's going to take to make everybody happy."

Della smiled wryly as she sat back. "I have to say, this fiery spirit of yours is what I need here. Your integrity is invaluable, commendable, and I feel fortunate to have you. I don't want you discouraged by decisions I may or may not make."

CHAPTER TWELVE

Shay crossed the great room, buttoning a new red checkered shirt over a white tank top. Misty eyed her from the breakfast bar.

"You look terrific. Very sharp. Very country."

Shay looked up quickly. "Do I look like a hick?"

"No, silly. You're fine." She pushed a wicker basket toward her along the countertop. "This is for you."

"A picnic basket? Jeez. Thank you, but that makes it an official date. It really isn't. I mean, it shouldn't be because I...shit. It *is*, isn't it?" Her shoulders drooped. "This is a mistake."

"What? Why?"

Shay paced to the living room window. "Because I've got to keep my priorities straight. Do you have her number? Christ, I don't even have her number. See? I don't concentrate well around her." She pulled her shirts out of her jeans. "This was a very bad idea, and I need to call it off right now." She paced back to the kitchen. "What was I thinking?"

"That you like each other and would enjoy spending a little time together?"

"I don't think I should be playing with fire, here, not with a job decision and a business future hanging over my head."

"Then why—"

"Because I can't help myself, goddamn it. Mel just..." She sent Misty a desperate look. "I can't help it."

"I think you need to calm down. There's nothing wrong with hanging out and talking."

Shay tossed a hand at the basket. "What's she going to think when I show up with that? Be serious."

"I *am* being serious. Stop being such a fart. Mel will be touched."

She lifted the linen napkin that covered the basket. "Just some crackers and cheese, some grapes. And a bottle of wine and some glasses."

"Misty. I hadn't intended for it to be anything special, and now I don't—"

"Right. Nothing you'd put on a new shirt and cool jeans for."

"I just didn't want her to think I was some slug, you know?"

"If she thought that, she wouldn't have agreed to this."

"I don't know. Danger bells are ringing in my head."

"Jesus, they're not wedding bells. Go and relax, for God's sake."

"So…" She wandered to the back door and stared toward the lake. With a heavy sigh, she turned back to Misty. "So, this shirt's okay?"

Coby entered from the back porch, eyeing Shay up and down.

Shay stopped tucking in her shirts. "Don't you start."

"You goin' a-courtin', I see."

"Jesus." Now a bit frantic, she looked to Misty. "See? I *do* look like a hick on the make."

"No, you do not. Coby, cut it out." She set the basket in Shay's hands. "Here. Strap this on the bike and get out of here or you'll be late."

Shay stared down at the basket. She really wasn't sure this was a good idea. *Time alone with Mel, some casual conversation about work, backgrounds, feelings. You know damn well where you want this to go.*

It was an isolated but bucolic fifteen-minute ride to the far boundary of the Maclin ranch, and Shay was grateful for every second. Her nerves were shot and her sweaty palms slid all over the bike's handgrips. She wiped each palm on a thigh. The wind was almost too warm in her face and did nothing to keep her hair from standing straight up, but the bedhead look couldn't be helped. Besides, putting on a helmet would only make her scalp sweat like the rest of her. The breeze was a godsend.

Just what they were supposed to talk about, Shay struggled to remember. But they did need time together alone. Hopefully, Mel would be relaxed enough to discuss her catch-22 lifestyle and even release some of that burden. *Mel can't expect to live her entire life in the closet because of her newspaper, can she? Is that what this afternoon will reveal? We'll probably never even open Misty's wine.*

But Shay had things to say, too, a catch-22 of her own, and her mind spun. *Mel seemed to accept my situation with Slattery. Maybe she knows too well what it's like, having to do one thing when you believe in another.* It crossed her mind that Mel just might be blind to what they had in common.

Shay slowed the Softail over the bridge and spotted the Subaru. Mel stepped out as Shay rolled up beside her and shut off the bike.

The perfect breeze wafted Mel's hair across her shoulders, and she reached up to draw it back. As usual, Shay was nearly swept away by the look of her.

"Fancy meeting you here."

Mel tucked her hands into the pockets of her khaki shorts and blatantly surveyed Shay's shirt. "Gotta say, Shay, you look really good in red checks."

Shay looked away as she dismounted. "Tell me you don't think I look like a hick."

"You? A hick? Hardly. What have you got there?"

Shay unstrapped the basket and held it up. "Misty."

"Ah. She figured we might get hungry?"

"I think so." Shay felt the color rise in her cheeks.

"Well, that's very sweet of her. She's always thinking."

"I'd say we both know what she's thinking." Shay pulled a worn wool blanket from a saddlebag and draped it over her shoulder. "So... Hey, is that a bruise at your eye?"

"Afraid so. Someone busted one of the big windows in our office yesterday and I turned away and collided with the door."

Shay stopped short and studied Mel's bruise. "Jesus, Mel. You're lucky."

"The EMT said that, too." She turned to show the bandage on her calf. "This took a few stiches, but, overall, yeah, I was lucky. Chunks of glass went everywhere."

"Come over here," Shay said, and hurried to an open, flat area where they would watch the creek flow, and shook out the blanket. "Sit. You probably should be resting that leg." She set the basket nearby and sat beside her. "So...who the hell...?"

"The police agree with us that, most likely, it was an irate reader, someone who'd had enough of the *Chronicle*'s position. We've been aggressively editorializing about Slattery's tainted project history, and stressing that quick-and-easy development demands severe oversight. I suppose we should have anticipated such a response."

"Do the cops know who did it?"

"Yeah. They pieced together a description of the passing truck from a few witnesses and they know the owner. A Chandler employee, a guy in his twenties."

"Shit, Mel. That doesn't sound like small-town stuff. Hell, Chicago, sure, but here?"

"I know. Another sign of how times are changing, I guess, and of how desperate some folks are to improve their situations."

Shay dragged the basket closer and pulled out the wine. "I think we need to tap this now." She poured Shiraz into both glasses.

"Thanks, Shay. This is all very nice of you. I don't remember the last time I did anything like it."

"I think…never, for me."

"The chivalrous Shay Maguire has never taken a girl on a picnic?"

"Ha. No." *She thinks it's a date, too.*

"I find that very hard to believe."

"And you, Ms. Baker, no picnics? Not even secret rendezvous?"

Mel sipped her wine and scanned the creek. "Another lifetime."

"Hmm. Back in the days of Triumphs and rough rides, I gather."

"Those ended quite a few years ago, Shay. I moved out here to care for Nana and run the *Chronicle*, and bang—a door slammed shut. So, it was another lifetime." She stretched her legs out and crossed her ankles. Shay looked away, surveyed the water just to keep from gazing upon her.

"Sounds like there are regrets."

"Eh, maybe. Sometimes, I wish I could pick it all up and move it to a more progressive place, you know? The world is different here. Change is slow."

"And difficult."

"It must seem downright prehistoric to you, coming from Chicago." She seemed to seek confirmation, and Shay wanted her to have it.

"At times, yeah. But I was prepared to be hassled a lot more than I have been. Sorvini is the only pain in my ass, so I guess that says a lot."

"He's a pain in everyone's ass."

"So I'm learning."

Mel kicked off her sandals and leaned back on her elbows. "I've thought a lot about what you said that night at the Exchange, about getting hit by the 'real world.' Does it mean you didn't date much in Chicago? You really seem to enjoy the bar scene here."

Shay chortled and looked down at her. "I've been single for a couple years, but the Exchange is the first bar I've been to more than once in a very long time. After Lee left, I put everything I had into my business and rarely dated. The *Chronicle* doesn't let you get out much either, does it?"

"People are stuck in their old ways and they see me as a reflection of them, and the *Chronicle* as a reflection of me. They'd flip out."

"If they knew you were a lesbian." *There. It's been said out loud.*

Mel nodded as she sat up and wrapped her arms around her knees. Shay turned to face her. "What could they do?"

"Turn up the homophobic heat, turn folks against me. But mostly I fear they'd pull their advertising, and we just make ends meet as it is."

"But you're the only game in town. Wouldn't they *have* to use the *Chronicle*?"

Mel shrugged. "They could cut back on us, go to the *Tribune*. It's a daily and more expensive, but it's something, even though it has only half our circulation."

"But people devour the *Chronicle* religiously, Mel. They love you."

"The Mel they think they know, maybe," she said with a self-deprecating little smile. "It's a step I can't afford to take."

"I would think the really good people would stand by you."

"Thanks, Shay. I wish I could count on that, because I'd love to just be me. It's difficult to editorialize about the changes in town when I don't dare do a thing about myself. I encourage Tomson to take cautious steps forward, while I sit behind that damn desk, wrapped in my own insular world. Hiding. I'm not proud of it. Makes me feel…"

"I understand the feeling. You remember me rambling on that first time we talked, frustrated about working for Slattery."

"It struck pretty close to home."

"We're more like comrades-in-arms than you realize."

Mel angled her head and looked away. "Good point."

Shay poured more wine. They had met at a crossroad and she wanted them to linger. She touched their glasses together.

"What are we toasting?" Mel asked.

"Courage."

"Oh, I'll drink to that."

They sipped the wine, and Mel peered into the basket.

"Cheese and stuff," Shay said, watching her, trying to ignore her insistent heart.

Mel selected a cube of cheese, but just stared at it instead of popping it into her mouth. "I don't want to be a hypocrite either, Shay."

The statement made Shay lower her glass. Mel dropped her hand and looked toward the water. Shay watched the delicate jaw clench, disturb the soft profile, and knew Mel wrestled with conflict as much as she did.

"Are we?"

Mel's eyes moistened. "Oh, I think so."

"I've never felt like this before, torn up inside. It makes me crazy sometimes." Mel's lips pressed together tightly as she nodded. "Look, Mel. It's not like no one's ever been able to figure out this difficult stuff. Right? It can be done."

Mel shook her head. "My life would be turned upside down, Shay. Nana's a tough nut to crack as it is, and the paper? God help me. I'd lose it all."

Shay couldn't quite see the severity of Mel's situation, considering folks hadn't turned her own presence in Tomson into a national crisis, but the loneliness in Mel's tone signaled a deep fear and begged understanding. "I get it, Mel. Well, I think I do. I'm looking at becoming a part of the Slattery operation in a big way, and my head's all screwed up about it."

"A big way? How big?"

"Della's asked me to be her project manager for the Fourth."

"Really? You'd be in deep with her, then."

"Believe me, I have mixed feelings about it."

"It's all just Heights propaganda, I'm sure you realize."

"Like I need to add that baggage to what I already carry." She touched Mel's chin lightly, turned her to face her. "But I think I need to take the challenge. For me. I'm going to make it worth my while. I think the same applies to you. And I think you agree."

"I've been seeing myself all too well lately, Shay, and I haven't been making me proud."

"Well, you should be proud, Mel, because it takes so much to go against the grain as much as you have. It's not always easy to stand your ground, especially when you're battling two highly emotional issues." She slid her palm over Mel's hand and squeezed. "I'm proud of you."

Mel's look probed Shay's self-control, made her question whether anyone had ever acknowledged Mel's efforts, made her want to say more reassuring things and bolster her spirit, be the one who made her smile. But Shay's breath caught when Mel leaned closer.

"You know, Shay? I'm proud of you, too." She touched her lips to Shay's and sat back.

"I, um…" Helplessly stunned, Shay chuckled at herself. "I think my brain just short-circuited."

"Obviously, mine is going in a million directions. I can't believe I just did that."

"I like that you did."

"Jesus, Shay, there's no way to…to be myself without losing everything I've got. You make me want to throw caution to the wind, when I know I can't."

"The first time I saw you, I knew you were special. You were drinking alone, wearing a USC shirt and your cap."

"I remember that night, too. Casanova Shay Maguire waltzed out with a dancing babe."

"What did I know?" She clinked her glass to Mel's. "We're all entitled to the occasional lapse in judgment." She hoped Mel saw it that way. She never wanted Mel to see her as a player again, and ignored the reason why.

It was a pleasure to see Mel's face brighten, for any reason. She wanted that glow to last, and despite the cautionary whispers in the back of her mind, she wanted those eyes to sparkle for her. And, as she knew it would, her self-control succumbed.

"You *are* special, Melissa Baker. So very special." She stroked Mel's hair and lightly cupped her head. She brushed her lips across Mel's and nestled their mouths together carefully. Mel's drew on hers so willingly Shay's heart pounded in her ears. Shay angled her head, intensified their kiss, and Mel draped her arm around Shay's neck, still holding her glass.

Slightly breathless, Shay drew back and rested her forehead against Mel's.

"Wow."

"Your kiss is a killer."

Shay whispered onto her lips. "Let's try it again."

"This is too dangerous, Shay."

"I know." Shay kissed Mel's upper lip. "We shouldn't."

Mel tightened her arm around Shay's neck, her mouth a breath away. "No, we shouldn't."

"Such a bad idea."

Shay kissed her slowly, fully, wrapped her arm around Mel's waist, and drew her against her chest. Mel moaned into her mouth, and Shay moaned in agreement and kissed her way carefully, luxuriously along the satin of Mel's jaw and throat, to the edge of her collar. Mel's free hand traveled up her back, into her hair, torching her scalp. She held Shay's lips in place on her neck.

"God, Shay."

"I know." Shay kissed her way upward. "Such a breathtaking… bad idea." She covered Mel's mouth in a long, deep kiss, squeezing her closer. She set her wine glass aside blindly and lay back, taking Mel with her.

Mel broke their kiss, gasped lightly as they went to the ground, and tossed her glass onto the grass.

Shay filtered her fingers through the airy silk of Mel's hair, let splayed hands wander across Mel's shoulders and back, and hugged her tighter. Her eyes closing, she watched her boundaries, her conscientious intentions melt away, and with Mel's urgent kiss, her head spun. Her entire body warmed beneath Mel's excited breaths, at the touch of plush, wet lips to her cheek, her ear. Shay squeezed Mel's ass with both hands and pressed their hips together with a groan. Mel breathed heavily in her ear, and Shay turned and took her lips hungrily.

Mel lifted her head to see her. "This is where I ruin things."

"No." Shay chased Mel's kiss. "Nothing can ruin this moment."

Mel took Shay's head in both hands and kissed her back onto the grass. "Something this sudden feels so good?"

Shay couldn't have agreed more. *How easily we could take each other right here, right now.*

"Don't ask." Shay rolled them over, off the blanket, her thigh landing between Mel's legs and causing Mel to arch against her. She reveled in the clutch of Mel's fingers kneading into her back, the grind of Mel's abdomen against hers, and sighed longingly beneath her chin.

Unconscious desire drew Shay's hands upward, her palms onto Mel's full breasts, and Mel groaned with arousal when Shay squeezed.

Another such moment could be forever away. Will there be another? Or is this as close as we ever get? It's meant so much, these first kisses, but our first time would mean the world...

Shay raised her head and Mel's look was glazed, lids half lowered as if in surrender. *She overwhelms all my common sense yet brings me to my senses in a heartbeat? Yes, so soon to be anything but special.* She rose over Mel on outstretched arms and studied the swollen lips, the high rosy cheekbones, the faint, finely arched brows. But the welcoming eyes allowing her the freedom to gaze gradually moistened.

"Shay." Mel palmed her cheek, beseeching. "We—I can't. I don't know what I was..." Shay drew back as Mel sat up. "I guess I stopped thinking. I shouldn't have let us get this far. I'm sorry."

Even though she'd been ready to halt this herself, Shay couldn't hide her disappointment. "I started this and got carried away. I'm the one who—"

"But I'm being...I need to apologize." Mel entwined their hands. "It can't matter how you make me feel or how I feel about you. I have to see beyond that." She shook her head. "I'm so, so sorry. God, this was such a mist—"

Shay pressed a finger to Mel's lips. "Don't. Just don't." She closed Mel's hands together and kissed them. "*I'm* sorry I pushed."

"There was no pushing involved, Shay. Quite the opposite." She cupped Shay's face in her hand and ran a thumb across her lips. "My life is a mess, yet I still let this happen. I think you're wonderful. God knows, I don't want to hurt you, mislead you. I just...can't."

Shay lowered her forehead to Mel's, feeling helpless to stop truth from pouring out. "I'll help you in any way I can. If you let me. Will you remember that?" She brought her lips to within a breath of a kiss and heard herself say things her heart believed were inevitable. "I'm not going away." She touched her lips to Mel's. "You feel so right. *We* are so right."

Chapter Thirteen

Buried in paperwork at her desk Monday morning, Mel jumped when Mike burst into the office.

"Hey, Mel. Come on. Big to-do at the lumber yard." He was almost out the door when Mel yelled.

"Wait! What? Moriarty's?" She grabbed a small notepad off her desk and hurried after him. "Did you give him the check for our window?"

"'Course I did." He swung open his car door. "This is about Sorvini with Bob and his boys. A guy at the diner just left them. Says there's going to be a fight."

She found it hard to imagine that Bob Moriarty could be set off, period, even by someone like Sorvini. Bob and his two sons were among the most likeable, hardest-working families in Tomson.

Two pickups from the Five Star, one of them Sorvini's signature red dually, sat at the loading dock on the side of the massive building. Mel could hear the shouting as they arrived.

"Told you we don't have all the inventory yet," Bob snarled up at Sorvini. "You think I'm moving heaven and earth for you now? Forget it!"

"All the business we give you? Listen, asshole. We oughta just march in there and take what we need!"

"You step foot inside and I'll take you on myself!"

Sorvini checked over his shoulder, apparently reassured the three Five Star workers still provided backup. To Mel, they just seemed amused. Sorvini loomed over him, and Bob's sons closed ranks around their father. She elbowed Mike and nodded discreetly, the signal to shoot.

"You don't intimidate me, you son of a bitch." Moriarty stabbed a finger into Sorvini's barrel chest. "I deal with Tom Rogers for a reason. He comes here, we'll talk, but you—you get off my property."

"Rogers, that idiot, should've been dealing with Home Depot all along. He's off today, so I'm here and you'll damn well deal with me. You've held up the work long enough." He summoned the Five Star men forward. "We'll take what we can now."

"The hell you will!"

"I'll call Sheriff Davis, Dad."

"Good!" Sorvini spat. "I want the cops to know you're holding out when we've paid good bucks already—and I won't push my schedule back any further because of you."

"Actually, it's *my* schedule," Shay interrupted, suddenly emerging between the Five Star workers. She strode up to Sorvini. "I'm coordinating work for the Fourth for Ms. Slattery as of today."

Mel's pen froze on the paper. Shay was the last person she expected to see. Sorvini obviously thought the same, except she doubted he felt that pleasurable heat rush through his system.

Sorvini stepped back, wide-eyed. "What the fuck are you talking about? Get lost."

Shay extended a hand to Bob. "Shay Maguire, Mr. Moriarty. Can we speak in your office, please?"

Sorvini looked ready to swing at her.

"Get the fuck out of here, Maguire. You don't know shit about what's going on."

"Excuse us, *Mr.* Sorvini. You're needed back at the office right away."

Bob, meanwhile, looked from Shay to Sorvini, back at his sons, and shrugged before cocking his head at Shay. "Maguire, you said?"

"Shay. Yes, sir. I think we can discuss our situation civilly inside, don't you?"

Sorvini yanked Shay around by the shoulder to face him. "What the hell are you doing? Goddamn dy—"

"Ms. Slattery asked to see you immediately."

Sorvini glowered, nostrils flaring. "You and I will have us a talk later. Count on it." He glared at Bob and spun away, waving the Five Star workers to follow.

With the trucks gone, Mel and Mike stood exposed in the lot.

"Hell of a start to the morning," she said. "Hi, guys. Shay."

Bob ran a weary hand across his face. "Morning, Mel. Wish you wouldn't print any of that. Business is slow enough." He looked fearfully at Mike.

"With his reputation, Bob, it might be *good* for business. You have nothing to worry about. Trust me."

Shay took several steps toward her. "I need to speak with Mr. Moriarty, Mel, if you're done." She took an extra second to assess the darkening bruise at Mel's eye. *And here I thought all this makeup would hide the shiner. Damn.* "Mel?"

"Just, ah…" Mel forced her attention to her notes. Looking at Shay was risky. The mussed hair, the authoritative stance, those soft mind-numbing lips…Strong, ready, sexy. A powerful visceral memory of that hard body yearning beneath her forced Mel to shuffle awkwardly.

"I, ah…" Her composure was slipping. The stall tactic didn't help and she looked up, smiling. Shay's frown lifted and she winked. A tremor weakened Mel's knees, and she fought to ignore it. *Damn that dark, windblown look. Jesus.* "Well, maybe you could just, ah, well, is there a chance the festivities won't go off as planned? Eh, are you really dangerously behind schedule?" Relief washed through her at having mustered a legitimate question.

"Well," Shay glanced at Bob, "we need to go over some things first, but I have a feeling we're in good shape."

Bob appeared to appreciate Shay's positive endorsement. He nodded eagerly.

"We always stand ready to help," he said and waved Shay inside. "Let's talk."

Shay backed away from Mel. "See? Sorvini will be the death of me, I swear."

Mel shook her head. "Don't let that happen, Shay."

"See you around, Ms. Baker."

Mel purposely avoided watching her go. She looked back at her notes as she returned to Mike's car, thankful for a getaway vehicle. Mike chuckled under his breath as he drove.

"What's so funny?"

"You didn't see Bob's son, Rick, checking you out?"

"Stop. You're sounding more like my grandmother every day."

"Shay knocks you off your feet."

Mel stared at him. "That's ridiculous."

"Is it? She really *is* good-looking, just in case you haven't noticed."

"Shut up."

"Kind of, hmm, I don't know, devilishly handsome."

"I know what she looks like."

"Well, I've met some butch lesbians before, but she's—"

"Will you stop already? I know she's hot."

Still grinning, Mike parked in front of the office, and Mel promptly went inside. He followed on her heels.

"You're not going to be able to avoid it forever, Mel. There's something between you that's electric."

Mel ignored him, tucking herself up to her desk. As if she needed to actually hear such words out loud.

"She makes you stutter, forget yourself. I noticed."

"That scene was awful." *Cripes. Everyone probably noticed.* The thought chilled her.

"I know you, how self-assured you are on the job. A few minutes ago, you couldn't have told me your name, for God's sake."

Mel leaned back in her chair and stared out the window. *This is hopeless.* "I like her."

Mike set his bag on the floor and sat in the guest chair. "It's more than that, isn't it? And Shay likes you. A lot."

Mel simply nodded. "She's special."

"What aren't you telling me?"

"Nothing. I just enjoy her company."

"Mel." He chortled. "That's pathetic, 'I just enjoy her company.' I saw you two dancing a while back, remember? You guys looked *very* content, cheek-to-cheek. There was some serious, full-body contact going on."

Mel flipped through the papers on her desk and found her pen. *God, I can't hear this.* "I'm not discussing Shay Maguire anymore. Go do something."

"Any more late-night rendezvous you want to confess?"

Mel raised her pen. "I'll throw this at you."

Mike sat back. "When did it happen?"

Mel frowned severely. "Nothing happened."

"Something did. When? Did she come on to you?"

"You are absolutely the worst busybody in Tomson."

"She did and you two clicked." He clapped his hands together gleefully. "I knew it!"

"She didn't come on to me, Mike. We are friends, yes."

He snorted. "Have you slept with her?"

"Hey!"

"It's just a question."

"And none of your business."

"Jesus, I hope you did. Told you you'd be great together. Does Misty know?"

Mel slammed the pen down. "No, Misty doesn't know. I mean, we didn't—There's nothing to know."

"Uh-huh. I'm going to grab a beer at the club tonight and I'll get the scoop from her."

"Unlike you, Misty is a good friend. She doesn't gossip."

"So there *is* a scoop."

"Mother of God. Give it a rest, would you?"

Mike straightened in the chair. "I'm shooting the work at the Five Star later. Maybe I'll run into Shay."

"Don't you dare put her on the spot. This is my personal life you're toying with."

He stood and picked up his bag. "I'd never say a word. I'm just razzing you because I care, but I *know* something's going on."

❖

Shay dismounted at the back porch to Della's office, debating just how much of Sorvini's character she should destroy. She reached for the railing but was abruptly hauled back by the arm, and Sorvini delivered a smashing backhand that knocked her on her ass.

The world went black for a second, the hum in her head deafening. Something warm and wet tickled her nose, then spread to her upper lip, and she blinked up at his raging face, much too close for comfort.

Instinct pushed her to her feet, but she swayed in place, too dizzy to retaliate. *Son of a bitch!*

Sorvini barked, and his hot breath made her cringe. "Mother-fucking dyke!"

Shay pressed a hand to her mouth and looked down to find it covered in blood. She'd also bled onto her favorite shirt.

Sorvini shoved her, and she staggered backward. He capitalized on that momentum and shoved her again. She threw up an arm to block his, but he fended her off and pushed again. Off balance, Shay hit the building hard. Her head spun and her vision went fuzzy.

"You fucking make an ass of me in public? You fucking dyke? I might just clean your clock right here and now." He seethed into her face, his bulk nearly blocking out the sky. "You know what it's taking, not beating you to a pulp?" He seized a fistful of her shirt by the neck and banged her against the building. Daylight dimmed. "Wanna play the man, huh? Come on, then, dyke, show me what you got."

"Get your hands off me, Sorvini," she muttered, blood and saliva mixing along a trail to her chin. A split in her lip stung when she spoke. And trying to breathe through her nose felt like she was under water. Her jaw throbbed.

Sorvini yanked her toward him and then slammed her against the wall with all his considerable might. Her head hit first, and her knees began to buckle. Everything went black again, for a bit longer this time, long enough for Sorvini to land a punch to her face. The impact snapped her head sideways, and then a follow-up punch dropped her to the gravel.

She had no concept of time, no idea how long she'd been on the ground before becoming conscious of a sturdy hand on her shoulder and a familiar male voice calling her name.

"Shay! Come on, Shay. Wake up. Jesus Christ."

Opening her eyes didn't accomplish much so she shut them again. The left one wasn't cooperating anyway. *Damn, this guy's persistent.* She swallowed, and the coppery taste made her gag. And that hurt like a bastard. Her cheekbone, jaw, nose, even her teeth hurt when the pain of everything else forced them to grind together. And someone must have glossed her lips with liquid fire.

She groaned as she was pulled into a sitting position against the building. Cautiously, she peered out at her savior, a tall, thin fellow squatting down, holding her upright.

"Shay? What the hell happened? Can you hear me?"

"Mmm."

"Can you see me? It's Mike. From the *Chronicle*."

"Hey."

"I'm taking you to the clinic. You need stitches. Can you sit there by yourself?"

"Mmm. Foggy."

"Yeah, no doubt. Listen, I'm going around front to get my car. I'll be right back, okay?" He backed away slowly, then ran.

Shay prodded her jaw, delicately worked it up and down, relieved it still functioned even though it hurt like hell to touch. Her cheek was wet, and she traced the moisture up to a slice across her cheekbone. Her nose was still straight and she had all her teeth, but her lips felt puffy and they were a bloody mess. And she estimated that her left eye would be swollen shut within minutes. *Sorvini. Christ, what did you hit me with?*

Suddenly, Della was on the back porch. "Oh my God!" Shay heard high heels hammer down the steps. "Chicago! Look at you!"

Mike's Volkswagen arrived in cloud of dust, and he scrambled around the car to crouch before Shay.

"Is she all right?" Della gasped.

"Does she look all right?" He draped Shay's arm over his shoulders and put his own around her waist. "Look, Ms. Slattery, do her a favor and call her house, her friends. Tell them I'm bringing her to the clinic."

Shay blinked repeatedly to focus on Della. She winced as Mike hoisted her to her feet, and fresh blood began flowing from her cheek, nose, and bottom lip.

"Della."

"Don't talk, Chicago," she said, and hustled to open Mike's side door. "Just take it easy." She retreated to let Mike maneuver Shay onto the seat. "Did she say who did this?"

"No. She was out cold when I spotted her. Who knows for how long."

"Well, I hate to assume it was someone on my ranch."

Mike shut the door and sighed as he rounded the car. "Y'think?"

"I have to reach my foreman immediately."

Mike drove carefully until he left the gravel driveway, then sped off. Shay just shut her eyes and tried not to vomit. She thought it grossly unfair that her stomach wanted to make her even more miserable.

"Mel, it's me. Listen up." Mike spoke rapidly into his cell as he approached the center of town. "I'm taking Shay to the clinic. Someone's done a number on her. Yes, Shay. I don't know. I just found her at the ranch. Yes, okay. Good." He threw the phone into the console. "Just when I thought you were becoming the most popular gal in town, Shay Maguire, *this* happens."

Shay moaned as her head bobbed forward, blood dripping from her nose and mouth to her jeans. Mike guided her head back to the headrest with a free hand, and Shay groaned again and put a palm over her stomach.

"Hey, no pukin' in my baby, okay? Hang on. We're almost there."

Shay lurched when the car stopped and was glad Mike had belted her upright. She also was thankful for whoever it was helping him get her inside, and for being able to lie down, finally.

Outside, Mel and Coby arrived simultaneously, and Coby fired off questions as they hurried into the building.

"What the hell happened?"

"Someone beat her up, Mike said."

"Jesus Christ." She pointed at Mel's eye. "Somebody hit you, too?"

"Huh? Oh. No. Somebody broke my office window, and I dodged everything but the door."

"Goddamn, you two are a pair. So, you know who did this to Shay?"

Frantic, they looked around the empty reception area.

"No idea. I'd just seen her this morning at Moriarty's Lumber."

"And? Jesus, Mel. This is like pulling teeth. What happened?" Coby glanced around the room again, impatient. She slapped the countertop several times. "Anybody home here?"

"Angelo Sorvini is my bet. He was furious with her and made a fool of himself, but I bet he blames her."

"Oh, this is going to be one hell of a mess." She pounded the counter with her fist. "Hey! Where is everybody? Screw it. Come on."

Mel followed Coby around the counter and down the hall to the exam rooms, letting her poke her head into each one. The third door Coby swung wide open.

"Found you, you pain in the ass."

"Shay!" Mel gasped from the doorway. Darkened by bruises and half-coated in blood, Shay's swollen face and bloodied shirt lay in stark contrast to the white exam table. Mel crossed the threshold but stopped. The automatic nature of her reaction startled her, the familiar reticence did not. Still, she knew her instinct had shifted.

The nurse finished situating pillows behind Shay's back and head and turned on them. "Both of you, out." She wrapped a blood pressure cuff around Shay's arm. "Hi, Mel. Only family, you know. Now out."

"I'm not going anywhere," Coby said from the foot of the exam table.

"Are you family?"

Coby folded her arms. "Yeah, I'm her sister."

A doctor arrived and recognized Mel as he squeezed past her.

"Hi, Mel. Friend of yours or are you here for this woman's story?"

"Friend first, Dr. Yarrow."

He opened the remaining buttons of Shay's shirt and reached beneath her tank top with the stethoscope. They watched him manipulate Shay's head, prod, lift, and generally cause her more pain. Again, blood trickled from her lips.

"We'll need some pictures to be sure," he said into Shay's one bloodshot eye, "but we may have a slight fracture here." He moved his fingers from her jaw to the bones surrounding her closed eye. "This concerns me more." A glance at the nurse earned him a nod. "I'd also like to rule out concussive injury, so we have some work to do."

He took Shay's chart from the nurse and started scribbling.

"Will she need to go the hospital?" Coby asked.

"Can't be sure yet," he answered, not looking up. "We'll take some X-rays to see. If you all would take a seat out front, we'll let you know shortly." He patted Shay's arm. "Ms. Maguire, you sit tight, okay? We'll see about getting you stitched up. And put on your prettiest face for the camera."

"Thanks a lot," Shay muttered as he handed off her chart and walked out.

"Just what we need," Coby sniped, "a comedian."

The nurse spread her arms wide to herd them out. "Have a seat, folks. It'll be a while."

Coby stepped around her. She went to Shay's side, placed a palm on her chest, and leaned down.

"Sorvini?"

"Never had a chance," Shay said. "Aww, think I'm gonna hurl."

"Nurse!" Coby grabbed a plastic basin off a nearby counter. "I gotcha. Roll this way."

"No. My head's splitting."

The nurse edged Coby away from the bed. "Outside. Now."

"I bet she's got a concussion. Be careful."

"I'm only saying this once more. Out!"

"We're not going far, Shay. Be strong."

Mel tugged at Coby's shirt. "You should call the Exchange, give Misty an update."

Coby nodded and squeezed Shay's hand. "Back in a bit." She glared at the nurse and stormed past Mel. "Try to stay with her."

The nurse guided Mel into the hallway. "So is your black eye related to this?"

"I just ran into my office door Sunday night. Someone threw a brick through the window and I turned too fast."

"Wow, Mel. Never a slow news day in the busy metropolis of Tomson, huh?"

"Count your blessings, Erica. Just wait till we're a thriving shopping Mecca."

"Ha. No kidding. Seems things are getting more hectic, the closer we get to birthing Slattery's dream child." She tossed a thumb toward Shay. "This one will give you a story, no doubt. I'd say she's as tough as she looks, too. I give her credit, though. That day we protested at the Heights, she stepped right in and rescued Joanie McGilvary. Took a wicked blow to the head for it. I saw the whole thing."

"I remember the pictures."

"My guess is somebody has a thing against her because she's, you know..."

"She's what, Erica? Catholic? Russian? I know—vegan."

"Oh, you know what I mean. A lesbian. Hard-core, if you ask me. Listen, if you really need to get your scoop, you go ahead in and talk with her. I'll stay right here, if you'd feel better about it."

"I'd just like a few words." She wanted far more than that. And the insinuation that Mel needed protection from Shay irked her. "You don't have to stay. She's no terrorist or psychopath."

Erica patted Mel's shoulder and went to the next exam room.

Mel turned to Shay. She leaned against the door frame and studied the tortured face. *How long since I kissed it?*

"Are we alone?" Shay murmured.

Mel went to her quickly. "As ideal conditions as we'll get for a while, I'm afraid."

"Then you're definitely not safe, fine lady."

"Such a tease." She ran her fingers lightly through Shay's hair and cupped her right cheek and jaw.

"Now who's teasing?"

"You're a mess."

"You make me feel like a million bucks." Blood threatened to spill off her lower lip.

"So, what's the other guy look like?"

"Sorvini. I never saw him coming."

"For that business this morning?"

"Yeah. For making him look like the ass he is."

"Okay. Shh. You're bleeding again." She found gauze nearby and dabbed at the thin stream heading toward Shay's chin.

"Christ, just two shots and he does me in. Well, two's all I remember."

"Shh, I said."

"Jeez, Mel. I must be losing my touch."

Mel's anger rose. Damn, she hated that man as much as she did Della. His beating Shay's face to a bloody pulp made her crazy, overwhelmed her self-control. She felt so emotionally raw, torn between vengeance and desire, she lost track of where she was.

She stroked Shay's right jaw with the back of her fingers. "You've got just the right touch."

Shay took Mel's hand and kissed it. They both noticed the blood she left behind.

"Gee," Shay said, her voice gravelly, "got lipstick on you."

"You certainly did, Ms. Maguire, and I'm going to leave it right where it is."

"Oh." From the doorway, Erica watched their hands lower to the bed. "I'm sorry to interrupt, Mel. I thought you'd left."

Mel took a deep steadying breath, her nervous heart thumping wildly, and she felt Shay squeeze her hand as she withdrew.

"No problem at all," she said as brightly as possible. "In fact, your timing is perfect. I'm leaving you to your chores." She rubbed Shay's shoulder briefly. "Don't run off on us, Maguire."

"No chance."

Mel elbowed Erica as she left. "Thank you."

Out in the hall, she dared congratulate herself for not crawling under the bed when Erica witnessed their tender moment. And once she pushed the ramifications from her mind, her nerves even settled a bit.

"Mel?"

Erica appeared at her shoulder and Mel fought to relax. She should have known Erica wouldn't let it go.

"Hey, um, about that, just then?" Mel offered only a questioning look. "I'm sorry if, y'know, earlier, if I said something I shouldn't have."

Mel gave every impression of struggling to recall that conversation. "All you said, really, was that Shay's a lesbian and even something of a hero."

"Yeah. I just wanted to make sure I didn't offend you, seeing as how you two are…close."

"We're good friends. She *is* tough and hard-core, but I got the scoop." She winked as she walked away, at least for this moment downright proud of herself.

But the drive home sank that emotional high into the depths of her stomach. She knew what Erica had seen, how rumors grew, and what they could cost her. Sensational headlines written by a replacement editor flashed through her mind, visions of her father's threatening face so real she had to stop the Subaru on the side the road and collect herself.

She'd succumbed to his power play, backed into the closet he made, and, in effect, closed the door on herself. And now, with only eight months left before he signed the *Chronicle* over to her, she could pay the price. In forgetting herself with that display of affection at the clinic, she'd taken a profound step she couldn't retract. *It was so right.* A step out of that damn closet was a step into oncoming traffic, a head-on collision with him and a substantial percentage of her readership.

Why in the name of God did I ever agree to this? Mel pounded the steering wheel. With rumors circulating, she knew she'd soon be the talk of the town, forced into public denials just to placate her father, and the struggle would be insufferable, both personally and professionally. As much as she hated every aspect of his game, the thought that he now might oust her at any time made her nauseous. She wrapped her arms around herself and fought back angry tears, as ashamed of herself as she was of him. He was that out of touch with the times, that afraid of "tarnishing" the family name and the newspaper he'd inherited but had no desire to run. Of course, she could beat him to the punch, tell everyone to go to hell, and finally pursue a relationship she wanted... and watch her father sell her newspaper to the *Tribune*.

She'd never have both the *Chronicle* and a relationship with Shay, not in Tomson, at least not in the foreseeable future. She knew she'd have to steel herself and make a firm choice. Damn her conscience, now whispering ever louder, reminding her of what really mattered and what didn't.

Chapter Fourteen

A nd your bike's fine and happy in the garage," Misty said, finally sitting down beside Shay on the porch. She'd been playing nurse for the past hour, getting Shay moved from the bedroom to the glider, and being such a burden frustrated Shay no end. She looked out at the lake with her one opened eye.

"Freddy Marsh drove it?"

"He said he hoped you wouldn't mind. Thought you'd trust him with it."

"He's a good guy. I need to thank him."

"Well, you're not going anywhere for a while. But he called this morning, asking how you were. He said some of the guys want to come visit, and I told them tomorrow. Day one, you need to rest." She sipped her iced tea and adjusted one of the pillows behind Shay's head. "It's very sweet of them."

"Did you call the cops for me?"

"Sure did. They should be here any minute. Mel, too. She asked if you were going through with this and seemed pretty pleased."

Shay grinned, then winced and touched her mouth. "Damn stitches."

"Hey, check this out," Coby said, carrying a bouquet of pink carnations from the kitchen. Misty hurriedly made room on the coffee table. "Moriarty's. You made a great impression, apparently."

"Whoa, that's awfully nice. Hard not to make a good impression when you follow an act like Sorvini." She glanced from Coby to Misty. "Jesus, word travels fast."

"Bob stopped by the clinic while they were stitching you up, you know," Misty said.

"Hell," Coby added with a chuckle, "there was a crowd. Keary and Doran, Freddy and a couple of other guys, even Sonny. Man, he takes up space, huh?"

Shay's laugh led to a moan, and she squeezed her eye shut.

"Even someone named Lisa," Misty said.

"Della's secretary."

"Hmm. She's a wild one. Was *very* worried about you."

"Yeah, Mel noticed," Coby said. "The more questions Lisa asked, the more irritated Mel got."

"Lisa's just a kid."

Misty tapped Shay's shoulder. "That's not the point."

The doorbell rang and Coby left to answer it.

"It's going to be a busy morning, I think," Misty sighed, "so no long visits. You need to rest, even if it is only a mild concussion." Mumbled conversation reached them from the living room. "I'm shutting you off from visitors in a bit."

"Yes, Nurse Kincaid."

"Morning, everyone." Officer Hennessey stepped out onto the porch, sizing up Shay's condition. "Maguire, we meet again." She surveyed Shay's battered face and shook her head as she pulled a notepad from a pocket on her thigh. "So you got the number of that truck, I hear? The clinic had to report the assault."

"Yeah, Angelo Sorvini."

Misty offered her chair and went inside. Hennessey wrote as she sat.

"Simple story," Shay said, "bastard bushwhacked me."

"Start from the beginning."

Somewhere during the tale, the doorbell rang again, and soon more conversation could be heard. Shay sighed. It was going to be a long day. Probably several. She wished Mel would arrive.

"What did he say to you, as specifically as you can recall?"

"Oh, his favorite term for me is 'motherfucking dyke.' Said I shouldn't have made an ass of him, that he was holding back, but wanted to clean my clock. 'Beat me to a pulp,' I think he said."

She watched Hennessey note every word.

"Witnesses?"

"Don't think so."

"Did he have a weapon of any kind?"

"None he showed, but he has hands the size of friggin' dinner plates. Hit like a brick, for Christ's sake."

"He struck you twice, then?"

"After the backhand, I think so. He slammed me into the building a lot. I think I went out a couple times before he finally put me down."

"Jesus. Didn't I tell you to watch out for him?" She closed the notepad and rose.

Shay couldn't look up that far to see her face. "Anyone ever call him on stuff like this before?"

"Once, maybe a year ago, but Della settled things before charges were filed."

Shay snorted. "She's not settling this one. No fucking way."

Hennessey patted Shay's shoulder. "Okay. We're done. Take it easy, huh? You'll be hearing from us."

She turned to leave and stopped, and Shay struggled to turn to see why.

Della stood holding flowers and something covered in silver gift wrapping. Shay hoped it was booze, that a few stiff shots would help the pain meds that had yet to do any good.

"Good morning," Della said, and Shay imagined that, confronting Hennessey, Della was picturing Sorvini in cuffs. "Chicago, Officer Hennessey." She came closer and pushed things around on the table to make room for her gifts. "I'm not going to stay because I'm sure you need your rest, but I wanted to see how you were getting along."

"Thanks, Della." *Worried I'm going to sue?* "I'm supposed to lay low for a while till my brain stops sloshing around and the eye opens. My vision is still cloudy, but I'll live. I'm giving it a week. Hope that doesn't put us too far behind."

"Your health is more important," Misty chimed in from the doorway.

Della sent her a look. "Absolutely. You're not to worry about that. I need you well and riding herd as soon as you're fit. Not before."

"Thank you," Shay said, hearing the doorbell ring again. "I'll do my best."

"I have no doubt." Della glanced up at Hennessey and back to Shay. "Forgive me, but I assume you're pressing charges?"

Hennessey fussed with her tactical belt and tucked both thumbs behind the buckle. Shay enjoyed the intimidating stance.

"Ms. Slattery, my meeting with Ms. Maguire will be public record soon enough."

Della nodded. "Of course. I had a feeling it might come to this."

"You did? Do you have information about this incident?"

"No. I just feel terribly about it."

"Uh-huh."

"Good morning, all," Mel proclaimed from the doorway. "Since I have everyone in one place, could I ask a few questions, please?"

"*Really*," Della said on a sigh, and studied Mel's shiner longer than was polite. "I hardly think this is appropriate, Ms. Baker. I'd thought you'd show more compassion for such a situation. After all, this woman needs serious rest."

"I'm fully aware of the situation, Ms. Slattery. I'm standing here at the invitation of the homeowner."

"I'm sure Ms. Kincaid's intent was *not* to provide you an interrogation opportunity."

"You're sure? What is your reaction to this assault by Angelo Sorvini?"

Shay and Hennessey shared an amused glance.

"I'm not commenting on this incident."

"Do you believe Mr. Sorvini was involved?"

"I'm not repeating myself, either." She turned to Shay and bent forward slightly. "My concern is that you are well. I hope you get some rest." She straightened stiffly. "Good day." Mel stepped aside to let her leave and turned back to Hennessey.

"Can I pick up a copy of your report before lunch?"

Hennessey smirked. "Sure, Mel." She paused and looked at Shay before heading down the back steps. "If you think of anything else you need to add, let me know."

Shay gave her a thumbs-up. "Thank you."

Mel drew a chair up against the glider. "Hi."

"Hi back. I'm happy to see you. Cute that we both have shiners."

"Just swell. Yours is far worse. And I'm happy to see you, too, especially here." With a fingertip, she grazed Shay's injured jaw. It was soft and so smooth, she could enjoy the feel forever, but it was also too warm and swollen. The dark purple bruise matched her left eye, which Shay still could not open. "How are you feeling?"

"No pain now."

Mel studied Shay's stitched cheek and lip. "I hate that bastard."

"Kiss me." Shay managed to push herself up on an elbow to get closer.

"No." Mel pressed her back down with a palm on her stomach. She kneaded her fingers into the cotton tee and the taut muscle beneath, and the coiling sensation in Mel's chest made her bite her lip. "Don't move so much."

"I like your hand there. It feels good."

"Your pain meds have kicked in."

"Wanna take a nap with me?"

"Sure, like that's what you have in mind."

Shay sulked, but peered at her through her half-opened good eye. "I enjoyed watching you with Della."

"She can be so full of herself. It's kind of fun sometimes."

"I like how you can be so gorgeous, sexy, *and* tough."

Shay's teasing warmed her. Without thinking, she ran her palm languidly across Shay's stomach several times. "I'm trying to make progress, Shay."

"Oh, you're making wonderful progress right now."

Mel slapped her belly. "I *meant* on me." She rested her hand back in her lap, the feel of Shay too distracting. *Too suggestive.* "I'm brave enough to do my job, and I *do* want to approach my life the same way, but the nerves, the risks are still there."

"I think that's normal, Mel. A person can't change overnight."

"But, Jesus, I have to play my cards just right, Shay, or I'll go insane. I have to bide my time."

Shay wrapped her fingers around Mel's thigh and squeezed. "You're making progress, you said?" Mel nodded. "I like that you're comfortable with me here."

"Here doesn't count. It's safe here. Misty and Coby are our friends. But at the clinic, your nurse Erica—"

"Saw me kiss your hand."

"Yes. And in the hall, I was a little…cocky."

"Naw, not *Chronicle* editor Melissa Baker. What did you say?"

"That we're close friends, and I suppose I looked pretty happy about it."

"Are you?"

Mel gazed into the lone, tired eye. The impulse to cup Shay's face in both hands and kiss her rose quickly. "Yes."

"She worries you, though, huh? Is she a gossip?"

"Hell, everyone in Tomson is a gossip, Shay. It's the town's official sport."

"So...?"

"So," Mel sighed deeply, "rumors will probably start, if they haven't already, and they're dangerous."

"Hey." Shay lifted Mel's chin. The touch tingled along her throat, but it was the weariness in that voice that struck Mel. She wished she hadn't broached the subject at all. "So, we're close, Mel. No one needs to know how my brain fries when I see you, or that I break out in a sweat and throb."

"Throb, huh?" The concept excited her. She watched the color rise in Shay's unblemished right cheek. "I think you're blushing."

"Yeah, probably. It got hot out here all of a sudden." Her good eye blinked.

"Well, at the risk of hiking the temperature further, I confess the same. I nearly made a fool of myself at Moriarty's. You looked so fine. And then did you *have* to wink at me? Jesus, Shay. I completely lost my train of thought."

"Mmm. Good to know."

"Mike noticed. God knows if anyone else did."

"I liked it."

"You're bad."

"What did Mike say?"

"Oh, he put me through the third degree back at the office. He was terrible. He had convinced himself that we'd slept together until I insisted we hadn't."

"Really? You *sure* you don't wanna take a nap with me?"

"You're incorrigible."

"He's no gossip, though. I just know."

Mel shook her head. "No, he's a sweetheart. But he knows there's something between us."

"Is he right?"

The question brought Mel up short. *Level with her. This split-second hesitation says...what?*

"Well," she felt heat rise in her cheeks now, "I suppose he is." The words surfaced from somewhere inside and popped out, honest and promising. Defiant and fearless—and damning. Mel heard them as clearly as Shay did, and she was as surprised as Shay was happy. They'd soared out of her heart, not her head, and left shadows in their wake. But the beaming expression on Shay's face brightened everything.

Shay tugged her down to within kissing reach. "No one needs to know more until you tell me otherwise. Then I'll scream it from the rooftops."

Enveloped by a surge of relief and gratitude, Mel set her nose to Shay's and let herself enjoy their connection. Shay's understanding calmed Mel's racing mind, pushed concerns aside, and allowed genuine emotion to surface. "You better hurry up and heal. There's a chance that delicate little kisses won't suffice much longer."

"So you're ready for lots of serious kissing?" Shay's good eye fluttered closed, but she opened it quickly.

"Ahem," Misty said. "Sorry, girls, but you'll just have to suffer for now."

Mel sat up and Shay growled at Misty.

"Killjoy."

Mel put her chair back in place and located her notebook on the floor. *Just drop everything, why don't you?*

"You need to sleep."

"Already dreamin'," Shay murmured, a goofy grin across her marked lips.

"And heal." Mel bent down very close. "And hurry up." She set a light kiss on her lips. "See you soon, tough guy."

She left Shay smiling sleepily on the glider before jogging down the porch steps, her mind abuzz with all she'd said and the repercussions.

CHAPTER FIFTEEN

Wednesday found Shay far more clearheaded, propped up on the glider in the early morning breeze, sipping coffee through a straw. With Mel beside her, however, a sleek leg pressed to hers and that freshly showered scent filling her senses, concentrating on a serious matter grew more difficult by the second. She wished she'd spoken to her about the Heights sooner—not when Mel was pressed for time.

"I'm sorry I'm cutting into your busiest day, but this is important."

"I do only have a half hour or so, but it's okay. First, tell me how you are? Did you sleep well?"

"I did. Yes. I'm sore as hell, but better. Your black eye is turning yellow."

"Gee, thanks. How to make a girl—"

"You are gorgeous, Melissa Baker. The yellow means it's healing fast." She squeezed Mel's hand. "I'm really glad to see you."

"Same here. I look forward to seeing both your eyes soon." She thanked Misty for delivering a cup of coffee. "Now, what is this that's so important?"

"I think something fishy's going on at the Heights."

Mel stopped in mid-sip. "Like what?"

"Like I heard Sorvini and Chandler are doing stuff that's not on the plans."

"Do you have any specifics? Who talked? When did—"

Shay exhaled hard. "Christ. I wish I talked to you sooner. But then this shit happened." She gestured toward her battered face. "And yesterday, I was…I think I was high most of the day."

"Shay, tell me." Mel set her coffee on the table and pulled out her tablet. "I won't involve you, but I need specifics, please."

"The guys said they struck rock so big excavating the leaching field that Sorvini told Chandler to dig around it, to move the field's location. They're already digging in the new spot. I don't know if foundation trenches have been moved, too."

Mel stopped making notes on her tablet and Shay watched her gaze take on an eerie blue haze, a vacant look beyond her toward the lake, as if seeing something in her mind. Then they flashed crisply to her.

"Mike and I will go out there to see. Damn it. I don't think there's a way to check everything in time for this week's paper, but I can try asking around."

"Well, these guys had no reason to make stuff up. I believe them because they saw the whole thing in terms of cash. They heard Sorvini say Della wants things sped up, so he's pushing."

Shay could practically hear the wheels turning in Mel's mind.

"It all sort of blew my mind, too," she continued, "so I went to Della and tried to get it out of her, see if she knew."

"Shay, I'm no fan of hers, but I'd be the first to admit she's sharp. She wouldn't allow Sorvini—either of them—to screw this up."

Shay shrugged. "She's shrewd, Mel. She didn't fess up to anything, but she endorsed Sorvini like he's some Wonder Boy and said he's got her blessing to 'expedite' the project. So, whether she knows the details or not—and probably not—the buck still stops with her."

"True." Mel sat back heavily, her tablet abandoned on her lap. "Damn it."

Shay stroked Mel's hand. "I don't know all this for fact, Mel, but I'd bet on it. Just how you go about showing it...Just be careful."

Mel nodded distantly. "Of all days."

"I'm so sorry. I should've told you sooner, I know, like at our picnic on Sunday, but...Well, it wasn't on my mind."

"It's okay." Mel entwined their fingers. "Sunday was...for us. And then, God, Shay, you were dragged through hell. I don't blame you at all." She squeezed Shay's hand as she sat back. "I just have to figure out the next step." She shoved her tablet into her satchel and grabbed her coffee cup. "There are a lot of pieces to put into place if we're going to run something this big this week. I doubt we'll make it, but I have to try." She gulped down two mouthfuls of coffee and palmed the uninjured side of Shay's face. "Thank you."

"Will you keep in touch?" Shay looked up as Mel prepared to dash off. "This worries me, Mel. There's a lot on the line here and it's bound to set them off."

"Believe me. I know." She ran a finger along Shay's jaw and Shay wanted to pull her back down beside her. "Mike and I have to do some quick work. Of course, if I can't reach the building inspector in time, this will all have to wait till next week. I'll call you soon, okay?" At the top porch step, she looked back and held up crossed fingers. "Won't this just make me the hit of Tomson?"

❖

Much to Mel's dismay, time conspired against all efforts to develop a news story off Shay's tip. Frustrated by a denial of access to the site prior to her deadline, she worried about alterations being made at the Heights before she could report them. She insisted on a site visit the next day, determined to obtain an accurate status of the project for the following week's paper.

She had Mike at her side as they stepped cautiously across the Heights's acreage Thursday afternoon, but that didn't deter workers from wolf whistling. Wishing she'd changed her skirt for slacks, she picked up their pace to reach the red dually truck. Sorvini and Chandler turned from the plans on the tailgate to watch.

"Figures he'd be out on bail." Mike swapped out a camera lens as they walked. "Della better fire his lard ass."

"Guaranteed he lands on his feet. Looks like he's already joined Chandler's army. They suit each other so well," Mel grumbled.

"You got that right. Can't trust either of them."

"After yesterday's stunt, I could crucify them. They knew exactly what they were doing, refusing to see us, pushing us back beyond deadline." Mel lowered her head, pretending to watch her footing as they reached the truck. "Regardless of what they say, shoot everything you can."

Chandler straightened his tie and adjusted his tan Stetson. "Good afternoon, Mel." He beamed at her and ignored Mike.

"Hi, Ed, Angelo."

Chandler surveyed her figure while Sorvini took off his suit jacket and tossed it over the plans. Mel's stomach turned. *What a disgusting, intimidating duo.*

Chandler stepped forward and placed a hand on her shoulder. "Too bad about that window of yours. At least it was a Sunday and you were closed."

Mel subtly shifted out from under his hand. "Glass flew right by me, Ed. I *was* in at the time."

"You were? Lord, Mel!" He took the opportunity to look her up and down again, and Mel was tempted to leave. "Were you hurt? Jesus, I surely hope not."

Looking like he didn't have a care in the world, Sorvini fought back a smirk. "Wouldn't mean you're pushing people to the brink, now would it?"

I'd love to push you on your goddamn ass.

"The police have a lead, so I'm sure whoever did it will be paying soon enough. It's a shame some people think intimidation is the answer to everything." She met Sorvini's eyes evenly and let her insinuation linger. "Are you here representing Slattery, Angie?"

Sorvini took a breath and Mel hoped the buttons would pop off his shirt.

"I've worked on this project since its inception," he said.

"And that's not changing," Chandler added. He clapped Sorvini's shoulder. "We're down to crunch time now and Della knows what an asset he is."

"So," Mel persisted, "you're still on the Slattery payroll?"

"Now, Mel," Chandler said, and stepped away from the truck. "I'm sure detailing our progress on Tomson's biggest commercial project is your purpose here today, so why don't we get to it, hmm?"

He strolled away, Sorvini followed, and Mel and Mike exchanged looks before tagging along. Mike clicked off photos as they went and Mel whispered at his side.

"Make sure you include them in a few shots," she whispered. "I'll try to get a straight answer out of Della later."

At a stack of cement forms, Chandler stopped and gestured broadly at the backhoe operating nearby. "As you can see, foundations will be framed in no time."

Sorvini said, "Everything's falling into place."

Mike wandered off, circling the pegged area and panning the scene as he walked, until Mel could no longer hear his camera's repetitive shutter action. She watched him circle the marked area closest to the river, counting on him to put easily identified perspective into his images.

"Nothing much that'll show in pictures," Chandler said.

That's what concerns me.

"Just dirt," Sorvini added.

"And holes." Chandler chuckled. "Nothing much has changed from the schedule I outlined for you a while back, Mel."

She swiped through pages on her tablet's screen and began walking toward Mike.

"I have an old note here, Ed, saying foundation forms would be in about now." She looked up at him and then pointed to the perimeter. "Didn't you hope to be done with this already?" *Come on, Ed. Admit you ran into a snag.*

"Oh, roughed-out time frames always get adjusted."

"That's the nature of the business," Sorvini said, adding nothing to the conversation except to remind Mel of Shay.

"So, you *are* behind—but it looks like things are really taking shape."

Chandler's frown disappeared as quickly as it had formed. "I'm glad you're seeing the positive here. This project is too important, and our operation is too big to let little things pull us off-target."

"Oh, I hear you loud and clear, Ed." Mel nodded as she wrote on her tablet. "Little things, like what?"

"Lord, Mel. Minutia doesn't matter. What's important is having the biggest outfit in this part of Montana on your side and getting the job done."

"Ahead of schedule, when possible," Sorvini added.

"Angie makes a good point," Chandler said. "With a little luck, we could finish *well* within the allotted time. When you've been in the business as long as I have, Mel, you learn to adapt. We're in very good shape, overall."

Mel wrote a bit longer, knowing both men figured she was logging impressive quotes, and put her tablet away. She couldn't get off the site fast enough.

Back in her Subaru, she swiped hair from her face with both

hands before turning the key. "Phew. They just disgust me. Did you get anything good?"

"Hard to tell." He was riveted to the screen on his camera, flipping through images. "I want to see these blown up on a tube. We might have something."

"We'll take a look as soon as we get back. We have the plans to compare them to."

CHAPTER SIXTEEN

Saturday morning, Shay rolled to a stop among trucks parked near the stage. Carpenters hammered and chatted away, and she was relieved to see Moriarty had come through with the long-awaited lumber.

Freddy waved as he approached. "Looking better than last I saw you."

"Second day riding and no headaches, no complaints." She scanned the vast, busy landscape. "He's gone now?"

"Sorvini? Yeah, and it's official, and a few of his boys are pissed. He came right here after his arraignment, cleaned out his desk in the barn, then took off for Chandler's."

She wondered how the two big goons were coping with inquiries about the Heights. She worried about Mel, stirring up controversy and stepping on toes with pointed questions. Shay called her every day to make sure things were still all right.

"Well, we have our own pressing issues. Like that piece-of-crap grader. I need it working in a big way. Do you know if Sorvini's had anyone on it?"

"Don't know. Tommy's been pushing this and driving us hard." He tipped his head toward the stage. "Hey, why are you here anyway? Don't you run Sonny's shop on Saturdays?"

"I'm still taking it slow."

"Don't rush it. Go cruise the grounds, take inventory or something." Freddy snorted. "Della's probably peeing her pants, being in the dark without her big man."

"You're probably right. I'll look around. Really pro job here, by the way. Looks great."

"Good as they have at Red Rock," he boasted. "Go see Tommy. He'll be glad to see you're back."

She rumbled across the acreage designated for carnival rides and midway games, only wincing occasionally when a bounce over a gopher hole or field rut rattled her jaw. Rogers walked out of the maintenance barn to greet her and shook his head.

"Well, you're a sight for sore eyes."

Shay joined him in the doorway. "Thanks for reminding me."

"You can see well enough to drive?"

"Looks worse than it feels."

"Hey, Angie's history. Gave me his keys just this morning. You heard, right?"

"I did. No loss in my book."

"Everyone agrees, except for a few of his pets, and they're the ones to watch out for."

Shay scrabbled a hand back through her hair. "Jensen and O'Brien?"

"And Peters, the crazy one."

"Figured. They were with him at Moriarty's, but I thought they looked ready to abandon him when he flew off the handle."

"Those clowns getting the drop on you would please them no end, so stay on your guard. And watch your bike."

"They touch my bike, they'll be sorry."

"Angie said Peters had a little go-round with Mel Baker early this morning at the diner. Guess she was interviewing him about working for Angie, temperament, that sort of thing, and Peters let the whole diner hear he thought you two had a 'thing' going."

Shay straightened and jammed her hands into her pockets. She tried to imagine Mel's reaction to such an accusation—in public, no less. *The counterpunching has begun.* She hurried to formulate an appropriate answer.

"Mel and I are friends and that's pretty low, twisting things around and putting her on the spot. Sorvini say what Mel's response was?"

"No, but he seemed proud of his boy, embarrassing her like that in front of everybody." Rogers took off his ball cap and scratched his head. When he shuffled in place, she knew there was more.

"Tommy?"

"Yeah, well, eh, I suppose you should hear it from me, if you haven't already."

"Now what?"

"Erica Brown was asking for you at the clinic the other night. I had one of my grandkids there for an earache, and Erica asked how you were coming along. Shay, she's a blabbermouth of the first degree. Nice lady, but damn, the woman never shuts up."

"What did she say?" Shay's nerves frazzled a bit more and she balled her hands into fists in her pockets.

"She said she saw Mel with you there and…you two looked pretty cozy." Shay half turned in anger, but Rogers rapped her arm with the back of his hand. "Hey, I'm not one to spread stuff like that. Hope you know. I just wanted to tell you that she's got folks talking."

"Mel doesn't deserve to be the butt of two-bit gossip!"

Rogers reared back. "Whoa, woman. You don't have to tell me. She's the darlin' of Tomson, but listen. It's all over town that Mel's nosing around the Heights for something, and if Angie and Ed Chandler think discrediting her will keep their butts out of hot water, they'll encourage all the rumors about her they can come up with."

"Got that right. Damn these people."

"Look, I don't really know and don't care what Erica's yapping about now, but I'll be honest. Half the guys in town have tried to date Mel and she plays close to the vest. Hard to get doesn't come close. And I say good for her. She should be picky. Hell, I've always figured she'd come back from some vacation with a city guy, that she must prefer that sort, you know?"

If Shay hadn't been so wound up about this escalation of war and Mel's reaction, she would have been amused. The temptation to level with him was great. Rogers was kind and honest, and she trusted him. There weren't many others in town about whom she could say the same.

"Shay, look. I got to say, that if Mel…" He frowned as he sighed. "If you and she, um…"

"If we what?" She was afraid to appear anything but curious.

Rogers shrugged. "I'm not sure what I was going to say there."

"Mel knows her own mind, Tommy, and I respect her immensely. She's up front with everyone, from what I've seen. Professionally and personally. I think we've become friends because I'm not from here and I see things a little differently, and she enjoys that change of pace."

Rogers nodded, then mumbled toward the ground. "You're from the city."

Shay studied him closely. "Are you saying I'm that *city guy*?"

"For what it's worth, Shay, I'm on your side."

❖

Mel set a glass of iced tea on the side table next to Nana and brought the knitting bag closer to her recliner. Settled into her comfortable spot, Nana would be happy for the several hours Mel needed to spend at the office.

"Must you work today, too, Lissa? Such a beautiful Sunday and you're going back to that little hole in the wall and coop yourself up."

"Things are busy lately, Nana. I just need a few hours of solitude with the Heights plans we got, to get a jump on the week. I'll be back in plenty of time to make us that pot roast I promised."

Nana grumbled as she rummaged in her bag and pulled out a tangle of needles and yarn.

"Are you seeing someone on the sly?"

Mel's jaw dropped slightly. "I beg your pardon?"

"You heard me. An outsider? From Chicago, I think?"

"What would ever make you ask that?" She wasn't ready or strong enough to engage in a battle with Nana.

"I may not get out very often, dear, but I *do* hear things, and there were a few whispers I caught this morning as we were leaving church. I was quite shocked."

Mel sat on the ottoman at Nana's feet, nervous but desperate to hear more.

"Like what?"

"That you and someone named Shay are an item. Why am I the last to hear? Why haven't I met him? Hearing Rachel Walker and Marybeth Starr whispering about it was very disappointing."

Mel sat up straight and glanced at the ceiling. *Erica.*

"Nana. You know how all those busybodies thrive on gossip, even if they have to create it themselves. They've got nothing better to do."

"Well, I couldn't hear all they were saying, but they were certainly aflutter over it."

She patted Nana's knee reassuringly. "Shay is in charge of the July

Fourth festival at the Five Star, so we've talked a lot. You know I have to keep up with things over there. We're friends. Don't fret over the likes of Rachel and Marybeth."

Not proud of avoiding the subject, Mel dreaded the moment she had to open up. She certainly didn't want to be forced into *that* discussion, but that's what it felt like. Dammed uncomfortable...untenable. Right now, all she wanted was to escape and just breathe.

"I don't like people whispering about you. It's not proper for a lady to be talked about like that. Casts you in a poor light. You'll get a *reputation*."

Mel swallowed and stood up with a sigh. *Tell me something I don't know, Nana.*

"You just consider the source," she said, wondering how many other sources were poised to rock her world. "I'm proud of my reputation."

"I am, too, dear. That's why I'm concerned."

Mel bent and kissed her cheek. "Shush. Now, I have to go get some work done."

In the Subaru, she started the ignition but dropped her hands into her lap. On top of all the news on her docket, she had this. Herself. Word was spreading already. The issue fought for priority in her brain, and she tried to find a place to stow it, just to be able to concentrate on daily life. But it refused back-burner status.

Her stomach became just as unruly as she drove into town. The *Chronicle* was on everyone's lips, and she couldn't have been more excited, more inspired, but now gossip would override that and the name Mel Baker would take precedence. Her character would be doubted, her work undermined.

She muttered a "thank you, God," that her father wasn't privy to Tomson's gossip mill from his Miami home. She doubted he corresponded socially with old acquaintances here. The idea that Nana might share Mel's "seeing someone on the sly" with him chilled her initially, until she realized Nana would elaborate and tell her father the "someone" was a Slattery worker. He'd assume "male" and be content. *And I could continue hiding...*

Eight months really isn't that *long. Just quit rocking the boat with this romantic fantasy. Do the job justice, return to a semblance of* normalcy. In the end, I'll own the Chronicle *and be free to enjoy the life I choose. It won't take forever, just patience and some time. And Shay... Will she really still be around in eight months, anyway? Already she's so special she's worth losing a lifelong dream? Smarten up and cool your heels.*

CHAPTER SEVENTEEN

Mel interpreted Mike's working on a Sunday as just another sign of how everyday life was changing. But she wasn't up for any of his teasing, and prepared by shoving every hint of her personal woes aside.

"What brings you in on a Sunday?" She headed to her desk as he went out to the front counter.

"Back issues for the Montana Press Photographers' competition," he said, his voice lost into the low shelves of newspapers.

"Are you entering all the categories again?"

"Yup. If I can find all the tear sheets I need. I'm going to claim a whole wall out here, you'll see."

"You better." She hoped Mike won for his work this year. He'd taken first prize in sports photography and third in features last year. He deserved the recognition. *The* Chronicle *will probably need the credibility by the time this mess settles.*

"If you can't find what you need, let me know," she said, firing up her computer. "I can dig through my stash at home." She picked a volume of town bylaws off a corner shelf as the front door bells jingled. *Don't people know it's Sunday?* She listened for Mike to greet the customer.

"Hey, Shay."

"Mike. You guys never take days off?"

"News waits for no one," he said loyally. "You still got some good color going there. Are you back in the saddle already? Where's the Harley?" He looked past her, out the door window.

"Across at the diner. I grabbed a sandwich and saw a certain car pull in."

Book in hand, Mel stepped toward the inner office doorway and wondered how she'd missed seeing the bike parked nearby. At least if she'd seen it, she could have prepared her body and mind for a visit like this, avoided morphing into a bundle of nerves like a schoolgirl.

She'd last visited Shay at Misty and Coby's place on Wednesday, and they'd spoken on the phone several times, but the void she felt inside said they hadn't connected in years. Seeing Shay sent a wave of longing through her so thoroughly, it forced her palm to the woodwork for support. *This is too physical for my own good.*

With windblown hair and the stitched slice below her left eye, Shay had the look of a surviving warrior, a dangerous renegade. *The "rogue."*

"Hi, Mel."

"Shay."

Mike stuttered. "Um, I'll, ah, I'll just take these back inside. Excuse me." He stepped around Shay with an armload of papers, and then passed Mel, whispering under his breath, "Go. I'll lock up."

Shay's presence was hypnotic. Mel tried to read her thoughts, found herself hoping Shay liked the strapless lavender sundress Mel still wore from church, that she preferred Mel's hair swept up as it was, that she thought the bare-shoulder look was sexy. *Stop. Don't do this. It's torture.*

Shay ran a fingertip up her arm. "Jesus Christ, you're beautiful."

"Your eyesight isn't back to normal yet."

Shay laughed. "I needed to see you. It's been too long. You look… God."

"Stop. You're messing with my concentration. Are you working today?"

"Not really. Do you have a few minutes?"

"Of course." She stepped behind the counter, needing some barrier to keep her from walking into those arms. Shay seemed to sense it and moved to face her from the opposite side. Her gaze went casually around the room as if looking for a topic to discuss.

"Everywhere I go, I hear people raving about the *Chronicle*. And you."

Mel's thoughts drifted back to what townspeople were *really* saying.

Shay leaned a hip against the counter. "How are you holding up?"

Mel shrugged and felt a wave of nausea pass through her stomach. "A bit tired, but hanging in there. How about you? No headaches?"

"No, thank you. Have you made any progress with the Heights?"

"From what we saw out there Thursday, I'd say they're in for a little time off. Your information was spot-on, Shay. Chandler's moved that massive leaching field at least partially within the buffer of a natural waterway. He never submitted a revised plan, never sought a variance. Not that he'd get one. Not for this. And he knows it."

"You're sure about the distance? Were you able to get any measurements?"

"Shay, believe me. I know these bylaws like the back of my hand. I see them in my dreams." She tossed a hand toward the door. "A leaching field this size should be as far away as that traffic light on the corner, not as close as Marie's Diner across the street. The plans I picked up—the approved ones—call for a much different arrangement."

"So, now what happens?"

"The conservation commission chairman told me he'd look at the plans and photos tomorrow morning, if I get them to Billings, where he works. He said, if he sees anything that doesn't jive, he'll bring it before the commission Tuesday night."

"That's really good news, Mel."

"I was *so* grateful, I almost cried driving home."

"The word around the barn is they start pouring foundations Wednesday."

"At least the project won't be too far along, if the commission sees reason to issue a stop order. I'm betting what we've got will warrant a review of the work. Chances are, Chandler will be ordered to comply with the original plan or submit new engineering, and it may set the project back a few weeks, but at least it will be done properly."

"Going to upset quite a few people, but credit to you, Mel. It's the right thing to do. Great job."

"Keep your fingers crossed, Shay. The fight hasn't even begun yet."

"I know." She moved uneasily at the counter. "Speaking of 'fight.' I wanted to let you know people are talking. About us."

Mel's system swirled as her emotions shifted.

"What have you heard?"

Shay looked down at Mel's fingers. She toyed with the trim, white-glossed tips.

"Tom Rogers told me about you and Peters at the diner, what he said in front of everybody." Mel took a slow, deep breath. "Tommy heard it from Sorvini."

Mel's rampaging thoughts almost made her tremble. Now the whole Five Star knew. It was only a matter of time before their families and friends knew. A day or two maybe. As it was, all the folks at the diner got an earful. *Shit*, she thought, *one of Nana's bingo chums will probably even call her to confirm*; they were that nosy, that rude. The strangulating loop of gossip soon would encircle her world and everything she did. *And Nana will be so beside herself, she'll call Dad.*

"This morning, Nana overheard women at church connect you and me. She even asked if I was seeing you 'on the sly.'"

"You're kidding."

Mel withdrew her hand from Shay's gentle, distracting touch. "All I can surmise is that Erica started it. I suppose I knew this would happen, but..." She exhaled wearily. "It's hard, Shay."

"I'm sure. And so unfair to you."

"To both of us, actually."

"It kills me to have to say this, Mel, but I want you to be prepared. Sorvini and/or Chandler, maybe even Della will try to use *us* against you."

"I've considered that. It's not sitting well, believe me."

"You can't let them. You have to hold your head up, face them. They'll use it to chop away at your credibility, your integrity, humiliate you so you'll lower your public profile and shut up. It's all they have, and you can't let that happen. If you do, they win."

Mel felt the weight of public opinion increase across her shoulders. "I haven't figured out how to deal with it yet, Shay. Hell, I'm losing sleep over this story, worrying about driving away pro-growth advertisers. And *now* I'm forced to worry about bigotry that'll shut doors in my face and cost even *more* revenue." *Not to mention Dad and losing the entire paper.*

"Sorvini and his types won't hesitate to play on that, Mel. That's why you can't show fear. You give them nothing. You play on Tomson's good side and carry on with your head high."

"But I have to interact with these people, Shay. I need their cooperation and respect. My job, my livelihood depends on it. I can't afford to have them look at me sideways or shut me out."

Shay straightened, and the energy seemed to drain from her chiseled face. She ran a hand through her hair. "So, what happened to 'making progress'? You're backing away, aren't you?"

Mel cocked her head. "I'm sorry, Shay, but, God, this is so…I'm, hell, I'm so damn blown away by you. I really enjoy being with you, in every way. I hope you know that."

"But?"

"It's not you, Shay."

"Jesus, Mel. Clichés?"

"I'd never give you some line. Seriously. I think that chivalrous heart of yours will look inward, and I can't bear the idea that you'd blame yourself, just because I—" She couldn't bring herself to admit that a career move had led her to sell her soul to her father. A stab of shame made her wince.

Shay's look hardened. "Because you what? You're having a hard time with us? I understand, Mel. I want to work through it with you." Shay's cell phone rang, but she ignored it.

"I need you to understand."

"I do, Mel. I know it's hard, but you can get through this."

"But do you understand, *really*?" Mel's gut twisted as she begged Shay to relate to a plight Shay knew nothing about. Desperate to convey the severity of her dilemma without confessing the details, Mel blurted out a makeshift defense. "You say you 'get' my situation, yet you've resigned yourself to yours, living with what Slattery's doing, and it doesn't look…Well, I don't see you fighting to do what's right for you."

Shay's face went blank. Her cell phone continued to ring, and Mel wished she could throw it against the damn wall. She could hear herself breathing hard. *Shit.*

Shay's jaw flexed. "So you're saying cashing a Slattery paycheck means I let them run my life?" She ripped her cell off her belt and practically slammed it against her ear. "What!"

Mel seized their pause to catch her breath and soothe her pulsing temples with her fingertips. She had to make Shay appreciate the magnitude of her position. *Or are you trying to convince yourself?*

Shay half turned from the counter and huffed into the phone. "All right. Maintenance, yes." She looked back evenly at Mel. "Yes. Give me fifteen minutes."

Mel snapped at the obvious interruption by Slattery. "What timing. They call, you jump. Where is *your* life, Shay?" *Throw another huge mistake onto your pile, why don't you?*

She needn't have pointed that out. Shay reattached her cell to her belt, her face taut. Mel hated the heat, the tension between them.

"Look, Shay. I've had a rough few days, and it's just the begin—"

"For the record, I haven't lost sight of what I'm after, Mel." Shay leaned against the counter. "I want my own shop someday, so yes, I'm playing their game for a while to get what I want in the end. But above all else, I'm doing it on my terms because *no one* tells me who I am or how to live. Maybe it's your time to stop playing and take what *you* want."

The correlation to Mel's deal with her father rocked Mel to her core. Shay's heated gaze didn't help. *She doesn't know the stakes of this game, that I could lose everything. She doesn't know. Why can't she simply accept what I'm saying? She can't invest in us. Certainly not now. And I let this happen.*

"There's a time for everything, Shay, and the *Chronicle*'s right in the middle of controversy now, risking advertisers. Jesus, for me to… This—this isn't the time, you know?"

She saw no agreement in Shay. Only disappointment. Then a wary curiosity.

"It really isn't about 'the right time,' is it?"

"Shay, the *Chronicle* has—"

"It's all about reputation."

"Please try to see the position I'm in."

"I do, Mel. Clearly. It's about finding the courage, and it looks like the last thing you need is to be seen with me." Stepping slightly away, she placed a hand over Mel's on the counter. "You don't know how sorry I am that you feel this way."

Bells jingled and Dick Turner strolled in, *Chronicle* tucked under his arm. At the sight of Mel's retreating hand, his congenial demeanor faded.

Mel spoke quickly. "Dick. How are you?" Her voice almost cracked.

"Good, thanks, Mel. Took a chance I'd find you in today." He glanced menacingly at Shay.

"Afternoon, Dick," she offered. "How's the Chevy?"

Turner took a half second to look at her and nod. "Shay." He opened the paper on the counter. "Little bit of business for you, Mel." He folded the pages carefully, and Mel lent her attention, feeling viciously yanked away from Shay.

Turner pointed to his advertisement, and Mel had to clear her throat before speaking.

"What can I help you with today?"

"Just a few changes I want to make for next week's paper." He glanced at Shay again. "No rush. If you're busy, I…"

"Oh," she said, looking to Shay, hoping she'd see this perfect example of what she'd tried to vocalize. "We were just chatting."

Shay gave them a short wave. "Yeah. I'm on my way out."

The door jingled shut, and Turner tugged a pen from his shirt pocket. He shook his head slightly as he scribbled on his large advertisement, wrote only two words before looking up.

"She bothering you, Mel? I mean, y'know, it's pretty obvious what that type has in mind."

Mel's entire system had already crashed. Blood rumbled in her temples, and her heart hammered so violently she feared her voice would shake. That whole scene went so wrong so fast. Shay left insulted, mad, hurt, and probably forever. The complete opposite of what Mel longed for. *But she got the message, didn't she? And what a pathetic, selfish, cruel message it was. Wasn't it? There had been no intention to hurt, but the facts are the facts. The* Chronicle *comes first. Right?*

"You okay, Mel?" Turner was frowning at her. "That Shay, she pushed herself at you, didn't she? Maybe you ought to talk to Sheriff Davis about her. Want me to swing by, have him send an officer over?"

Mel blinked and replayed Turner's words in her head. "Excuse me?"

"Can't deny she's one of those *dykes*, pardon my language, and deserves a talking-to by the law before she goes after someone else in town. No telling who she's got her eye on."

The sheriff? Seriously?

"Now, Dick. I appreciate your looking out for me, but relax. There's absolutely no need to involve the police." She touched his shoulder reassuringly. "Shay's a friend and as curious about Tomson as any newcomer would be. She fixed your truck, so I'm sure you'll admit she's skilled, polite, and very pleasant. Whatever her sexual orientation—and it's no one's business, by the way—it has nothing to do with how she treats people."

Turner mumbled "If you say so" as he went back to writing on his ad, but her words echoed in her head, a thunderous mocking she felt to the pit of her stomach. She watched him cross out prices and jot down new ones, carefully list several items in the spaces available. She watched but didn't see. All she saw was the dimmed light in Shay's eyes, the flinch of that sultry jawline. The bold stride of those long legs out the door. *It's about your reputation.*

Finally, Turner stood up. "There. You can read all that, right, Mel?"

"Perfectly." She wanted him gone. She needed to think. "Great job, Dick. I'll make sure those are done by tomorrow afternoon, if you want to stop in and proof it."

He tossed a dismissive hand her way. "Nope. You always get it right." He snorted. "Hell, half the time, you know what I mean even when I don't. We think too much alike." The words chilled her to the bone. "You take care, now, Mel."

She thanked him as he left the office, and thought her brain would implode.

Courage.

She took the ad and wandered to her desk and sat down hard, completely distracted. *We think too much alike.*

From the doorway of his workroom, Mike coughed discreetly. "Want me to grab you a coffee across the street?"

"Only if it's one hundred proof."

"Maybe you should just go for a drive. Let some wide-open spaces help clear your mind."

Driving all the way to Canada wouldn't do the trick, she mused, not even if she stayed. *Damn you, Dad. Damn me. Sticking to my guns, building a future shouldn't feel like this.*

"You heard all that?"

He walked quietly to the guest chair in front of her desk and settled in. It was a while before he answered.

"Don't you think, with business about to explode in Tomson, that it'd be safe to stand your ground?"

Mel stared out the window until she realized she was holding back tears. *The last thing you need is to be seen with me.*

She fought for composure and uttered a self-deprecating snicker. "You mean there's no more room in the closet back there?"

"Just might be time you moved out of it."

❖

Coby elbowed Shay and almost knocked her over.

"Wake up or you'll fall in."

Shay squinted in the sunset off the lake and unfolded her legs over the edge of the dock. "Must have dozed off."

"Again. You're pushing yourself too hard, my friend, picking up Sonny's slack every night on top of this Fourth stuff."

"He finally admitted it's all too much for him, so I don't mind. Things will ease up after this weekend, anyway. Once the holiday's past, I'll get back to regular ranch work."

"You have three days to charge your batteries, Shay. You'll have nothing left for the bash if you don't. You're brain's frazzled enough."

"How did I get so caught up by her, Cob? I knew better." She shook her head at the lake. "I told myself coming out here, looking for a new start doesn't mean hooking up with someone. That was the last thing I should've done. So stupid."

"Nothing stupid about it. Just a natural thing. You two were drawn together. Still are."

"No. I don't want to go through that again. Mel obviously doesn't have the guts she supposedly wants. She's too scared, and I've been too taken to see."

"We can't force someone to make this kind of change, Shay. But I do think Mel has what it takes, even though she might not think so."

"I can't get her off my mind. I know better, but I can't. Plus, she called yesterday."

"And?"

"She just left a message that she'd like me to call back."

"You going to?"

"What good would it do? We'd just hang on each other's every word and get nowhere. I'm not going to beg and blubber like a fool."

"Maybe she wants to apologize."

"Yeah, like that will get us anywhere. 'Sorry, Shay, but if you put on a dress and some makeup, maybe we could meet for tea.'"

Coby whacked her arm. "Cut that shit out. Mel's not like that and you know it."

"But isn't that what all this says?" Shay shook her head at her thoughts. "I should've known better. Just when I thought this would be the place, where I could get into something I liked and make a go of it. How can I hang around Tomson now when she's everywhere? When the damn *Chronicle* is everywhere?"

"Listen, you're taking this too far too soon."

"Now *that* sure sums everything up, doesn't it?"

"Damn it, Shay. I know it's frustrating, but give it time. Give Mel time. What did you expect? That she'd come out on the front page of her fucking newspaper? She's got baggage to handle, the paper and this Heights mess, not to mention her grandmother and the ignorant asses in Tomson who will turn on her. Damn, give the lady a fucking break."

Shay wandered to the far end of the dock. "You think I'm pressing?" She stuffed her fists into her pockets. "I just want her to give herself a chance, give us one."

"Give yourself time, too, Shay."

"Time." *That's a familiar theme.* She turned and they headed back to the house. "Maybe I *am* pressing."

All she could see was Mel's desperate look, that see-what-I-mean resignation, with Turner at the counter. It hurt seeing Mel fall back to form. It hurt more than expected, being shoved under the rug, no matter how reluctant Mel appeared. It certainly felt like more than their exchange had ended. More like something much bigger had ended. *Before it even started.*

Shay scrubbed a hand over her face, pushed images of sun-kissed hair and excited smiles aside, tamped down the sensations of warm hands and the draw of sweet lips. She tried to minimize the emotional high of the connection they shared, place it into a manageable perspective. If time was what they needed, dwelling in self-pity wasn't going to help. The distraction of a heavy workload would pass the time.

"I need to get to Sonny's."

"You ought to take the night off."

"No. God knows what mess Bailey's made out there today. Sonny's leaving him there alone more these days, and he's good at what he does, but slow, and shrinks away from customers." She veered off from Coby, headed toward her bike in the garage.

"Don't stay till freakin' dawn, Shay."

"Just a few hours." The work would occupy her mind just fine. Just what she needed. She was glad Coby understood, like best friends did. She stopped and looked back to see her watching from the porch.

"Hey?"

"Hey what?"

"Thanks."

All the way to Sonny's, she wrestled with what to say when she returned Mel's call, which she'd already decided to do. She didn't really think she had much choice. She'd go nuts if she didn't. But she wanted to let Mel do the talking, mostly because she needed to hear what was on her mind, and needed to hear her voice.

Once in the office, Shay dialed in a classic doo-wop song on Sonny's dusty old radio and dug into double-checking Bailey's paperwork. She was relieved to find his mistakes simple enough to resolve within a half hour, despite the songs of love and longing that demanded her attention. *Maybe I should shut it off.* She took her own coveralls off the hook nearby and stepped into them. Her objective tonight was to have a new exhaust system on the Ford in the second bay, come morning.

I need to call. Now.

She lowered the volume on the radio, but picked up the desk phone receiver with hesitation. On Mel's schedule, Wednesday evening meant they were "on deadline," as Mel referred to crunch time, so Shay hung up. *Damn it. Who knows what she's dealing with right now... interviews, a crucial phone call, late word on the Heights...* She kicked herself for waiting so long. Then picked up again and punched in the numbers anyway.

"Good evening. *Tomson Chronicle.*"

Shay's throat jammed.

"Tomson Chronicle. May I help you?"

"Hi, Mel. It's Shay." She could hear Mike and a woman talking and another phone ringing in the background.

"Shay? You sound funny. Are you all right?"

"Yeah. I'm fine. Eh, well, look, I'm sorry to call now. You're busy. I can call back at a better time."

"No, wait! Don't hang up." Rustling on the line quickly changed to silence, and Mel's voice came back hushed. "Hi. I just moved out to the door. It's crazy in here on deadline. So, you're okay?"

"I am. Are you?"

Mel sighed. "I'm really glad to hear your voice. I left a message, but I wasn't too sure you'd call."

"I wasn't either."

"Well, I'm happy you did. Thank you. Misty said you're working nights at Sonny's?"

"I'm here now."

"God, how do you manage? Are you running yourself ragged?"

"I'm only going to push it tonight and tomorrow. Friday night, I'll be at the ranch till late."

"Are things still set to go?"

"Is that the reporter talking, Ms. Baker?"

"Don't be fresh. No," she added hurriedly, "I take that back. *Be* fresh. I-I miss that."

Shay set her forehead onto her arm on the desk. *I don't want to be patient. I know, deep down, you don't, either. You're killing me, Mel.*

"We're set to go. All the guys are up for it, even though only a few will get the overtime to work the events."

"Um. Listen, Shay. About Sunday here in the off—"

"Let's not get into it. Not now, Mel."

"I know, but things were said that—"

"We don't really want to do this over the phone, do we?" *Look me in the eye and tell me you've had a change of heart, that we really can make something happen together.*

"No, I suppose you're right."

"Hey, how'd you make out with the conservation people? How's the story?" Mel didn't respond immediately and Shay tensed. "Mel? What's happening?"

"Tomorrow morning. The commission is delivering a stop order."

"Really? God, Mel, excellent work!"

"The leaching field issue went before the commissioners last night and they agreed to meet in emergency session earlier this evening. I just got back a half hour ago. We'll have the announcement tomorrow."

Shay wanted to cheer Mel's hard-won success. The Sorvini-and-Chandler tandem would finally learn it didn't have free rein and that a town as meek and seemingly complacent as Tomson actually *could* do the right thing occasionally. However, the idea of repercussions unnerved her. She decided not to mention it for Mel's sake. *If anyone's aware of what this means, she is.*

"You're stronger than you know, Mel."

"Thank you, Shay, but we'll see." Her voice was so soft, Shay wanted to wrap her arms around her and steal her away, but Mel was just as wary of them as a couple as she was of the Heights fallout.

"Good luck with putting it all together. Listen, I know you're swamped right now, so I'm going to go."

"I need to talk with you, Shay. Could I catch you at the garage tomorrow night?"

"I'll be here. Friday morning, the carnies are due first thing, so you know where I'll be."

"And all weekend."

"Through Monday. It's going to be a madhouse."

"I'll be there through it all, too. And I'll stop by tomorrow night."

"I look forward to that." *Because I'm a glutton for punishment and can't help myself.*

"Me too, Shay. Thanks for calling."

"Good luck with your deadline. Be strong."

CHAPTER EIGHTEEN

The *Chronicle* hit the stands at its usual six o'clock Thursday morning, and at nine thirty, armed with a dapper, silver-haired attorney, Ed Chandler raged at Mel over her desk. Refusing to sit, he slapped the edition down and papers blew everywhere.

"What the hell have you done? You know damn well what's at stake here, Mel."

She leaned back with an air of strict, professional calm. "I asked for your position on the board's emergency session, Ed, but you said you were too busy to talk. You gave me that 'no comment' knowing full well how it would look. Not one of you even attended the session."

He shook a finger at her. "These town boards take forever, and now you've pushed them to reconsider the entire first phase of my project. Do you know what that means?"

"Apparently, the Conservation Commission believes putting a hold on things is necessary. When I reached the planning board chairwoman last night, she deferred to the commission. The *Chronicle* simply asked questions, Ed. What town officials do is their prerogative. Your business is with them, not us."

"We're headed over there now to settle this. And I want it put in the paper."

"For any dealings with the project, the boards have to be in formal open session. They can't have—and I'm sure you don't want—personal discussions about town business. You'll have to wait for the hearing in two weeks."

Chandler's chest inflated and his face reddened. "And that's another thing. Two weeks will destroy my schedule!"

"Please lower your voice."

"I will not lower my voice. I'm furious, goddamn it! This will cost me a fortune."

She raised her hands in supplication. "Both boards have to advertise with us first, and seven days in advance. We can't print it before next week, Ed."

He spun to his attorney. "Are you sure that's cast in stone?"

The stoic man nodded. "State law."

"Jesus, Mary, and Joseph." He eyed Mel sideways, his pallor rolling from red to scarlet. "So I just let this simmer? Stew in it until I get to say my piece? And by the time those guys cough up some decisions, it'll be a month, if I'm lucky? Son of a bitch!"

"Look, Ed. If you want, we could sit down and you could detail your side. We could run the interview next week. You could explain the issues as you see them."

"Huh." He seemed to consider the invitation, but then menace returned to his eyes and he pointed into her face. "You generated all this with your damned crusade. My timetable—for the Heights and projects I have lined up behind it—is shot to hell now because of you, and I'm not going to forget it. And neither will all the help I've contracted. Do you have any idea what this delay of yours is costing *them*? How furious they are already? I won't be held responsible for their actions, Mel. Remember that."

Mel looked to the attorney and wondered if he construed his client's words as a threat. The man's steady gaze revealed nothing.

"I'm sorry, Ed, but it's not our delay. The *Chronicle* doesn't make the laws. Our offer stands."

"You can rest assured you haven't heard the end of this. You just might be sorry you played this game of yours."

The attorney tapped Chandler's shoulder.

"That's enough, Ed." He nodded at Mel. "We'll consider your offer and let you know."

"Very well."

The front door jingling shut signaled it was safe for Mike to emerge from his workroom, and the *Chronicle's* part-time correspondent, Ida, trailed out behind him.

"You were awesome, Mel!" she exclaimed, and hurriedly collected scattered papers off the floor. "The man's a beast. Anyone taking his time can see—plain as day—that he screwed up. Like, him taking that extra hundred and twenty feet wouldn't be noticed?"

Hands in his pockets, Mike rocked back on his heels. "That shot we got of the inspector and commissioners out there, looking at the dig was right on." He shook his head. "Chandler had to know things would blow. What did he expect?"

"He expected the usual, I imagine, to be cut some slack," Mel said. "I just hope this was the worst of it."

Mike stared down at her. "Did my ears pick up a threat in that tirade?"

"Yeah, mine did, too. He's such an intimidating guy, but that just made me mad. He brought all this on himself—with Sorvini. Was all I could do to hold my temper."

Ida tapped her desk and bent closer. "You got guts, Mel. I'll give you that."

"Only Della could give you more grief," Mike said. "If she was planning on a big opening for the Christmas season, she just might be a *tad* upset now."

Ida rolled her eyes. "Cruella-Della. Don't you let her get to you either, Mel."

"Let's just be thankful she's not our landlord."

"Got that right," Mike said. "You know, stands to reason the public will see Chandler's mess as some Slattery scheme. She hired the guy."

"It *really* exposes her big July Fourth bash as the propaganda ploy it is, and not some generous, heartfelt effort."

"She'll be beside herself."

Mel nodded at him and imagined Shay right in the middle of it all. "Well, it's too late for her to cancel now. Besides, that would look even worse."

"Oh, folks will still go," Ida said. "It's going to be a blast, even though Della's motives are pretty obvious. I mean, people will jump to take advantage of such a fun time. Don't you think?" She looked from Mel to Mike and back. "That doesn't make us all a bunch of hypocrites, does it?"

❖

Thursday was "polish it up day" for the Fourth event, and Shay's stops at the main barn and 10B, the performance arena, found Rogers's carpentry crews on the final phases of work. When the Tomson health inspector appeared for a surprise inspection, his approval boosted her spirit even higher.

By lunchtime, Shay was thankful the Softail's gnawing growl always reminded her to focus on the task at hand. As she rumbled across the acreage, she saw only sapphire where the horizon met the sky, and felt the sun's golden aura melt into her pores. She relaxed her grip on the throttle and let the Softail roll to a stop in the middle of acres of open ground. *Has hell swallowed her up this morning? Call and check as soon as you can.*

Mike's Volkswagen bounced up beside her.

"Hey, Woman in Charge," he sang out the window.

"Mike, what's up?"

"Town's buzzing, Shay. We smoked a grand slam over the damn fence this morning."

His excitement was contagious and Shay was glad Mel had his wholehearted support. *She needs it.*

"Great job, you guys did, Mike. Important in so many ways."

"Phone's been ringing off the hook. I don't think either of us got more than a few hours' sleep. Mel was already in when I got there at seven thirty. Chandler showed up with a lawyer, totally pissed off, and Mel stood her ground."

That's how it's done, Mel. You're better at it than you think.

He stared off through the windshield, still smiling and looking a bit dazed by the *Chronicle*'s achievement. She wondered if he'd be lured by the excitement to seek employment at a bigger paper, a daily. She hoped not, for Mel's sake.

"Anything I can do for you?"

"Oh, um. Sorry." His cheeks pinked. "Just amazes me that we pulled it off, that the timing was perfect. That's so hard, so rare for a weekly to break such a newsy story, y'know?" He shook his head. "Yeah, so, the fair. Is it okay if I wander around some? Get some shots of the locals at work?"

"Yeah, sure." She turned on her seat and waved back at the landscape, the carnival, fair, and stage areas dotted with workers and trucks. "We've got electricians finishing up, the main barn is practically done inside, but the guys have to rebuild the front steps. The grandstand is nearly done, too. Take your pick. Toilets arrived a while ago—a *lovely* shot, I'm sure," she added with a grin. "There are folks from different groups in town putting their own touches on their booths. That might make for better pictures."

"Got a few minutes to show me, tell me what's happening so I can get some stuff?"

Della's directive replayed in her head. Good PR, she heard her say, that's what this is all about. *Or was.* She smiled inwardly.

She circled back to the fairgrounds with the Volkswagen close behind. They left the vehicles at the entrance, and Shay led him into the maze of newly constructed booths and pointed out each community organization as they walked.

Three women from the Tomoon Fire Department Ladies' Auxiliary were putting up hooks and light shelving in their booth when Shay brought Mike to the counter.

"Hello there," she said. "I'm Shay Maguire, project coordinator for Slattery, and you might already know Mike Richards from the *Chronicle*. He's looking to take some pictures of how hard everyone's working."

The women giggled at each other and tried to wave him off. One stepped forward while the others shared a whisper, and Mike slid right into professional mode.

"You ladies just pretend I'm not here," he said, camera to his eye. "Go right back to what you were doing. Shay, let me get one with you inside, too. Hold up that board with them."

Shay was reluctant, if a bit sadistically amused. *These women and the dyke: such a telling picture for the quaint little weekly.* She sighed helplessly as Mel came to mind.

"You come right over here, honey," the lead woman beckoned, and Shay did as she was told, despite feeling that the others weren't thrilled by the idea. "You just stand with us and we'll pretend we know what we're doing." They all shared short, polite laughs as Mike leaned and crouched and ran around the booth, shooting from different angles.

Positioned between the whispering women, Shay summoned her most casual, welcoming posture. The middle-aged bleached-blonde at her left looked up with a feigned innocence. "So, where's Mel Baker today?"

Shay's irritation mounted. *Oh, she's recovering from our wild night of wet, steamy sex.* She returned the innocent look. "Ms. Baker? Well, it's Mike's job to take pictures, so I'd say she's busy doing hers, but what that involves, I couldn't begin to guess."

"Uh-huh."

"We're good," Mike declared, finished. Shay was relieved to leave the booth while Mike recorded the women's names.

"We've got the best pies in Tomson due in," the jovial woman called to Shay. "Make sure you come by for some!"

One of her whispering friends chimed in. "And tell Mel we expect to see her, too!"

"Thank you," Shay said, and mumbled to Mike when he caught up. "Sometimes, I just don't know how to read this town."

He appeared not to hear, his photographer's eye evidently preoccupied by everything in sight. "Mel said to say hi to you, to make sure I did."

Shay grinned at her boots as they walked.

"And make sure you tell her I said hi back." She stopped them halfway to the concert area. "The word is out, isn't it?"

Mike nodded. "When I checked in at the office for the okay to shoot here, the secretary asked if it was true that you two are dating."

"Jesus, Lisa? You're kidding."

"I don't think I'll tell Mel. She's worried enough about what her grandmother will hear today at the hair salon. That place is the Fox News of Tomson, for God's sake."

"Just great. She'd sounded optimistic on the phone. Or maybe that's what I wanted to hear." Shay rubbed a hand across her tumbling stomach. "We're not, you know. Dating. I mean, I'll confess to wanting to, but…"

"I think she's trying, Shay. That performance with Dick Turner really messed her up. She was pretty shaken. It put her worst fears right on the table. But," and his face brightened, "I think she saw that she needs to take a stand."

"I don't want to add to the pressure she's under, Mike, and I know I have."

"You're good for her, Shay. She's the nicest person I've ever met. Hell, I couldn't ask for a better boss, she's so bright and talented. But she's also a really considerate and fair person, hardworking and honest, and someone like that deserves to be happy. You make her happy. It's plain to see."

Despite his sincere endorsement, Shay still worried. *Plain for all to see.* Being paired with her sure added a rousing fanfare to Mel's everyday routine.

"It's so much more than people just learning who she really is."

Mike chortled. "Oh, for sure. And being with you makes a statement, no offense of course. Around here, it's nothing to see a woman in jeans and boots come in off a ranch riding a bike or an ATV, but a stranger on a show-stopping Harley, a strong-looking city woman with hair as short as mine?" He elbowed her arm. "She gets noticed."

"I've put her on the spot, I know." *Will being patient be enough? Will time enable Mel to climb out of this hole? Or will time just add rungs to the ladder?*

Mike pawed through the bag hanging off his shoulder and produced a different lens. He swapped it for the one on his camera as he softly spoke his mind. "Some people fall back into their comfort zones when they come face-to-face with change. Like the ones dead set on killing the whole Heights project, for instance. Rather than think it through, they throw up barriers like stereotypes and preconceived notions. They perceive a threat to something they're used to, they get very protective." He snorted as he looked through the new lens. "Ironically, the Heights *did* turn out to be a threat."

"Well, I couldn't care less if I'm perceived as a threat. What matters is how they treat Mel."

"Hey, she's stronger than she thinks. That's my opinion. And you're you. Only one's got a right to make you change is you. You aren't going to start wearing lipstick and carrying a purse, are you?"

Shay laughed lightly. "No."

"Well, all right then. Everyone's entitled to that self-determination the long-timers brag about out here, and sometimes I think they forget that. It's important for people see a woman standing tall. Important for Mel to see and be that woman."

"I'm glad you work with her, Mike. I get the feeling you add a lot more than pictures to the *Chronicle*."

CHAPTER NINETEEN

Mel expected Sonny's place at least to *look* deserted when she pulled in, but seeing both bay doors open, a gleaming motorcycle inside, and the overhead lights on told her otherwise. Riding this damn emotional roller coaster was going to kill her. She needed this, to see Shay and try to mend what they'd ripped apart several days before. *Is keeping a lid on us until spring too much to ask? Is it possible?* More than anything, she yearned to be herself, even though her self-discipline was worn and tenuous at best.

These past few days, she'd used up almost all the strength and confidence Shay had lent her. She conceded that it had been one bitch of a week; that Nana brooding about God-knows-what the biddies said at the salon had been infuriating, and that impacting the lives of everyone in town with a monster news story had drained her. But she'd come to acknowledge that the void widening inside her felt like heartache. Unwise of her to feel this connected to Shay, Mel knew, considering she still held the *Chronicle* as the center of her world, and needed to placate her father for eight more months. But God knows, she'd done a pitiful job showing how much she valued the connection to Shay the last time they saw each other. And being connected to Shay had started to mean a great deal.

A classic Chuck Berry song rocked out into the lot as she looked around the bays.

"Good evening! Anybody home?" She peeked into the empty office, then turned and spotted the motorcycle boots extended from beneath a Honda in the second bay. She nudged one with her foot and crouched.

Shay rolled out on a creeper from under the car and checked out

Mel's denim cutoffs and the tight red tank top. A brilliant smile took control of the smudged, rugged face, and Mel felt her body temperature rise. An overwhelming rush filled her chest, and she shook her head at the powerful, physical effect Shay had on her.

"God, Mel, you're hot. Wow." Shay sat up and dropped the wrench to the concrete floor. "If I wasn't such a wicked mess, I'd risk pulling you down here right now."

Mel laughed and they rose together. "And I think you look just fine. Grease and all." She rubbed at a smudge on Shay's cheek with her thumb. "It's so good to see you."

Shay stepped closer, a hint of caution in her normally care free manner.

"I hoped I'd see you tonight."

The intimacy hummed through Mel's system and she wanted more, but the hint of uncertainty in Shay's bearing reminded Mel that she had to make things right. She forced herself to focus on the brown paper bag in her hand. "I wasn't sure if you'd had time to eat, so I brought you supper. Some of the fried chicken and potato salad we had tonight."

Shay quickly grabbed the rag in her back pocket and wiped her hands. "Oh, Mel. That's…thank you. Did you make this?"

Mel's chin jutted up haughtily. "Fried chicken is my specialty."

"You are an amazing woman. Let me wash up." Shay bolted for the rest room. "Make yourself comfortable in the office. I'll be right there."

Mel wandered out to the front counter. She tried to settle her jittery nerves by scanning the merchandise on shelves, the miscellaneous notes and signs on the walls, and then lowered the blaring volume on the radio. Shay returned with Diet Pepsis for each of them and hurriedly cleared away clutter on the desk and rolled the spare chair closer. Finally, she stopped bustling and abruptly took Mel's face in her hands. Mel's toes literally tingled. Her eyes moistened. *There is no way in hell I can turn this off.*

"I'm so sorry, Shay."

"Shh. Don't. I owe you an apology. I'm sorry I pressured you."

Mel held Shay's hands to her own cheeks. "I was terribly unfair, selfish, and that's not me at all. Why, how I could be like that with *you*, of all people, someone who…I…I'm sor—"

"Mel. I should have understood. I was frustrated, only thinking of myself, and that's not me, either. I don't want 'us' to end." She bent her knees enough to meet Mel's eyes directly. "Just tell me there *is* an 'us.'"

Short of throwing her arms around Shay, all means of conveying her answer paled. Words wouldn't measure up. Yes, she wanted an "us," to her body and soul she could feel it. *But...*

She reminded herself that eight months could pass in a blur, that she could survive it if Shay meant what she said. Having an "us" was just *right.*

She reached around Shay's waist and drew them together, fit herself to the length of Shay's filthy coveralls.

"There's no denying it, Shay." She brushed her nose along the side of Shay's, across the scar on her cheek. "I don't know how I ever thought I could set this aside or, God forbid, let it slip away. Not you." She brought her lips to Shay's, tightened her arms around her, and offered all the sincerity she could. Shay squeezed her closer, but kissed her with a reservation Mel knew was her own doing.

She drew back and ran her palms reverently over Shay's shoulders. "For so long, I've been ridiculously consumed by my work, not giving *my* reality an ounce of attention, maybe because it's been easier to juggle that way. These things *do* take time." She spoke steadily, with hope that Shay understood the need for patience. A lot of it. *Eight months' worth.* "Everything about this, about us, feels so powerful. No one has ever taken my heart in her hands the way you have."

Shay's fingertips guided a strand of Mel's hair from her cheek, a tender stroke from a powerful hand that weakened Mel's bones, sank her into a deep, rich contentment she recognized as complete surrender. She laced her arms around Shay's neck and Shay's lips met hers, softly at first, and then with growing hunger.

Heavy, reassuring hands roamed her back, firm along her spine, and one ventured lower, covered her hip pocket and squeezed. Breathing heavily as her sex clenched, Mel kissed her hard, drove encouraging fingers up into Shay's hair. Shay's tongue skimmed hers, again and again until Shay momentarily gripped Mel's between her teeth. Mel moaned and leaned upward into their kiss. She needed this, craved it, and sensed she'd shatter irrevocably without this connection. She clutched Shay to her, drew on her upper lip. Shay uttered a low growl, slid both palms beneath Mel, and lifted as she covered Mel's mouth with her own. Mel teased her tongue into Shay's mouth and wrapped her legs around her hips.

Urged back against the door to the bays, Mel gasped, the sensation of Shay crushed against her, pressed between her opened legs, made her mind blur. She buried her face in Shay's neck and kissed the solid muscle down to the neckband of her T and back up to her jaw, along her chin and up to Shay's mouth. *Home again.* Shay's fingers dug deeply into her ass and massaged, crawled lower, her breath hot and sporadic on Mel's throat and shoulder.

Shay's mouth fell to the scooped neck of Mel's tank top, and she kissed all the bared chest within reach. Breasts aching for attention, the urge to shed top and bra so strong, Mel fisted Shay's hair and dove into her mouth. Shay growled louder, and Mel's pulse quickened. She sucked Shay's tongue greedily, her drive heightened by those long fingers beneath her, nearly at her overheated crotch.

She squirmed as arousal mounted, shifted higher in Shay's arms, and Shay plunged her face into Mel's breast. Head and shoulders bumped the door as Mel reflexively leaned back, offering. She hissed when Shay claimed a taut nipple through all the fabric.

"I want you, Mel." Her voice a muffled, agonized moan, Shay pressed fingertips fervently between Mel's legs, rubbed upward along the seam of her shorts.

Mel's body spiraled. "Jesus, I want you, too." She wanted Shay over her, under her, inside her. Everywhere at once.

Shay looked up, as if seeking permission. *She wants it all and so do I.* Mel smothered her with a kiss. She wanted to please Shay more than anything she'd ever wanted before. She needed to back up her promise, those words of apology, demonstrate the care she felt so sincerely. And she wanted to return the thrill Shay delivered with such raw, selfless passion.

A car door shut outside, and they jerked apart.

"No!"

"Damn it!" Shay said on an exhale.

"Ladies' room." Mel straightened her tank top as she spun away. *Somebody's bound to put two and two together. Us two. Really smart.* At the sink, she steadied herself with several much-needed breaths. *Jesus. Now, if only my knees would stop shaking.* The heated cheeks had to go.

She splashed water on her face to restore her usual coloring and dabbed at her smeared makeup with a paper towel. *She's incredible and we need so much more of that.* She madly swiped her hair back into its clip and concentrated on the conversation reaching her from the office.

"Hey, Shay. How's it going?"

"Mike. Hi. What brings you out here tonight?"

Thank God.

"I was just coming back into town and it dawned on me to ask about credentials for the weekend. Mel's here?"

"Eh, yeah. She stopped by. Credentials?"

"Yeah, for Prairie Fire's concert Sunday night. Maybe I should've asked about this earlier, because they probably will want a list of who's authorized backstage."

Mel joined them, relieved not to be a disheveled mess, even though her flushed cheeks were a lost cause. Mike raised an eyebrow and she scowled back as many comments rushed to mind. *Thanks one hell of a lot* was one.

"Guess you forgot that I submitted our names last week when I requested interview time." She removed the clip she'd shoved into her hair and reworked it a bit neater. She saw him glance at Shay, curious and all-seeing. *Ever the photographer.*

"Oh, yeah. Damn, that's right. Jeez. I-I'm sorry, you know, eh, for interrupting."

"Shay was about to eat," Mel said, and stepped behind the desk and opened an aluminum foil package of chicken. *Shit, did I just say that?*

Shay shoved a hand back through her hair. "Yeah. Mel swung by with some supper."

"Well, I'm glad you two are on good terms again." Mike rubbed at the smirk he couldn't hide. He shook his head. "Look, next time, at least make the place look closed, okay?"

Shay grinned as she sat down and bit into a chicken leg. Mel busied herself setting out the container of potato salad, napkin, and fork, all while hoping he'd disappear.

"We're the talk of the town and then some, Mel."

She looked up sharply. Shay stopped eating.

"The Heights stoppage story," Mike explained. "People

approached me about it at the coffee shop, the gas station, and a little while ago, at Home Depot. Everyone agrees it's a shame. What's even more interesting, though, is that nobody seems surprised."

"We're not the bad guys?"

"Well, one guy said he didn't think it should've cost everyone time off from work, that it didn't seem like a big enough deal to him. He felt pretty bad for the construction guys."

Shay snickered and reached for the fork. "Wonder how he'd feel if his neighbor ignored the law and put a leaching field beside his well."

"Exactly!" Mel quickly turned to her, bolstered by the support. She squeezed Shay's shoulder. "Thank you."

"No thanks necessary, Mel." She swallowed a mouthful of potato salad and groaned appreciatively. "God, this is wonderful." She wiped her mouth. "The *Chronicle* did a big time thing today and you guys should be proud. But there are bound to be folks who don't see the merit in it, so prepare yourself for some backlash."

"Just what I need," Mel said, slumping into the adjacent chair.

Mike stepped to the door. "Yeah, I was thinking the same thing. Thought I'd go by the office and make sure our windows are still intact."

"And your house," Shay said. "Who knows what some people would do, if they're mad enough."

"I suppose you're right," Mel said, her focus now far from romance. "I probably should check on Nana. Hopefully, there's no lynch mob with torches and pitchforks on our front lawn."

Mel picked up her keys and headed for the door, ushering Mike out ahead of her.

"Sorry I interrupted, Mel."

"Uh-huh."

"Well, y'know, you two need to find a better place than a wide-open garage."

"If you're insinuating that—"

Shay moved to her side, slid an arm around her waist, and drew her to her hip. "He's not insinuating anything. He being pretty flat-out direct."

Mike sent her triumphant grin. "Caught you red-handed, Mel."

Shay turned slightly and whispered into Mel's hair. "Red-handed is just about right."

Mel pinched Shay's stomach. "You be quiet. Don't get him going. He's bad enough on his own."

Mike winked at Shay. "Gee, Mel, now you'll have to deal with both of us."

"God help me," Mel sighed. "And no winking. Don't think for a second you're getting into cahoots with this one." She eyed Shay sideways. "You're dangerous, you are."

She couldn't help but grin at Shay's mock innocence. She knew, when Shay pulled her into a tight hug, that Shay and Mike were sharing some victorious signal. But what truly mattered was freely holding Shay at this precise moment. *I owe you honesty, Shay, no matter how it'll make you'll feel about me.* She backed away, sliding her palms along Shay's arms until their fingers entwined.

"Finish your supper."

"Yes, Mom. This was fun. We'll have to do it again sometime."

Mel cocked her head. "Yes, won't we."

Mike opened his car door and looked back to the doorway. "Lay a big wet one on her, Shay!"

Mel yelled over her shoulder. "Get lost or you're fired."

"Hell no. I'm not missing this!"

"Pervert."

Shay stepped up. "Let him watch," she whispered.

Mel almost lost her breath when Shay swept her off her feet. Swirling in circles, laughter came automatically, a simple profound joy, and Mel squeezed Shay as close as she could. If only they could do this any time, any place, she thought, and when Shay set her down and softly cupped her face, she knew she saw the same desire.

"I *so* wish I didn't have to go."

"The carnival opens at six tomorrow night."

"I'll find you."

"I just bought a straw cowboy hat, so look for that."

"Oh, right. That'll narrow it down." Mel raised up on her toes, linked her arms around Shay's neck, and felt every muscle melt as she was drawn in snug against Shay's body. Their lips met, eager and comfortably familiar, and Mel moaned as their kiss lengthened, lost within Shay's embrace, lost in their kiss.

❖

Shay drank her second cup of coffee while she stared out the front windows at the morning deluge. There were lakes in the driveway. She hated rain. Hated the look of it, the feel of it, the way it killed a motorcycle ride, the way it put a damper on everything, except making love in bed. Thoughts then took a decidedly different turn, until Coby ran in the back door.

"Our garden is happy, but it better not do this all goddamn day."

Shay imagined the carnival arriving in the mud, reducing the fairgrounds roads to troughs of slop. "I envy you," she said, and brought her cup to the sink. "Wish I could spend my workday in the loft." Her phone chirped and she snatched it off her belt and listened. "Shit."

"Now what?" Coby said. "It's too early and too friggin' miserable out to have a crisis."

Shay was equally thrilled to hear Della's voice at that hour. She clipped the phone back into place. "Seven o'clock and she's in the office. I gotta go."

"Here." Coby tossed her the Jeep keys. "If we need to go out, we'll call you. And if this mess ever lets up, bring it back."

"Thanks." She shrugged into a rain slicker and headed for the garage. "Wish me luck."

Coby yelled after her. "Don't forget your hat. That's what you bought it for, city girl."

When Shay pulled up to the office, she had no place to park. Trucks and trailers of every size were scattered like toys on a front lawn. Shay drove around back and ran into the building through the torrential rain. She could hear commotion in the front office as she peeked into Della's.

"Chicago. Get in here and shut the door."

"Carnies here already? Ain't that swell."

Della pointed at the coffee carafe on the bar. "Get yourself one for the road. You have to get out there and direct traffic, organize that circus."

"They drive all damn night to get here?"

"Looks like it," Della said. "I want them settled in place and kept there. I don't want carnies poking around. The vendors will throttle me and that's the last thing I need."

"But the building inspector isn't here yet. He's due around ten o'clock."

"Then you tell them there are no hook-ups until he's done."

"Great."

Shay stirred her coffee and could feel Della's clandestine inspection creep from head to toe. She snickered under her breath. *I'm her personal Texas Ranger, for God's sake, cowboy hat, slicker, jeans, boots. It's a wonder she hasn't given me a damn gun. Probably wise.*

"It's awfully quiet out there," she said, and snapped a plastic lid onto her cup.

"If you need help, call me. I'll be here all day."

Dealing with lawyers, the Sorvini-Chandler show, and a much greater mess than this.

Shay nodded and shut the door behind her. Glad to be on her own, she was relieved Della hadn't mentioned the Heights. And she dreaded the craziness ahead. *God help me if the carnies create trouble. Della will vent all that pent-up rage on me.*

The front office was abandoned when she entered; even Lisa was missing. *Probably hiding or being held hostage.*

She took a breath and stepped out into the rain on the porch. A sea of colorful rain gear surged forward and several dozen people yelled at once. Shay hurriedly assessed the situation as water poured off the front brim of her straw hat. Her hand went up quickly.

"Hang on! Everybody quiet!" The group hushed. "I'm Shay Maguire, project coordinator. I'm going to get you all settled, okay? This rain's no fun for any of us, so let's get it together. Who do I work with?"

A small, older man waved at her. Water rushed off his cowboy hat, too, front and rear, down the back of his orange nylon poncho. "Eric Bass," he yelled. "What's your setup here?"

"I'll get my car and lead you over to the site."

The damp paperwork in her hand said it was going to be a long day, especially if this damn deluge didn't let up like the weatherman promised. With the festivities scheduled to kick off tonight when the carnival opened, all the elements of Della's PR extravaganza would fall into place, as long as Shay hit every item on the list.

The parade of vehicles followed her through the mud to the field that had been flagged off for their amusement rides, refreshment stands, and game booths. Luckily, the field was grassy, slightly higher ground, conditions better than the road itself.

Walking back to the first truck, Shay wondered what the hell she was doing out here in the first place. She was a motorcycle mechanic. *Jesus*, she thought, as Bass rolled down his truck window one measly inch, *I hate rain*.

"However you circle your wagons is fine with me," she shouted over the downpour. "There's no power out here yet. The inspector should show in about an hour or so. Once he signs off, I'll let you know and you'll be all set."

She drove off to the side to observe the convoy and the madly scurrying workers who obviously knew their craft. She sipped her coffee and ran through the upcoming days' schedule. This afternoon's agenda had Shay visiting the police and fire departments for a final review of the physical layout, traffic plan, the events schedule, and overall safety issues. In light of the conditions the day had offered thus far, she looked forward to sitting anyplace dry for a while. Grimly, she hoped everything was still in accordance with all the preliminary work that had been approved prior to her arrival in Tomson. She dreaded being responsible for things she didn't even know existed.

She jumped when her cell phone rang.

"Hi, it's Lisa. I'm sending the kids out to see you. The bus is on its way."

"Wait. What kids?" She flashed a look to the rearview mirror just as a school bus appeared in the distance.

"The high school's student government council. They're here to help."

"You're kidding." *What else did they forget to tell me?* She tucked her paperwork back inside her slicker and pulled the hood up over her head.

The bus stopped behind the Jeep, and an athletic-looking man Shay estimated to be considerably younger than herself jumped out. He met her at the front of the bus, hand extended, eyes narrowed against the pelting rain.

"Shay Maguire? Jack Lawrence, student government advisor."

She shook his hand. "Hi. Sorry, but I wasn't told you were coming."

"Don't know which is worse, academia or corporate America. Such efficiency." He hunched his shoulders as rain slid down the back of his neck, the windbreaker he wore hardly sufficient. "The kids brought a supply of donuts and muffins and big urns of coffee to help get everyone off to a great start. Good thing we packed a tarp for sunscreen, huh?"

"I'll get some heavier rope and stakes," Shay offered. "You situate the bus so it opens to the field and the road."

Shay spent the next half hour fending off a wide-eyed student in a Taylor Swift sweatshirt while erecting a green vinyl roof off the end of the bus, and then another hour dealing with the building inspector. Thankfully, he issued the festival go-ahead Shay anticipated, but had precious little else to say. Shay imagined him strolling onto the Heights site and presenting the conservation commission's stop-work order—for work he should have stopped long ago. Another Tomson "name" on the hot seat, and she was glad. *Tough luck, Della.*

By the time Shay parked downtown next to the sheriff's cruiser for her meeting with officials, the day's torrent had relaxed into a light rain, and she eagerly took the letup as a promising sign. She'd managed to get past the *Chronicle* office without stopping and losing time she couldn't afford, even though she did slow to a crawl to peek in the windows. The meeting went well, as the sheriff and fire chief and their seconds perused her plans carefully. Shay found she liked all four of them, despite the curious stares they'd lent when she walked into the conference room.

The morning's monsoon frenzy evolved into an endless day of damp, continuous errands, questions, adjustments, and quick fixes that left her worn but quite satisfied and more excited than she'd expected. But Shay was glad to steal away later in the afternoon and recharge before the gates officially opened at six o'clock.

"Jesus, it's like a sauna out here." She joined Coby and Misty on their porch, opening her faded denim vest. Both it and the white tank she wore beneath it fell just short of her jeans, and she welcomed the air cooling her midsection.

"All that rain and eighty-six-degree sunshine make for genuine Boston muggies," Coby quipped. "Make you homesick?"

"Hell, no. Humidity sucks."

Coby raised her sweating glass of iced tea. "Got time for some?"

"Yeah, sure." Shay dropped into a chair and sighed. "To think the day's just begun."

"Well, it's good you're taking a moment for yourself," Misty said.

"At least after this weekend, you can go back to normal ranch hours. And get a chance to talk to Sonny."

"Yeah, I really want to do that." She'd been giving the purchase idea serious thought for some time, but the decision to buy and operate her own business in Tomson was big.

"So, you said Mel brought you supper last night?" Misty asked.

"She did."

"A peace offering?" Coby asked.

Misty winked at Shay. "I gather by the smile on your face that you two are back on the same page?"

"Definitely. In fact, we were a bit indisposed when Mike popped in."

"Whoa!" Coby lurched forward. "It was supper you were eating, I hope."

Misty slapped her arm. "Coby!"

Shay shook her head. "My best friend. Such a pig."

"She coped well with Mike showing up?"

"She did. Maybe embarrassed at first, but not for long. Mike's kind of a confidant anyway, and he's been nagging at her about us for a while. He's 'safe,' in her mind. Like you guys."

"Time will tell," Coby muttered. "I hope she's buckled up, because it's just started. People are talking."

Shay scrubbed at her face, annoyed. "You can figure Sorvini into that group. I'm sure he'll spread every rumor, every sick thought he's ever had about Mel, about us, to the assholes in town, to get attention taken off him. At the very least, he'll make Mel's job ten times harder." She snorted. "Hell, he's stupid enough to think he can force Mel to avoid the spotlight and shut up about what he's done."

"Then it sounds like his game has started, Shay," Coby said. "Your name came up at the diner this morning. That Franny Whatshername, all pissy about *someone like you* preying on Mel, how before you, she was their innocent all-American girl. I wanted to knock the woman out of the damn booth."

"She's a horribly misguided woman," Misty stated. "And Dickie Turner's wife, her partner in crime, is no better. She's filed complaints about the Exchange attracting the *wrong element* and jeopardizing the town's reputation and property values."

"Jesus. Some people are so damn blind," Shay grumbled. "Turner better not screw the paper. His is a regular income the *Chronicle* depends on. Mel will be hurt in more ways than one if he cuts back, or worse." *Who do I sound like now?*

"But wait. Get this, Shay. Marie stuck up for you." Coby raised her glass in salute. "She came out from behind the counter, all fired up, and went over to the booth and told those bats right off. Told them that spreading hate was un-Christian-like, and that she liked you very much and they would, too, if they'd quit acting like immature schoolgirls. I was floored."

"Maybe they talked loudly for your benefit," Misty said.

Coby shrugged. "Maybe. Serves them right, getting chastised by Marie."

"Mel needs to hear all this," Shay said.

"And Eli, Mr. Winston, the elderly butcher?" Misty added. "He asked how you were getting along. I'd told him we had an old friend staying with us, right after you arrived, and he'd read how Sorvini was arrested for beating you up. He was quite upset about that. Then he shocked the crap out of me and asked if our houseguest and Mel Baker were dating."

Shay slammed back in her chair. "No."

Misty looked ready to burst. "Then guess what he said. I wanted to kiss him. He gave me one of his big, toothless smiles," she glanced knowingly at Coby, "and he said, 'Just like you and your Miss Palmer, finding someone who makes you happy is the most important thing in this world.'"

Chapter Twenty

Shay stood alongside the bonfire stack of oak barrels, watching a worker in a bucket truck wire the last one into position. Her neck hurt, she'd been gawking too long, but she left the scene smiling, pleased that the event would be ready for tomorrow, that the day's downpour hadn't thrown the build that far off schedule.

The carnival venue, meanwhile, had come to life an hour ago, and cars were filtering into the parking fields as the supper hour progressed. Most folks went straight for dinner, as vendors sold hot dogs, pizza, chicken, and a myriad of other delights in ever-increasing numbers. Smoke from the mammoth barbecue hung in the air like edible fog. It wafted over everything and competed with an ever-changing mixture of delicious aromas, all of which made her stomach growl.

She left the Softail behind the popcorn stand and prowled the two-sided row of vendors, weighing the options of strawberry-rhubarb pie versus fried pickles, corn dogs, or bread bowls of buffalo chili. She'd never tasted buffalo or the fried pickles. She wished Mel was at her side.

"Shay! Come over here this minute. You need pie!"

The jovial woman at the Fire Department Ladies' Auxiliary booth waved vigorously, and Shay spotted Mel at the counter. That sly smirk gripped her where she stood. The white shorts, coupled with a telling blue-and-white striped jersey, delivered an electrical surge from Shay's brain, through her chest and into her groin with such force she broke out in a sweat. *Jesus. Keep your tongue in your mouth.* With considerable effort, she greeted everyone equally.

"Hi. Good to see you all." She noted Mel's pointed look at her hat, and addressed the familiar trio manning the booth. "I need pie?"

"Don't tell me you forgot you were coming back for some," the jolly woman said, and pushed several pies together in front of Shay. "Now—and back me up on this, Mel—these are the best you will ever taste. Hands down. Isn't that right, Mel?"

"Without a doubt." Mel replied. "The apple has taken the county blue ribbon four years running. I'm partial to the blueberry, though."

Shay studied the pies. *Anything you suggest.* "Blueberry's always been my favorite."

"Well, we also have pecan, buttercream-and-chocolate, apple, lemon meringue, and strawberry rhubarb. Fresh from the oven just an hour or so ago. And there are more coming. Part of Tomson's claim to fame and a newcomer to town simply *has* to know firsthand."

Shay sent the woman a narrow, evil look. "You're just too smooth at your job for my own good, you know. I hate these decisions." She earned a smile for her remark.

"I bet you haven't eaten much all day, have you?" Mel asked.

"That rain this morning did a number on my schedule. It's been crazy."

The bleached-blonde stepped around her jolly friend. "I bet you two want matching blueberries." Shay and Mel looked up as the third woman spun away and busied herself folding pastry boxes. "I'm right, aren't I?" The bleached-blonde offered an arched brow and gestured with a pie knife.

Shay knew Mel picked up on the innuendo. "Two blueberries sound great. Thank you."

"Want the works?" The jolly woman pointed to the vat of vanilla ice cream.

Mel held up a palm. "Thanks, but I can't. I'll have to walk for hours just because of pie."

Shay placed money on the counter and the blonde set two paper plates of pie before them, then poked Shay's hand. "I don't imagine you think she has to worry about that figure, do you?"

Shay's blood now boiling, the image of blueberry pie all over this woman made her grin despite herself. She lifted her plate and looked from it to Mel and then to the blonde.

"As a matter of fact, no, I don't think she has anything to worry about. It doesn't matter what kind of figure Mel has."

Mel stepped away slightly and sent them an admonishing head shake. "Contrary to public opinion, *if you asked her*, Mel would say she does." She held her plate aloft. "Thanks, ladies. We're back to work. Sell out tonight."

She walked away and Shay glanced back to the blonde before following. The wink she received nearly pushed her patience over its limit. She caught up with Mel instead.

"Hi."

Mel paused before putting a forkful into her mouth. "*So* glad you didn't heave that. I know you wanted to."

"She deserved it."

Mel looked at her thoughtfully, watched her devour her slice. "Maybe we should've fed each other a taste. They would have flipped."

Shay chortled at the idea. "Well, Ms. Baker, it's *so* nice to meet the devil in you. She's very attractive." Mel "stepping out," no matter how boldly, meant progress, and Shay couldn't wait

Mel took a long look at Shay's hat. "That brings out the desperado in you. Very…sexy."

Shay shook her head. "You just tell me how I'm supposed to keep your admirers away tonight with you looking so hot?"

"You're determined to make me blush, aren't you?"

"You're already turning heads, Mel."

"Stop. It's you in those low, tight jeans. That white tank and vest. I like them a lot." She executed an odd maneuver and stepped ahead enough to move to Shay's opposite side—and discreetly dragged a fingertip along the sliver of Shay's bared stomach. "A real lot."

Shay's entire midsection twitched at the sensation. Her fork trembled, her last bite of pie fell back to the plate. "Shit, don't do that. It's not fair."

"And I like you sleeveless," she continued. "You have such long, strong arms."

Shay's head spun. She *really* liked the sassy Melissa Baker. Self-confidence always looked so good on her. She sidestepped behind her and headed for a trash barrel. "All the better to snatch you up, little girl." She covertly pinched Mel's ass.

Mel yelped and passersby glanced her way. Shay laughed and casually strolled away through the foot traffic. Three strides later, she checked over her shoulder and then turned fully as Mel's quickened pace brought her closer.

"You're fresh, Maguire."

"Mel, it's illegal to be so god-awful sexy," she growled, glad to be beside her again. "I'm losing my mind like a horny high school kid, for Christ's sake. I want to trace those stripes on your jersey all over you, all over those gorgeous—"

"Hush!"

"I want to squeeze you to me, feel you."

"Shay."

"I need to kiss you."

Mel lowered her smile, and Shay watched a flicker of pink tongue wet those glossy rose lips. *Let me.*

"I want to kiss you too," Mel whispered.

Do it. Right here and now. Fuck everybody.

Shay stopped and closed to within a step.

Mel studied her warily. "Shay." Her eyes flitted to an elderly couple strolling by.

"To hell with everyone, Mel." Shay reached for her hand but a foreign one slapped her back. She turned and looked up at a smiling Officer Hennessey.

"Evening, Shay, Mel. Looks to be a great night, considering the weather this morning."

"Jen. Nice to see you." Mel sighed under her breath.

Close enough to feel that warmth against the back of her neck, Shay straightened, proud that Mel hadn't backed away. "Hopefully, you'll have a quiet night."

Hennessey nodded and looked evenly from one to the other. "It'll be quiet unless you two start a riot. Go do what you were going to do in private."

Shay reset her hat. "So, you're preventing me from giving the lady a kiss in public?" She wondered about Mel's reaction and hoped verbalizing her intention hadn't jammed Mel's heart up into her throat with fear or embarrassment. *But it needed to be said.*

Hennessey looked past her to Mel. "Is that okay with you?"

Mel apparently needed an extra second to compose a response, and her extended pause threatened Shay's confidence, but finally Mel spoke up.

"With all due respect, Jen, it simply isn't a concern of yours."

Hennessey nodded again. "Fair enough. So, you two, you're...?"

Shay bristled. "It's none—"

Mel stepped closer. "Jen."

Shay *really* wanted to kiss Mel now.

"Enjoy your evening," Hennessey said, and feigned a salute and walked away.

Shay turned and they stood toe to toe.

"May I kiss you?"

"*Now* you ask?"

"I wasn't going to ask at all, a second ago."

"I know."

"So, may I?"

"Right here?"

"Right now."

"Shay, just your kiss alone melts me into my shoes, but out here, in the middle of—"

Shay sank back on a hip and tried her most incredulous voice. "You think I'd tear your clothes off and make passionate love to you thirty feet from the corn dog stand?"

"Well, no, but—"

"Maybe at the merry-go-round or the teacup ride, but not the corn dog stand." Mel's surprised laugh was exactly what Shay hoped to hear. "Let's go for a ride."

"What? Shay, I can't leave."

"Not leave, *ride*. As in Ferris wheel. Come on." She backed away, grinning, waving Mel to follow.

Their five-minute walk took an hour, as people stopped Mel to chat about the Heights and the fair. And Mel approached just as many, and logged "some great quotes" from seemingly everyone. No one dissed her or them with gossipy innuendo or even castigating looks. Folks spoke to them both, as if they were a team. *Together.* And conversation flowed comfortably. In her element, openly relaxed and confident, Mel simply glowed, and Shay enjoyed every second proudly.

Are you seeing what I'm seeing, Mel? You need to. Tomson has more fair-minded people than you think, and it just can't be that big a risk to take charge of your happiness. Don't let the haters, the ignorant ones run your life. Shay compiled a mental list of townspeople who had welcomed her, not turned their backs on the *dyke from Chicago*, and was surprised at the number. *You'd be surprised, too, Mel. They're out there and they think the world of you.*

The American Legion band director drew them over, eager to promote his group, and Mel dazzled him with her smile and genuine interest. Student government advisor Jack Lawrence stopped them in the heart of the midway crowd, and after making sure Mel credited Shay for helping his group, he introduced his life partner. They all shook hands, and the men left them with an invitation to gather at the Exchange sometime soon.

"So," Mel began as they resumed their stroll, "how many people do you think saw us as a couple?"

Shay fought the exasperation born from Mel's concern. She longed to help her over the mountain Mel believed blocked her path. "Well, it's hard to say. The fair coordinator and the newspaper editor have reason to walk the grounds, to check on things, get feedback." A glance at Mel's thoughtful expression told her she expected more. "But then again, maybe everyone *did* think we were together. And if you have to ask, then they didn't show they cared. The idea—any rumor—that we're a couple obviously didn't matter. Did it?"

Mel stared up at the stars for an extra beat. She puffed a strand of hair off her forehead.

"Jesus, Shay. But it does matter. Maybe not to the folks we just talked to, but to a lot of others. Especially the ones who help pay my bills."

Shay drew her to a stop. "Do you truly know what they think? No. Granted, somebody like Dick Turner wears his attitude on his sleeve, but it's all just ignorance, Mel. These people tonight surprised you, didn't they? Who's to say those others you worry about won't surprise you too?"

"There's a lot of ignorance in Tomson, even hate. The *Chronicle* can't afford—"

"Looks to me like times are changing here in more ways than one, Mel. I'd say there are more open minds here than you realize. Hell, just the fact that no one's burned down the Exchange says a lot."

Mel just scanned the grounds, nodding ponderously, and Shay figured mentioning such a tragedy hadn't been too bright an idea.

"I desperately want to put all my chips on faith in human nature and just spin the wheel, Shay. But it's a gamble I'm not allow—" She huffed out a breath. "It's a gamble I can't take." She started them walking again and Shay sighed heavily. Mel bumped her shoulder.

"Please know I treasure your support. God, so much. I treasure everything about you."

Carnival boss Eric Bass beckoned Shay from his station at the Ferris wheel and she whispered as they neared the ride. "I'll help you any way I can."

She introduced Mel to Bass, and he regaled them with an endless string of tedious but hilarious tales of past fairs. He helped lock them into their seat on the big ride and manned the switch himself.

"I haven't been on a Ferris wheel since I was a kid." Shay grabbed her hat as they rose into the sky. Wind blew Mel's hair across Shay's face, and she let it tickle her nose until the wheel stopped for others to get on below. Their seat swung.

"It's been quite a few years for me," Mel said. "A carnival in Cascade, right before I moved in with Nana. It was a memorable night."

The wheel took them up another notch and stopped abruptly, the swing rocked hard. Mel whimpered and Shay laid her hand over Mel's on the cross bar.

"Memorable, huh? Back in the days of Triumphs and rough rides?"

"Yeah, before that door slammed shut, you know?"

The wheel advanced and stopped once more. Now at the apex, they swung gently, and Shay ran a finger along the back of Mel's hand.

"Someday will you tell me about that door slamming shut?"

"It's not an easy story to tell, Shay. I was a grad student at USC but might as well have been fifteen. Pretty emotional."

"She had the Triumph?"

Mel nodded. "A bit rough around the edges, let's say, and, well, getting surprised by my dad just led to bad things."

"Oh, shit. One of *those* stories. Ouch."

"There's a lot more to the tale, but…some other time." Mel slipped her hand out from under Shay's and entwined their fingers on the bar. "The world looks so different now."

They gazed down at the bustling carnival, so small beneath them, the dark bonfire and stage areas, the many pastures and riding rings, and the muted landscape sprawled out in every direction.

"Does it look better now?"

Mel drew her focus from the scene below and squeezed Shay's hand. "You make it look better. Because of you, I want to find the strength I should have found long ago."

"You deserve to be happy, Mel, not just successful. And now, not some future day."

Mel ran her hand up Shay's arm and carefully drew her near. "I'm enjoying this wild ride with you, Shay Maguire, more than you know." Mel boldly leaned in for a kiss, and Shay's breath left her. Every nerve in her body registered the touch of their lips, the exhilaration of a first kiss. Her sex pulsed insistently, and she felt herself dissolving into that gorgeous mouth, onto the rocking seat. It was as wild as anything she'd ever experienced. She slipped her fingers into Mel's hair, cupped the back of her head as their kiss lengthened, Mel's mouth a molten velvet around her tongue. Mel's moan rolled softly into Shay's mouth as they kissed slowly, deeply.

The wheel lurched and so did they.

"Mel, I don't want this ride to end."

Mel kissed her lightly and drew back before they swung to the bottom of the wheel and up again. A hand on Shay's bicep, she gave her a long look.

"God, what you do to me."

Shay swallowed hard. *I'm falling and there isn't a damn thing I can do.* She interlocked their fingers on the bar again.

"We have to hang on."

"I promise to do everything I can *not* to let go."

They zoomed down, past Bass at the controls, yelled hello this time, and soared skyward. Mel laughed, a free, uninhibited sound that made Shay smile from the inside out.

"Think I'm going to be ready for popcorn," Mel shouted as they reached bottom and swung back up.

"I'm with you, if my stomach holds."

"You have a weak stomach?" Mel shook her head at her own question. "No way." She tossed Shay a sly glance. "No weakness in that stomach."

"I refuse to blush."

"Go ahead. I love your shy side."

Shay knew she'd treasure this moment, this sight for years, probably forever, the bronco-busting look of a sensuous blonde riding wild against a backdrop of stars. *You're a goner, you are, Maguire.* She could only grin and hang on to her hat.

Chapter Twenty-one

Saturday night, the bonfire ramped up the crowds and proceeded without a hitch for Shay and her massive crew of volunteers and Five Star employees. Firefighters dutifully misted the surrounding grounds, while police officers meandered through the welling crowd and mounted deputies patrolled the perimeter.

Sheriff Davis drew his palomino to a halt beside Shay and tipped his hat.

Shay beamed up at him from beneath her battered straw brim. "Howdy, pardner." She ran a soothing palm along the horse's withers.

"Goes well, Shay. Nice job so far."

"Thanks, Sheriff. Fingers crossed."

"We're estimating the crowd at around five thousand, and it's early."

"We're going to blow those numbers all to hell."

"Agreed. Tomorrow should be the biggest test. The whole damn town should show up, not to mention area towns, and we'll probably top twenty thousand. What time does Prairie Fire arrive?"

"Trucks should get here around noon, the band buses about four. Opening act goes on at eight." She didn't show her concern for the concert, the weekend's biggest feature. The Nashville celebrities' tour company would be providing its own security, and she hoped it and Tomson's finest would get along.

"Captain Anderson and his detail will want to meet with those folks right away," Davis said.

"Oh, they'll be the welcoming committee, don't worry. I'm getting them together immediately. I don't want any misunderstandings, no turf wars. This is Tomson territory, not theirs."

He chuckled and his horse stepped sideways, impatiently. "Good to see you're on top of things, Shay. Della chose right with you." He tipped his hat again. "Stay sharp."

He moseyed off across the field and she took a moment to reflect on her present situation. *Who would've thought...?*

She scruffed up her heated scalp and settled her hat back on her head. After a day of supervising the parking fields, the carnival and the vendors' areas, the barns and farm corrals, and the growing bonfire crowd, she still hadn't seen Mel. She pictured her cornered somewhere by a gaggle of biddies, being harped at by vultures. Before steam rose in her again, she dismissed that image. Mel wouldn't put up with that. She'd stand her ground. *Wouldn't she?*

Ending another monotonous trip past the exhibits in the main barn, she descended the ramp and surveyed the bonfire throng once more. Flailing arms caught her eye this time, and she waved back at Misty, Coby, Keary, and Doran and felt a bit more secure in her solitary role.

An ice-cold drink was in order, and she turned toward the nearest beer stand without looking. And knocked Mel right off her feet.

"Holy shit!" Shay scrambled to help her up and brush dirt from her blouse and shorts.

"Wow, Maguire, you're a force!"

"Jesus, Mel, I'm so sorry!" Shay was panic-stricken. *Was that a flicker of pain?*

"It's okay. I'm fine, honest." Mel chuckled. "I just won't try sneaking up again."

Shay scanned Mel's adorable backside, brushed at every speck of dirt she could find along her legs and up to her hip pockets.

Mel whispered. "Shay Maguire, come back here."

"I was just, you know..."

"Yeah, I know."

"Buy you an ice cream? Cotton candy? Ride the Ferris wheel? Make out behind the barn?"

"The devil in you—"

Mel cut herself off so abruptly, Shay stilled. The sudden intensity in Mel's eyes gripped her with the surety of hands on her shoulders, and Shay's pulse quickened.

"Mel?" *Look at me like this much longer and I'll kiss you.*

Mel sighed. "God. You're irresistible. I need ice cream in a hurry."

Shay led the way past the crafts vendors and the high school booth, ridiculously eager to please.

"Hey, Shay!" A wide-eyed teenager suddenly had Shay by the arm. "Remember me? Kenzie, freshman class president. I helped you at our bus yesterday." She tugged Shay back to the booth. "Come see what we've got." She removed Shay's cowboy hat, and replaced it with a gold ball cap emblazoned with a black letter "T." "You're an honorary Tomson Trailblazer now." Shay took it off to adjust the band, then fitted the cap to her head and bent the brim into a tight arc. She took back her cowboy hat and looked to Mel.

"It's *so you*, Shay," Mel said, appraising her openly.

Gleeful, Kenzie turned to the adult advisor behind the table. "See? This is Shay. I told you about her. She's in charge here." Her eyes followed Shay's hands as Shay pulled money from her jeans. "No, the hat's from me. It's a gift. You aren't paying for it."

Shay tried to speak, but Kenzie kept protesting. Shay glanced helplessly to Mel, but the sly look told her she was on her own. The advisor was no help either.

"Here, then." Shay put a twenty on the table. "A donation to the Student Government Council." She backed away. "Thanks very much, Kenzie. I'll wear it proudly."

"Sure, Shay. See ya 'round."

Shay shook her head as they walked. "How about something stronger than ice cream?"

"She's adorable, Shay."

"Great."

"I think it's sweet. And no, ice cream will be perfect. Thank you."

Shay shot Mel a resigned look. "Thanks for your sympathy." Forgetting that they were surrounded by hundreds of fair goers, she set her cowboy hat on Mel's head and whistled at the sassiness it lent Mel's all-American image.

A middle-aged couple maneuvered around them and smiled approvingly at the hat. The man gave her a nod. "Lookin' good."

Mel blushed as she eyed Shay. "You like this?"

"God give me strength."

She fought the urge to take Mel's hand as they roamed the busy midway. As it was, she thought a second straight night of them simply appearing together would have every tongue wagging that wasn't already. But then Mel moved closer, and Shay's confusion grew. Just how Mel wanted to be seen with her was a mystery. She didn't want to push. No doubt Mel was just as frustrated. But Shay needed to know where she stood, at least where their boundaries lay. She was relieved when Mel glanced her way and spoke.

"Last night...I can't remember the last time I felt so good. And I want to enjoy tonight with you."

The words warmed Shay to her toes. *I'd enjoy every night with you.*

"How about we don't limit us to tonight?" She bumped her shoulder into Mel's. "Last night really was special, Mel—even with cotton candy up your nose."

"That was your fault, you know."

"You pushed me."

"Ha! You pushed *me!*" Mel poked her chest.

"I did not. I pulled you."

Mel grinned. "Yes, you certainly did."

"So, are you really okay with this?" Shay waved a hand between them, afraid to rejoice. *Whatever you do, don't kiss her, for God's sake.* "Us being seen together?"

Mel took a noticeable breath. "Shay? I'm going to hold my head up. Screw them."

Shay stopped so fast she stirred up dust. "What?"

"I said, screw them. I've put up with enough."

Shay's mind hummed erratically and she looked hard at Mel's keen stare. "I, um, wow. Yeah?"

"There's nothing I can do about people gossiping, is there? Why should I change who I am to satisfy someone else, especially low-life idiots? I'm not going to. I'm done."

"Mel? Am I dreaming here?" She squeezed Mel's arm. "No, you're real. What the hell happened today? Did somebody get to you?" Mel fidgeted with her hat again and resumed their walk. Shay tugged her back. "Something happened, didn't it?"

"Let's enjoy the fair, Shay, okay? It took me since five o'clock to hunt you down, practically three hours, and we've finally found each other."

"Who was it? What happened?" The idea of Mel being attacked in any way had Shay's chest in knots.

"Please, Shay. This is the highlight of my day, so—"

"If somebody hurt you, Mel, I'll—"

"Now, please listen." Mel exhaled hard and urged Shay out of the path of foot traffic.

"Mel, so help me, if—"

"Promise me. I need you to listen, not explode."

"I'm listening." Blood pounded through her veins, and at the sight of Mel's tears, she started to breathe heavily.

Mel glanced at the scene bustling around them. "Turner pulled his ad today—"

"What? That fu—"

"And we lost Home Depot." Her voice cracked, and Shay knew she was about to crumble. "Nelson called to say he negotiated a better deal with the *Tribune*, so he's not renewing his contract for the supplements. He's got two more left with us."

Shay couldn't believe Mel still stood before her and hadn't simply shattered in disappointment. And yet Mel was here, covering the fair and keeping everything inside, as if her day hadn't included two crippling stabs to the heart.

Shay pulled Mel behind the barn and wrapped her arms around her. Mel broke into sobs against Shay's chest.

"They'd do this just because of rumors?"

Mel nodded vigorously and coughed as she tried to catch her breath.

"They spread like wildfire. After the Heights piece, rumors about me personally must've just sent them over the top."

"That's crazy, Mel. Can't be. It's just stupid." Visions of Sorvini & Company whispering in the ears of *Chronicle* advertisers came to mind. "Did the *Tribune* make ol' Dick-face a better offer, too?"

"I-I don't know. Marie...I went for coffee and...Marie said she heard them. Their cronies from church will follow."

"Unbelievable." She squeezed Mel closer. "Shh, now. You'll get through this. You'll beat them at their damn game."

"I was under control until now," she cried. "Oh goddamn them, Shay."

"Screw them, Mel. You're right." She rubbed her hands all over Mel's back, desperate to ease her pain. "You'll get through this. You're tough. Sometimes we get knocked down, but then we come back stronger. Trust me, honey. You'll see." She rocked her from side to side as Mel cried. "I'll do whatever I can, if you need me."

Mel sniffed again and straightened within Shay's arms. Trails of mascara started down her cheeks.

"*If* I need you?" Mel asked, and set a hot, damp palm on Shay's cheek. "There's no *if*, Shay. I'll need support, yes, because I intend to fight the war that's coming, and you have no idea, but I *want* you."

An emotional torrent of desire, defeat, triumph, and rage roared through Shay's system with abandon. She held Mel out at arm's length to speak earnestly.

"I want you, too, Mel. Without reservation. Through whatever war you see coming. I swear to God, if I could turn into some superhero for you right now, I would. Seeing you cry makes me lose my friggin' mind. I don't want you ever to have reason to cry. Ever." She watched Mel fumble with the clasp of her shoulder bag. "Do you have tissues in there? Because you need some. You're not going back out into that crowd looking defeated. You're tough, proud, and gorgeous. And you kick ass."

Mel sputtered as she dabbed her face with a tissue. "You should coach a football team."

"Hey. Pull on a helmet, honey. You're going to lead a winning drive. I just know it."

"Going to give it my best shot, Coach." She blew her nose and tucked the tissues away. "God help me."

"You are an extraordinary woman, Melissa Baker. Jesus, how you sweep me away."

Mel's tightened lips labored into a smile as if with renewed purpose. She flattened a palm on the center of Shay's chest and leveled a look at her that seized Shay's breath.

"You know, Shay Maguire, I think every woman has dreamt of someone wonderful riding into her life. I know I have. You've materialized in mine like a fantasy, and I'd be a fool to let you go." She took Shay's face in her hands and kissed her powerfully, slowly, masterfully. Shay groaned with pleasure and fought against staggering, unable to feel her feet.

❖

They bought vanilla and strawberry cones and walked on as the bonfire waned. Shay was grateful that the crowd was diminishing. It had been one hell of a long day, and it was almost time to relax. She wanted time alone with Mel, knew they needed it.

They checked back at the main barn, where various town organizations swept and tidied up and draped sheets over their wares for the evening. Around them, lights went out and moonlight emerged.

"I needed tonight so badly," Mel said.

"I'm glad it took your mind off things for a while."

"Off some things," she said, as they walked in and out of the shadows of the barns. "But everyone loved the fire. It really was fun, what we saw of it."

Shay loved the fire in Mel's eyes, the desire on her lips when she kissed her. She loved her newfound resolve, too, but just hoped Mel was ready for what it would take to maintain—and what it would take out of her personally.

"I did see the fire, off and on," Shay said. What she really enjoyed most was studying Mel's supple mouth and tongue as she worked on her ice cream.

Those plush lips curled flirtatiously, and Shay knew she'd been caught watching. Mel raised an eyebrow. Topped by that damn cowboy hat with its cocked brim, the look grabbed Shay's crotch and squeezed. Mel sidled closer and breathed, "Want some?"

Shay looked up at the moon. "Help me."

Mel held out her cone. Shay did likewise and their eyes met as they sampled each other's ice cream.

"Come back to the house with me, Mel. Stay." She watched Mel's lips go where her own had just been.

A deep frown hardened Mel's delicate features. "I'm sorry, Shay. I can't leave Nana alone much longer. And I take her to church in the morning."

"I want you, Mel. I want us together, completely."

"Oh, Shay. I wish…" She brushed her hand along Shay's arm. "I'll figure out a way."

They took back their cones, and as Mel started to lick hers, Shay bent forward quickly and licked it, too. For a second, their tongues touched. The arousal was instantaneous.

Mel gasped softly. "Jesus." She pulled away.

Shay cleared her throat nervously, unsure how much she should push. She knew she had to temper her nagging impatience.

"Things are pretty much shut down here. We can walk for a while, at least."

The line of red taillights crawling out to the paved road had their attention when Tom Rogers and his family came up from behind.

"Shay, I want you to meet everyone. Nice hat, Mel. You getting the news from the source, I see?"

"Actually, I'm enjoying the evening." She smiled at Shay.

Rogers acknowledged Mel's gesture with a nod to Shay and she felt her face heat. She smiled at his wife. "Hi. I'm Shay."

"I'm Barbara, and these guys are our grandsons, Joey and Josh. They're with us for the month of July."

"The *whole* month," Rogers stressed, and everyone chuckled.

"We're twins," Joey declared, "and we're in the first grade."

Shay crouched to their level. "What kind of grade would you give that bonfire tonight?"

"An A," Joey said. "It made my face hot."

"I give it an A, too, 'cause the top came crashing down!" Josh added, and demonstrated with a swing of his arm.

Shay helped Joey finish zipping his jacket. "Maybe you guys will be back tomorrow night for the concert or the carnival?"

"Yeah, we can't wait!"

"Grammy said we can go on the Dino Blaster!"

Shay looked up at Barbara, then back to the boys. "Wow, you're a lot braver than me. That thing scares me to death!"

"I'm not scared," Joey stated.

"Grampy says you ride a Harley." Little Josh had different priorities.

"Yup, I do. Sometime when you come to visit him, I'll show you."

"Cool!" Josh's miniature Five Star ball cap almost fell off his head. "Like, tomorrow?"

"Sure. Like tomorrow. Make sure you guys come find me."

"We will!" both boys declared.

"So, Mel," Rogers asked. "I think you've been one of busiest people in town lately. How goes it?"

"The stoppage has drawn lots of mixed reaction so far. Seems like people are either seeing it as lost jobs or as sneaky business getting caught. Ed Chandler and his lawyer paid me a visit. You can just imagine how that conversation went."

"I bet. And Angie?" He flashed Shay a look.

"He's been unusually quiet," Mel said. "Maybe he realizes he needs to lay low, with his court date a week from Monday. Have you seen him since the Heights was stopped?"

"Only this morning when I ran some supplies out to the site. Looks like he hooked up with Chandler pretty quick." He elbowed Shay. "And he's got nothing good to say about you." He turned back to Mel. "Or you."

"Or me?" Mel asked.

"Yeah, well, he's got you in Shay's camp now. Sounds like you've 'fallen under her influence.'" Shay waited for Mel to look at her, but that sassy cowboy-hat look remained focused on Rogers. "He's not calling you all the names he calls her, yet, but it's pretty clear that in his book," and he lowered his voice, "you're a lost cause because you're gay."

"Tommy!" Barbara scolded in a hush. She checked to see the boys were preoccupied with deflated balloons nearby. "Don't be spreading Angie's—"

Mel stopped her with a hand on her shoulder. "Thank you, Barbara, but it's okay. I understand. It's Angie's problem, not Tommy's."

"Hell no," he said hurriedly. "I got no problem with it. Jeez, Shay and I are good friends, and, Mel, we've known each other since, well, since you were a little girl visiting your grandma."

Shay warmed at their exchange. She needed—Mel needed to take the next step.

"Never had a doubt, Tommy," Mel said and took Shay's arm. "I'm very happy, very excited that Shay's come into my life."

Shay took a subtle breath. *I like the new Mel Baker.*

Barbara looked from Shay to Mel. "It's good to see. Does your grandmother know?"

"Has there been any fallout about it around town?" Rogers asked.

"I haven't sat down with Nana yet. Needless to say, it'll be one of the great challenges of my life. And yes, there has been fallout, in a big financial way, I'm afraid. But it's made me see how I've been bullied into a corner. It's time I was a big girl and stopped allowing it, as difficult as that will be. But seriously, I can't afford it in more ways than one. It's as simple as that."

Shay wanted to applaud. Her face hurt from smiling.

Tommy hugged Mel. "I'm real proud of you. You've got guts. But I always knew that."

After all the good nights were spoken and high fives with Joey and Josh were slapped, Shay and Mel returned to their stroll toward the parking field, and Shay longed to put an arm around her.

"I can't begin to tell you all the ways you impress me."

"Shush."

"I hope you're as proud of you as I am."

Mel puffed her cheeks and blew out a breath, as if relieved. "The worst is yet to come, Shay, and I have to walk the walk."

"Well, you see you have good friends. You won't walk alone."

Mel turned Shay's face and kissed her. It was a light kiss, fleeting, but bold for Mel, not hidden by any building or shadow, and the significance of it warmed Shay deeply. "You are an absolute dream, Shay Maguire. After all, I don't wear just anybody's hat."

"It means we're going steady."

"In that case, you're not getting it back." She shifted it into a decidedly seductive tilt.

"Oh, that's foxy. And very risky out here." They were at Mel's car and Shay wanted to press her against it and kiss her till the sun came up. "We lost time together today. I wish we'd found each other sooner." She tipped the hat up to let moonlight illuminate Mel's face.

"I wish I'd said that, Shay, but I'm covering the fair right through Monday, so we'll do better."

"Quality time together. Promise?"

Mel put a fingertip on Shay's lips. "Promise."

"I don't want you to go, Mel. I need your kisses, your smile, your—" She cut herself short. "God, I'm fumbling like a kid again."

Mel set a palm to Shay's neck, and the warmth, the intimacy made Shay's heart pound.

"Shay." The softened voice caressed her lips. "I've been thinking the same things about you…and how amazing all this is, how you make me feel."

"You make me crazy inside, wanting you."

In another move Shay thought quite daring, Mel stepped into her arms. "I'd throw myself at you right now if I could."

Shay's insides liquefied at the image of Mel shedding all reservations. She steadied her breathing and dared to lean against her until the car door met Mel's back. The curves, the softness of Mel pressing into her stole her mind. "I want you, all of you."

"We're pushing our luck out here."

Shay kissed her upper lip, then the lower.

Mel stroked Shay's hair back. "We have to behave."

"Let's not," Shay whispered. She squeezed closer and nuzzled her neck, Mel's fingers in her hair making her dizzy. "God, I hate behaving."

Mel took Shay's hand and held it against her leg. Her voice shook at Shay's ear. "I'm not so fond of it myself, so…God, Shay. I'd better go now."

A hollow ache rose in Shay's chest. She braced an arm against the car roof to keep their bodies separated and offered only a resigned sigh.

Mel closed her eyes. "I can't see that soft, hurt-puppy look. I lose my mind over you."

"I like that," Shay said, and put light fingertips to Mel's cheek. She kissed her tenderly. Mel reached for her, drew her shoulders in tightly, and Shay felt her tremble.

She lifted her lips from Mel's just enough to whisper against them. "You are all I think about, Mel." She kissed her briefly. "When my head aches from all this, I think of you." Again, she touched her mouth to Mel's. "When I'm lying in bed, I think of you…and wish you were with me."

Mel brought her lips to Shay's this time and kept them there, kissing her deeply, clutching her. Mel squeezed her shoulders, sent a hand up into her hair, and lengthened their kiss. Shay shifted her hips into hers, kneaded Mel's ribs, adrift in the feel of her, in Mel's passion, in her own desire. She grazed a palm over Mel's breast, closing her fingers around it, and groaned against Mel's neck.

Shay almost shuddered as the moan in her ear fanned the flame between her legs and searing heat threatened to take control. She stepped in farther, edged between Mel's legs, and hugged her tightly. Mel's fingers dug into the muscles across her upper back and her tremulous breathing pushed Shay closer to the edge.

"Mel, Jesus, I want to make love with you."

"Shay, we're…here…Oh, please, don't let go."

"I won't. I can't."

"You feel so good."

"Let me kiss you, caress you everywhere."

Mel lifted her head. "Shay." She trailed a fingertip along Shay's jaw, over her lips, then spoke against her mouth. "Come home with me."

"Are you sure?"

"No, but I don't want you to let go, and I can't let go of you."

Shay kissed her deeply, Mel locked within her arms. "I could kiss you all night. Your kisses…You absolutely destroy me."

Mel's head thudded onto Shay's shoulder. "You make me throw every care away. I've never felt want like this, Shay. It's you. I know it's you."

Shay could barely speak. "Let's get out of here."

CHAPTER TWENTY-TWO

Mel shut and locked the shed doors, wrapped her fingers around Shay's hand, and led her into the old farmhouse kitchen, never more thankful that Nana went to bed early and slept like a rock. Rolling the Harley across the yard and into the shed had taken some doing, but they'd succeeded and now headed up the back stairs.

Mel closed her bedroom door and turned on a lamp. "Once we leave for church, the coast will be clear." She hated sneaking around like schoolgirls. Hated that she hadn't the courage to do this right. But at the moment, Shay just stood in the middle of the room, hands in her pockets, grinning, and nothing else mattered.

Mel shook her head. "I can't believe you're standing here."

Shay drew her into a snug embrace, and Mel linked her arms around Shay's neck.

"It's just us now." Soft, warm kisses landed on Mel's shoulder, her cheek, and Mel captured Shay's mouth with her own. Shay's hands slipped beneath her blouse, glided up her bare back, and the sheer breadth and strength of them made Mel quiver. She didn't care that Shay knew how willing, how thoroughly swept away she felt.

Mel rubbed her nose along the underside of Shay's jaw before settling her lips against her throat. The smooth skin was warm and soft as she pressed a long kiss to it, enjoying the resistance of the hardened tendons that underscored every part of Shay she'd touched so far. And she wanted to touch them all. Shay's moan rumbled against her lips, and Mel nipped at her throat, excited to have roused her.

"Jesus, Mel." Shay kissed her hard.

Mel drove both hands into Shay's hair and returned the kiss just as thoroughly. The flood of pure, raw want sent her into an uncontrollable tailspin, a high she could not—did not have to stop. She squeezed Shay's shoulders and felt the response with a surge in her heart and groin.

Shay pulled her blouse up and off, and Mel groaned with want. She felt her knees quake when Shay released her bra, and watched as Shay cupped her breasts with a tender, reverent touch, just as she'd expected. *And you waited so long.* Her breasts filled Shay's palms, dissolved into weightlessness as long fingers surrounded them and kneaded lightly.

Shay lowered her head. "God, you're so beautiful." She kissed each taut nipple and Mel shuddered. Her eyes fell closed, and as a warm hand claimed each breast, she felt Shay's mouth meet hers. "Breathe," Shay whispered. "When you're this close, it's easy to tell when someone's not breathing."

"It's your fault," she said on a sigh. Slow, seeking kisses milked her throat of all her strength, and she was almost too overcome to stand.

Shay's breath on her skin tingled everywhere. It made her chest tight, her arms and legs dangerously weak, her sex cry for attention. She belonged to Shay at that moment, and there was only the urge to give. No urge to resist, no thought of turning back or of tomorrow, just surrender.

"I want you so much." She set her palms on Shay's chest and kissed her with a longing that left them both breathless. "Such an incredible kisser, Shay Maguire."

She unbuttoned Shay's shirt and laid it back off her shoulders. Shay drew her arms out and let it drop to the floor, and Mel ran fingertips along the straps of the white tank top, recalling those urges to touch it every time she'd seen Shay wear one. She loved the lines of Shay's shoulders and torso, how they swept to her hips and thighs, the straight and solid musculature that extended along her limbs. She wanted to touch them, too, feel them around her, wanted them relaxed and at ease in her hands.

She ran a palm lightly down Shay's arm and relished the sensuous texture of skin over the hard bicep, the corded forearm. "So incredibly sexy." She explored the curve of Shay's neck with her whole hand, grazed down and over her breast, and paused to massage it through the cotton. She rubbed firmly across the width of Shay's abs and exhaled hard. *Mine.*

She pinched the fabric. "Take this off. Now." Shay obeyed, and small breasts and eager nipples appeared in the dim light. Mel leaned forward and kissed the center of Shay's chest, then each nipple. She covered them with her hands and squeezed, pleased when Shay took a steadying breath. She slid her hands up to Shay's shoulders and marveled at the solid feel of them. "Heaven help me."

Shay went to one knee.

"My turn." The heat of Shay's kiss on her stomach made Mel inhale, the sensation of Shay's tongue along the inside of her waistband made her squirm. Mel sent both hands into Shay's hair to steady herself, and looked down as Shay unbuttoned and unzipped her shorts. Shay pushed them and Mel's bikini briefs to her knees and pressed a kiss into the narrow triangle of blond curls between Mel's legs.

"Shay. I don't think I can st—"

"Sh." She kissed Mel's thighs as she lowered her clothing to the floor.

Supported by a shaky hand on Shay's head, Mel stepped free of them, and Shay stole her sandals as she did, and slid those expansive hands up the back of her legs. From her knees, Shay flexed her fingers into Mel's rear and slowly looked up.

"You are a goddess. My goddess."

The tousled hair, the wondrous half-smile on that shadowy face drew Mel's fingers to Shay's chin in an enchanted daze. She urged her to stand, entranced by the ardent smokiness of her eyes. Shay stood taller, it seemed, and, broad-shouldered and naked to the hips, more dominant and arresting than ever. The simmering air between them rippled the length of Mel's nude frame, and she was never happier to be so completely exposed and available.

"You are the hottest thing I have ever seen—especially in just jeans." She exhaled hard. "Such a stud you are, my God." She reached for Shay's belt and unbuckled it, then unbuttoned her fly. She grinned into Shay's smile as she slid her palms beneath the waistband and forced the jeans to the floor. Sharply contoured pelvic bones and thigh muscles, a dark thatch of hair appeared within easy reach, and Mel labored to contain her throbbing eagerness to touch.

"My boots."

Mel simply pointed to her bed. Shay sat, and as Mel removed the second one, Shay grabbed her hand and pulled. Mel went willingly and landed atop her, an electric first connection that shimmered between them. Shay wrapped her up tightly and they sank into a lengthy, penetrating kiss.

Shay rolled nearly on top of her, her kisses fierce and hungry. Mel held on firmly, pulled on her shoulders and back, clutched at Shay's ass. Abruptly, Shay stopped and shook her head.

Gasping for breath, Mel looked up in wonder.

"I cannot kiss you like that," Shay stated. "I have to kiss you like this." And now her kisses were soft and deliberate, languorous and wet. Mel reached for more with her tongue, felt Shay take it, suck it deeply. Hands squeezed her hips and made Mel writhe beneath her, wound her sex so tightly she nearly begged.

Shay sat back, straddling one of Mel's legs, and Mel would have whimpered if not for Shay's finger at her lips.

"I want to look at you like this." She ran her hands delicately over Mel's stomach and up to claim both breasts. "I want to worship every single inch of you."

All modesty abandoned, Mel gloried beneath Shay's attention, immeasurably pleased to see Shay liked what she saw. She watched Shay caress her stomach, the slope of her hipbone, the top of her thighs, the pale blond hair between them. She writhed at the touch. Sensation constricted her lungs, gnarled her abdominals, and twisted in her groin. She nearly doubled over with yearning.

Shay slowly kissed her stomach, ran her nose along the underside of each breast, and then across and around each nipple. She sucked contentedly on each one for some time.

"Shay, God, I love your touch."

Shay licked between her breasts and up to the base of her throat. Mel's arms crossed over Shay's back, and she sought Shay's lips.

"Kiss me."

Shay lay on her slowly, her thigh settling between Mel's, and licked Mel's lips steadily as she pressed up into her. Mel's hips rose and her senses whirled. Shay's tongue ventured into her mouth, inside each lip.

Mel's hands roamed Shay's back, absorbed its strength, and she thrilled to possess its power. She wanted to lay her face on it, to taste it. Mel grabbed a fistful of blanket and sheet when Shay's bare thigh snugged farther into a tight, perfect fit between her legs.

"Oh, God, yes." Mel felt the heat and wetness on her own thigh as Shay rode it, as Shay slipped her arms beneath Mel's shoulders and melded to her body completely.

"I want you, Mel," Shay whispered into her mouth. "I want to please you, to thrill you."

Mel hooked her leg over Shay's hip, and Shay pressed into her with purpose. At Mel's gasp, Shay rocked harder. She lifted Mel's breast and took possession of the nipple, sucking firmly, tugging on it every time Mel moaned.

"Shay. I want…"

"What would you like?" Shay whispered, kisses moving to Mel's stomach. "Tell me. Anything."

Mel pressed the hand covering her breast. Her mind reeled. With the warmth of Shay's breath on the inside of her thigh, she thought she would explode with desire. No one had touched her in so long, she'd almost forgotten what the sensation did to her. Emotionally and physically, she tried in vain to focus.

"I…" Words were so difficult. Shay's kisses, her open mouth, her tongue traveled up her thigh. "Oh God."

"Tell me." Shay nuzzled her hair and Mel squirmed.

"I want to be yours." With an exquisite urgency, she reached for Shay's head, combed fingers into her hair. "Take me."

At the touch of Shay's tongue, Mel's body arched hard off the bed and a steel-like arm encircled her hips. Shay's long fingers held her open as she lapped at her wetness, at her clit, with scorching, wide strokes, slowly from every direction.

She shuddered uncontrollably, and her hands and arms collapsed onto the bed. Somehow, she uttered Shay's name. How inconceivable, she thought as her mind raced blindly, to find a special someone after all this time, and then beg to be taken, to invite her to feast on her, make her come…how euphoric…

Shay kissed her clit, blew on it, ran her lips over it, and teased her devilishly.

"Jesus, you're evil."

"Come to me, Mel." She delivered deep, heavy kisses into the wet heat, and Mel shook violently.

"Sh—Shay. Yes, Shay. Please."

Shay claimed her clit and sucked hard. Mel quivered repeatedly as Shay commanded her every bodily function, and Mel grew wetter by the second. She reveled in the feel of that handsome face immersed in her. Shay slid both palms beneath her and drew Mel to her mouth tightly. *Possess me.* A wave of surrender rolled through Mel at Shay's primal, muffled growl against her flesh, and she welcomed Shay's unrelenting worship of her clit so much it dazed her.

Her body rocked as Shay pressed deeper, took every ounce of her. Mel struggled not to scream Shay's name as every muscle grew taut, strained for release. Her strength never more evident, Shay kept her in perfect position to devour her, and Mel couldn't have pleaded for a more exacting touch. Mel's connection with reality frayed. Shay sucked ravenously, took her mercilessly until, at last over the top, Mel shattered.

Shay gently released her hips as the shuddering subsided and Mel worked to steady her breathing. She twitched as Shay continued to lick her sex.

"Can't get enough of you," Shay whispered into her.

Mel brought her hands to Shay's head. "My God. Please come here."

Shay lowered herself as gently onto her body as she did her mouth to Mel's lips. Desperate as she was to crush Shay to her, Mel knew she lacked the strength. But Shay seemed to know, and carefully gathered her in her arms. She rolled them as one onto their sides, and kissed her deeply.

Shay burrowed her face between Mel's and their pillow and kissed her ear. "So, so beautiful."

Mel shivered at the breath along her neck. She sighed inside, thankful to be held together in one piece, thankful and joyous that it was Shay holding her.

"Incredible." She stroked Shay's neck, squeezed her shoulders and back.

"*You* are incredible, Mel. I could make love with you till I pass out."

Eyes closed, Mel smiled. "Another one of those and I might."

Shay raised her head and kissed her slowly. "I want to give you stars," she said, and kissed each lip. "Stars, thunder, lightning."

"Shay, I saw, I felt all of them."

"That's all I want, Mel. I want to give you everything."

Mel's voice was meek, broken against Shay's lips. "Where have you been, Shay Maguire?"

Shay took Mel's mouth tenderly. "Searching for you."

❖

The sun blazed through both windows at seven o'clock, when Nana yelled up the stairs.

"Melissa! Are you coming down for breakfast?"

Shay yanked her arms and legs free from Mel's, and saw her lurch upright.

"No thanks, Nana. I'll be down in a little bit."

Shay lay in place, completely taken by the lustrous hair, the fair skin, the luxurious texture of Mel's bare back. She ran her hand across it. "At least we didn't wake her during the night."

Mel lay down and trilled light fingers around Shay's breasts. She stimulated a nipple with her thumb and Shay's heart rate spiked.

"We really have to be quiet now," Mel whispered, and straddled Shay's waist.

Claiming both nipples with a snarl, Mel slid her mouth over Shay's, and rubbed her wet center against her abs, sent fingers into her hair. Shay groaned, struggled to be patient as Mel's hair feathered onto her face.

"God, you're so good," Mel breathed between kisses. "You make me so happy."

Shay clamped both hands on her hips and squeezed, worked her fingers between Mel's legs, eager to claim. Mel responded with impassioned kisses, and tugged, twisted both nipples. Shay's muscles slackened, her sex screamed for action.

"Mmm." Mel smiled onto her lips. "Gotcha." Shay couldn't respond. Mel's tongue slipped into her mouth, licked hers, and Shay sucked needily.

She tripped her fingers through Mel's sex before sliding two inside and causing Mel's attention to fail, her mouth to fall away. Shay sat them up, her fingers still deep inside, and Mel's head dropped limply onto her shoulder.

"Now I've got *you*," Shay breathed into the sweet slope of her neck. "And I love it. God. You're so deliciously wet. I love being inside you, Mel. I love touching the softness of you...such a lady." She stroked the hot inner walls, explored as deeply as her fingers would reach, and Mel's arms tightened around her shoulders. Her breathing quickened in Shay's ear.

"Jesus, Shay, feeling you inside me like this...Stay there."

Their lips met softly but the kiss heightened. Shay shifted her fingers, crazy with the feel of her, to be exactly where she was.

"Let me stay inside you like this all day," Shay murmured against her throat. "I will always be gentle."

Her words breathy and heavy, Mel tongued her ear, whispering, "You are just...fucking amazing." She rotated her hips slightly on Shay's fingers. "So perfect inside me. God, you feel so good, all over. I love your strength, your muscles, and how hard and smooth you are."

Shay's stomach grumbled loudly and she chuckled against Mel's chin.

Mel's head lolled backward as she sighed. "Sounds like someone's hungry."

Shay tightened her arm around Mel's waist and wiggled her fingers inside, made Mel squirm. "You know what I'm hungry for, Mel." She covered Mel's neck with long, wet kisses.

"Shh. We have to be quiet. Oh, that feels— Shay, somehow we should...need to stop. Nana could make her way up here. Oh, God, yes."

Shay couldn't think about anyone's grandmother. Not right now. She swirled her fingers again, and relished the steaming, wet clench of Mel's muscles. Mel shuddered and inched down onto them for more. Her head returned to Shay's shoulder.

"Oh, please stay inside me." She gripped the tendon at Shay's neck with her teeth.

I'd crawl inside you, if I could.

Shay laid Mel back, eased in deeper, withdrew smoothly. She moved down on the bed and used both palms to spread Mel's thighs farther apart, open her fully. She tickled the glistening flesh, kissed it, twirled her tongue around Mel's clit and took it. Hungrier than she'd ever imagined, she sucked firmly, relentlessly, and Mel moaned, drew Shay's head into her. Mel's hips rose and shook, and Shay followed.

She refused to give less than everything she could, refused to part with the treasure in her mouth. Mel's body became rigid and beckoned. Shay bore down and drove Mel up, off the bed.

Clutching at the sheet, Mel threw her other hand over her face. "Shay, yes!"

Shay nibbled her clit, forced her into a thrashing orgasm, and held her at the peak of ecstasy, trembling, whimpering. Shay groaned at their pleasure, and as Mel succumbed, Shay relaxed between her legs, content to lap her moist sex.

"Shay Maguire," Mel exhaled in a hush, exhausted. "Dear God. I am helpless against you."

"And I just can't get enough of you." Shay nuzzled into her.

"Oh, Christ, yes." Tremors rocked her with every movement of Shay's tongue. "Nothing on earth has ever felt so good."

Shay set Mel's thighs on her shoulders and kissed from the inside of one to the other, paused between them to dip her tongue for more. Mel shifted encouragingly, and Shay could feel the throbbing against her lips. She kissed the swollen clit gingerly.

"You're so sweet, so tender. I am starving for you." Shay sucked steadily and slid inside again. Mel sighed and her palm skittered across Shay's hair. Shay kissed the thigh that reclined against her shoulder, then flicked her tongue across Mel's exposed clit and made her twitch.

"How can I let go?" she whispered, pleading. "Holding you inside like this, tasting you this way, there is no outside world. Just you."

"Just you. Only you, Shay."

Mel drew a fingertip across Shay's wet lips and Shay thought her heart would burst. She wanted Mel and everything that meant. That Mel somehow knew, that she was willing to surrender so much, simply completed her in every way.

Shay pressed her mouth to Mel's clit. "You are a treasure."

Her yearning mounting, Shay increased the pressure, the strength of her kiss, the swipe of her tongue, and Mel shivered. Shay sucked harder, tugged the enlarged bud deeper into her mouth, and heard Mel struggle to remain quiet. The thighs on her shoulders stiffened, and Mel shook. A trickle of warmth coated Shay's cheek and chin. Her own clit pulsed wildly as she licked Mel's opening, swallowed Mel's essence. The urge to touch herself nearly distracted her. She practically pounced on Mel's clit, seized it with her lips, then between her teeth. Mel hissed and twisted against her mouth, and Shay nearly lost her grip on the soft hips.

"Come to me, honey," Shay said on a breath. She slid her fingers deep within the taut flesh as she sucked with as much force as she dare. Mel uttered a long, muffled groan.

"I'm com—" She hugged a pillow over her face as her body curled upward and muscles clenched around Shay's mouth and fingers. Wolfishly, Shay persisted, clung to her, feasted, and Mel's climax vibrated long and hard against her tongue. Mel's hand fell atop Shay's head, and Shay stopped. The tremors at her mouth slowed. The pillow cast aside, Mel gasped for air, spent. Shay drank from her, kisses searching and soft.

Then, crisp knocking on the bedroom door changed everything.

Shay withdrew swiftly, rolling over and off the far side of the bed to the floor. She snatched her clothes back out of the line of sight as Mel struggled valiantly to collect herself.

"One second, Nana!"

Breathless, Mel gathered her legs under her. Forcing her knees to flex and her body to bend upright, she nearly crumpled to the floor. She staggered against her thrumming heart and managed to reach her robe on the bathroom door. She flipped her hair into place as she tied the sash and blindly swiped perspiration from her face. Steadying herself with a deep exhale, she opened the door.

Nana stood, eyes wide and fearful, offering a cup of coffee.

"Morning, Nana."

"Are you okay? My God! I thought you were hurt!"

"Ah, oh no, Nana. I just whacked my toes on the bureau." Mel managed to chuckle for Nana's sake and worked to ignore the incredible throbbing, the slick wanting between her feeble legs. "That's what I get for being a sleepyhead this morning."

"Oh, Lord, that's all." Nana was noticeably relieved. She patted Mel's shoulder and put a hand to her cheek. "Are you feeling all right, dear? You look flushed." Her hand went to Mel's forehead. "You're so warm. Feels like a fever."

"Nana, you are a worrywart, bless you. Now, let me help you down these stairs." Mel turned her around in the doorway. "And I am scolding you for coming up here," she kissed her cheek, "even though I needed the coffee so badly."

Step by step, Mel labored, her knees and legs frighteningly worthless as she helped Nana down the stairs to the kitchen, where ham and eggs had been prepared earlier.

"I made you breakfast anyway, young lady. You are too thin. You need to eat."

"Nana, I have to shower and get dressed."

"Yes, you do. Here. Take this plate up with you and get a move on."

Mel kissed her cheek again and hauled herself back up to the bedroom. Church, she thought, noting the irony of it all. *Jesus, are you watching?* She shook her head as her racing heart finally returned to normal. *That was close.*

She held up the plate sheepishly when Shay peeked out from the bathroom.

"Unique room service you got here, Mel." She grinned as she walked to her, powerfully naked, and set the plate on the dresser. "Don't you dare ask if I want that for breakfast."

Mel would have preferred to simply enjoy the view, but the vision of Nana in the doorway was slow to fade. She concentrated on Shay, on the sinewy body that now contained her very essence, and her mind reeled at the concept. When Shay reached for her, opened her robe, Mel eagerly stepped into Shay's embrace. *This is where I need to be.*

Shay slipped the robe off Mel's shoulders and squeezed her closer. "I hate letting go." She pressed a lingering kiss to her neck.

"God, Shay." She nibbled along Shay's jaw.

"If we don't stop now, I won't be able to."

"Me neither." Mel pulled back and led Shay to the bathroom. "At least Nana will hear the water running," she said, adjusting the shower. She turned and glazed a palm across Shay's abs.

Shay backed her into the shower and wrapped her up beneath the spray. "Guess I am very late for work."

"Is that right?" Mel rose on her toes and kissed Shay's nose. "And God is waiting for me."

"We're gonna disappoint everyone."

CHAPTER TWENTY-THREE

One of Sorvini's mechanics stirred up a trail of gritty, brown dust as he graded the perimeter road, and Shay really longed to be gazing at something quite different in this bright morning sunshine. She was thankful the sweet breeze didn't carry dust to where she sat on the Softail, deliberately conspicuous in the middle of the beaten parking fields. The heat bearing down was just ridiculous, but the view was invigorating, empowering, and her lingering high from the glorious morning just put a fuzzy warm glow around everything. Only an occasional wisp of cloud interrupted the morning's tender blue sky, lofting above the distant, sensuously rolling hills, so like Mel's consuming eyes, the easy, velvety curve of her hips, breasts, shoulders…

She inhaled deeply and exhaled slowly, taken by her newly expanded reality, humbled by the gifts she'd been granted. She looked over the hushed fair and carnival grounds, the concert area, caught up in their serenity. Intermittently, workers appeared at the rides, booths, the main barn where a delivery truck sat. Somewhere, a dog barked and a tractor grumbled. She marveled at the transformation due in just a few hours, the transformation of her life.

Thousands of acres, she thought, *and here I sit*. No asphalt grid for granite giants, no crooked maze among triple-deckers, no traffic, no nine-to-five, no makeshift commercialized reality. Such a storybook world so foreign to a born-and-bred city girl. Boston to Chicago to *this*?

It feels so right because it is. It's the hypnotic power of the open spaces, the wonder of an endless blue sky, the warmth that reaches your bones, the breath of wind that fills your lungs. It's everything Mel is.

"Amazing," she said on a sigh.

She had to admit, pieces had fallen into place like some damn

Hollywood movie. Life had never "clicked" before, always packed with troubles, worries, obstacles, and all that stress. Only those final months in Chicago had offered promise before they, too, dissolved into just one more tough break.

But here, here the world hadn't stopped spinning since she'd come to town, from the moment Coby and Misty suggested she stay. And, Jesus, it'd been quite a ride. A mind-boggling fine one.

Here, she was free to work, to make the most of her talents, to meet challenges and thrive, to let her heart breathe. Here she was stretching out, growing, even at her age, and she didn't want it to stop. Banking Slattery's attractive paycheck was all well and good; it gave her a solid start, but she couldn't allow it to take control. Filling these open spaces with subdivisions, traffic, and business bustle felt like a sin against nature, and she couldn't—didn't want to be a contributor. She'd left that life, where people, the very air and land meant nothing. Here, they meant everything, and so could she. Yes, she conceded, this place demanded she let roots take hold, because *this* was where her soul needed to be.

The "big decision" came easily. She would sit Sonny down and force him into a reality check. Tap her savings and investment money, if she had to, and put her offer on the table. And if her luck held, she would settle in. *With Mel.*

Coby and Misty would be thrilled.

Mel, she hoped, would be overjoyed. Staying put in Tomson meant investing in her life, and she wanted Mel to be as much a part of that as the damn wild grass beneath her boots, as the big sky overhead. Their relationship might still be new and fragile, but it was real. The sincerity Mel brought made their relationship worth every effort required to make it work.

She removed her Trailblazer cap and wiped the sweat from her brow with the hem of her shirt. *Damn heat.* She rumbled slowly across the field to begin status checks, an eye on the slow-rolling BMW convertible that looked destined to intercept.

Della drew alongside as they stopped in the vendors' area. The tailored white linen skirt and jacket dazzled in the sunshine, and Della's air of calm was welcome, if rather curiously uncharacteristic.

"Morning, Chicago."

"A gorgeous morning. Hot start."

Hands on her hips, Della surveyed the grounds through black Gucci sunglasses, the captain at the bow of her ship.

"Sure is. The place looks good, considering yesterday's turnout was bigger than anticipated."

"I think so, too," Shay said, and performed the same scan. "So far, everything's gone like clockwork. Should I be worried?"

"Don't jinx it. I already have a nightmare on my plate. *Something* has to go right. I just got off the phone with Glen Davis. He said they only had to deal with one disorderly conduct yesterday, something about a fistfight over a damn parking space. He spoke highly of you and hopes these next two days won't be too much of a test."

"I like being on the sheriff's good list. Our biggest challenge will be tonight."

"Prairie Fire."

"Yup. Major feather in your cap, getting them to come, Della. They won some national award on TV just last week and are all over the radio. This place will be packed."

"Friend of a friend in Nashville tipped me off about them last fall, said they were going places, so I took a chance and got lucky."

Shay wondered how many other well-placed connections figured into Della's success.

"So what brings you out here this morning?"

"Well, I'm looking for your opinion on something." She seemed to study the mechanics' barn in the distance for too long. "Is there someone you'd recommend to take over up there?"

"For Sorvini?"

"A big hole to fill. Don't misunderstand, but losing him has hurt." Shay crossed her arms, waiting for Della to spout his praises. "His temper cost us, Chicago—and you, obviously. Stupid on his part, so childish and hurtful to you and our mission. I've had to add finding a replacement to my list of priorities at a most inconvenient time."

"How inconsiderate of him."

"Regardless, he's gone and his loss here could be profound. From a business standpoint, we're fortunate he's working with Ed Chandler until the damn court finishes with him, and that should help get us through some of these Heights *issues*."

"From what I've heard, it sounds like his influence *contributed* to those issues, Della."

"Oh, we'll get past this mess the *Chronicle* caused, Chicago."
Shay scuffed the turf, sorely tempted to defend Mel. "Granted, it looks
as if they overstepped out there, and, believe me, I'm not the least bit
thrilled about this delay, but we'll be back on track quickly. With Ed,
and Angie helping for the time he has left, I'm not too worried." Della
adjusted her sunglasses. "Meanwhile, I'm faced with a critical vacancy.
Tom Rogers endorsed someone I feel might be too young."

"He told me he recommended Tim Kasparian. He's twenty-four."

Della nodded. "He's only been with us for two years."

"Smart kid, though, and a really hard worker."

"The next six months are big on our calendar, very big."

Shay geared up for what she hoped she wouldn't hear. She didn't
want the job. "Well, I do *not* recommend Sorvini's pets, Peters, O'Brien,
or Jensen. They're trouble. And only work when watched."

Now Della removed her glasses. "I need someone with
management smarts, someone willing to be hard-nosed about things
when necessary. I'm considering you."

"I appreciate that. Thank—"

"You're interested?" The sunglasses went back on.

"Jesus, Della. Thank you, but Kasper's a real workhorse. He's
young but honest, sharp, and reliable, and I think he'd do a great job
for you."

"Uh-huh. I'm disappointed. I don't mind saying." Della drifted
to her car door. "You've become a key member of the Slattery team,
Chicago, and I'd rather it be you." She settled in behind the wheel.
"Let's get through this weekend and we'll talk again." She started the
car and grinned. "Maybe one of us will have changed her mind by
then."

❖

"Young people today don't sing and play like the real ones," Nana
declared. She refreshed her Jean Naté with a dab behind each ear while
Mel waited. "In fact, no one does the good songs any more. Who sings
like Jim Reeves today?" She closed her bureau drawer and shuffled
toward Mel, finally ready to leave. "No one, that's who. Or Hank
Snow? Tennessee Ernie Ford? And must you wear that hat? Where'd
you get it? I don't recall ever seeing it before."

Mel minimized her smile as best she could. "Oh, it's a fun hat, Nana. It belonged to a very special friend, but I've got it now."

"Oh, did it?"

"Listen. If you don't want to go back later for the concert, you don't have to." Mel followed patiently behind. Her mind spun as she took along the folded walker by the entry and stepped ahead to hold open the screen door and guide Nana onto the porch. They'd already performed this routine to attend church just to get to the fair at a decent hour. The recollection of Shay upstairs brought a buzz to her system. She looked forward to more of their time together tonight and secretly hoped Nana wouldn't want to attend the concert.

"We'll see, dear. Helen expects me to sit with her at the Grange table today, so I might not have energy for a concert—especially one where the music isn't what it should be."

"Their lead singer does Patsy Cline very well, you know. You might enjoy it. Prairie Fire is the newcomer of the year in Nashville. LeAnn Rimes was, too, when she started out, and you like her. So you might like some of the music tonight."

They edged down the three porch steps, and Nana maneuvered her walker to the car.

"Helen will have talked both my ears off long before then, Lissa, so I think I'll be looking forward to some peace and quiet this evening."

Mel helped her buckle up and went around to the driver's side. Just what Helen would profess to Nana began to eat at her. From the moment they'd kissed good-bye in her bedroom, Mel had been trying to formulate a way to introduce Shay to Nana. Today was the day. It had to be, the way word was zipping around town, but exactly *how* to tell her was the question.

She headed off to the ranch, deep in thought, convinced that Helen's wealth of gossip included the "new couple in town." Having Nana learn of them from someone else would make Mel's effort twice as difficult. She covered her concern with sunglasses.

"The bonfire last night was great," she offered. "Big turnout, too."

"It confounds me," Nana said, "how folks love to watch fire. Such a scary thing. Never could see the attraction in it."

"Well, the concert and tomorrow night's fireworks will draw even more people. There are lots of events going on, actually. We'll get programs when we go through the gate." She tamped down her rising jitters and took a breath. "Shay Maguire's been super as Della's project manager and has done a fantastic job with this. So much to coordinate and prepare."

Nana shook her head and gazed out the window as they drove through town. "I know business is business, Lissa, but being chummy with one of Della's cronies doesn't look good." Mel could feel the small gray eyes level at her as she drove. "We've already discussed your association with this Maguire character."

"Nana, stop. Everything is fine. You'll see. I'll introduce you." She urgently wanted Shay to turn her charm loose on Nana upon arrival.

Nana exhaled a resigned sigh. "I expect to get an earful today about what you did to the new shopping center."

"You mean the liberties Angie Sorvini, Ed Chandler, and Della tried to take?"

"Seems to me, being nitpicky has cost a pretty penny all around. What am I supposed to say when people ask why you put the kibosh on all those jobs, those shops?"

Going to be a very long day.

"I had information about what they were doing out there and gave it to the proper authorities, Nana. Town officials issued a temporary stop; *I* didn't put the kibosh on anything. Remember that. Nothing's been *killed*, just delayed until they go through channels and fix what they did. Folks who know the facts are thankful it'll be corrected." They slowed at the Five Star gate and pulled up to the ticket booth. "So, are you going to be my ally today, Nana? Or are you going to let folks use me as a punching bag?"

"Hi, Mel. Good morning, Mrs. Baker." The young redhead who ran a register at the supermarket eagerly thrust two fair programs through Mel's window.

"Doing double duty, Janice?"

"Never turn down a little extra cash," she said. "Glad you're here. Shay and Mike have both been by, asking if you'd come in yet."

"I'll hunt them down," she said and wondered what Nana was thinking.

Janice gestured toward the programs Mel set on the dashboard. "Range Riders go on in twenty minutes. Ring 10B."

"Thanks, Jan." Mel pulled away, and they waved to the two men in suits seated beneath a patio umbrella, a shiny red Ford Escape beside them to be raffled off this weekend.

"Come buy a ticket, Mel!" one shouted, and Mel stopped politely. He trotted to Nana's window and bent down to greet them. "Mrs. Baker, you're looking younger every time we meet. Honest to God."

Nana chuckled at him. "Always the car salesman, Henry."

"Can I talk you ladies into buying a couple of tickets? Just fifty apiece and the money goes to the Winter Fuel Fund. Can't pass up a beauty like this, can you? Won't find a better deal on the planet."

"Thanks. Nana and I will discuss it," Mel told him, eager to move on.

His associate joined him at the window, and Mel was tempted to roll away. From too many past encounters, she knew Grayson Cochran would make his intentions known immediately.

"All set for the Harvest Ball, Mel?"

"Working it this year."

"Really?" He elbowed Henry. "I figured you'd be on the arm of *someone special*."

"Sounds like you've got your figures mixed up. Sorry, guys, but it's almost show time and we've got to run. Good luck with sales."

She left them grinning as she drove to the performance arena and found Nana's quiet almost as disturbing as her nagging. Letting her stew over what she'd heard wasn't wise.

"Want to gamble on a new car, Nana? If we won it, we could sell it for the cash."

"I wish you'd attend the ball. Why did he think you were going?"

"Lord, Nana. You *know* Grayson's even more of a car salesman than Henry."

She bypassed the public parking fields and pulled in among the many horse trailers at the arena. Mel set up the walker and scanned the grounds as they made their way ringside.

Chapter Twenty-four

S hay rumbled over to the PA booth for one final check, waved a two-minute signal to the horse barn, and drove to the arena gate. Parked in the shade of a lone spruce, she was eager to watch Dolan's Range Riders drill team perform.

A small voice called her name and she turned in time to catch the youngster stumbling over his own feet. "Whoa, cowboy!" Shay caught him before he hit the turf.

"I sorta almost tripped," he said. "Hi, Shay."

"Hi." She squatted to see beneath his red cowboy hat. "Hey, you're Josh?"

The round face lit up. "Yeah, it's me. Grammy and Grampy brought us again. We had to see the Rangers 'cause me and Joey are gonna do that next summer and then I saw you 'cause we're over there on the fence and you said you'd show me your Harley if I came again and so can I see it? Here I am."

"Yeah, you sure are." Shay looked around for Rogers and his family. Her breath caught when she spotted them and an elderly woman—and Mel wearing dark Jackie-O sunglasses.

They all appeared engaged in lighthearted conversation with the older woman, who sat in a folding chair very close to the rail. At her side, Mel pointed out something in the program to the others.

Her hair was loose, and Shay was hypnotized by the glossy waves lolling about her shoulders in the breeze. She knew how they felt, as she did all Mel's curves, outlined by that rosy T-shirt. The khaki shorts just shouted for Shay's hands.

Shay's mind flipped into playback mode as she lost herself in the view, and she reveled in the sensation of those lips melting into her own, the feather-light touch of that hair dancing across her eyelids, the trembling on her tongue…

"Hey, Shay." Josh yanked on her belt. "Can you take me for a ride? This is so cool!" He ran both tiny palms across the Softail's leather seat.

"I can't right now, Josh, but if you want to sit on it, that's okay."

He heaved himself onto the seat, head first, and almost fell off the other side. She dashed to rescue him by his back pockets.

"Okay, not that way," she said, laughing, and set him on the seat properly. He grabbed for the handlebars, and even though he could barely reach both at the same time, it didn't seem to spoil his fun.

Josh yelled with all his might, "HEY, GRAMPY, LOOK!"

All heads in the immediate vicinity turned.

Mel's heart pumped a bit harder at the sight by the motorcycle. Josh was adorable. Shay was hot.

She watched Shay place his hands on the gas tank and then sling a leg over the seat behind him. With tactile clarity, Mel recalled the weakness she had brought to those legs just hours ago in the shower, how Shay had clung to her as she shuddered, so vulnerable during climax. Standing beside Nana, Mel welcomed a familiar rush of arousal.

Shay straightened the bike and heeled up the kickstand. She threw her weight forward to coax the Softail into motion, then pushed off with her feet. Josh beamed at his grandparents.

Shay rolled them to the railing and raised her voice over Josh's rapid-fire exclamations to greet everyone. Joey whined for his turn, so Shay hoisted Josh off and him on, and gave him a few minutes to gawk and preen from the seat.

Nana peered out from under her sun hat at the scene. Once again, Mel wondered what was going through her mind. *Ready or not…*

The children examined the Harley thoroughly while Tommy and Barbara picked up the conversation about motorcycles, horses, the Five Star, the fair, and, thankfully, not the Heights. Mel didn't want that heavy topic to surface. She already had one to think about. Determined to wait for the right moment, Mel remained cool, silent, and smiling behind her black lenses.

Little Joey got his quiet ride as Shay walked the heavy Softail to the arena gate and back. Marveling at the strength in Shay's legs, Mel just shook her head. Joey waved and she extended both arms and revved an invisible motorcycle. Shay flashed her a sideways grin, rolled to a stop, and set Joey next to Barbara.

Shay remained seated, pointedly looking everywhere but at her. Mel could feel Nana sizing up this infamous Shay Maguire person she'd heard precious little about. In fact, Nana blatantly stared. *Courage, remember? Open your mouth before she does.*

"Do you work for Della Slattery?" Nana abruptly said.

Too late.

Shay removed her Trailblazer cap, and Mel wished that seductive look had a smidgeon of the impact on Nana that it did on her.

"Yes, ma'am. The fair is the biggest responsibility I've ever had. I hope you're enjoying it."

I could listen to that deep, creamy voice all day.

Nana turned away to take Mel's arm and pull her down. In a poorly-disguised hush, she asked, "Lissa, is this a man or a woman?"

Mel felt her face drop. She was mortified. Graciously, Shay grinned at the ground. Tommy and Barbara immediately began discussing food, but had to silence the boys, who thought the entire issue was hysterical.

"Nana, this is Shay Maguire. *She* is the project manager for Slattery."

"*This* is Shay Maguire?"

With a mixed expression, Nana turned back, and Mel cringed, having no idea what would come out of that mouth next. Nana most likely would insult Shay's gender, her appearance, or her employer, or all three, and Mel simply shook her head at everyone.

Shay leaned off her seat toward Nana. "How do you do, Mrs. Baker? It's very nice to meet you."

"You don't dress the part of a boss," Nana said. Mel's attention went skyward.

Shay sat up straighter and offered a humble smile. "Well, I'm lucky that my boss didn't hire me for my wardrobe. I tend to get pretty involved in my work, and I never know when I'm going to end up really dirty."

"Oh, so you don't just ride around on that thing giving orders to folks?"

"No, ma'am, I don't. I'm working with police and fire officials, vendors, townspeople, even those Nashville bigwigs about the concert.

I have a lot of ground to cover every day, and I have to make sure things get done on time. And if somebody needs a hand, I jump in. I believe in earning my paycheck."

"Well, that's mighty refreshing to hear these days. I like that," Nana said and nodded her approval.

Mel dared to think Shay was racking up points. She glanced at Tommy and Barbara. Both appeared quite amused.

"Are you from Chicago?"

So much for points.

Shay looked surprised. "Ah, yes, ma'am."

"I'd heard that."

"Have you ever been?"

Good for you, Shay.

"Lord, no. No city for me. I'm proud to say I've lived here all my life."

"Honestly, Mrs. Baker, I've only been here a short time, but I wish I could say the same. You're a very lucky lady."

"You know, you have such a pretty smile. Why don't you let your hair grow?"

Mel bent down to whisper. "Nana, stop embarrassing her."

"I was just asking an honest question, Lissa. Look at her," she went on, and pointed with a crooked finger. "She should let it grow. It would look so nice, and right now, it's just so…mannish. Just look."

Mel dropped her sunglasses to the tip of her nose and connected with Shay's eyes. The impact swirled to her depths like a fine liqueur, and she bit her lower lip. Shay noticed and shifted on her seat. Unable to control her smile, Mel turned away briefly and reset her sunglasses. *Jesus,* she thought, *I can't even look at her without melting. And it shows.* She collected herself as quickly as possible.

"Nana, if she wanted longer hair, she'd have it, I'm sure. You know, with this weather we've been having, I don't blame Shay for wearing it that way. It's much cooler. And speaking of that," she rounded on their group, "I am parched. Anyone for lemonade?"

"Me! Me!" the boys chorused. Everyone but Nana smirked.

"Hey, guys?" Shay reached into her pocket and drew out a quarter. The boys gathered closer. She quickly flipped it into the air and slapped it down onto her thigh. "One of you picks heads or tails, and the winner rides up front, the other rides behind me. We'll roll over to the lemonade stand with Ms. Baker, okay?"

Mel sighed with relief.

"Yeah!" Josh shouted, then apparently remembered to ask for permission.

"I call heads!" Joey yelled, as if Shay wasn't less than a foot away.

The boys pressed against the motorcycle and Shay's leg to see. She slowly lifted her hand and the three of them leaned in to peek at the results. The adults were amused, but Mel was busy thanking her sunglasses because every part of Shay made her mind race and her vision blur. *I want you* completely, *too.*

"Tails! I win!" Josh blurted, and jumped up and down. "I'm sitting up front! I'll drive!"

They left Nana with Tommy and Barbara and made their way across the grounds. The boys talked nonstop, and Mel strolled while Shay worked up a sweat to keep the bike rolling.

"Sorry about Nana, Shay."

Joey tapped Shay's back. "Did she hurt your feelings, Shay, not knowin' you was a girl?"

"No. She was just being honest about what she was thinking. It's just that, sometimes, it's polite to think about the other person's feelings before you say or do things. I bet Ms. Baker's grandmother just forgot, that's all."

At the concession stand, with the boys content waiting on the bike, Mel gazed appreciatively at Shay's profile. "You're terrific with them, you know." Shay chuckled, and Mel reached into her shoulder bag for her wallet. "I'm buying. This was my idea."

Shay unfolded a wad of wrinkled bills she'd pulled from her pocket and didn't look up. "To save my ass, so I'm buying."

"No, you're not." She bumped her shoulder to Shay's and murmured, "It's a really nice ass." She rushed money onto the counter and lowered her voice. "I can't keep my eyes off you. It's going to be an awfully long day."

Shay spoke toward her boots. "I hate not seeing *your* eyes. All I want to do is kiss you—everywhere." She chuckled and Mel glanced her way.

"What's funny?"

"Well, it's not really *funny*, funny," Shay said as she watched the woman pour their drinks. "I, ah, riding the bike...the vibration..."

Mel looked over the top of her sunglasses again and smirked. She loved the lines of Shay's face, the determined set of the lips she now knew so well and ached to touch. She rose on tiptoes to whisper in her ear.

"Somebody's horny."

Shay's eyes flashed. "Do tell."

Mel pushed her glasses back into place. Teasing was as arousing as a touch. She took the carrier with lemonade for the boys, Nana, and herself, and they headed back to the bike.

But nearly light-headed with happiness, Mel couldn't let it go. It simply felt so good. "And whose fault is that?"

"It's your fault."

"Thank you."

"Oh, God, no. I thank you."

"Nana doesn't know what to make of you."

"Who?" Shay asked. "Him or her?"

"I'm so sorry, Shay."

"It's okay. I'm used to it. I just don't want her to dislike me."

Mel was lost in thought as Shay carefully mounted the Softail between the boys. Approaching the group along the fence, she walked closer to the bike.

"We'll be going up to the barn in a bit. Nana's friends are expecting her at the Grange exhibit. Mike and I have work to do here before I take Nana home."

"You're coming back, though, right? I mean, for the concert and all."

"Seriously?" She watched Shay lift each boy off the Softail. "For the concert. Oh, of course."

Shay leaned toward Nana again. "I better get back to work. It was a pleasure meeting you, Mrs. Baker. I hope we see each other again soon."

"Good afternoon, Shay."

Mel tempered the longing from her voice. "Good seeing you. Don't work too hard."

"Can't. I'm pretty worn out already," Shay said. "Pedaling this thing is hard work."

❖

Nana didn't waste any time getting to the point, just held her words until Mel left the ranch and turned onto asphalt. Mel had been about to ask if Nana reconsidered attending the concert, returning to the fair after a nap and supper, but didn't get the opportunity.

"Are you carrying on with that…that woman? She's a *lesbian*."

Mel froze. This certainly wasn't the way she'd hoped to deal with the issue. Not that she'd come up with any suitable way yet.

"'Carrying on'? What do you mean, precisely?"

"You know perfectly well what I mean. Please take those glasses off and look at me."

"Nana, I'm driving."

"You're avoiding my question. It simply cannot be true. I won't hear of it."

"Can we talk at home?"

"I am just so upset. It's all so disturbing." She pulled tissues from her handbag. "To hear from several people that my granddaughter is associating with someone who…who thinks she's a man, that Melissa Baker is being played for a fool, has been taken in by—"

"Okay, that's enough." Mel braked hard and pulled off the road. Nana stopped dabbing her eyes to grab the door handle. Mel threw the shift into park, turned in the driver's seat, and flung her sunglasses onto the dashboard.

Nana looked at her fearfully. "Why are you angry?"

"Why?" Mel took a breath. She had to calm down or Nana wouldn't see past the fury. "I'd thought we'd have a calm, mature discussion in the privacy of our home, Nana, but you leave me no choice."

"You need to do something immediately, remove yourself from the dangerous game being played by this *woman*, if that's what she really is. I can't say as I'm sure. No one is sure."

Mel was so mad, she didn't know where to begin. *That's it. This insanity stops here.*

"First of all, I'll associate with Shay Maguire in any way and for as long as *I* choose." Nana's eye widened. "Secondly, I'm a grown woman and don't 'play games,' as you so crassly put it. Do you think I'm a fool? Is that what you think?"

"Well, no, Lissa, dear, but—"

"You need to acknowledge that I've been properly raised to be a kind, honest person. A good person, one with a brain. I am smart enough to recognize and appreciate sincerity in others. I've earned your respect. Hell, I *deserve* your respect."

"Well, yes."

"Do you respect me?"

"Good heavens, yes. I know how you were raised, how smart you are, how much you care for others. I *know* you, Lissa, that's why this is—"

Mel shook her head and held up a hand for Nana to stop. "There's a part of me, Nana, a very big part of who I am that you do *not* know." She set her upraised hand on her chest. "The heart of the matter is that I'm gay, Nana, and I've always been gay. It's the part of me I've wanted to share with you for so, so long, but I feared you'd put credence to gossip and negativity and overlook my happiness. Obviously, my fears were justified, and that hurts me terribly."

"You're claiming to be a lesbian?"

"It's a fact, Nana. And I am tired of living my life in fear of ridiculous attitudes. Yours included. I'm done with it."

Her voice a tear-choked mumble, Nana stated, "Our pastor reminds us that homosexuals—"

"He's wrong, Nana."

"Melissa! His is the word of our Lord!"

"No, Nana. It isn't. It's Pastor Rooney's interpretation. And I'm not going to debate the *Bible* with you here on the side of the damn road, nor confess my years of frustration having had to listen to him rant about innocent people...*about me*," she added, leaning toward her for emphasis.

Nana sat dumbstruck, tears wet her blouse. She shook her head slowly, turned away as she wiped her face, and spoke out the window.

"I refuse to believe it. Three people spoke to me about you today. I shudder to think what the entire town must be saying."

Mel touched her arm. "Would you let someone tell you how to live your life? No, I know you wouldn't. It'd be a cold day in hell. Well, I'm being honest with you, Nana, because I love you, and I'm being honest with myself. Please hear me." Nana sent her a guarded look. "These are the indisputable facts: I'm extremely attracted to Shay Maguire and she is to me. I find her refreshingly exciting, kind, and fun, and I'm envious of her courage to be her own person. I respect that immensely. Being with her makes me happy, stronger inside, and I enjoy being with her. I think the world of her, Nana. She's very special to me."

Mel had no idea what either of them would say next, but when Nana removed her glasses, she braced for more.

"Melissa Baker. What in the name of God's green earth are you saying?"

"I'm telling you that I've buried myself in my work long enough. I've found someone who makes my days brighter, who makes my heart happy."

"But, Lissa, that's what good friends are for. This Shay Maguire, well, if she insists on taking you as her friend, you have to be aware of what people will say, how the *Chronicle* could suffer."

"I'll repeat myself. I am done living my life to please other people. As for the *Chronicle*, well, I guess we'll see how fair-minded Tomson people really are, won't we?" Mel swallowed the scream that threatened to leap from her lips. "And Shay hasn't *taken* me as a friend. Shay and I have *grown* to become friends. And I don't want Shay to become something someone else wants. She is wonderful the way she is. It's why we're close. We're different and we complement each other amazingly well. I love it. And I love her for it."

Nana issued a tired sigh and Mel reset herself behind the wheel. Shifting the car into drive, she noticed the tremor in her hand. *My heart rate must be over a hundred.* So much was said, yet she knew she stopped short of admitting she was falling in love. *And it's time you admitted it to yourself.*

"Let's get home and I'll fix us a couple tall iced teas." She glanced at Nana, but found her staring out the window again. Mel exhaled, feeling a bit lighter around her shoulders. "We can talk more at the house, if you want." She gave Nana's knee a little squeeze.

"I don't think there's much more to be said."

A million more things need to be said, but not if they'll fall on deaf ears.

With not another word between them, Mel helped Nana out of the car and into her recliner. Tempted as she was to resume their discussion, she mentally logged all her points, and hoped, given some indication that Nana was willing to talk—and listen, that she'd be able to express them.

But Nana made her unwillingness quite evident throughout Mel's supper preparations, and Mel's patience dwindled as rapidly as her frustration and anger mounted. *If I don't get out of this house right now, I'll lose my mind.*

Twenty minutes later, Mel sat staring at the creek flowing beneath the old stone bridge. She downed an entire bottle of water, unable to remember driving, Nana's desperate whining still loud in her ears. *Too bad it's not in me to show her the same pathetic respect.*

Mel chuckled through her blank stare, hearing Nana humph and tsk-tsk around Mel's every other word. *"Your father told me you'd outgrown that fad in college! Is this how desperate for companionship you've become? Cooped up with your damn newspaper? Maybe Robert should sell it just to bring you to your senses!"*

The only thing Mel salvaged from their confrontation was Nana's exasperated refusal to call her son for reinforcement. Nana had sobbed hard at the prospect of telling him that all of Tomson now knew of his deviant daughter.

Mel cracked the seal on a second bottle and drank. *His ultimate nightmare.* My *ultimate nightmare. What a naïve fool I was, so young, trading the personal life for the professional.* She tipped her head back against the headrest. *Thirty didn't seem so far away then. If only it wasn't so far away now.*

As long as he was unaware of this firestorm, the *Chronicle* was hers to run, complete with its own set of political and financial woes; hers to own outright, as long as… She knew keeping him in the dark about herself until the end of March was unrealistic, at best. *Maybe ride this for just a few months? Hot heads will be cooler by then. The Heights opening will help soothe tempers, too. Can I hold him off till then? Till January? His Christmas visit should be lovely.*

She wondered, again, if he kept in touch with any townspeople, he knew so many long-timers. Did they exchange email? Did his friends here go to vacation with him in Miami? He received the *Chronicle* by mail every week, so he was well up on its content, but what personal conversations could reveal was another matter.

He'll call by the beginning of August. Somehow, I have to lure back Home Depot and Dick Turner, and, hopefully, others will follow like sheep. If not, page reduction will strike Dad like a blow to the face. Jesus, if he shows up…

She drank heavily and wished it was stronger stuff. *How the hell do I stand my ground and keep it all quiet? The* Chronicle *will be lost.* The calm and security of Shay's embrace, her support and companionship called to her. *What was I thinking? Hard to imagine having you* and *the* Chronicle, *especially when you learn my whole pathetic—shameful story.*

Mel took another blast of water, primped a little in the rearview mirror, and drove to the ranch with as much determination as possible, thoughts tumbling out into the breeze. "You've no idea what this stupid, scared college girl did, Shay, how stuck she is now. I wouldn't blame you if you wanted to just get the hell out." She wondered if it was too late to be honest, if she could take Shay aside, explain well enough to make her understand.

Her mind far from where she now stood, Mel worked her way through the crowd to the blanket Misty and friends shared at the rear of the concert venue. She was desperately eager to escape and destress, even for a couple hours, and welcomed the group's laughter and upbeat mood.

CHAPTER TWENTY-FIVE

O h! I *love* this song!" Keary wiggled with glee, and a wave of her beer sloshed onto Mel's thigh. Doran tossed extra napkins across Keary, onto Mel's lap.

"Down, girl!" Misty said from Mel's other side.

"The band's really happy to be here, too," Mel reported. "The bass player grew up in Cascade, did you know that?" Keary spared her a surprised look. "They're doing three shows in Helena next weekend."

Doran pressed forward to see around Keary. "She's preoccupied."

"I'd worry if I were you," Coby told Doran from the far end of their blanket. "That lead singer is a knockout."

"Not my type," Keary injected absently. "Now, the banjo player, *she's...*"

Doran elbowed her and knocked her into Mel. More beer spilled.

"Will you finish that before I wear it all?" Mel laughed. "I'm getting all wet."

Coby leaned forward again, but Misty poked her shoulder. "Don't even go there." She reclined on her elbows, angling her head to see through the crowd. "Can't believe you got to sit and talk with them, Mel."

"Neither can I. After five minutes, I just forgot about my notes and we just hung out." She bent close to Misty's ear. "Don't say anything now, or I'll wear the rest of Keary's beer, but the banjo player is family."

"I love it. Is she out?"

Mel nodded. "I met her girlfriend, too. They said nobody makes a big deal of it in Nashville anymore."

"Wonder what Tomson would say if it knew." Misty raised an eyebrow when Mel simply nodded again. "Times have changed, Mel."

Mel had begun to give that serious thought, but Shay arrived in broad, easy steps over and around legs, chairs, coolers, and blankets.

Keary whispered, "You don't really need to hear this, Mel, and don't you *dare* tell Doran I said it, but Shay makes me hot."

"Hot doesn't even come close."

She heard Keary chuckle and wished Nana could muster an ounce of respect for Mel's happiness. *It's okay to go after what you want, regardless of Nana's tears. This is* my *life,* my *heart, and if it was wrong to give it away to Shay, it wouldn't feel so...*

Hard to stay on point, with Shay reaching their blanket. The low-cut jeans practically made Mel drool. She was startled to actually feel her thighs enclosing those hips, those shoulders. Her eyes shut briefly, and she squirmed a bit at the all-too-tangible recollection of Shay's mouth, ravenous at her center. Deep, wet arousal forced Mel to adjust her butt on the blanket.

She exhaled heavily. "Jesus."

Keary teased her with an elbow to the ribs. "Oh, you got that right."

Sitting on the ground, Mel had to look a long way up to meet Shay's eyes, and she deliberately took her time. The body-hugging burgundy shirt with its top three buttons undone was nothing short of criminal.

This time, Keary elbowed Doran, who looked past her to Mel and then up at Shay.

"Hey, Don Juan." She hissed at her and tugged on her pant leg. "Friggin' take a seat or we'll have to chain your woman down."

Shay quickly settled in beside Mel and leaned back on outstretched arms. She pressed one against Mel's back, and Mel offered a knowing smile.

She whispered over her shoulder. "Is it unladylike to be this turned on?"

Shay's breath warmed her ear. "Nothing you could do would be unladylike."

"Wish I dared lay my head on your shoulder."

"It's better this way," Shay answered, her voice low, "otherwise we'd definitely miss the show."

Mel knew that to be a fact. Sitting so close made resisting Shay nearly impossible. "Nice shirt." She slipped a finger between two buttons to feel Shay's bare stomach. "Delicious body."

"Don't tease the tiger, young lady."

"Hey, Mel." Coby pointed to the edge of the crowd. "That your guy Mike, waving like a lunatic?"

Mel craned her neck to see Mike hopping over people to reach her. She felt Shay grip her arm.

"What's got him so wound up?"

Mike stopped some fifty feet away and yelled. "Mel!" He waved her toward him. "Come on! Hurry!" He turned and rushed away.

"Shit." Mel scrambled to her feet. "Kear, I'm deputizing you for this show." She dug a pen and small notepad from the side pocket of her satchel and dropped them onto Keary's lap. "Play reporter for me." She took off after him.

Shay stood up and watched for several seconds. "I can't stay here." She high-stepped her way through the gathering.

Mike's Volkswagen skidded to a halt as Mel ran up, and he shoved open the passenger door. "Get in!"

"Wait!" Shay called. "What's up?"

Mike sent Mel a desperate look and then shouted to Shay. "Fire at Mel's!"

Mel gasped and Shay stopped dead at the car.

"Fuck! I can't leave the fair, goddamn it!"

"Send the others," Mike yelled, and put his foot to the gas just as Mel shut her door.

They flew along the isolated country road to the source of flickering red and blue lights and the fog of black smoke, while Mel feared for Nana and struggled to absorb this nightmare. Mike wove through the collection of volunteers' cars, onto the front lawn, right up to the ambulance, and Mel raced to Nana, who sat in a porch chair with an EMT crouched alongside.

Nana peered up at Mel around the heavy-gauge plastic of an oxygen mask, her eyes watery and blank with shock, and Mel dropped to her knees and took the frail arms in her hands.

"My God, Nana! Are you all right?"

"She's okay," the technician said. "This is just a precaution. She smelled smoke and called us right away. I guess then she went outside to see what she could see, and it's a good thing she did."

Smoke and mist drifted across them in the shifting breeze, but Mel just blinked away the sting, refusing to take her gaze from Nana. Then the questions, self-doubt, and guilt set in. *What happened? How? Supper was baking. The timer should have shut the oven off automatically.*

And they'd fought. A lot. About her "personal choices," her reputation, the family's "good name." She'd left in a blinding rage, craving Shay's support...*and wasn't here for Nana when the ultimate fear took hold. Thank God she called, got herself outside. How did the poor thing ever manage? How terrified she must have been.*

Mel broke into tears and lunged forward, taking Nana in her arms.

"Thank God, Nana. I'm so glad you're okay!"

Breathless from the run from her car, Misty set her palms on Mel's back.

"We're here, hon." She asked the technician for some water for Nana.

Coby gripped Mel's shoulder. "I'm going to see what I can find out and call Shay."

Misty nodded and knelt next to Mel, slid a steadying arm around her waist. "Mrs. Baker. I'm a friend of Melissa's. My name is Misty." She patted Nana's shoulder and gave Mel a squeeze. "I'll stay with her, Mel. Go with Coby."

Mel nodded numbly, still staring at Nana's face.

"Nana? You let Misty know if you're not feeling well, all right? I have to talk to the firefighters, but I'll be back in just a few minutes." She stood and kissed the top of her head. "Thank you, Misty."

She hurried around the house, stricken by the activity, the surreal sight. The ladder truck, two engines, and a pumper truck occupied the well-groomed lawn, and firefighters bustled about with hoses and axes. Sparks and shrapnel filled the air, shreds of asphalt shingles, tar paper, and wood littered the shrubs, the ground, flattened her flower beds.

Mel was taken aback by the pile of blackened wood and the charred lawn tractor where the oversized shed had stood until a few hours ago. And it literally pained her to see firefighters with axes widen the hole in the roof on the house, one story above her bedroom. A solid cable of water bridged the gap from the extended ladder to the black chasm on the roof while three-inch hoses fired into upper windows from the ground.

Coby hustled to meet her, put an arm around her shoulders, and the security made her tremble. Fire Chief Madden approached, and Mel nearly broke down at his sympathetic expression.

"So sorry, Mel. From what we can tell, it started in the shed." They turned to the pile of black, steaming rubble. "Jumped to the house roof here. Overall, though, you're pretty lucky. This end of the house took the brunt of it, but for the most part, it's workable. I suspect what Elsie smelled was the shed."

Through her tears, Mel watched clouds of black become streams of gray, then white as firefighters tamed the flames.

"There were some gasoline cans in the shed for the yard tools and stuff," Mel mumbled.

Madden nodded. "Well, something sparked it. I'd say the inside was pretty well soaked down for the thing to go up like it did. The cans old? Could they have leaked across the floor?"

"Ah, um, no. Not old." Mel shook her head and leaned into Coby's shoulder. "I bought them last summer. Two five-gallon plastic ones. And they were full."

"We'll have the investigation up and running real quick, Mel, but it seems pretty suspicious. When's the last time you were in the shed? Past few days? This week?"

"Just last night." She wiped her cheeks with her fingers. "It was locked. I always locked it."

"I'm sure the investigation will prove that," Madden said, "which means there's a good chance we're looking at arson."

Mel stared up at the house, her bedroom, and that upper corner of the structure blackened and mauled. Her head dropped as tears began in earnest.

Coby gathered her into her chest. "Hang in there, hon. It's going to be all right. Chief said it's fixable, so that's really good news. And your grandmother is okay, Mel, and that's the most important thing."

Mel sobbed against Coby's shirt, hearing the words and struggling for their comfort. Through it all, her mind kept returning to one face.

"Shay will be going crazy."

"Shh." Coby steered them toward the front yard. "Let's get back to your Nana and Misty, and I'll call her. You can talk to her."

❖

Shay took a deep breath and knocked softly on the hotel suite door. When Mel opened it and threw herself into her arms, she felt the tension in her chest subside, despite Mel's instantaneous flood of tears. She held her tightly, as fully as she could, inhaling the scent of wood smoke off Mel's hair and clothes.

She let her cry right where they stood, but wanted to take them inside. Nana was there at the River House, too, Misty had said.

Mel straightened and tried to brush the wet spots from Shay's shirt. She tugged her in and shut the door quietly.

"Nana's asleep in the other bedroom," she said, leading Shay to hers.

Shay closed the door, dropped the duffel she'd brought on the floor, and took Mel to the bed. The smell of smoke was pervasive and made her temper rise. She drew Mel to sit beside her, took her wet face in her hands, and kissed her softly.

"It's going to be all right." She enclosed her in her arms again.

"I'm so glad you're here. I don't know where to start."

"Shh, honey."

"I-I feel so...lost. What a m-mess this is. My whole life is a m—"

"Sh." Shay ran her hands over Mel's back, pressing her close. "You need sleep. It's very late."

Mel shook her head against Shay's chest. "There's no w-way I could. First the window, now my house, and Nana, and I need to talk to y—"

"First, you're going to shower." She took Mel up with her as she stood. "Misty threw some clothes in a bag for you. Some sweats and stuff, a toothbrush, so you'll have something in the morning. Tonight, you're sleeping with me, and we're not wearing anything for that."

Mel caught her breath and looked up, tears still trickling. Shay lightly rubbed them away.

"Don't argue, Ms. Baker. I don't give a damn if Nana finds out.

Of course, I'd rather she didn't, for your mental state right now, and I hope to be gone before she wakes, but if she does, she does. You're what matters to me, and I intend to see that you get a good night's sleep. Now come on."

She went to the duffel and pulled out a small toiletries bag, then took Mel's hand. It was cool and weak in hers as she led her into the bathroom and locked the door. She started the shower and unbuttoned Mel's shirt.

"I have to admit," she whispered on the tip of Mel's nose, "I never envisioned taking your clothes off under such circumstances."

Mel blurted out a chuckle as her shirt and bra fell away, and she kneaded her hands into Shay's hips. "That makes two of us."

Shay knelt and pulled down the rest of Mel's clothes. She kissed her stomach, nuzzled into her hair, and hugged her around the hips. "Smoke isn't the scent I enjoy from you, my goddess." She stripped quickly and took Mel's hand again. "Let's go."

Shay lathered every inch of her, shampooed her hair patiently, thrilled for many reasons. She couldn't wash away the despair and worry, but she could provide comfort and security, and love. More than anything, she wanted to convey love. Mel stood vacantly still, blinking through the cascading water.

"I am in such awe of you, Melissa Baker, your strength, your beauty. Your heart. I'm so grateful you're a part of my life."

"There's so much I need to say to you." Mel combed Shay's wet hair back with her fingers.

Shay hardly heard her. "Shh." Tingling raced from her scalp to everywhere else.

Mel cupped her face. "I didn't think knights in shining armor existed anymore." The half-smile pulled at Shay's composure. "Guess I never thought I'd ever need one, but I do." Her arms slid around Shay's neck. "And she's you."

Mel's heartfelt words sent Shay's emotions reeling, glazed her mind and body as thoroughly as the water raining from the wall. Reality became the surface of her skin, of Mel's skin, where their bodies met, where passion and desire passed between them. She swallowed hard and heard herself speak.

"We all need someone who'll…How did you put it once? Take

your heart into her hands?" She kissed Mel lightly. "I cherish yours. And you have mine to hold, Mel. I love you."

Mel blinked, and Shay saw sadness slowly rinse away. She held her breath as Mel brought her mouth close and spoke against her lips.

"And I love you, Shay Maguire, so very much."

CHAPTER TWENTY-SIX

Shay's eyes fluttered open at the sound of her cell phone alarm beneath her pillow. She switched it off hurriedly, before Mel stirred at her side, and rolled over, spooned against her, and kissed her back and shoulder. *Warm satin. Given to me. With love.*

Shay dressed silently and slipped away. She walked the Softail from the parking lot to the road before firing it up, knowing life was about to change in a very big way.

Home within ten minutes, she'd just poured herself coffee when Coby shuffled out of the bedroom and uttered a raspy, "Hey."

"Hey yourself. Go back to bed. It's early."

Coby squinted at the clock over the sink and then at Shay. "Not even six thirty. You stay with Mel?"

Shay nodded and reached for the coffeepot. "Ready for a cup?"

"Sure." Coby sat beside her and ran both hands back through her disheveled hair. "How is she?"

"Sleeping like a rock. Her grandmother, too, thank God."

Coby snorted into her coffee. "You mean you two didn't wake her last night with orgasmic screaming?"

"No, asshole. Well, we didn't wake anybody. And we didn't do it all night…just in the shower."

"Ah."

"Not good timing for all-night 'orgasmic screaming' anyway. She needed sleep."

Coby nodded thoughtfully. "You did good, Shay, going to her like that, regardless of the grandmother. Good job."

Shay looked up from the depths of her coffee.

"No question where I'd be. I love her."

"About time you admitted it."

"I said it and *she* said it."

Coby's sleepiness vanished. "Yes!" She threw an arm around Shay's neck and hugged her.

"Who woulda thunk, huh?"

"You just know when it's right, Shay. I'm really happy for you. Both of you. You're so good for each other." She raised her cup to Shay's. "Oh, man, wait till Misty finds out."

"But Mel's got a tough road ahead." She stared off at the stove, wondering what else she could do, what would help Mel most. "As if she needed to add the damn house to her worries. The grandmother hasn't said more than a few words to her, the arson investigation starts right away, her position in the paper puts her in jeopardy, and now—*now* her folks are coming."

"What? Oh, fuck." Coby sat up straighter. "Her father's a son of a bitch, I hear. Mel's said they barely tolerate each other."

"Well, that's just great."

"And her grandmother's mad at her? For what? She can't blame her for the fire."

"Oh, on top of being gay and 'ruining the family name,' now Mel wasn't home when she should have been. She 'abandoned' the grandmother to fend for herself."

"Ha. Now, you *know* that's gotta be your fault." Coby snickered. "She's been a thorn in poor Mel's side from the beginning. This is just what Mel needs on her conscience."

"Exactly. I don't know what to do that won't make things harder for her. I'd like to fix the house, start right away, but God knows how her grandmother will interpret that. Besides, the fire department will be all over it now."

"When are her folks due in?"

"Wednesday. Mel is completely beside herself with worry. She tossed and turned all night. Plus, she's mad they're coming on her deadline day, the worst possible time. How she's ever going to deal with them, I don't have a clue."

"Man, talk about pressure."

"Should be swell, huh?"

"Hey, wonder if she'll introduce you. I mean *really* introduce you."

"It's her call. Totally. I'd just love to get going on that house for her." She finished her coffee and rinsed the cup in the sink. "I could round up some guys, I know Moriarty would loan me the stock, and we could have it back in shape in no time. Maybe even before Mel gets the insurance check. It kills me to wait."

"Misty's going to see her this morning, go with her back to the house and get a good look in the daylight, grab some things. There really isn't anything you can do right now."

"Maybe Chief Madden will let me in there sooner than later. It sucks that today's the damn Fourth of July. I doubt anybody's working."

"Except you."

"Right. One more day of this. Christ, this fair's been endless." She untucked her shirt as she headed toward the bathroom. "We were looking forward to the fireworks tonight."

Twenty minutes later, she was pulling on her boots when Misty appeared in the doorway, holding out the phone. She pulled it back just as Shay reached for it, then yanked Shay into a tight hug and gushed into her ear.

"I'm so damn happy for you two, I could scream." She kissed Shay's cheek and thrust the phone into her hand. "Here's Keary."

Shay had to grin as she answered. "Morning."

"Hi, Shay. Sorry to bother you so early, but I figured you could let Mel know I'll drop off my notes on the concert around lunchtime. How's she doing?"

"She got some sleep," she said, following Misty to the kitchen, "but today's not going to be fun."

"I'm sure. Things aren't always better in the light of day."

"Not in this case." She hung up and smiled dimly at Misty and Coby. "Concert notes for Mel."

Misty said, "Keary's the *Chronicle*'s new reporter, huh?"

"Yeah." Shay wondered how long Mel could afford the staff she already had. "It's going to be really difficult for her in the days ahead. Torching that shed was a message. She knew she wasn't winning friends in the construction trade, but this is scary now. At least she enjoyed Prairie Fire, for as long as that lasted. Did she tell you she lost the Home Depot and Dick Turner accounts?"

Coby glared. "No way."

"Aw, Shay." Misty sagged against the bar. "That's terrible news."

"The paper's politics may have ticked them off, but learning that a lesbian has been running their newspaper all these years, well, that was the crowning touch. They're homophobic pricks, that's what it boils down to."

Coby crossed her arms. "Because they heard Mel's gay? You're not serious."

"Dead serious. Mel said Marie overheard them at the diner. Ironic, that advertising income from the Heights businesses could end up saving the *Chronicle*."

"Yeah," Coby said, "after the little guys downtown are crushed."

"Well, that won't happen this year," Misty added, "not with the project delayed like it is. Everyone is saying it won't open until well after Christmas now."

Shay ran a hand through her hair. "It would be so great if those two accounts came back, if they missed the good thing they had. Even if Mel has to cut them a deal. If they did, the smaller ones might be tempted to hang on and ride those coattails."

"Good luck convincing the likes of those assholes," Coby said.

"Well, think about it," Shay continued. "Pretty stupid business move to pull out when the paper stands to have Heights' businesses advertising. The *Chronicle* could use the Heights to its benefit, right?" She cupped a hand to her mouth. "Hey, Dickie, you asshole. Look at all the people reading the *Tomson Chronicle* now. Too bad you're not in it, dickhead."

"I like that approach, Shay," Misty said. "I bet Mel would, too."

"First things first." Coby pointed at Shay. "You find out what Madden says. Maybe he *is* doing his investigation today. You get the okay, we'll fix us a house."

Shay joined dozens of onlookers later that day, applauding as the winning ribbons were awarded outside the livestock barn and Mike took everyone's picture. Despite her aching feet, she started a new supervisory sweep of the grounds, the midway, in particular, and considered sending a few fastballs into milk cans, just to vent her frustration. The crowd grew steadily as the day pushed toward six o'clock, and folks streamed in, eager for prime seats for the fair's fireworks finale.

She hadn't been back in the office with her feet up on Lisa's desk for more than five minutes before pounding on the door nearly startled her out of the chair. *Now what the hell is it?* Her anxiety disappeared when she opened the door and Coby, Misty, Keary, Doran—and Mel— started talking at the same time.

"Oh my God! The lesbians!" She shut the door.

Coby shoved it open and strutted in. "We're here and we're queer. Deal with it."

"How you holding up?" Misty asked, as they filed in.

"We were a little worried about you," Keary said. "It's insane out there."

Coby slung an arm around Mel's shoulders. "Yeah, so we brought the queen of all troublemakers in to see you."

Shay went to Mel and leaned in for a light but lingering kiss.

"Hi," she said gently.

Mel tugged Shay into a hug by her belt. "God, it's good to see you."

"I'm all set now," Shay announced to the room.

"Any crises?" Doran asked.

Shay knocked on the wooden desk three times. "So far so good. In fact, it's gone so well that I'm worried, like something should have happened by now."

"God damn. Enough already," Coby said. "Don't go thinking that."

"How about you, Mel?" Shay asked, brushing her nose against Mel's.

"I'm...better." She kissed Shay's chin.

Keary steered Doran toward the door. "Time we all found something unhealthy for supper."

Coby retrieved a blanket from the Jeep and they cut across the parking area, headed for the concession stands, hopelessly undecided about what to eat. Ultimately, they purchased a smorgasbord of food and planted themselves amidst the growing crowd in the fireworks field.

Shay spoke softly into Mel's ear. "Think kissing you right now would be too much?"

That drew a chuckle. *It's good to hear you laugh.*

"Too much in more ways than one," Mel said, and yanked the brim of Shay's hat down.

"I love you."

Mel wiped a speck of chili sauce from the corner of her mouth. "I love you, too."

Shay leaned to her ear. "You make me break out in a sweat."

"That's the chili."

"Uh-uh. I want to lay you back right here and get lost in your kisses."

"Shh. I can't hear that right now. Makes me woozy." She grazed a finger along the inseam of Shay's jeans.

"I can't wait for this fair to end. I have to do another sweep now and the last thing I want is to leave your side."

"Can I go with you?"

Shay brightened. "Of course." She rose from the blanket and offered Mel a hand up. "Time for another patrol," she told the others. "We'll back in a while, hopefully by the start of the show."

They picked their way out of the crowd and meandered along the midway.

"I talked to Madden a little while ago," Shay said, an eye on four teenage boys loitering by the beer stand.

"Anything new? I was surprised to find an investigator at the house this morning. We spoke briefly, but he didn't reveal much."

"Well, the chief said his guy did collect evidence of arson. They hope to have a report typed up by tomorrow afternoon." Mel was quiet, and Shay tried to be optimistic for her sake. "It means repairs can start immediately."

"My father will be glad of that. I just hope he focuses on fixing the place instead of why the fire happened. He thrives on righting wrongs." She snickered. "And those wrongs include me."

"You can't let him get to you, Mel. This wasn't your fault."

"Wasn't it, though?"

Fireworks lit up the fairgrounds, and explosions made talking nearly impossible. Shay urged Mel toward the side of the pizza booth.

"Don't think that way, Mel. Someone lit up that shed. Could've been in the middle of the night while you were both sleeping, for Christ's sake. *Then* what would have happened?" She placed her hands on Mel's shoulders. "You, amazing woman, can't be ruled by nutcases who flip out about your paper's position. And you can't stay glued to your grandmother every second of the day."

"I *am* responsible for her, Shay, for her well-being, and I—"

"No one should fault you for having a life, Mel. Like I said, this could've happened at any time, regardless of whether you were there with her."

"Dad is going to freak. For starters, he's going to look at the politics and say it's just one way I've embarrassed the family. He'll probably side with Della and think I've stirred the pot recklessly and cost the paper dearly. He'll basically believe I asked for this."

Shay hadn't even met the man, but knew she didn't like him. "He has that little faith in you?"

Mel swiped angrily at the tendrils of hair that tickled her face. "Once Nana gets at him, God knows what he'll think. She'll out me, Shay, and then...It'll all come crashing down."

Another massive explosion sounded, right on cue. Shay ducked instinctively. "He can't force you to do anything you don't want to do."

"Oh, he'll be beside himself, resenting that he's been backed into a corner, that I've not only become reckless with the family's legacy but shamed the Baker name, and that means...I'm *so* not looking forward to this. I've been trying to keep from dwelling on it, but not doing a great job."

"Your grandmother will just fuel his fire?"

Mel nodded. "I'm sure of it. After meeting you yesterday at the Rangers show, she fell back on all the gossip she'd heard about you, about us, and went on a rant."

"I thought she actually might have liked me."

"I was hopeful, too. I tried to explain what you mean to me, and why, and of course I couldn't do that without leveling with her. So I did."

"You did?"

Mel nodded. "And we fought all afternoon. Reasoning with her was impossible, and she said so many ignorant and mean things, I refused to listen anymore, so I left in a huff. I was furious—and so glad to get back here to you."

"So you told her?" Shay was afraid to be happy. "And I've perverted the all-American girl."

"Yes. My father will cruise in here Wednesday and take up her cause."

"Is there anything I can do?" Mel's face fell and Shay frowned at the expression that looked too much like shame. "Mel, things in town will settle down soon, honest. I don't think you need to worry about the majority of folks. I don't think your dad does, either." She was desperate for the right thing to say. There had to be a way to sort through this mess, at least for the sake of Mel's sanity. Her world was disintegrating, and Shay's gut told her to come up with something.

Mel smiled ruefully and squeezed her hand. "Thank you, Shay. Aren't you glad we met?"

Shay took Mel's face in both hands and the sky's brilliant colors flickered across her cheeks. "Melissa Baker, you're the greatest thing that's ever happened to me. Do not think for one second that I regret falling in love with you. I'm here for you, Mel, at your side. And that's where I'm staying for as long as you'll have me."

CHAPTER TWENTY-SEVEN

Tuesday, Mel tackled work like never before, trying not to question if she was staying ahead of the onrushing Robert Baker disaster or simply burying it. Tomorrow, her deadline day, would be total chaos once her parents arrived, so she compiled columns and news articles, laid out advertisements, and edited photos as if there was only an hour left before going to press.

"The damn fair might be our saving grace," she mumbled to Mike as she sketched a photo layout on paper. He leaned over her shoulder and watched. "I'd worked in a double-truck of photos, but it won't be enough to make up for Turner's hole on page three, so let's do two."

"A four-page spread?" His eyes lit up like a kid's at Christmas.

"And I'm going to jump the Prairie Fire interview off page one, so we'll take it inside with a handful of shots. I think another full page, but we could end up at two-thirds."

"Sweet!" He grabbed her sketch and headed for the workroom.

"Remember: kids, animals, faces." She raised her voice once he disappeared. "And give me something kick-ass of the band for our lead!"

She was as happy as he was to showcase his work, but allocating so much space to unpaid content gnawed at her business sense. *After this, we really have to start cramming, pinching pennies. For as long as this run lasts, goddamn it.*

"You sure you want to go with all this, Mel?"

"Biggest weekend in forever. Why wouldn't we? Besides," she tossed a hand at her paperwork, "we have space to fill."

He leaned pensively against his door frame. "Well, yeah, but can we really afford this?"

"We're going to hold out as long as we can. You're thinking we'll lose more, aren't you?"

He shrugged. "Aren't you? The trades guys may stir up more trouble, and then there's the animosity toward you personally."

She massaged her temples. "Yeah."

"I don't think folks in general give a damn, Mel, but they aren't the majority of advertisers. The old-timers with the money, they're the ones who don't get it, all stuck in their ways. And any one of them on the fence about our Heights story could easily be pushed to the wrong side, swayed to join the gay-bashing party. Cripes, I wish things were different for you and for the *Chronicle*."

"And for you," Mel added, knowing her father sat among those "stuck in their ways." He'd soon drive right into a town roiling in controversy, *scandal*, in his mind, and she knew how he would react. She'd not only jeopardized her role and the *Chronicle* itself, but Mike's job, as well. *Finally getting mad, standing my ground on all fronts was my only choice.* Mike deserved better, and certainly deserved to know the score.

She waved him over to her guest chair. "There's more to this damn nightmare that you need to know. I should have told you sooner." *You're not the only one.*

"Told me what? We're a well-oiled machine here, Mel. We'll survive this."

"You're sweet to say that, and I couldn't be happier or luckier than to have you on board, but I've neglected you. See...this naïve college girl made a very wrong, very long-term decision many years ago that she can't undo. And today, unfortunately, it affects you."

"Oh. So, let me think. You need cash for the secret love child you've hidden away?"

Mel smiled at his levity. "Not a bad guess. Her name is the *Tomson Chronicle*."

"Uh-oh."

"You already know my grandfather was the founder, that he handed it down to my father, and then—"

"He refused to be tied down here and hired an outsider to run it. And then came you."

"Right. It's mine, free and clear, when I turn thirty next March."

"I know all that, Mel." He frowned and leaned forward. "What don't I know?"

Mel took a breath. "Provided I stay in the closet."

He sat back hard. "Whoa. Shit. You're kidding."

"I wish."

"All this time, I had no idea." He sat forward again. "You *agreed* to this?"

"I was twenty-two, looking at a dream come true, my own newspaper, and thought I was clever enough to live under his radar until the inheritance became official."

"For *eight years*?"

"Sad to say, but there are many in the gay community who've gone far longer." She paused to summon difficult memories long-since locked away. "I was a total mess from a relationship gone terribly bad, your classic emotional wreck for months. He took advantage of my youth, my vulnerability, just to hide his 'deviant' daughter. At the time, I'd given up on every goddamn thing. I didn't care about living. Hell, when you think you're going to die from heartache anyway, you *don't* care. It's easy to do something crazy."

"Like make a deal with the devil."

Mel nodded. "I convinced myself it would be worth it in the long run. I'd keep the paper in the family and have a future I'd be proud of. The problem is, my father's always been a bigoted fool, and it was well after the fact when I actually began to *feel* the impact of what he'd done...what *I'd* done." She leaned back in her chair and hoped her words wouldn't send him out the door for good. "He threatened to sell the *Chronicle* if the Baker name is 'tarnished,' if I don't stick to the straight-and-narrow." Mike's eyes widened. "And you know as well as I that the *Tribune* will buy it to kill it and eliminate the competition."

He flexed his shoulders and readjusted himself in the chair. Mel couldn't imagine his thoughts now, with his livelihood on the brink of disappearing. She knew she'd write him the finest letters of reference in the world, make phone calls, personal visits, anything, but none of it would make up for jeopardizing this job he loved.

"I can't believe it." He folded his hands on his head, dumbfounded. "Does Shay know?"

"No. If she thought her arrival in my life led to losing the *Chronicle*, I-I have no idea what she'd do. As it is, she's furious that talk about us is costing the paper revenue. I don't want her feeling guilty, shouldering the blame."

"But she— Mel, you *have* to tell her."

"Believe me, I know. I'm not proud of any of it. I've been trying to gather up the courage, and the timing's been horrible lately."

"Look, what about your mother? She's awesome. She'd help, right? She can*not* side with your father."

"Mom is the only other person who knows. She's nowhere near as closed-minded as he is, but she stays quiet. Dad's…well, he's a very old-school, domineering man."

"Obviously. Hmm. So let me get this straight: he subjugates his daughter for the 'family name' yet doesn't care enough about his legacy to keep it in the family? I have to say, Mel, he's fucked up."

"It's bad, I know, and I'm as much to blame. And now—"

"And now he's coming here, with talk of you and Shay all over town and just eight months left on your sentence."

"The single rumor that grew," she reflected, toying with her pen. "All because I went with my heart for the first time in…I don't remember when. Hearing why we lost Turner and Home Depot just made me blind mad at them and their attitudes, at Dad, at myself. I hated being so helpless and bullied into servicing them all—servicing my own goddamn agreement—all while I watch this love I've found twist in the wind." She shook her head.

Mike went to the window and stuffed his hands into his pockets.

"Whether you lose it or find it," he said toward the passing traffic, "love can take charge."

"I've had nightmares of Shay leaving Tomson, of me making yet another colossal mistake. I *had* to step up."

He turned to her, his baffled expression painful to see. "You were just *months* away, Mel." He exhaled hard. "Jesus Christ. He'd really sell us off?"

"It's his trump card."

"Goddamn it!" He pounded the wall. "Isn't there anything we can do?"

"I suppose Dad could have had some epiphany since I saw him at Christmas and won't flip out, but…"

The phone at her elbow rang and she jumped. She looked from it to Mike.

"Take it," he said quietly. "I've got photos to crop."

She watched him leave for his workroom, his head down. A now-familiar chill crossed her shoulders. *Shit.* She answered the phone on the fourth ring.

"Good morning, *Tomson Chronicle.*"

"Hello, Melissa. This is Mae Sullivan at Chandler Construction."

"Oh, hello, Mae."

"So terrible, your house fire. So sad to hear. You and your grandma are okay, though?"

The image of a vengeful Ed Chandler popped to mind. "Yes, thanks. We were very lucky. What can I do for you?"

"Just calling on Ed's behalf. He and his attorney would like to sit with you today, go over some revised elements of the Heights project, if you can spare some time."

Mel felt her mind twist, squeeze ahead of her heart. *Revised? Damn, that's big. But time? What's that?* "Of course, Mae. This has become an awful week for me, as I'm sure you can imagine, but if they could stop by later this afternoon?"

"I'll let them know. You take care now."

"Thank you, Mae. You, too."

She hung up and scanned her to-do list, searching for a time slot for the interview, the related phone calls, the writing required for such a substantial piece. *You offered. He most likely won't even mention the fire.*

"Morning, newspeople!"

Mel's correspondent, Ida, jingled through the front door, set her tote bag on Mike's desk, and began rummaging through it. *Yet another person who needs to know the score.*

"What've you got for me?"

"Well, I have a piece on Marie's total redo of the diner's menu. She's adding tons of that vegan stuff, Lord knows why. And I did my first official personality interview! The new trainer out at Gronlund's ranch is a hunk!" Mel rolled her eyes as Ida slapped a flash drive onto the blotter. "Even took a couple of pictures. Hope Mike doesn't mind."

"You saved us. Great job."

"I went by the sheriff's office for the log, like you asked. Your Shay Maguire is sure making a name for herself, Mel. She's mentioned in a few places."

My *Shay Maguire?* She raised an eyebrow at the cavalier assumption.

"She's the spokesperson for the fair."

Ida hurried into Mel's guest chair. "So gimme the scoop. You two really dating?"

"Wow. Some interview technique."

"That's just the word around town. I didn't know that you, I mean—"

"Was I supposed to broadcast to the damn town that I'm gay?"

Ida sat back. "Well, no, Mel. I just didn't know."

Mel took a breath. "Sorry to snap. Yes, we've become very special to each other. I don't expect it's going over too well in town, but folks will simply have to adjust, won't they?" She snickered. Until very recently, she never would have considered such a thought, let alone voiced it. "The *Chronicle* has always been my priority, and I live every damn day trying to keep readers and advertisers happy, but I've never given any priority to my personal life before."

Ida giggled. "Before Shay."

"Yes."

"Well," Ida whispered, "she *is* tall, dark, and handsome."

"She certainly is."

"A great smile and a sexy bod, especially in boots and jeans." Ida squirmed in the chair. "I've read some novels about women like her. Pretty hot stuff."

God, spare me, please.

"'Women like her'? We're all the same inside, remember."

Ida guffawed. "Not like her, we're not! Come on, Mel. That deep voice? Those hunky shoulders? And a Harley, no less." She bent so far forward, her ample bosom touched the desktop. "It's not the same as a guy's, but she's quite the package, if you catch my drift." She fanned herself with her hand as she stood. "Phew! See? Boy, even *I'm* getting all worked up."

Mel really needed to wipe the perspiration from her forehead but didn't dare call attention to her body's reaction. And she appreciated feeling relieved, even a bit emboldened by Ida's obvious glee.

"But, Mel, I have to warn you. Some folks are all turned around by it. Honestly, I don't quite understand it myself, but that's your business, not mine."

"And not the town's either. As I told Dick Turner a little while back, it has nothing to do with business or how townspeople interact. It's about respect for others. Some people have forgotten that that's how we *all* were raised."

Ida's expression lightened. "You know, I like that. Very well put."

Mel pointed to her chair and Ida sat. She had to broach the painful subject of her father and the *Chronicle* again, and it hurt to think Shay could be the last to know the score.

CHAPTER TWENTY-EIGHT

When she drove up to her homestead, exhausted at ten o'clock Wednesday morning, Mel fell into speechless shock. Her parents and Nana bemoaned the charred siding and naked roof joists, while Mel scoured her memory for a previous conversation about repairs. Obviously, they had begun.

"Honey," her mother began from the back seat, "I thought you said the insurance check was due tomorrow."

"It is. All this is a surprise to me. I haven't been able to get out here because of work."

Her father stole looks at the house as he helped Nana from the car. "Well, thank God it's not all that bad, Connie. At least someone's been tending to it."

The snide comment registered, but Mel shoved it aside as she walked around the structure, still gazing upward at new wood. In the backyard, an overloaded twenty-yard construction bin sat beside the shed's blackened fieldstone foundation. All other remnants of the building were gone.

Surprised as she was, the one person she suspected came to mind automatically. Her entire system surged at the idea of taking Shay to new heights, and she was shocked by her body's physical reaction. She crossed her arms over her chest firmly, her nipples insisting on being noticed, and stared up at the new window frames in her bedroom.

"Lissa, you didn't authorize this work?" her father asked, still supporting Nana by the elbow.

"Well, no, but I'm pretty sure I know who's behind it. My friends are amazing."

She met Nana's eyes and could read the irritation.

"Don't forget that your grandmother has many friends in town. It could be any or all of them," her father said.

Nana turned to her, chin raised. "So where are your friends now?"

"Maybe they've given us some privacy for our first look," Mel offered, and knew a battle was in the offing. "Maybe they'll be here tomorrow."

"We'll see," Nana said.

"Well, honey," and her mother squeezed Mel's arm, "I can't wait to meet them, whoever they are. Such generosity."

Thank you, Mom.

Mel followed her father into the kitchen and was surprised that the smell of smoke did not overpower them. Two walls in the kitchen had been stripped to the studs and the back staircase was about to be assembled. New wide pine flooring had yet to be sanded and finished.

Her mother stood with Nana in the back doorway while Mel and her father roamed the downstairs. He seemed impressed. She definitely was.

"Wish we could get upstairs," he mumbled. He eyed the ladder in the corner and wasted no time setting it into the opening on the second floor. He climbed up with Mel right behind him.

They examined the hallway, Mel's vast bedroom, its adjoining bath, and the new drop-down hatch for the attic. Plywood, drop lights, bundles of studs, stacks of drywall were everywhere.

"You're a very lucky lady," her father said. "I still can't get over that you were not here to prevent this." He turned to her directly. "You've pushed your limitations since you were a little girl, but this… This irresponsibility goes far beyond excusable. Your grandmother could have been killed."

Here we go. Mel nodded and slowly turned to leave, but he took her upper arm firmly.

"I'm talking to you, Melissa. Do you realize what could have happened here? Maybe you don't."

At the limit of her stamina and patience, Mel met his glare evenly. "What do you think, Dad?"

She backed out of his grip and felt just as hollow as the sound of her footsteps on the new plywood. If only her mother had come alone.

They settled back into the car, and her father muttered and sighed at the house as they drove away.

"Once we drop Mom and Nana off at the hotel, we're going to see Louie Madden," her father declared. "You and I should hear what he's got to say."

"Dad, I can't. I told you I spoke with the chief this morning and they aren't finished with the investigation yet. I have to get back to the office. I'm on deadline."

He flailed a hand in the air. "Just when are you going to take charge of this mess, Melissa?"

"It's out of my hands at the moment. Besides, who'll put out next week's paper?"

He turned in his seat. "You know, your grandmother implied you'd changed your priorities lately, and obviously, she was right."

Mel glanced at Nana in the rearview mirror and found her looking out the window.

"Please don't start. That couldn't be further from the truth. I have a job to do. And I intend to do it."

"It's more important than putting a roof over your grandmother's head? Your own? The *Chronicle* will do just fine if it's a day or so late. This is your priority."

"The *Chronicle* has never been late and never will be, as long as I can help it. I have obligations to publish on time. Legal advertisements are date-sensitive. You know I can't just drop the ball."

"Get off your high horse, and stop reaching."

Steam built as Mel struggled for control. "I told you on the phone, when Mom first said you were coming in today, that it was terrible timing for me, but you wouldn't wait. Not a day. What do you expect to accomplish that isn't already being done?"

"To have someone here who gives a goddamn about the Baker name. Someone I can trust. You've lost that."

"Fine. Do what you want. I'm dropping you off at the River House and going back to work. Wednesdays are all-nighters for me, so I'm sorry, but I won't be free for dinner."

Her mother reached forward and set a hand on her shoulder. "I'm not convinced it's safe for you there all night, Melissa. Nana told us about the window. And now there's this."

"I'll be fine, Mom, honest."

"Well, will you come to the hotel for brunch, then?"

"Yes, Mom." *If I can stay awake that long.*

"Nice of you to make it," her father sniped. He swore out the window before making the last point Mel cared to consider. "And I want to know who the hell's been roaming around the house."

"You mean *working*?"

"I want to meet them face-to-face. Who knows what you've got going on."

❖

It was almost one a.m., but Shay sat on the Softail, thinking, before going into the *Chronicle*. The window at Mel's desk revealed a room bustling with activity and cast the only light in the downtown district, save the overhead lamp four blocks away at the Exchange's door. She wished she could bring Mel there for a quick beer and a few moments of peace. Instead, she watched her dart between desks, check computer screens, sit and type, shuffle through papers, and then cross the room again in an endless, tiresome dance.

The voice mail she'd received in the maintenance barn that morning kept replaying in her head. Mel's voice, weary and a bit breathless, was both overjoyed and distraught. Mel was blown away by Shay's surprise. And battered by her father.

Shay sighed as she shifted weary muscles and her leather seat creaked in the quiet night. She needed to hold Mel for just a moment, reassure her that she wasn't alone and that things would work out.

Shay was hell-bent that they would. She'd taken half-days off from the ranch yesterday and today and worked on the Baker homestead till very early each morning. Coby, Misty, Doran, and Keary did as well, when they could get away from the Exchange. After four o'clock each afternoon, several Five Star guys had joined in, brought supplies and more power tools they'd "borrowed" from the barn. At this rate, Shay figured the house could be occupied by Sunday. Insurance check be damned.

Father be damned.

She opened the office door, and the jingling bells gave her away. Shoulders drooping heavily over the paperwork on her blotter, Mel looked up, her honey complexion shadowy with fatigue, ponytail askew. She rushed around the desk and into Shay's arms.

"Oh God, I love you!"

Shay wrapped her as fully to her chest as her arms would reach. *I need this as much as you do, Mel, more and more each day.*

"And I love you, sweetheart. I just had to see you. You're busy, I know, but—"

Mel kissed her lips hungrily, her neck hard, buried her face in Shay's collar.

Shay cupped her head and leaned back. "I'm not staying. I just had to see you, connect with you."

"How can I ever thank you for what you're doing out there, Shay? I was completely shocked. You never let on."

"I had to do something, Mel. To hell with paperwork. You need your home back and so does your grandmother, even if she does hate me." She shrugged and Mel kissed her.

"Jesus, you are truly amazing." Mel clung to her, arms desperately tight around her neck. "If only my family could see what you mean to me, see who you are."

"Well, I suppose we'll all meet sometime." She attempted to lighten the futility of the situation by grinning. "Us good guys are hard at work over there as of lunchtime, even more of us tomorrow. Will you and your family be coming by?"

Mel nodded and stepped back. "Unfortunately, Dad wants to grill everyone, practically take Social Security numbers, for God's sake. I'm not trustworthy, you see, since my 'way of thinking' has gone south, so I can't be the one taking care of things maturely."

Shay shook her head. *What a pathetic, unnecessary mess. How cruel can a parent be?* She removed her cap and scruffed up her hair. Mel quickly pulled her hand down and did it herself.

Shay groaned at the soothing sensation. "How about you do that in front of your father?"

Mel kissed her again. "I just might, he's being such a bastard."

"Bring them to the house tomorrow."

"It might bring on World War Three, Shay, but I intend to stand up for us. I just wish I could say he'll be reasonable." She snickered. "I don't even expect he'll listen."

Shay took a breath, then gathered Mel's hands to her chest. Mel had to see she meant every word because she'd never meant them more in her life.

"I should meet your folks, and I have no qualms about squaring off with him, if that's what he's after, but not if he's going to take his prejudices, his anger out on you. I won't risk that. I'll just let him say what he's got to say and I'll shrug it off." She kissed Mel's fingers. "But one thing I *won't* do is watch while he beats you down the way he does."

"Shay, he's—"

"I won't stand for it, Mel."

"My badass dyke."

"I've had my moments." She set her forehead against Mel's and hardened her voice. "There's no negotiation here, sweetheart, not when it comes to taking shit—from anyone. I love you and I'm more than willing to say so joyously, but if he lashes out at you, he'll learn it the hard way."

"All right, Shay!" Mike pumped his fist in the doorway.

Mel rested her head on Shay's chest. "Michael. Again?"

"I have exquisite timing, y'know." He grinned at Shay. "I've met her Dad and—sorry, Mel—he's a sonuva-B. But you can take him, Shay."

Shay chuckled and held Mel out at arm's length. "You are what matters to me, Mel. That's all."

She practically lifted Mel off her feet, kissing her, and yearned to kiss away Mel's anguish, wished they had the whole night to enjoy each other.

"I'm leaving now." She stroked back some of Mel's runaway hair and kissed her forehead. "You get to work. One thing at a time. Go make that newspaper that everyone itches to read on Thursdays."

Mel ran her hands over the breadth of Shay's chest and down her arms.

"You always make me smile, Shay Maguire. Please be safe."

Shay backed away and opened the door. "Always."

Shay fired up the Softail, shattered the quiet along Main Street, and rolled away. Cool air shot into her lungs and freshened her heated blood. *How could such a warm, compassionate woman be related to such a prick? God, what are we in for?*

CHAPTER TWENTY-NINE

The two-hour catnap at dawn bolstered Mel's stamina through brunch with her family the following morning, but wore off by the time she and her mother arrived at the homestead. Thankful for the caffeine buzz off several cups of coffee, Mel gathered her wits for the emotional showdown that awaited her.

"Melissa!" Her mother gasped as the car came to a stop. Mel was just as surprised to see so many hard at work. She recognized one face after another, and knew there were more inside. Shay was inside.

A beaming Barbara Rogers approached, arm waving, and Mel shook her head in amazement as Barbara gathered her in a hug.

"What do ya think, honey? Surprise!"

"Oh, God, Barbara. I don't know what to say, honestly. Mom? This is Barbara Rogers. Barbara? My mother, Connie Baker."

Barbara's enthusiasm wouldn't quit as she shook her mother's hand. "We look out for each other in Tomson, Connie." She set an arm around Mel's shoulders. "Your daughter has done so much for this town. We're more than happy to help."

"I can't thank you enough. All these people. How amazing!"

"C'mon," Barbara said, steering them toward the house. "Let me introduce you."

Proud of her friends and humbled beyond belief, Mel doubted her father would recognize such support. She looked haplessly at her mother. "You think *this* would impress Dad?"

"Oh, you'll see. He'll be along soon. You know your father, Melissa. He simply *had* to see Frank Brennan at the bank and assess Nana's affairs as soon as he could. He's thrilled that Frank's become manager. He and your father still correspond now and then, you know."

"I didn't know." *But I should have guessed.*

Barbara brought them to meet every worker, yelled up to the roof, coaxed people off ladders, and ventured inside toward the newly installed staircase. Stunned at the assemblage of people, Mel expressed heartfelt appreciation to each one, provided some background about them to her mother as they went.

"And who's this?" came the deep voice.

Barbara turned to Tommy and slid an arm around his waist.

"Honey, this is Mel's mother, Connie Baker. Connie, my husband, Tom."

"Pleasure meeting you, Connie."

"Mom, Tommy's the maintenance foreman at the Five Star. A lot of his guys are here today. And it looks like they provided the stuff to work with, too."

Her mother's expression was glazed. "All you people are so wonderful. Thank you so much."

Mel hugged him. "Thank you, Tommy. I am beyond shocked. Does Della know what her guys are up to?"

Rogers simply winked.

"Connie, your daughter is the town's sweetheart. Any lady as smart as Mel who decides to stay here in our little town deserves all our support. She's raised our culture level a notch or two, let me tell you." Mel felt her mother set a maternal hand on her back. "Of course," he added, leaning closer confidentially, "once Shay explained you folks were in town, we jumped. It's our pleasure, believe me." Tommy pecked Barbara on the cheek and was gone.

Her mother whispered, "This Shay…The boss is here, too? My God, Melissa. I think my daughter is a celebrity."

"Well, ladies." Barbara rubbed her hands together eagerly. "Let's not dillydally. Let's go meet the 'boss.'"

Mel's insides knotted tighter with each step. Her heart pounded mercilessly. She met Barbara's twinkling eyes and wondered if she had any idea of the trepidation rattling Mel's bones.

Barbara led the way up the new stairs, narrating. "Shay Maguire was project manager for the big Fourth of July Festival we just had. Too bad you folks didn't come in last weekend. What a terrific time. Tomson's biggest bash ever."

"The project manager?" her mother repeated. "Oh my."

"Yup," Barbara rolled on. "Kinda new in town, but she's done one heck of a job since she's been here. Tommy thinks the world of her. We all do."

"*Her*? Well, isn't that unique."

Mel steadied her breathing. *Thank you, Barb.*

"I really want you to meet her, Mom. She's, well, she's just terrific."

In the stifling heat of the second floor landing, as an oldies radio station blared from down the hall, Mel tried to read her mother's reaction to Misty, armed with a cordless screwdriver and pouch of screws hanging from her waist. Sheetrock dust frosted her dark curls, her shoulders, arms, and knees, but Misty's shapely figure left no doubt that a woman was hard at work.

Shay stepped into view and grunted a four-by-eight sheet of drywall into position. Misty dodged around her, driving in screws to take up the load. Mel swallowed hard. With Shay, her mother might have doubts.

"Lord, Melissa, that looks awfully heavy."

If that's her first reaction to Shay, there's hope.

Shay's mint green tank top was covered with everything that would adhere to sweat-soaked cotton. Every muscle flexed and clenched as she held the drywall in position, and moisture shone off every inch of available skin. *Mom could never appreciate this.*

As Misty set the last screw, Mel cleared her throat to gain their attention.

"Hi," Shay and Misty said in unison, and each reached for cloths to dry their faces.

Misty extended a dusty hand as she approached.

"I'm sorry we're so—"

"Not at all!" Mel's mother interrupted, accepting the small hand. "Not to worry."

"Guys, this is my mother, Connie Baker. Mom, this is Misty Kincaid and Shay Maguire."

Shay stepped forward. "I'm very glad to meet you, Mrs. Baker," she said, and shook her hand.

"You girls certainly know how to get all worked up."

"It's this July heat," Shay said. "It's a killer."

"Barbara's giving us the tour, meeting everyone, Shay." Mel tried not to gaze, feeling helpless at the rush of affection that vibrated through her. "I truly can't believe all this. You got all these people here?"

Shay grinned, and the sparkle in her eyes warmed Mel to her core.

"Shay's a slave driver, Mrs. Baker," Misty said, drawing attention from the intimate exchange. "But we love Mel, and this is a labor of love."

"Absolutely true," Shay stated.

Mel's mother moved forward suddenly and squeezed Shay in a long hug. Mel felt faint.

"You are so special," her mother said, a tremor in her voice. "Saying thank you is nowhere near sufficient."

Shay chuckled, her cheeks reddened, and she eased her away by a shoulder. "Please, no. Look at you now. Your gorgeous outfit is a mess from me."

"Hush, you!" She playfully slapped at Shay's chest. "I wish Melissa's father was here to see what you all are doing, you girls."

"He didn't make the trip with you?" Shay asked. She wiped her face again.

No such luck, Shay.

"Oh, he'll be right along, all right. He took his mother to the bank. Money, money, money. He's a stickler."

Mel caught Misty watching her every move. *Yes, I need to start digging in.*

"Mom, I'd like to take the three of you to dinner tonight…"

"Oh, how nice. Thank you, honey. That's sweet of you."

Mel moved to Shay's side and placed a hand on her upper arm, oblivious to the slippery grime coating the bicep. "And, Shay, I'd love to have you join us—if you're free, that is."

"Just so happens, I am. Thank you."

"Of course you should join us," Mel's mother insisted. "It'll be fun."

"Excellent," Mel said, unable to break her visual connection with Shay. *I wish Mom could see what I see.* She gave the bicep a discreet little squeeze but didn't let go. She inhaled deeply, exhaled, and Barbara and Misty faded from view. *They know what's coming. Do I?*

"Mom?"

Her mother eyed her curiously, but noticed Mel's hand still on Shay's arm. Mel let her see.

"Mom, there's..." She released Shay's arm to take her hand instead, and entwined their fingers. Her mother's eyes followed. "I want you to know, we...Shay and I—"

"Melissa?" She turned to Shay. "You...?"

Shay rested her hand atop Mel's. "Mrs. Baker—"

Mel's mother raised a palm for silence and looked from Mel to Shay several times.

"Don't, Please, don't. Not a word. Not right now." She glanced at Misty and Barbara, who stood offering a chair and glass of water, respectively, and then at Mel. "I'm not sure I can handle what I think you're saying."

Misty set a hand on her shoulder. "Would you like to sit a minute?"

"Please." She sat slowly, obviously stunned, and accepted the glass from Barbara.

Mel crouched in front of her mother, palms on her knees affectionately. Her mother stroked her cheek as if for the first time—or the last—and a flashback struck Mel at that moment, of sitting with her grandmother, trying to reason with her, comfort her as she sobbed.

"It's real, Mom," Mel whispered. "It's very real. Unexpected and undeniable. And wonderful."

Now her mother studied Shay, and Mel knew what she was seeing, the tall, lean, sweaty *butch woman* with the rocky jaw and the filthy clothes, far from the sophisticated businessman her parents had always hoped she'd find. Mel looked up at Shay, and Shay fumbled briefly with the rag in her hand, but lifted her gaze back to her mother's. *She won't be stared down, Mom, whether you're analyzing her stature or her soul.*

"So, you, Shay...and my daughter?"

Mel took a breath and waited.

"Yes, ma'am. Totally."

Her mother swallowed so hard Mel heard it. Her water glass shook in her hand. "Melissa. As much as it confounds me to ask... Heaven help me. How do I ask this?" She sipped her water hurriedly. "Are you...You and Shay...?"

"We love each other very much."

Her mother exhaled a ragged breath and sipped her water again before standing. Mel rose also.

"Dear Lord," her mother said, and pinched the bridge of her nose. "I thought all I had to deal with back here was a house. I can't believe this. How am I ever going to break this to your father?"

"I will, Mom."

"I will," Shay said. "I'll tell him."

Her mother grimaced. "Oh no, no. Not Robert. I wouldn't wish that on anyone." She went absently to the window, sipped her water, and sighed. "I don't want either of you speaking to him. At least…not until I do. Somehow."

Mel shared a dubious look with Shay.

Her mother turned back to them. "Obviously, Shay, you have an enormous heart. What you've done here for Melissa is truly thoughtful and incredibly generous, but…" She sighed again. "Unfortunately, it won't matter a damn, once Robert learns what the bottom line is. *Our daughter is in love with a woman—again.*" She shivered. "Melissa, I-I thought you'd…Well, I don't know, I thought you'd *outgrown* whatever this is. It's hard to even verbalize."

"It's who I am, Mom. Who I've always been." She jiggled Shay's hand. "And this is for keeps."

"We really should discuss this, Melissa. It's a shock, I'm sure you realize, and your father, my God, he'll, well…I shudder to think. But this comes with some very serious repercussions, and it's a matter we need to discuss as a family. You know what I'm talking about."

Mel set her mother's glass aside and took her hands. "Discussion as a family won't change this, not anymore. There's no changing who I am. This means everything to me, and I want to share it with you," she glanced brightly at Shay, "share my happiness with you."

Her mother cupped her cheek. "Well, there's certainly no denying the happiness I see in you, dear. Your father…Oh, sweet Melissa. You know I want you to be happy."

Mel squeezed her hands reassuringly. "I have incredible friends, a spectacular love in my life after all these years, and the most wonderful mother on earth." She pulled her mother into her arms and hugged her tightly. "I love you, Mom."

Loud, racing footsteps cut into the moment, and an agitated voice called out.

"Hey, Shay! Mel's dad is here and her grandmother, too, but—"

Coby bounded into the room and came to an abrupt halt. Then turned scarlet. She tugged at her denim vest and wiped a hand on her paint-spattered cutoffs. Everyone chuckled and Barbara left to start another tour downstairs.

"Ah, hi. I'm Coby Palmer." She offered her hand. "You're Mrs. Baker? Pleased to meet you."

Somewhat bewildered, Mel's mother accepted the handshake. "You make quite an entrance, Ms. Palmer."

"Ah, sorry about barging in." Still antsy, she glanced around the room.

Shay frowned. "You said Mel's dad and grandmother are here 'but'?"

Coby's face dropped. She pointed over her shoulder. "Downstairs, they're going through the first floor. He's with Angie Sorvini."

"What?" Shay surged forward, but Mel tugged at her shirt.

"Let me go," Mel said. "You guys forget about him."

"Get him the hell out of here, Mel."

Mel sensed her mother's curiosity, knew she saw Shay's fire rise, and wasn't surprised when she commented.

"Angelo is still in Tomson? I'd thought he'd be long gone by now, looking to buy up the entire Northwest. Whatever is he doing with your father?"

"My question exactly," Mel said with a snarl. "He's no good."

"He never was, dear."

"He attacked Shay a while back and goes to court for it next week."

"Gracious!" She looked at Shay quickly before turning back to Mel. "That man does think he's superior to everyone, but not to worry. Your father's known him for ages and knows what he's dealing with."

"Excuse me," Coby injected, "but I'm heading back down." She sent a foreboding look to Shay. "My paint, y'know? Gotta go."

Mel's mother set her glass on the chair. "I'm going with you, Ms. Palmer."

"And so am I," Mel stated and stuck a finger into Shay's chest. "Please stay here." Shay ran a hand back through her hair, exasperated, and Mel knew she was asking a lot. "Please."

❖

Two sets of heavy footsteps sounded on the stairs.

"Too late," Coby muttered and grabbed a short two-by-four off the floor. She hefted it in one hand as she and Shay exchanged concerned looks.

Misty mumbled into Mel's ear as she moved to stand closer to Coby. "I'm dialing nine-one-one in a heartbeat."

Mel braced herself. The very last person she expected to see on her property—ever—was Sorvini. *God. Shay with Dad and Sorvini? Could this nightmare get any worse? And Shay's keeping cool for me, for us.*

Her father reached the landing first. "Sounds like a rock concert up here, with the music so loud." He stepped into the doorway, and Mel felt the walls inch closer. Someone turned down the radio.

Her father surveyed the room possessively. "Good to see things being tended to." He stared at Shay, Coby, and Misty as he spoke to Mel. "Found Angie downtown, asked him to tag along for old time's sake. He's surprised so many Five Star men got the time off to work here today, Mel. How'd that happen?" Before she could answer, he blurted, "And who are you three?"

Mel cringed. Sorvini lurked in the hall behind her father like a hand grenade eager to blow. *The minute he realizes Shay's here...*

Coby brought the end of her two-by-four to rest in her other hand. "We're friends of Mel's, Mr. Baker. I'm Coby Palmer, this is Misty Kincaid, and Shay Maguire."

Boom.

"Maguire?" Sorvini hauled her father from the doorway by the shoulder and stomped into the room. "What the hell?" He spun to him in a frenzy. "You know what this one's up to?" He jutted a thumb toward Shay.

Mel stepped up, tempted to spit in his face. "Get your disgusting ass out of this house."

"Melissa!" her father snapped. "*I'm* in charge of this house, Jesus Christ!"

Always self-assured, Sorvini calmly nodded at Mel, and she wound up for what might come next. He pointed at her severely. "Maguire finally got to you, eh? And you let her in?" He squinted at Coby and Misty. "These her sicko friends?" He turned to her father and lowered his voice. "You got to get them out of here, Bob."

Mel watched her father's eyes flit from her friends to her mother. "Connie? What's this all about?"

"Angie," her mother tried, "I'd appreciate it if you'd leave this matter to our family."

Sorvini turned crimson with restraint. He glared at Shay.

"You—you know what you are. These people, they don't want—"

"Get the hell out!" Mel shouted.

Her father pulled Mel to him by her arm, and Shay took a step forward as he barked into Mel's face. "What the hell is going on here?" Mel tried in vain to wrest her arm free of his grip. "Did you hear me?" He shook her.

"Hey!" Shay moved a few steps closer. "Take your hands off her."

"Who the hell are you again?" His fingers slackened, and Mel yanked her arm free.

"Her name is Shay Maguire," Mel said. "She's brought all these people, coordinated all this to help us, me and Nana. And you've brought *him*. He's not welcome here, Dad."

Sorvini closed in, sandwiched her between his bulk and her father's. Her skin crawled when he leaned over her shoulder to whisper to him.

"She's a dyke. They all are, you can bet. This is the one the whole damn town knows about, the one who started a thing with your daughter."

Mel shouldered him back. "You're a sick son of a bitch. And just days from going to jail for it. You tell Dad that? That you're going to jail? I bet you didn't. My father's out of touch with the pile of human waste you've become, how big a sleaze you are."

"Melissa!"

She ignored her father. *A long time coming.*

"Did you take advantage of his invitation to nose around our house? For what? To see how much you could offer for it? Fill his head with your shit?"

"Melissa, that's enough!" her father yelled, but Mel wasn't deterred.

"You're a pathetic excuse for a man, Angie, a closed-minded, hurtful bastard, and the whole damn town knows that, too! I can't believe you're in my house. I can't imagine *anyone* in Tomson would want you in their house."

Sorvini stared at her as the heated silence in the room expanded. He looked past her to her father and raised an eyebrow.

"You notice she didn't deny what I said?"

She could feel her father's glare boring into her, expecting her to contradict Sorvini. Around her, everyone waited. *Take a breath. Use your head.*

She turned to Misty. "Please call the sheriff's office. Tell them we need a trespasser removed immediately." Misty hurried into the hall where all their friends had gathered.

"Wait just a minute!" Mel's father ordered, watching Misty go. "I'm not removing—"

Mel thrust her hand up. "*You're* not removing someone. *I* am. And as for a response to such a degenerate, forget it. Friends of mine are staying—if they choose, considering the *hospitality* they've been extended in the Baker home. I'm ashamed of what's happened here and you should be as well."

"I can't believe what's come over you, Melissa, but I'm putting my foot down." He looked to Sorvini. "I'll meet you out back, if you don't mind." Sorvini nodded and edged his way past them. "Angie, I apologize for this. For my daughter."

"Oh, no." Mel shook a finger at him. "Don't you dare apologize for me. He caused all this. *You* should be apologizing to my friends."

"They're leaving," he countered, and met each face evenly. "Collect your things and go. Now."

"That's not happening, Dad." She looked to her mother for support.

"Melissa, dear. For now, we should just let all this go and let cooler heads prevail."

Mel's temples pounded as viciously as her heart. Disappointment in her mother nearly crushed her. *He holds the cards…Nana's power of attorney, the mortgage, the* Chronicle.

Her father's voice was tight. "You've overstepped for the last time, Melissa. We're finished here. Every single one of you, out."

"Have you lost your mind? Don't you see their effort here? Don't you care? Don't you care what it means to me?"

From the doorway, Misty nodded and held up her cell. She tucked it into her shorts and unfastened her tool pouch. Coby gave Mel's arm a little bump as she passed and joined Misty.

Shay didn't move. Mel's father stepped into her personal space.

"And you. Are you going to tell me what Angie said is a lie? What've you got to say?"

Mel held her breath as she envisioned Shay bashing her father's face. *She loves me. She won't.*

Shay turned away and gazed at her for several seconds. Mel absorbed all she could of the always-adoring eyes, now fierce but steadfast, reassuring. And she tried to imagine what her parents were reading into their exchange.

Shay refocused on Mel's father. "Ever since Mel said you were coming, I figured we'd meet. And now I've seen enough to know just how little you care for your daughter."

Red-faced, he scrutinized Shay from top to bottom, and his look soured. "Scum like you dares to judge me? Get the hell off my property Your kind has no business here or near my family."

Shay inched sideways until her shoulder touched Mel's. "We're all here to help *your family*, and I'm staying until Mel tells me otherwise."

He snickered and shook his head. "Is that right?" He moved crisply up to Mel. "Spending just the past hour in town, I heard things I never dreamed I'd hear, things I couldn't believe. How you've turned people against the *Chronicle*, particularly, and then rumors of *this*, of all things. As if the Baker name wasn't being painted in a bad light already, you've added this to it?"

"Dad, advertisers—"

Ignoring her, he bellowed at Shay. "I told you to get the hell out!" He whirled back to Mel. "What a foolish girl you've been, Melissa, and I'm thoroughly ashamed. This will cost you dearly, and you knew full well it was coming. Or did you conveniently forget our arrangement?"

Mel glared at him, frantically searching for the right words. She saw Shay retract a turn of her head and knew he'd piqued her curiosity. Her father didn't wait for an answer.

"My own daughter. Never did I think you'd ultimately choose this route, Melissa. Once upon a time, you were smarter than this. Well, you've fallen back to your schoolgirl ways and made the wrong decision—again—and this time it's over. You've dragged the Baker name through Tomson like so much disgusting laundry and I'm putting an end to it."

"Stop, Dad. There's no dirty laundry, for God's sake. You need to see—"

"*You* need to see there are consequence for your actions. Do you seriously think you can repair the damage you've done? Was our agreement a game to you? Something you could just walk away from?"

Shay shifted uneasily beside her and Mel's mind spun in a tumult of anger, heartbreak, and fear. *I love you. Why didn't I tell you sooner? Please don't think you brought all this on.*

"There is no damage, Dad. Damn it!"

"Watch your mouth! You know full well you've forced me into this. You *signed* that contract and now you've shattered it. You know you have. You want this depraved life?"

Shay did turn her head then and looked at her curiously. "You have a contract with him?"

Mel's father nearly jumped at Shay. "Until you showed up!"

"Dad! Don't talk to her like that! And do *not* blame her!" Mel angrily swiped at the start of a tear and knew Shay, especially Shay, waited for more. "It's *my* life, Dad, and there's nothing dep—"

"You're done taking the Baker name down with you. There's only one sure way to quash this once and for all, and you know what that is. So, tell me now that you'll end this perverted nonsense, or that damn newspaper goes on the market tomorrow. Tell me!"

Shay turned to face her fully. "Mel? The *Chronicle*'s on the line here?"

"There's no need to clean up our name!" Mel gulped down a breath. Words clogged her throat and made it hard to speak, hard to breathe. *My heart's in the way.* She blinked back tears of frustration.

Her father lowered his voice to a restrained simmer. "I'm waiting. What's it going to be?"

It had come to this. Nightmares had told her it would. How could she have let it get this far? She'd ignored the nightmares, the written restriction, the ultimate decision. *That's exactly what this is and has always been: a decision, a step I have to take.*

The prolonged silence weighed heavily on her exhausted shoulders. Mentally, she scrambled to summon strength, to keep her head above water and not be pushed back under like so many years ago. Where was all the courage she'd mustered in recent days, the bluster that had helped her fight back? The guts to choose love over her dream? She forced back more tears.

Shay shuffled her feet and looked down. Mel could feel the somber change in her presence. Her nerves spiked when Shay cleared her throat to speak.

"Mel?" Shay didn't reach out, but the hurt in her hushed voice did. The uncertainty, the sadness and defeat Mel now saw on Shay's handsome face had appeared only once before—when Shay said good-bye as Dick Turner looked on in the *Chronicle* office. "Mel. I'm so very sorry."

"Sorry?" Mel froze, mouth agape as Shay stepped around her father and left the room. She disappeared into the crowd on the landing and Mel felt her heart break. "Shay, no!"

Her mother stepped up quickly. "Please *think*, dear."

"Jesus Christ, Melissa. Let that…that deviant leave," her father said. Mel hurried toward the doorway, but her father grabbed her arm. "What's the matter with you? My God. After all she's done to you, to us, you're chasing after her? Show some self-respect, for Christ's sake, some respect for the Baker name!"

"How dare you call her that! I know you, and *still* I can't believe this! Let go of me!" She struggled to peel his fingers from her elbow. "Damn you, Dad! Can't you see what you've done?"

He pulled her farther into the room. "You brought this on yourself! And it's plenty obvious what recourse you've left me."

Mel freed herself with a savage yank of her arm. "Goddamn you and your sick mind!"

"You curse me?" He shook a finger in her face. "You can forget the *Chronicle*. This game you're playing is over and you are finished. I'm calling my attorney as soon as I get back to the hotel. Count on it!"

Mel ran to the landing and everyone in the gathering looked away or down.

"Where is she?"

Coby muttered toward the floor. "We heard the bike leave, Mel."

An icy swell started at the back of her neck and rippled downward until her entire body shivered. "This is all my fault."

"No, it's his, Mel," Misty said. "I think Shay may need a little time."

Mel shook her head with increasing vigor, her awareness returning with clarity.

"No, it's mine. And mine to fix."

She walked to where her father stood waiting and glanced at her mother before locking eyes with him. Heart pounding and her breath falling short, she released her deepest thoughts in her sharpest tone and with no reservation.

"This has gone on far too long. I should have done this so, so long ago, but didn't. And you know why? Because I hadn't met someone who truly mattered until now." His eyebrows nearly met above his nose, but Mel railed on, undaunted. "I know you won't even *try* to understand, but you need to hear it and you're going to. I love Shay. No one's ever made me happier. So go ahead and do what you want. Even if it were possible—which is isn't—I wouldn't change my mind about her. I'm not letting her go."

"Melissa." His tone had reverted to the slow, stern sound she'd dealt with since childhood. "You're talking foolishness. This is ridiculous. If this is what you've become, it actually scares me."

"Typically, you'll see things any way that suits you." Mel shook her head. "As much as I dreamed you'd be happy for me, I knew you'd never see beyond what matters to *you*. I'm disappointed that I won't be able to share my happiness with my father, but not so much that I'll set it aside. I'm not putting myself second anymore. Not to you *or* the *Chronicle*."

He looked at her mother, but returned to stare at Mel with a hardened, resolved ire. "Your work here in our name used to make me proud. I'm removing you from all of it, Melissa, *all of it*, because I have to."

"You didn't listen to a goddamn word I said!"

"Oh, I certainly did. And I'm ashamed."

"Fine. Be ashamed. Be anything you damn well choose. Be blind to my finding happiness at last, be blind to how much I care about the *Chronicle*. But know this: I'm done being bullied by you and that damned agreement. I won't have hurtful people in my life, and that includes you."

"What did you say?"

Mel looked back. "Mom? I'm sorry it's come to this." She faced her father. "You wield the power, Dad, so go ahead and take the

Chronicle, and you know what? Take the house with it, and this work that's been done *for us* out of the goodness of my friends' hearts. And you can take responsibility for your mother while you're at it. You want me removed? Fine. It's all yours, because I'm out of here. I'll get what's left of my things in the morning."

She stormed through the crowd on the landing and down the stairs.

CHAPTER THIRTY

You're all dressed again." Coby eyed Mel suspiciously around the open refrigerator door. "Going back to work?"

"Staying busy keeps me sane." Mel glanced at the phone but no red light blinked; there were no messages. Lately, she'd started wondering if there ever would be any.

"For the first time in a week, the three of us are awake in the same house together, and you're leaving again just as *I'm* about to make us this exotic supper?"

"I hope you haven't gone to any trouble. What are you cooking?"

"Burgers."

Grateful for Coby's effervescent humor, Mel had to chuckle, but noticed how odd it felt. She hadn't done anything close to laugh since Shay walked out of the homestead. Seven days of no contact were taking their toll. And staying in the guest room Shay vacated bordered on the masochistic; Misty and Coby ordered her off their couch after the third night. Sleepless nights and reduced appetite were now the norm, and she spent a bit more time making up her face each morning to hide her drawn look.

"We've yet to catch you for morning coffee on the deck, Mel."

"And, again, we didn't hear you come in last night," Misty said. "You can't keep this up. Eighteen-hour days will make you sick."

"They'll have to get in line behind the workload. We lost another advertiser yesterday, and holding us at twenty pages is a financial marathon, not to mention agony." She snickered abruptly. "Maybe I'll just let it crash, then the *Tribune* won't have to buy it." She swung her satchel over her shoulder.

"I'm amazed you still go back to it, Mel," Coby said, "that you're still giving."

"It's not like a job you can just dump. A newspaper is a living, breathing entity." Mel sighed toward her shoes. "There's duty involved, not to mention what's left of my pride and self-respect. The *Chronicle*'s been a part of me since I was a little girl. Just letting it run aground isn't in me. Out of the question."

"I wish your grandmother had come around, talked some sense into him."

Mel sent Misty a sardonic chuckle. "*That* was never going to happen. And now that she's in assisted living just two miles from him, it never will. I'm sure they get together regularly to bitch about how I cost them everything."

"Amazes me that some people just don't get it." Misty shook her head. "Did your dad's attorney say when he's meeting with the *Tribune*?"

"We're down to three weeks. Then it's over. Selling a paper never happens in a month, so Dad obviously moved mountains."

"Fucking idiots," Coby muttered. "How can family or readers do that to you, someone they've known and loved for so long?" She wiped her hands on a towel and leaned on the breakfast bar. "Can't you just let tonight go, stay here with us? You need a night off."

"Thanks, but actually, tonight I'm working on my resume. Last night I helped Mike with his and wrote him three letters of reference. Pretty hard, especially considering everything else."

Out of habit, she searched her bag for her cell. "Damn. Be right back."

She found it on the nightstand, where she'd left it during her failed attempt at a nap, and headed back out. Coby's lowered voice didn't prevent Mel from overhearing the conversation that continued in her absence.

"I don't care that she took off to God-knows-where. I don't even care that she's okay. I get one bizarre voice mail message? And her cell's full, probably with Mel's apologies, so I can't get through. Jesus, I want to kick her ass."

"Sweetie, we're all relieved to hear she's okay. Wherever she is. But you're right. She should speak to Mel, at least. No doubt she sees herself as the catalyst in this mess and is trying to figure out the right thing to do."

"Yeah? Well, I get more pissed off at her by the day. She should be here. Mel needs her. Does she even know Mel told her father to kiss off? I bet she has no clue what Mel's going through now."

Mel entered the room as Coby threw her dish towel into the sink with a frustrated "shit."

"Hey, so, the happenings just keep coming," she offered sarcastically, and accepted a bottle of water from Misty. "As if there needs to be more."

"Now what?" Coby crossed her arms and leaned against the counter.

"I was on a rare high this afternoon because the piece on the Heights restart was going together smoothly, and then the real estate office called *me* by mistake, instead of Dad's attorney. He got a nibble on the homestead, just two days on the market, and was giddy as a kid."

Misty slumped onto a stool. "Wow. Already?"

"You know what's really a kick in the teeth? Because it's one of the first homes built in this damn town, I'm obliged to write about it."

She headed for the door, thanking them for their hospitality, as she did every time she saw them, and reminding them not to wait up. She thanked God constantly, too, it seemed, that Misty and Coby were "family" in all the right ways.

"Where would I be without you guys?" she sighed as she drove to the office. Their unwavering support meant the world because these days she felt too much like an exiled captain on the *Titanic*. She issued a snide laugh through the windshield and snapped off a crisp salute. "Down with the ship, Dad!"

On top of having no home, a dying job, and no waking hours to look for replacements, the heartache threatened to break her. It dwarfed the horror she'd endured in college. Those weeks of introspection and depression, the sessions with two of her father's psychologists, all paled in comparison to these mere seven days. The nausea, spontaneous tears, and exhausting expectations wreaked havoc on her concentration and made work doubly difficult, and breaks from the tedium simply allowed debilitating loneliness to regain control.

She locked herself in the office and put on the slippers she now kept beneath her desk. *Always as comfortable as an old friend, like taking comfort in this job. Or has it been refuge all this time?* Suddenly, words Shay whispered during their only dance—as they took turns sharing intimate thoughts—returned to her so clearly Mel looked toward her office door, then to the quiet evening outside. *There's no more hiding from the real world now. I made the right decision, Shay. Your turn.*

❖

At nine thirty the following Friday morning, Ida jingled through the *Chronicle*'s front door, and Mike joined her at Mel's desk. The closing of another week without Shay and facing only two more with the *Chronicle* had Mel resorting to coffee to stay sociable and sharp, but despite the double espresso in this third cup, she was bone-tired of explaining, rationalizing, and just talking. Misty and Coby now walked on eggshells around her and tried to hide their aggravation with Shay's silence.

Mel knew she wasn't entitled to such anger because she'd brought this on herself, but she simply didn't know how to interpret Shay's absence anymore. Frustration competed with shame as a growing part of her believed Shay was gone for good. She considered leaving town, that starting fresh somewhere, anywhere, would be best. However, seeing that parallel to Shay's past only deepened her depression and pushed rational thought into a corner of her mind she avoided at all cost.

Mike rolled his chair closer, Ida settled into the guest chair, and both seemed eager to speak. Leaning forward on her arms, Mel looked from one to the other.

"What's going on? I'm sorry, guys, but there's no retracting the 'Letter to Readers.'"

"Absolutely not," Mike stated. "You took the high road, Mel. Classy."

"I liked the part where you basically told people to open up," Ida said, turning to the editorial page and the "good-bye" that had taken Mel days to write. *"Today, residents need to ensure Tomson offers everyone the welcome, nurturing, and respect of a true hometown."*

"The beginning was best," Mike said, "where you sorta say 'suck it up and deal with change.'"

"The epilogue of my life, I suppose. Lessons learned." She

shrugged. "My point was fairness first, that when change is inevitable, it often doesn't come easily, and it's in everyone's best interest to give it a fair, open-minded review." She sat back and sighed. "No more hypocrisy."

"And this is good, Mel," he insisted, and read from Ida's paper. *"Whether building a shopping complex, having a youngster's two moms join the PTA, or selling the local newspaper, changes often ask a lot of us. Our responses must be guided by fairness and foresight—not lust for superiority, not fear of the unfamiliar."* He sat back, beaming. "Excellent."

It was a relief to hear that the most difficult piece she'd written in ages hit its mark, and the satisfaction lent Mel a pat on the back she sorely needed. She'd reached deeply to put all that in print. It had forced her to admit, to herself as much as the readership, that confronting change—not denying or ignoring it—was part of living life to its fullest and, if approached fairly, respectfully, would enhance the greater good.

It had been hard enough to generate the small boxed news blurb above the fold on page one, announcing the *Chronicle*'s imminent sale by her father, and Mel's upcoming resignation. Telling readers that Tribune Publishing, Inc. planned to introduce a new *Chronicle* editor after next week's final issue had phones ringing off the hook once the paper appeared yesterday morning. Readers protested, voiced disappointment, and offered her well-wishes, and Mel took a bit of comfort in their reaction.

"Anyone out there who's glad about the *Trib* buying us or who's happy you're leaving must be hiding," Ida said, "because I haven't run into any." Mel's desk phone rang and Ida pointed at it. "Want me to hang here and take calls?"

"Thanks, but they're slowing down." She let it go to voice mail, no longer willing to hear it wasn't Shay.

"Ida and I each have been nabbed on the street a few times already," Mike said. "It is nice to hear readers are upset, you've got to admit."

"They think it stinks that you're not being allowed to stay on," Ida said.

Mike snickered. "The *Trib* won't waste any time shutting the doors."

"That's what you two are all pumped up about?"

Ida moved to the edge of her seat. "No, silly. It's payday and there's something we want to do." Mel unlocked a side drawer and brought out their checks, but Ida pushed them back across the blotter. "We've made up our minds and you're going to like it."

Mel frowned. "Really?" She hoped she would. Anything good was welcome these days.

"Really. We know things are getting awfully tight, financially, so we're not taking any more money." Mel opened her mouth to protest. "Before you start, it's a done deal."

Mike nodded. "I've picked up some freelance stuff that should work out fine."

Mel sat back hard. "I don't believe you two."

"Let us do this," Ida said. "This is our way of helping. Don't argue."

"No. It's totally unfair to—"

"I said don't argue."

"We've got it all worked out, Mel," Mike added.

"I-I don't know what to say. Jesus, I don't believe this is all happening. I hate it so much."

Ida tapped the desk. "Hey," she said playfully, "it's not like what I earn covers my mortgage or anything."

"And I'm ahead on my rent, so I'm good, too," Mike said. "Plus, this freelance job at Gronlund's will bring in some major bucks. He wants a whole promo package for the ranch."

Mel sent him a wary look. "The hotshot news photographer we're so proud of isn't selling out for PR work, is he?"

"Hell, no. You know my thing is running around like a crazy guy, getting off on the variety, the deadlines. It's in my blood, Mel. Like the *Chronicle* is in yo—" He caught himself. "Sorry."

"Well…" Mel leaned back, wondering where to begin. "What you've offered is beyond generous. I don't want to accept the offer, but honestly, it would give the *Chronicle* a real shot in the arm right now. Staying at twenty pages won't be a problem after all, and that's…" She took a breath as emotion rose to the surface. "The *Chronicle* will go out looking good. Thank you."

Ida stood. "Glad that's settled. Now, I've got work to do." She patted Mel's hand. "Chin up, kiddo."

She bustled out the door, and Mel watched her through the window. "I'd forgotten how much fun this job used to be."

"We could have one last hurrah as a staff, Mel." He edged forward. "Guys at the Heights told me this morning they heard Chandler talking about tearing down the old railroad depot so Della can put up a restaurant."

"I wondered when she'd get around to that property. Damn, Mike. That's a great old building."

"Neither of us may be around to see Ed tackle the site," he said, "but we can break the story. Folks will remember *our Chronicle* as a feisty paper." The gleam in his eye almost made Mel forget their days were numbered. "Those shots of dynamiting at the Heights last week were the best we ever ran, Mel, dirt and rock going sky-high. Nothing like letting everyone see and *feel* that the Heights is back—on the right track now, thanks to us. I'm saving that front page for next year's photo contest."

"Leave it to Della. She must be ecstatic to be getting the *Chronicle* out of her hair."

He sighed dreamily. "Wouldn't you love to have a tenth of her money? She didn't flinch when Ed was ordered to redo all that excavation."

"She didn't, did she?" As proud as she was of the *Chronicle*'s effort, it pained her to think Slattery would now be free to run roughshod through town without a watchdog. "You know, things will only stay on the up-and-up around here for so long. Angie will probably do only a few months, so he'll be back."

"Well, at least Peters will go away for a long time, Mel. Madden's got an airtight case against that sicko for your fire. Nasty stuff, arson of an occupied dwelling."

"I'm thankful they wrapped that case so quickly, and hopefully, the trial will go as fast. Testifying will hurt like hell, and…I'm tired of hurting."

Mike nodded companionably and sat back. "So, still nothing from her?"

Mel shook her head. "And I wish I could just be angry about it, but I can't blame her for having had enough of me and my mess. There's just so much I need to say."

Mike leaned on the edge of her desk. "Mel. I don't believe Shay would—or could—do this. I think you need to hang in there."

"Thank you, Mike." She reached to the far side of her desk and gripped his arm. "No matter where we end up when the *Tribune* takes over, I don't ever want us to lose touch."

He put his hand over hers. "Hey, I'm the number one man in your life. I won't give that up."

CHAPTER THIRTY-ONE

Mel's Tuesday morning visits to the town assessor's office hardly compared to today's, as she fought a numbing trepidation in collecting the latest real estate transactions. She opened the voluminous antique ledger and the clerk suddenly set her palm atop Mel's hand.

"I'm just so sad about all you're going through, Mel."

"Thank you, Patsy."

"Lord, it was hard, reading your letter in the paper. Those suits from the *Tribune* were here Friday, going through our books. Can't you stop them?"

"It's not my call, I'm afraid. Dad's made up his mind. But thank you for the support. It means a lot."

"Well, he's the stupidest man in the world and I don't mind saying so. We're all different in our own ways, and it's just plain cruel what he's done to you. Everyone coming in here, at the market, the post office, Lord, everywhere I go, someone has something to say about it. I mean, I'm sorry folks are so into your private business, but they're really unhappy. You're one of us. He hasn't been for years."

One of us?

"Again, thank you, but lots of people aren't upset at all. One look at the *Chronicle* tells you there are quite a few in my father's camp."

"Yeah, well, the paper has shrunk a lot, I know, but it would bounce back, given the chance. I believe that. Now that the Heights work is moving again, the idiots who blamed you will smarten up—and the fools who think like your father, well, they'll come around, too. And if they don't, you don't need them anyway." She grumbled indignantly. "It's all over town, how he forced you out. A decent person doesn't do such a terrible thing, care so little for his daughter and his family roots. Pretty easy to see how unlike us he is, so they'll change their tune."

Mel figured Patsy was right, but held little hope things would change that much, fast enough to improve her situation.

"Mel," Patsy said with renewed vigor, "do you know that last week, Eli Winston had three of us customers there for half an hour while he paced behind his meat case, working himself into a tizzy about all this? But good Lord, if that man isn't wise in his old age. He made the best point." She tapped her pen on the counter. "Like he said, deep down, people in territory like this have always respected someone who stands up for herself. Folks have been standing their ground here for generations, like my grandfather and yours, you know? And when it comes down to love, family, and homestead, they relate to that."

Mel took a steadying breath. Patsy's pep talk wasn't helping. The willpower Mel had mustered just to get into the shower this morning was washing away, along with her cheerful façade. "Oh, I'm sure, eventually, Tomson will see the light, Patsy, but my father's not changing his mind, and the *Chronicle*'s his to do with as he pleases." She took Patsy's hand in both of hers. "I haven't decided what's up with me yet, things have been so crazy, but please know I think you're a love. Thank you so much for all your help over the years, your friendship. I'm really going to miss you."

Patsy squeezed Mel's hand before pulling away to grab a tissue. "Now, knock that off or the waterworks will start."

Mel opened the ledger to the current date. She was surprised when Patsy covered the page with her splayed hand.

"No matter how discouraged you get, Mel, remember you're better than this and you'll pull through." She offered a sympathetic pat before returning to her desk.

Smothering a sigh, Mel ran her finger down the recent listings until a new one made her breath catch. *Patsy knew.* The sale of the Baker homestead to some corporate trust processed through county land court late yesterday morning.

It's gone.

Mel stood, weakened, as memories and visions of people, things, events that would never recur drained from her system. She lowered her head, and felt Patsy stuff a tissue into her hand.

"It's been my experience, Mel, that when a trust like that buys a residence, it's a corporate move just so the high and mighty can write off a second home. Some legal firm did this. I'm so sorry, honey." She went to the front of the counter and draped an arm around Mel's shoulders. "Notification came through around lunch yesterday. I didn't have the heart to call you."

Mel mustered a smile and hugged her, but had to get away. Every day, reality struck a bit harder, and, more than ever, she ached at the loss of Shay's companionship.

The five-minute drive in the compact security of her Subaru ended too soon, and Mel regretted not having walked. The fresh air would've helped clear her mind, but she'd reserved that energy to tackle the work ahead. *One week at a time.* Discipline pushed her through the week's production with hardly a flare of interest. *Next week it's all over.*

❖

Thursday night, with Coby and Misty at the Exchange, Mel took advantage of the private time and sought refuge in a long, steamy shower to ease her tension, and the pain in her heart and mind, fully intending to escape into early, much-needed sleep. *God, how did I make it through the week? And will I survive this final one? Damn it, Shay Maguire. Was I a fool to love you? After all that's happened, you just vanish and leave me with…with what?*

A towel wrapped around her, she forced down the lump in her throat and clicked on the nightstand lamp. A soft knock on her open door startled her.

"Dear God!"

Shay stepped into the dim light, hands in her pockets, and an uncharacteristic air of vulnerability about her that only enhanced her appeal. Mel swallowed hard. *If you've finally found the nerve to say good-bye, thanks a lot. And make it quick.*

Shay slid a small backpack from her shoulder and dropped it by her feet.

"I didn't mean to scare you, but you didn't hear me at the front door and it was unlocked." She edged farther into the room. "I'm so happy to see you, I can't think straight."

"I-I'm…" Mel took a breath. "*Three weeks*, Shay." She struggled to collect herself, but too many emotions were in play and she was just too exhausted to sort them out. "Where have you been and why didn't you call?" Her voice wavered.

Shay ran a hand through her hair.

"Don't do that," Mel ordered. "Just tell me why."

"I had to think things through and make some serious decisions, and I had a really hard time taking emotion out of the equation. I couldn't see things for what they were with my heart screaming in my face."

"My love screams in your face? Gets in your way?"

"No, no, Mel." With negligible effort, she moved to within arm's reach. "No. Please, you need to und—"

Mel blinked away moisture to send a stern message. "No, *you* need to tell me why you walked away, Shay, why I didn't even warrant a few words on the phone while I've been here going through hell."

Shay took Mel's shoulders, backed her up to the bed until Mel had to sit, and knelt before her.

"A lot has happened in three weeks."

"That's all you've got?"

"No, of course not, Mel." Shay set a hand on Mel's knee.

"Please don't touch me. I'm trying to see things clearly."

Shay retracted her hand. "I'm sorry, first of all, and not just for taking so long to apologize. I'm deeply sorry for so many things. For being mad that you never spoke of this agreement with your father. For my role in your breaking it. For being so damn inconsiderate and self-centered." She cleared her throat and briefly looked down. "When he made you choose, I expected…Well, you hesitated, Mel, and all I saw was that, deep down, the *Chronicle* came first, that you *really* wanted the paper, not me, not us. Please forgive me for being an idiot. I hurt you, I know, and that's what I'm most sorry about."

Mel worked to steady her breathing. This was hard to hear, Shay getting everything off her chest so she could ride off into the sunset, start anew, again. Mel didn't want to hear more. She wanted to escape, to run out back and jump in the lake, go lock herself into her office. *It's only available for two more days, then where will you hide?*

"You shocked the hell out of me, Shay, walking out. Dad had me so furious, so disappointed, and so damn scared, I was speechless, and you walked out. Jesus, Shay. I couldn't believe it. Everything in me emptied in that instant."

"Mel, I couldn't have been more wrong. I'm so very sorry."

"I haven't even had the strength for anger—at you *or* him. I've just been too sad. I *did* realize what I needed to do, you know, and somehow I did it. And I still believe it was the right thing to do, but you left, goddamn it. You have no idea what's happened here."

"Wait. Yes, I do." Shay's frown deepened. "I was in Cascade—"

"You rode all that way?"

"I wasn't thinking, Mel. I grabbed things here and just kept going. And the Exchange band, Tracy was playing at the bar—"

"What? You were with Tracy?"

"Don't. You know better."

"I thought I knew, but after three weeks of noth—"

"She'd talked with Coby and told me what happened."

"And still you let three—"

"That spun me around, Mel, had me back at square one, rethinking everything. It took even longer to know what to do. Maybe I needed to prove to myself that I...that I can't be away from you, that you make everything right—regardless of what we do for a living or where. Part of me prayed you'd see it, too."

Mel straightened. "So...you're not leaving? Saying good-bye?"

"No, Mel!" Shay gathered Mel's hands quickly. "Just the opposite."

"Have you been *testing* me? My feelings for you?"

"Actually, my feelings. I was completely thrown by that scene between you and your dad, learning he held the *Chronicle* over your head all this time. Having a relationship with me, you risked so much more than advertising money. It cost you your dream, but I never knew." Shay brought Mel's hands to her lips and kissed them. "When I heard what happened after I left that house, what you told him, it woke me up, thank God. I *can't* take emotion out of the picture, Mel, because I'm so in love with you."

"I'm so in love with you, too."

Mel's moist eyes overflowed and Shay cupped her face. "Nothing will ever make me leave your side again. Nothing. Please forgive me. Please."

"Oh, God, Shay. I-I did this to you. I should have—"

"Stop, Mel. You're not to blame."

"I was so ashamed of what I did."

Shay touched Mel's lip. "Shh. No. You've no reason—"

"Yes, I do. I'm still ashamed of it. You deserved to know, and my cowardice hurt y—"

"No more." Shay drew her into a hug. "So we each screwed up. We know better now."

Mel leaned back enough to kiss her, softly, slowly, as Shay's familiar arms closed out the world and sensation soared through her system. She locked hers around Shay's neck, unable to get close enough. *Each kiss is finer than the last.* Need and desire blurring into uncontrollable urge, Mel sucked her tongue deeper and surrendered fully when Shay bent her back onto the bed. Kisses pressed to her cheek, her chin. Shay's firm, determined lips wet her throat, seared across her shoulder, along her arm, back up as ragged breath heated her neck, ear, mouth. *She needs me as much as I need her.*

She clawed greedily at Shay's back, dragged her shirt out of her jeans and over her head. She lost her towel just as swiftly. Shay kicked off her boots, stepped out of her jeans, and seized Mel by the ribs with both hands, growling as she rose over her.

Mel gasped at being taken bodily with such urgency. Shay's weight sent a surge to her sex that opened her legs in welcome, and Shay nestled their bodies together, her mouth hovering above Mel's breast. Shay licked the nipple, stroking upward repeatedly, circling, teasing until Mel drove her fingers into her hair and pressed her face down onto it.

Mel's unstoppable tears trickled to her ears, and her body screamed for more as Shay sucked voraciously. Mel captured Shay's thighs within her legs, ground their hips together as her clit throbbed and yearned to be touched. Shay moved to her other breast, tugged the nipple between her teeth, and made Mel gasp. She kissed her way along Mel's side, across her abdomen to her hipbone, and pretended to gnaw on it like a starved beast. Mel lurched upright and a short, tight squeal escaped.

"No tickling!" she protested, but broad hands slid beneath her hips and pulled her right into Shay's mouth. Mel fell back to the mattress, gloriously helpless. "Oh God, yes."

She writhed beneath the long, heavy strokes of Shay's tongue, her mind flashing, her clit twitching each time Shay circled it. Her flesh dissolved, her bones softened as Shay consumed her, tripped electrified nerves and moaned for more.

"Shay!" Mel's body contracted, twisted against the unrelenting strength of Shay's arms, and she dropped back onto the bed only to arch off it again.

Shay would not be swayed. Mel felt her securely attached. *Permanently.* Palms held her in place as Shay claimed her, and Mel's every muscle coiled tighter with each draw of Shay's mouth. Shuddering, Mel searched frantically, mindlessly, for purchase in Shay's hair with one hand while the other thrashed pillows to the floor.

"Shay, I'm—Shay!"

Tremors rocked her. In a chest void of breath, her heart hammered wildly, constricted her throat, and pounded in her ears. Fingers plying her sodden sex glided perfectly inside and took hold. The entire length of her body stiffened and shook.

A euphoric eternity passed before she succumbed. Shay withdrew slowly and her wet face coated Mel's thighs, stomach, breasts, and throat with tender caresses as she inched her way up.

"Mel. I love you. Every inch of you."

"Baby, how I love you." She draped limp arms around Shay's neck and pulled her into a kiss. "Dear God Almighty, Shay Maguire. I surely do."

Shay kissed her lips delicately, kissed her jaw, her neck, and nuzzled into the crook of her shoulder as she snuggled closer.

"So, do you want to talk some more?"

"Now?" Mel laughed, so emotionally drained she couldn't control thankful tears. She ran her hands across Shay's back, absorbing what she'd missed so desperately. She'd had enough talk for a while. She wanted to disappear within Shay's hold, to crawl all over her, inside and out. Now.

Shay rose up on an elbow, suddenly serious, and guided some stray hair from Mel's face. "About the house, Mel."

Mel traced Shay's cheek with her fingertips. "Probably the *very* last thing I want to think about at this moment."

"I think you want to stay in Tomson."

"Yet *another* romantic topic."

"I mean, I know the *Tribune* is moving in—"

"Aw, Shay, you're batting three for three. *Now*? Let's not—"

"I was told that's happening soon."

"A week from Saturday, and I'd really rather not—"

"But, Mel," Shay sat up, "couldn't you start your own?"

Mel stroked Shay's arm up to her shoulder. She wanted to think about *this* and luxuriate in the best sex of her life. She sighed. "There's just a little matter of being homeless and poor. You're killing me, Maguire. Stop or I'm getting out of this bed."

Shay looked crestfallen. "You *do* want to stay in town, don't you?"

Mel frowned. *So much for my threat. Staying in Tomson is what's on your mind?* "Yes, Shay. Of course I want to stay here, ideally, but income matters, remember? And I'm not looking at any after next Friday."

Shay clasped Mel's hand and looked at her earnestly. "What if you start your own paper and I buy Sonny's?"

"What?" Mel's face blanked. "You're not serious."

"Never more."

"Be real, Shay. You're talking about a lot of money. And neither of us even has a place of her own." As soon as she said it, she knew she'd opened that painful door.

"Mel, about the house—"

"Please, Shay." Resigned to Shay's insistence, she sat up and faced her. "It's gone now. A moot point. The end. Must we talk about it now?"

Damn, she didn't want her bitterness in bed with them. But she definitely wasn't up for house talk. That wound was so fresh she could practically feel her heart bleed. And now Shay most likely would bring up the old von Miller spread again. Her fondness for the place was touching, but Mel's heart just wasn't in it. Besides, she didn't have anywhere near enough money to pay her share of the work required to make that house livable. Buying it was out of the question. On top of the outlay to start a newspaper? They'd spent a few evenings toying with such dreams, but fantasy was fantasy. Mel hated to burst her bubble.

"Shay, I'm sorry, really, but I can't—"

"But yes, you can."

"No. I'm really strapped now, baby. I can't. I hardly have enough to put down on an apartment, everything I had went into my printing costs. I'm so sorry. I know you've fallen for the von Miller place, and I feel terrible."

"And I know how much you want a home."

Mel looked on curiously as Shay leaned away to turn on the other bedside lamp. Then she pulled a bulging envelope out of her backpack. *Show me bundles of hundreds, Shay Maguire, and I'll scream.* Instead, Shay laid a folded set of legal papers on her lap.

Mel looked at them and back up. "What's this?"

Shay unfolded the documents and held them patiently for Mel to read.

"This fax," Mel's eyes raced down the page, "it's from a Boston bank?" She glanced up again, then read for several seconds more. "It's to *you* from—"

She grabbed the pages from Shay and reread what she didn't believe on her first scan.

"This trust..." Her escalating heartbeat sounded louder in her ears than her voice. She raised the pages and her voice cracked when she spoke. "This is the trust that bought my—" She couldn't speak. Her lips began to tremble and her eyes filled. When Shay moved the papers aside and took Mel's face in her palms, tears rolled down over her hands.

"Yes. Mel, the trust is me. I put a chunk of my insurance settlement into it before I left Chicago. The rest I invested. The legal firm and the bank are ones I've used since college."

"You bought my homestead?" Mel blinked repeatedly and tried to catch her breath.

Shay nodded and kissed away the tears on Mel's cheeks. "Yes, sweetheart. Because it's a part of you and you need it. And I need you just as desperately."

Mel collapsed onto Shay's chest and cried harder than she'd ever cried before. Shay wrapped her up securely, rocked her as Mel sobbed beneath her chin.

"I can't believe it. Thank you doesn't come close to what I'm feeling." She thrust her arms around Shay's waist, and her body shook as she cried.

Shay pressed her face into Mel's hair. "Once I got my head on straight, I took it as a race against time. I was in such a damn hurry, I almost complicated things too much and screwed it all up. The whole thing almost fell through because..." She held Mel out to look at her. "I, well, see, I put money down on Sonny's, too."

Tears still falling and her nose dripping, Mel stared. "Sonny's? You did?"

"Yeah, and boy, did I make a huge mess of everything. For such big transactions so fast, they made me go in person."

"Oh my God, Shay. You went to Boston?"

Shay combed her fingers through Mel's hair. "Chicago, first."

"No way."

"It got kind of hectic."

Mel drew back and pressed a hand to Shay's face. "I don't know what to say. There are no words to describe how wonderful you are."

"No," Shay whispered, shaking her head. "After what I put you through—"

"Shh. None of that matters. We're together now."

She pressed her mouth to Shay's, but the kiss felt so inadequate. Her lips trembled. She kissed harder, the desire to convey her feelings so incredibly strong and growing. Tears found their way along her nose, into her mouth, their mouths. Smiling, Shay withdrew and used a corner of the sheet to wipe Mel's face.

"No more tears, honey. Hey, in due time, we'll get the Baker name back on the deed where it's always been, where it belongs. Meanwhile, the purchase agreement includes a proviso that keeps that roof over your head, specifically, for as long as you choose. Your father no longer has a claim to any of it."

Mel could barely breathe as her mind ran through the homestead like a child on a playground, as she proudly watched Shay at work in her own shop. *My job hunt starts today. I've avoided it long enough. Regardless of what it is, we'll have what matters.*

Inconceivably, Shay had righted the most important part of her world, exchanged defeat for victory, despair for joy, and Mel was dizzy, shocked, overwhelmed, thankful, jubilant. It was all beyond her wildest imagination, almost beyond her ability to cope. She struggled to sit up straighter and collect herself. She'd soaked them both with tears, and she rubbed some of the moisture across Shay's breast.

"Your heart is pounding as hard as mine."

"It sure is."

"My God. You are such a wonderful woman. I am so lucky, so thankful we found each other. I love you with all my heart, Shay. Truly. I'll never be able to tell you how much."

"Every time I look into your eyes, you tell me."

Mel rose to her knees on the bed and cupped Shay's face in trembling hands. "Then take a good, long look, Shay Maguire. There's a lot more where this comes from."

CHAPTER THIRTY-TWO

M el telling Ida about the homestead on Monday morning set Tomson abuzz within the day. Congratulatory hugs, handshakes, and phone calls made coping with the *Chronicle*'s final week considerably easier, even though the end of her dream and its weekly paycheck still loomed.

It took herculean effort to write the last few articles she'd ever do for the *Chronicle*, and her fragile concentration broke easily when Mike jerked out of his desk chair.

"Did I just hear her pull up?" He checked the street.

Mel hit the Save button and sighed. "Who's more excited to see her, you or me?"

"Are you kidding? Hell, I'm going to kiss her. Stealing the homestead from your father? Shay's my hero."

"Have you finished all four of those layouts yet?"

He tore himself from the window, frowning. "I'm getting there. Jesus, you'll always be a slave driver, Ms. Baker. You still want four?"

"I'm not leaving him a cent in our account. Our last dime's going into twenty-four pages. We will not give up that centerfold. I want that pullout to be a photo keepsake, our thank-you to readers."

She watched for his understanding and was surprised when he turned back to the window.

"You've taught me a hell of a lot more than I ever learned in school, Mel. I never dreamed I'd love a job this much."

"Please, Mike. We'll never make it through today, let alone through Friday."

"Hey," he said and stepped closer to the glass, "Shay *is* here. She must have parked beyond that beat-up truck. And Tom Rogers is getting out of it."

Mel labored to focus on her screen. Concentrating was nearly impossible as every thought rolled back to saying good-bye in some fashion. Tommy probably was next, and would wax nostalgic about "the good ol' days."

"Mel, now they're on the sidewalk, talking to someone I can't see."

"Will you get to work? It's eleven o'clock already. If they're coming in, they'll come in."

He backed up and looked to the outer office just as the door jingled, and Shay's dashing smile struck Mel like a breath of fresh air. She stood and reached for her hand, a gesture she was thrilled to offer.

"Hi, you."

Shay took it as she rounded the desk. "Hi, honey." She kissed her cheek and Mel felt the color rise in her face. "Look who I found wandering the streets."

Mel nodded at Tommy. "Fancy seeing you in our neighborhood, Mr. Rogers."

Blocking the inner doorway, Mike stood shaking the hand of someone she couldn't see. It appeared there were now three men beyond him, and when he finally stepped aside, Mel's mouth opened in silent surprise.

Dick Turner and Garret Nelson offered humble smiles as they entered her office, and elderly butcher Eli Winston followed.

"Gentlemen. Good morning." Winston shuffled forward and Mike hurriedly provided the guest chair. "Mr. Winston. It's lovely to see you."

"You, too, dear girl." He settled in and Tommy handed him a rumpled collection of papers.

"Eli has some business for the *Chronicle*, Mel."

"Oh?" She looked to Winston and then the others. "And you're...?"

"We're with him on this," Turner said, and looked at Shay. "We all are."

Tommy grinned and crossed his arms.

Nelson concurred quickly. "We are."

Mel cast Shay a glance before leaning over her desk toward Winston. "It must be serious business, if you've rounded up this impressive escort."

"That it is." Never one to be rushed, he removed his spectacles, wiped them on his shirt, and methodically wrapped the wire stems back around his ears. He flattened the papers across his thigh, pressing his palm over the creases as if to iron out the wrinkles, and, at last, handed her the fourteen stapled pages.

"Want all that in a full-page ad."

With a hand on her desk to steady herself, Mel read the opening paragraph of what amounted to a letter of support—for her and the *Chronicle* under her editorship. She quickly flipped to each subsequent page. They were filled with signatures. Hundreds of them she knew and didn't, of those who held town, county, and state positions, of those in civic organizations, of ranchers, farmers, business owners——all her advertisers, it seemed—and of those readers she had and hadn't met.

She sat down hard. "Wow."

"Mel?" Mike asked, sounding afraid to know what she'd read.

She handed him the papers. "I can't believe this." She sent Winston a sly look. "Are you the mastermind here?"

"No sense in everybody whining and complaining and never doing nothing about it. I put a paper on my counter a while back and told folks to put their names down if their yapping meant something. Got to put your money where your mouth is, y'know? You putting this in the paper might help this damn town see the light of day. And you deserve to see that *you've* made a difference."

Mel bit her lower lip. *No more tears.* Shay gave her shoulders a squeeze.

Camera now at the ready, Mike put the papers back in Mel's hands and waved her to stand among Nelson, Turner, and Winston. Somehow, Mel found herself properly positioned and heard Mike take the shot.

"Now, Mel," Winston kept on, "I want a big spread. These fellows here, they know about advertising big." Mel eyed Turner and Nelson, wondering how their ad dollars were serving them in the *Tribune*, wondering if they squirmed at the sight of Shay by her side.

"Yes, sir, that they do."

"Uh-huh. So they're gonna make sure this is done up big. From the top of that first sheet to the very last name." He jerked his thumb at Nelson. "Mr. Home Depot here has the cash to cover it." He maneuvered in the chair to look up. "Hand over that envelope, Garret. Quit wasting the lady's time, not to mention mine."

Mel stifled a grin as Nelson scrambled to do Winston's bidding. He handed her an envelope stuffed with bills of every small denomination.

"Ah, that should meet your full-page price, Mel," Turner said. "The non-contract price. No artwork worries, so should be easy."

"Should one of us come by to proofread, say tomorrow night?" Nelson's sudden acquiescence surprised her, but his eagerness to point out errors just rubbed her the wrong way.

"If you'd like, of course, but I guarantee you, gentlemen, we'll do our best."

They all nodded and took Winston rising from the chair as their cue to leave.

Turner stepped forward and offered a handshake.

"I-I'm sad that this...I'm sorry for your loss. The end of the *Chronicle* in the family feels like...Well, I know how much it's meant to you. It's always been a pleasure, Mel."

"Same here, Mel," Nelson said. He shook her hand. "I'm sure you'll find bigger and better."

Shocked by their gesture yet glad when they left, Mel had the urge to wash their traitorous touch from her hand.

"Mel?" Winston said. He worked himself up to his full height and knocked on her desk severely. "I'm pretty damn mad about all this, you should know. Mighty hard to sit still."

She slid a palm across Shay's back as she stepped around her, and then Tommy, to get to Winston. "Thank you from the bottom of my heart," she said, gently gripping his arms. "You are what Tomson is really all about and I am proud to know you, someone who fights for what matters."

"Look who's talking, young lady." A corner of his mouth rose with satisfaction and Mel almost broke down.

"Mr. Winston, I have never been so honored. Thank you for being such a special man." She hugged him as tightly as she dared and kissed his scruffy cheek.

"You're welcome," he mumbled toward his shoes, and began his shuffle out. Mike hustled ahead and opened the door.

Mel turned and stared at the papers on her desk, the envelope of cash. She looked at Tommy, and then Shay.

"Did you know he got everyone to do this? Them, especially?"

"I didn't have a clue until this morning. I was telling Tommy about buying Sonny's and he only said we had to be here at eleven."

"I just don't believe it." She queried Tommy. "Do you?"

"That Winston's still got the nuts to make those two jump? You bet I do."

"That you and the *Chronicle* are being saluted in style?" Shay asked. "Thank God. You *so* deserve it." She wrapped an arm around Mel's waist. "I'm so glad it's being done publicly. Your father will never show his face in this town again, once he knows all these people see him for what he really is." She picked up the papers. "Here. Take a good look at all the people who signed for you and the *Chronicle*."

"I took a sheet to the office," Tommy said, leaning both hands on Mel's desk, watching her read, "and I think everybody at the Five Star signed."

Mel inhaled sharply. "Oh, my God! Della signed!"

"I couldn't wait to see your face," Tommy said. "No offense to you personally, Mel, but she knows the best advertising deal when she sees it. Everyone knows the *Trib* is expensive and doesn't have half your circulation. You're a pain in her ass, but the *Chronicle*'s the best bang for her buck. No way she wants the paper to go to the *Trib*."

Mel wandered back to her chair and sat. She dropped the papers on her blotter and stared at them, until Shay scooped them up.

"I can't wait to see this in print." Shay grinned at Tommy. "What a statement this makes. Listen.

"To the editor: The following residents of Tomson wish to express our sincere objection to the decision of owner Robert Baker to sell our town newspaper, the Tomson Chronicle, *to one in a distant city and thereby deprive us of the informative, helpful, and necessary media outlet available here for generations. The* Tomson Chronicle *is and has always been vital to our community. It is an integral part of our town with a proud heritage. Closing the doors on a Tomson family institution not only dishonors its founders, but weakens a cornerstone of our town for present and future generations."*

Shay looked dazed. "Whoever put this together deserves a medal." She stole a sip of Mel's coffee and kept reading.

"Additionally, we voice our deepest disappointment at the departure of Tomson Chronicle *editor Melissa Baker, who has served townspeople tirelessly during her six years. Every town organization, department, and business has benefited by her professionalism and her*

dedication to family. Removing her from her key role subtracts one more precious element of Tomson we cannot afford to lose in these ever-changing times, and therefore, we believe it to be an ill-thought action, detrimental to the town and its residents.

"We hereby record both our opposition to these decisions by owner Robert Baker, and our endorsement of the Tomson Chronicle *and its editor, Melissa Baker."*

❖

"I expect one of the attorneys will let us know when the ink is dry, probably before noon," Mel said, her voice a lifeless drone as her personal files transferred to an external hard drive.

She checked her watch again, wondering how she'd made it to Friday, through days wherein every routine step dredged up precious memories. *Chronicle* assets were being signed away at that moment in Billings, but she refused to leave six years of achievements to rot under some figurehead editor.

Mike scanned his empty desk, the packed boxes by the inner doorway. When the front door jingled open, the scent of flowers from consoling readers wafted through the room on the incoming breeze. It overpowered the coffee aroma from the urn Marie had brought from the diner.

Mike glanced at the clock again. "S'pose I should take the bells off the door."

Saying "hello" in passing, Ida went to Mel's desk and the assortment of cookies, brownies, and breads sent by townspeople, and the fragrant bouquet of crimson roses.

"Wow, Mel, these are spectacular. Shay?"

Mel nodded. "Sam was waiting at the door when I arrived to open up. He said he had 'penalty of death' orders to deliver first thing."

Ida patted her hand and turned in place, inspecting the emptiness of the office, the missing pieces, and the many flowers and plants.

"So many lovely arrangements. Those two on the front counter are beautiful and these are gorgeous in the window, but the place is starting to look like a funeral parlor."

"I was thinking hospital room. You're more accurate." She watched Mike drop the leather strip of bells into an open box, and the significance of the gesture struck her painfully.

Ida tipped up Mel's chin. "If you start, I'll start. No telling who'll show up today, so let's not ruin our faces."

The next few hours passed in a haze for Mel, who set herself on autopilot to handle the steady stream of visitors. Ida jumped into hostess mode and established the coffee urn on the front counter, along with all the confections, and Mel was grateful. Having kept a close eye on the clock all morning, wondering about the progress of the sale and when *that* call would come, she finally was able to lose track of time. After two thirty, however, the periods of quiet grew longer and heavier.

Ida sighed and leaned against the inner door frame. "Well, at least it felt more like a bon voyage reception. And now a lot of the goodies are gone, so they won't end up on my thighs."

"Thank you, Ida. You're a peach."

"Can't say it was easy, and I damn sure wish it wasn't necessary."

Mike emerged from his workroom and flopped into his chair. "So, seriously, how long do you think they'll keep the *Chronicle* afloat?"

"No clue," Mel said. "Maybe they'll see how advertising goes through the holidays. Or maybe they'll wait to evaluate the Heights advertising, like into the spring."

"Or maybe not," he mumbled.

"They're just going to fill our pages with canned crap and articles from the *Trib* that nobody here cares about," Ida added as she swept the outer office. "Before you know it, the advertising will drop to a minimum, and bye-bye."

Mel stared down at her bare desk, knowing Ida most likely was right.

"Short of locking the doors here," Mike said, "that's their cheapest out. I think we can guess what they'll do." He pulled a battered envelope from his hip pocket. "I, ah, I have an interview on Monday with the *Frontier News*."

Mel sat back and forced a smile past her aching heart. "In Cascade? Mike, that's big. You'll be great on a daily."

He shrugged. "It's a long shot and it would mean moving. It's only thirty hours a week, but they pay a little more, so I might be able to swing it."

She already missed his optimism and eager spirit. *Jesus, this sucks.*

CHAPTER THIRTY-THREE

S houldn't the attorney have called by now, Mel? It's four thirty."
She looked from Mike to the clock, which now lay on her desk. "Yeah, I'd have thought—"

The door swung open and Shay stepped in and stopped abruptly, looking up for the bells. She shook her head and strode directly to where Mel sat, barely acknowledging Ida and Mike.

"Shay?"

The look on her face was hard to decipher, concerned, maybe, and Mel could only watch as Shay took her by the shoulders and urged her to stand.

"Shay, what—"

Shay cupped her face and kissed her. Deeply. Back against the wall, deeply. Mel's mind whirled. She envisioned something tragic Shay couldn't verbalize, imagined Shay was making a quasi-public statement about their love, wondered what Ida and Mike thought of this display. And Shay wasn't stopping. Her kiss was firm, hungry, consuming. She slid her arms around Mel's waist and practically lifted her off the floor.

Mel seized Shay's shoulders, tried to ease her back, but that familiar comfort, pressed against her full length, so perfect and so welcome, especially today, won out. She encircled Shay's neck and responded in kind.

It took Ida's giggle to distract them. Shay lifted her head and her eyes glowed.

"I love you, Mel."

"I love you, Shay." She fingered Shay's mussed hair away from her face. "And thank you for my roses. They're fantastic. What's gotten into you?"

Ida giggled again, Mike snorted, and Shay backed up just as the door opened again.

Mel sighed. *Timing is everything.* She looked around Shay's shoulder to see their newest visitor and hurriedly straightened her blouse before Shay stepped aside.

"Mr. Brennan," she said, moving to greet the Commerce Bank manager with a handshake. "It's a pleasure to see you."

"Very nice seeing you, Melissa." He nodded to Ida and Mike and fidgeted with his tie as he gave Shay an extra beat of attention. "It's been a while."

"Too long," Mel said and recalled her winter meeting with him about advertising. Her father had met with him a month ago. "We still have some cookies, if you have a moment. We're, well, this being our last day, folks have been very kind."

He helped himself to a cookie off the platter Ida extended and sat in Mel's guest chair.

"Thank you for stopping by," she said. "Seeing everyone today has been heartwarming."

"I'm not surprised by people's reaction, Melissa. You're an important part of Tomson. I've never known a community to respond the way this one has. That full-page advertisement with the hundreds of signatures—"

"Eight-hundred-and-sixty-three of them," Mike boasted.

Brennan nodded as he chewed. "And the biggest names in town among them. Truly remarkable, but actually, not surprising."

Certainly a surprise to me.

Brennan wiped his mouth with a napkin. "And that's what I told your father."

"Excuse me? You spoke with my father?"

"Last night. At length. Twice, in fact." He shook his head. "Long as I've known Bob, he's never changed. And never admits when he's wrong."

"Sounds like Dad."

"Well, last night we ended up arguing over this situation you've got here. Not that arguing is unusual for us. Hell, every conversation we have includes at least one." He chuckled at that. "I had him so frustrated he hung up. So I let him cool off a bit and called back, had your mother get him to the phone."

"Well." Mel struggled to imagine her father discussing his "shameful" nightmare any further. "I...That's so thoughtful of you. Thank you for the support, but I'm not surprised he—"

Brennan held up a hand. "For once in his life, he had to wise up. I told him I'm not the only one thinking he's a pigheaded ass. I told him to check his email right away and we'd talk in the morning—when he came to his senses."

"Wow. I appreciate your gesture, Mr. Brennan. God knows I do. I'm sorry that Dad's just blind to reason. He's always been that way."

"Melissa. Your father canceled the sale of the *Chronicle*. I'm here to notify you that he transferred full ownership of it to you, effective immediately."

She stopped breathing. "He what?" Her hands went to her face in shock.

Ida screamed and burst into tears. Mike cheered and called Robert Baker several creative names. Shay literally hoisted Mel from her seat and hugged her.

Mel squeezed Shay's shoulders with all her strength. She sucked in a breath so deeply she thought she'd hyperventilate.

"Oh, my God, Shay!"

"Yes!" Shay twirled her in a circle. "It's yours, honey. As it should be!" She kissed Mel's temple and set her on her feet.

Mel's knees wobbled and she felt the blood draining from her head. "I-I think I better sit." Shay guided her back into her chair. "No. I can't sit." Mel grabbed the edge of her desk and bobbed up, shoving a hand into her hair. "I can't believe it." She studied Brennan's bright expression. "You're serious? He changed his mind?"

"He did," Brennan said with a nod.

"Impossible. He'd never back down." Mel leaned toward him on outstretched arms. "He actually changed his mind?"

"Yes."

Mel stared at him hard, as if he'd look away and reveal his deception. Slowly, she checked each face around her. Shay's was last and Mel posed the question again, this time via raised eyebrows and her bottom lip between her teeth nervously.

Shay nodded. "For real."

Mel jammed her eyes shut, thrust both arms to the ceiling, and shouted. "YES!"

She threw herself at Shay, seized her face, and kissed her hard.

Shay spun her around as Mel punched the air repeatedly.

"YES! YES! YES!"

Shay joined the cheering until Mel kissed her again, twirled free, and rushed to Brennan. She grabbed his hand and shook it. Then she hugged him.

"Thank you. A million times, thank you."

Shay shook her head in amazement at Brennan. "Must've been some email you sent."

"Pictures I took of the farewell editorial and the people's advertisement. I knew he wouldn't get his own copy until this afternoon at the earliest, and by then it would've been too late."

"No way," Mike said, both hands on his head.

"I suggested he take a hard look at what the *big names he knows so well* think of his daughter, and to just imagine what they all now think of *him*."

"Tell me," Mel started, "tell me this isn't a dream, that it's no sick joke on his part?"

"No joke." Brennan shook his head emphatically. "The ink on the transfer is dry, Melissa. He's washed his hands of it completely. We do need you to sign, of course, and I can make the paperwork available to you as soon as you're ready. I have a little pull at the bank."

Mel straightened her shoulders and took a deep, ragged breath as reality hit home. The dream for which she'd sacrificed so much materialized right where she stood.

Mike rocked back on his heels and beamed with satisfaction. Ida squeaked from behind her hands as she bounced on her toes. Mel grinned at them, ecstatic to the point of silly.

"As new *owner* of the *Tomson Chronicle*, I would like to offer you both jobs."

Ida shrieked again and rushed to her, crying. "I accept! I accept!"

Mike pulled out his letter from *Frontier*, ripped it to pieces, and threw them at the ceiling. "Where do I sign, boss?" He extended a handshake and Mel hauled him into a hug.

"My God. This is unbelievable." She turned to Brennan. "You didn't have to do what you did, calling—"

"Of course I did. Your father made a massive mistake, Melissa, one that affected an entire town, not to mention what he did to his only child. He needed to realize that, needed to see it. Believe me, I was only too glad to win this argument. I'm happy he did the right thing this time. And I'm very happy for you."

"Everyone at the bank is elated, Mel," Shay told her. "I went in to deposit some checks from the garage and they mobbed me. *Me!*"

Mel shook her head again. "Mr. Brennan, you saved the *Chronicle*, you know." Her voice caught in her throat.

"The full-page ad is what did it," he said, "all those people. Can you imagine what he thought when he saw Garret Nelson's name? Or Eli Winston's?"

"Or Della's," Shay added.

"And Sheriff Davis and the fire chief," Mike said. "Mel, you said he's known Chief Madden forever."

"Correct," Brennan added. "Bob, Louis, and I played ball together here many a summer. Damn, you know? I didn't even hear about the petition until Wednesday when my wife said she signed it for the both of us. I hope Bob was sitting down when he read it."

Shay turned Mel by the shoulders. "They wouldn't have signed if you weren't somebody special, sweetheart. But you are. And everybody—including your father—knows it. *You being you* saved the *Chronicle*."

EPILOGUE

More than two dozen townspeople milled about the Indigo Country Club's portico, taking in the September sunset, when Shay stepped out of the rented ivory Cadillac. Eyes and whispers focused on her in her black tuxedo as she reached back for Mel's hand.

All week, Mel wondered how folks would react to her attendance at the Harvest Ball, but now *their* arrival set her mind adrift. She found herself more curious than nervous, playfully eager and strong enough to grab the status quo by the throat and shake it. *Yes*, she mused as she wrapped her fingers around Shay's, *this is how it always should have been and how it's going to stay.*

She set both stilettos on the pavement to a scattering of wolf whistles and let Shay guide her to her feet. "High-class crowd."

Shay chuckled under her breath. "Damn, I was tempted."

Mel straightened to her new height and let all heads turn and stare. She gave Shay's chest a reassuring pat and whispered suggestively, "You can morph into a wolf later, my handsome stud." She linked their arms as they headed toward the door. "This is Tomson's version of the red carpet, so eat it up."

"Oh, I'm already enjoying it. Believe me."

Now almost equal to Shay's height, Mel knew they made an eye-catching couple, and she was damned pleased to have her arm clutched possessively to Shay's side. *Go ahead. Do double takes and take notes.* They greeted familiar faces and exchanged compliments as they entered the ballroom, and she picked up many a comment about the revealing black halter dress she'd chosen earlier in the week.

A camera flash caught them sharing a suggestive smile, and Ida emerged from the crowd.

"Gotcha."

Mel dipped her head. "I didn't mean for you to get *our* photo."

"You look gorgeous, Mel. And Shay's just to die for! Go knock 'em out."

Shay urged them onward, but a tug at her sleeve brought them to a halt.

Mike beamed at his fiancée. "Honey, you remember my boss, Melissa Baker?"

"Mike, you doofus," Mel sighed, reaching for the slim brunette. "Of course we remember each other." They hugged quickly. "Tammy, you've been away too long. How's Tahoe?"

"Damn hot."

"Well, thank God you're here. He's missed you *a lot*. Trust me."

Mike hurried to divert the attention from his blush. "This is Mel's partner, Shay Maguire."

Shay shook Tammy's hand and sent Mel a sly smile at the designation. Mel winked back. *I like the sound of it, too.*

Tammy leaned covertly toward Mel's ear. "You two are just *steamy* together. And that dress is supremely wicked."

"Too much, you think?"

Tammy shook her head definitively. "I feel like I'm going to prom, for Christ's sake. You, you're on the attack."

"Aw, not really. I'm celebrating." Mel took Shay's hand. "We have what we've always wanted."

"Shall we get drinks?" Mike cupped Tammy's elbow and glanced back at Shay. "Beware of salivating dogs tonight."

"Aside from me?"

Mel squeezed her hand, and as they neared the bar, Fire Chief Madden looked from Mel to Shay and back.

"Good evening, you two. Nice turnout tonight. Glad to see you here, Mel. You look sensational."

"Thank you, Chief." *Good to be here on my own terms.*

Shay ordered brandies from the bartender and Mel set a palm on her lower back, not willing to sever their physical connection.

Madden noticed and looked away. "How's your grandmother doing in Miami?"

"Well, I can't say we've been in touch, but Mom tells me Nana's in good health." She accepted her drink from Shay, lingering over her fingers around the glass. *I'm so happy to be with you.*

"Well, hubba hubba!" The boisterous voice made everyone turn. Ever the car salesman, Grayson Cochran leaned against the bar and visually stripped Mel naked. "Our all-American girl newspaper owner is a fox! Looking real fine, Mel. *Real* fine."

"Thank you, Grayson. Your wife let you loose here tonight? I think all the women are in danger."

He raised his glass. "None more so than you. How about a dance later? I might even keep my hands to myself. *Might*, I said." He laughed.

Shay hovered just behind her. "Who is this guy?"

"Grayson, I'd like you to meet my partner. Shay Maguire, this is Grayson Cochran of Bissett Ford."

Shay simply nodded. "Grayson."

He cocked an eyebrow at Mel. "Your date? I'd heard that, but you know how rumors are. I don't pay them any mind. I make my own decisions."

Mel slipped an arm around Shay's hip. "Not date, Grayson. Partner."

"That so?" He peered at Shay as if she'd just taken his last drink. "Lesbians, huh? Damn shame." He strolled away, shaking his head. "Such a waste."

Shay sighed. "That went well."

Mel gave her a squeeze. "I thought so." She sipped her brandy and nodded for Shay to follow her line of vision. "Here comes a political package if I ever saw one."

Headed for the bar, Della and Garret Nelson cut short their conversation to greet them and Mel wondered how long Della would ogle Shay before speaking.

"Good evening," Nelson said. "You're dazzling tonight, Mel."

"You're quite dapper yourself." She noted Shay shifting uneasily beneath Della's inspection. "Shay, this is Tomson Selectmen Chairman Garret Nelson. He manages the Home Depot. Mr. Nelson, my partner, Shay Maguire."

Nelson nodded to Shay's hello. "So you bought the Baker place."

"Proudly."

"And moved right in."

"Yes, we did," Mel stated, and brushed a hand along Shay's arm.

"Buying it was the right thing to do for Mel," Shay told him. "Much like you helping her by signing for the *Chronicle*." She extended her hand. "Thank you for that."

"Ah…" Nelson looked down at her offer, obviously surprised.

Mel sipped her drink to hide a smirk. *Shake the butch's hand, Mr. Chairman.*

Nelson accepted hurriedly. "You're welcome. It was, wasn't it? The right thing to do."

Mel turned her grin aside and caught Della still perusing Shay's tux. Shay, meanwhile, stepped into Nelson's insecure moment and lowered her voice.

"Rumor has it Dick Turner's unhappy in the *Trib* and probably will return to the *Chronicle* soon. How about Home Depot?"

"Oh." Nelson appeared even more flustered. He took a breath and adjusted the knot in his tie. "Well, that's a business matter I—"

"A wise move, in my opinion," Shay observed. "I mean, harvest and winter prep are upon us, then the holidays. And you *know* the Heights's businesses will have everyone getting the local paper. Sounds like Turner's capitalizing on that opportunity."

Nelson shrugged, but when Mel turned his way, he nodded. "I'll admit it's crossed my mind, Mel. Maybe I'll stop in and we'll talk numbers."

"I look forward to it."

Della swirled the ice in her Scotch for attention and touched Shay's shoulder. "Guess there's no such thing as too much business talk."

Mel had had enough of Della's fixation. "Are you having a good time, Della?" *Sure looks like you are.*

"I see someone changed your mind about joining us this year."

Shay put an arm around her and Mel was proud to lean into it. Shay grinned matter-of-factly. "Who can resist my charm?"

"A lot of things are changing around town these days," Nelson injected, glancing at Shay's hand curled into the curve of Mel's waist.

"And amazingly, most of them for the better," Mel added. She considered Della over the rim of her glass as she drank. *So damn cocky in Armani and diamonds.* "The Heights is coming along. You must be pleased." Shay's little squeeze reminded her to behave.

With Nelson dutifully on her heels, Della walked to the bar as she responded. "You're aware we'll miss the holiday shopping season because of the...delay." Mel and Shay took a few steps toward her, and Mel fumed at having to trail after her in mid conversation. "For your little newspaper, I can't imagine the impact of that revenue loss."

Up yours. The "little newspaper" you need so badly.

"Every business takes a hit now and then—as we all know." Mel sent Nelson a knowing glance. "The *Chronicle* is bouncing back energetically. I expect our holiday season to be as bright as ever. And that's good for everyone."

Della left Nelson at the bar and sashayed up to Shay. "Very suave tonight, Chicago."

Mel grazed her fingertips across Shay's back and allowed the luxurious feel of it to calm her. *Do not slap the bitch.* She turned openly to Shay and winked as she needlessly straightened her tie.

"She certainly is, isn't she?" She accepted Shay's offer to link arms.

"Well," Della began again, "things must be good in the car repair business."

Shay tilted her head cavalierly. "Oh, those emergency ranch calls add up. This," she waved a hand at herself, "just a little something I grabbed out of the closet."

Della smiled coyly as she leaned closer. "Really, Chicago. Where you're concerned, I seriously doubt anything except Ms. Baker has come out of the closet in a very long time."

Mel almost choked on her brandy. "Excuse me?"

Shay tossed back the last of her own drink and set it on a nearby table.

"We're done here." She took Mel's hand and led her away. "God, she pisses me off."

"Shay." Mel stopped her halfway to the other bar at the opposite end of the ballroom. "We're not letting her spoil our evening."

"Someone needs to take her down a few pegs, the condescending bit—"

"Shh. Calm down."

"She doesn't have half your guts, Mel. And none of the class."

"God, you're adorable. Thank you, baby, but please shush. If I can rise above her, you can, too. We're not letting it get to us, remember? Not anymore. Okay?" She ran a finger along Shay's jaw and watched the anger subside. "Good."

"Hey." Mike breezed up, Tammy in tow. "Escaped from the Dragon Lady, I see. Damn. And Nelson?" He raised his eyebrows at Mel.

"I know. Shay got our point across." She tugged her closer and narrowed her eyes. "So, what's this you told him about Dick Turner being unhappy at the *Trib*?"

Shay shrugged. "I know I heard it somewhere, just can't remember where."

Mel punched her stomach playfully. "Oh, you're *very* good."

"The music's starting," Mike announced. "Come on."

They danced to the upbeat songs as a group, shouting amusing, suggestive comments to one another until the music slowed and Mel found herself eager to be in Shay's arms. Yearning for that intimate escape from the crowd, she settled in against Shay and boldly laced her arms around her neck. *Eat your heart out, people.*

Shay's hand arrived at her bare lower back, warm and firm, and Mel relaxed, her cheek against Shay's.

"You're incredibly sexy in this tux."

"Just part of the package, ma'am, being your stud."

Mel hummed in approval. "Oh, you're so much more than that."

"You're simply devastating tonight, Mel. Breathtaking. God help the person who tries to cut in while I'm holding the most spectacular lady in the room."

"I don't want anyone's hands on me but yours." Mel kissed Shay's jaw lightly.

Shay snickered against her neck and Mel was ever so pleased she'd swept her hair up for the occasion. Kisses on her shoulder sent a titillating charge almost too deep to control. Shay's hand tingled at the base of her spine, and fingertips teased beneath the fabric just above her rear.

Mel closed her eyes and enjoyed the intimacy. She'd never felt so liberated. No longer was this a fantasy. Neither was falling so completely in love and letting the whole world see.

"I've dreamt about this for so long, it's hard to believe that I'm not dreaming, still."

"Only good dreams from now on. Our dreams and we'll make them come true."

"The summer of a lifetime," Mel whispered, and nuzzled Shay's ear.

"I love you, Mel," and she brought her lips to within a kiss, "so very much."

"You are my everything, Shay Maguire. I love you, too."

About the Author

A recent telecommunications retiree, CF "friz" Frizzell is the recipient of the Golden Crown Literary Society's 2015 Debut Author Award for her novel *Stick McLaughlin: The Prohibition Years*. Friz discovered her passion for writing in high school and went on to establish an award-winning twenty-two-year career in community newspapers that culminated in the role of founder/publisher. She credits powerhouse authors Lee Lynch and Radclyffe and the generous family that is Bold Strokes Books for inspiration. Friz is into history, New England pro sports, and singing and acoustic guitar, and loves living on Cape Cod, just an hour from Provincetown, with her wife, Kathy.

Books Available From Bold Strokes Books

Best Laid Plans by Jan Gayle. Nicky and Lauren are meant for each other, but Nicky's haunting past and Lauren's societal fears threaten to derail all possibilities of a relationship. (978-1-62639-658-6)

Exchange by CF Frizzell. When Shay Maguire rode into rural Montana, she never expected to meet the woman of her dreams—or to learn Mel Baker was held hostage by legal agreement to her right-wing father. (978-1-62639-679-1)

Just Enough Light by AJ Quinn. Will a serial killer's return to Colorado destroy Kellen Ryan and Dana Kingston's chance at love, or can the search-and-rescue team save themselves? (978-1-62639-685-2)

Rise of the Rain Queen by Fiona Zedde. Nyandoro is nobody's princess. She fights, curses, fornicates, and gets into as much trouble as her brothers. But the path to a throne is not always the one we expect. (978-1-62639-592-3)

Tales from Sea Glass Inn by Karis Walsh. Over the course of a year at Cannon Beach, tourists and locals alike find solace and passion at the Sea Glass Inn. (978-1-62639-643-2)

The Color of Love by Radclyffe. Black sheep Derian Winfield needs to convince literary agent Emily May to marry her to save the Winfield Agency and solve Emily's green card problem, but Derian didn't count on falling in love. (978-1-62639-716-3)

A Reluctant Enterprise by Gun Brooke. When two women grow up learning nothing but distrust, unworthiness, and abandonment, it's no wonder they are apprehensive and fearful when an overwhelming love just won't be denied. (978-1-62639-500-8)

Above the Law by Carsen Taite. Love is the last thing on Agent Dale Nelson's mind, but reporter Lindsey Ryan's investigation could change the way she sees everything—her career, her past, and her future. (978-1-62639-558-9)